twisted

BOND

the Holly Woods files

BOND

the Holly Woods files

EMMA HART

Interior Formatted by Tianne Samson with E.M. Tippetts Book Designs

emtippettsbookdesigns.com

books by

EMMA HART

For Danielle.
Because you reminded me that it's okay to do something different –
and that I have to write what my heart wants me to, and that it's okay
to do that, too.
And for calling me a whore when you found out I was writing this in
secret. That could be one of the best things you've ever said to me.
Thank you for keeping me sane every day. This one is yours.

chapter ONE

IALWAYS wanted to be a Bond girl.

When I was seven, I proudly declared to my family that I would one day be beneath Sean Connery on a haystack, a la Pussy Galore. My mother laughed, my father choked, my brothers looked at me like I'd gone batshit crazy, and my Nonna yelled that I would only ever be beneath a good Italian boy, preferably a Catholic, and only on my wedding night.

Of course, their reactions were pointless. At my tender, young age, I hadn't considered how much older Mr. Connery was—or that, by the time I'd be at a suitable age to bump uglies with him, he'd be replaced several times over.

Now I'm not saying that Daniel Craig is a sight for sore eyes. The man is drops for pinkeye, if you know what I mean. I'm just saying that, when I decided to be a Bond girl, I meant Hollywood, California, and James Bond. Not Holly Woods, Texas, and Bond P.I.

Not that I hate my job. I sure don't. When I quit my job as a cop two years ago and left Dallas for my shoddy yet adorable hometown after a case gone wrong, my best friend immediately enrolled in a private investigator course. Bekah nailed the course, flew through the police academy training, and passed her concealed carry test with so many damn colors that there isn't a rainbow in existence that hasn't turned green with envy.

Maybe the shooting thing is a Texas perk. I don't know.

Still, this wasn't my life plan. Neither was becoming a cop. But when your grandpa was a cop, just like your daddy was and your three brothers *are,* it's pretty much a given. I was basically born in the Holly Woods Police Department building.

So it was the parking lot, but close enough.

Being Noelle Bond is kind of super shit—not least because my mom decided Christmas day was a good day to have a baby, but because people hear my surname and assume I have a fucking Aston Martin DB5 in my garage.

I don't.

I have a freakin' Honda that needs a good seeing to by a scrapping machine because I'm too damn lazy to drive to Austin and visit the dealership. I also really hate cars salesmen. They think that, because I'm in possession of a pair of breasts and a vagina, I don't know anything about cars. Well, I know how to drive one, so suck on that, fancy-suited assholes.

"I don't think Mr. Luiz is cheating on his wife." Bekah lowers her binoculars. "He's been watching that porn for a while."

"I agree." I drop my zoomed-in camera. "At least he isn't tonight. But I'd bet that Mrs. Luiz doesn't know about her husband's interest in gay porn."

Bekah purses her lips. "Well, no. For the sake of easiness, though, I'd rather my husband watch gay porn than cheat on me."

"You don't *have* a husband, Bek. You don't even have a boyfriend."

"I know that." She rolls her eyes. "Wait. Who's that?"

I snap the camera to my eyes and stare at the car pulling onto the Luiz's driveway. "That isn't Mrs. Luiz's car."

"She drives an Audi TT, right?"

"Yep. A bright-pink one."

"Yuck."

"Who is that?" I narrow my eyes.

"Oh, shit. He hasn't turned off the porn. Or put his pants on!" Bekah whispers harshly. "And he's going to the door! Noelle!"

"I can see," I hiss, snapping a couple of pictures. And boy, can I see. Mr. Luiz is packin', and I ain't talking about a suitcase.

"What's he… Oh my sweet baby Jesus."

"Nonna would have a fit if she heard you using his name in vain."

"I called him sweet," Bekah argues. "Where did they go?"

"Upstairs, I think." I keep my camera trained on the bedroom window and zoom in. How the fuck did I forget my binoculars? "Oh, yep. Yep. Upstairs."

We watch in silence as Mr. Luiz and the mystery man come together in a mash of tongues. And hands. And penises.

"Ooookay. I think we have enough." I tuck my camera into my purse and swing my legs around to climb from the tree.

"Are you sure?"

My eyes shoot to my best friend. "Um, yes. I'm all for equality and rainbows and all that, but I can't say any of my interests lie in observing gay sex."

"I'm kind of fascinated by it," she says thoughtfully, still watching.

Jesus. *Don't kill me, Nonna. I say it fondly. Fifty times a day.* "We're going. We have to compile this for Mrs. Luiz tomorrow morning. Come on, peeper."

Bekah begrudgingly drops the binoculars and follows me down the tree. "I just wanted to see how it works."

"Presumably the same way heterosexual anal sex works," I retort dryly. "If you're that interested, I'll get you a subscription to PornHub or something for your birthday, okay? Then you can watch all the gay porn you like—on your own time."

"But—"

"I am not payin' you to watch gay porn." I switch my Chucks out for my shiny, new Prada heels. Yes, my car is shit, but my shoes are sexy. A girl has to have her priorities.

Bekah pulls a face and gets in the driver's side of her Mercedes.

Rebekah Hough has been my best friend since I was five and Jean Thomas pushed me off of the monkey bars. Bekah saw her do it, and when Jean swung upside down and showed all the boys her panties, Bekah pulled her off of the bars and into the sand.

I knew right then that the carrot-haired girl in the tartan dress was my soul mate.

Of course, now, her hair is more of a dark auburn than carrot colored, and I'm more accident-prone than I was then—despite my permit to carry a deadly weapon (or several)—and we're some twenty-three years older than we were in kindergarten, but I was right.

She's my soul mate, best friend, and faithful cupcake buyer. And out of the three, the latter is by far the most important. She drives to Austin to Gigi's Cupcakes three times a week just so I can get my cupcake fix. That's true love right there. Who needs a man with a best friend like her?

Of course, my other employees also do it, but I have to pay them gas money for that. Bekah does it for a bottle of wine on a Saturday night, and that's way cheaper.

She parks outside my office building. The two-story, painted-white building is a converted four-bedroom house that works perfectly for our needs. Besides me and Bekah, I have two other PIs, Dean and Mike. Dean is an ex-marine, and Mike an ex–FBI agent, so between us all, we have a wide range of experience.

So I'm still waiting for Bekah's experience as a sales assistant at Forever 21 to show itself, but you never know in this job.

Aside from my badass boys as I call them, there's Marshall, a twenty-two-year-old college graduate with the hacking skills of an alien. The guy can find out anything I want, whenever I want it, and it's perfect. All I have to do is give him a name and I have their life stories on my desk within the hour. Then there's Grecia, my secretary-slash-receptionist-slash-assistant. My little Mexican girl makes killer nachos, so she's basically hired until she quits, retires, or dies. And she has her own little space—so it has no door and I think it used to be a bathroom, but don't tell her that—so she's happy.

If my employees are happy, I'm happy.

I also get paid, which makes me even happier. Because getting paid means more shoes. But shush. My family think I'm saving for a deposit on a new house.

I'm not. Since I already own my house, I'm kind of saving for a vacation I'll likely never take, but I only buy expensive shoes when they're on sale, so it doesn't really count. Everyone does that.

Don't they?

I drop into my office chair with a sigh and plug the small digital camera into my laptop. Every other private investigator I know—which is a grand total of two—have big-ass Polaroid cameras or fancy professional cameras. Fact is, my little Samsung camera has a kickass zoom and hasn't failed me yet. It also fits in my purse for the times when I need to go from heels to Chucks and vice versa. My purses are

Mary Poppins style for that reason and that reason only.

God bless you, Coach.

Taking my mind away from the sale I know Coach is having thanks to this morning's e-mail, I highlight the best photos from our trip to the Luizes' and send them to print at my picture printer. That's right. My picture printer. I'm too lazy to change the paper to photo paper every time I need to print them, which can be a few times a day, so I have two printers set up in the corner of my office. Everyone laughs at me, but it's just one of my quirks. It goes along with the adorable trait I have for randomly appearing bruises all over my body.

What can I say? I'm a catch, and it's a wonder I'm still single.

I dial through to Grecia and ask her to call Mrs. Luiz to set up an appointment at her earliest convenience. Minutes later, Grecia returns my call and tells me that Mrs. Luiz will stop in after work tonight at around four p.m. It's a little sooner than I'd like, especially since it's Friday and Friday night is family dinner night, but it'll do. I have to write a report out of necessity, but all she'll have to do is look at the pictures for her confirmation of Mr. Luiz's sordid activities.

Telling someone that their spouse is cheating on them isn't nice. I've seen every reaction possible over the last two years. It doesn't matter to the person in front of me that they walked into my building, into my office or one of my employees' offices after hiring us. It just matters that we've proved what they didn't want us to.

Some go crazy. Like call-the-mental-hospital crazy. Some cry, and that varies from hysterical call-the-mental-hospital to silent tears. Some nod, thank me for my time, and hand me my check. I like the last ones the best. Simple.

I have the horrible feeling, though, that Mrs. Luiz won't be a nodder and a thanker.

I thought right.

Mrs. Luiz yelled a number of curse words in Spanish. So many, in fact, that I had to do a quick Google translate on some of her obscenities. Needless to say, I have a brand-new vocab to piss off my Nonna with. Add that they're in Spanish and not in Italian and

I'm set for a fun hour of discipline on how I'm disgracing my family legacy by speaking another language.

Ignore the fact that my name is derived from French and it makes total sense.

Of course, my name's being French is no coincidence. My mom and nonna get along like oil and water, so my mom took it upon herself to name all four of her kids anything *but* Italian names. My father, half Italian and more than accustomed to the dressing down my nonna can give someone, attempted to convince Mom to give at least one of us an Italian name.

It didn't work. Obviously.

Mom argued that, since she did the baby-growing and the whole labor thing, she was damn well picking our names. And I gotta say that it's really freakin' hard to argue with logic like that.

Add to this whole situation that my mom is your perfect Southern belle who uses "bless your heart" the way I use the word "fuck" and my nonna wishes she could disown all of us.

It makes Friday nights fun. Not wine-and-nachos kind of fun, but fun all the same.

I push the door to my parents' house open quietly, biting my bottom lip as I wait for the standard greeting.

"No!" Nonna screams. "You cook-a the pasta for longer!"

I've no sooner shut the door than I rest my forehead against it. Here we go again. Fucking pasta.

"Dang it, Liliana!" Mom shouts back. "One day, you will leave me to cook in my own kitchen!"

"Pasta! From-a a bag!" Nonna follows it up with a stream of Italian.

Honestly, the woman has lived in the States for almost fifty years. You'd think she'd give up the accent, but nope. She's as stuck on Italy as she was when she came here. Which explains the pasta disagreement.

I run past the kitchen and into the living room before either of the crazy old bats notice me and drag me into the pasta debate. I've been there way too many times, and it's never pretty.

My little brother, Brody, is relaxing on the couch next to my big brother, Devin.

"Where's Trent?" I ask, squeezing between them.

"Sick kid," Devin replies. "Aria."

Ahh, Trent. The favorite grandchild because he married a Catholic woman with a tenth of Italian blood and gave both their children Italian names. Golden boy.

I love Alison and she's one of my best friends, but, pah.

"Nasty. She's okay though?"

"Just a bug," Brody grumbles. "Her third one this year, mind you."

And it's barely April.

"Such a fucking liar," I mutter. "I'm gonna get married and have a kid to be sick all the time so I don't have to come to these dumb dinners."

Devin snorts. "When you find a man who'll marry you, I'll pay you five hundred bucks."

I cut my eyes to him. "What does that mean?"

"Noelle, you fall over thin air."

"Maybe clumsiness is attractive to some guys."

"Yeah. The kind who hope you fall over when you wear a skirt," Brody retorts.

"So, if I weren't your sister, you'd be attracted to me?"

He screws up his face. "I'd rather be attracted to a fuckin' bobcat."

"Look in the mirror and you'll find one." I poke my tongue out as he prods my side.

"Do you ever stop fighting? It occurred to you that you're no longer in your teens, yes?" Dad stops in the doorway when Nonna screams in Italian again. He takes a deep breath and closes his eyes. "I'm in the wrong room."

I grin.

Dad has serious and final words with both Nonna and Mom, which end with him telling Nonna to cut the Italian sassing and get her ass into the front room before he makes her move.

My smile drops.

Fuck me. The man hates me.

"You married yet?" she demands the second she sits down.

"Yeah. Last Saturday, I found a good Italian boy who's so Catholic he bleeds the Bible and snores your favorite passages. He even sings hymns in the shower. Bagged him before I closed my open infidelity case," I reply, my eyes on the television. "He'd be here tonight but you can't see him. He's invisible, and I think you might be sitting on him."

She curses in Italian. "I should-a have taken you back to Italy years ago. I might-a," she threatens.

"Not a good idea to threaten kidnap in a cop's house."

"I'm-a saving you."

"Pretty sure you kidnapping me and dragging me to Italy is closer to murder. Attempted at the very least."

"Noella!"

After twenty-eight years of her changing my name to make it sound something close to Italian, I've given up trying to correct her. "Yes, Nonna?"

"Look-a at me!"

I swallow down every thread of annoyance and look at her. "Yes, Nonna?"

She raises her eyebrows.

Sweet fucking Jesus. "*Sì,* Nonna?"

"*So un sacco di veleni.*" She raises her eyebrows even higher.

"Nonna, I don't give a shit how many poisons you know," Devin interrupts without taking his eyes from the television. "I'll arrest you for every damn one of them."

"I know-a love spells," she replies, waggling her eyebrows.

"Never consuming anything you give me," I squeak.

"Cops. You-a so suspicious."

"Not a cop," I remind her.

Brody frowns as Nonna gets up, presumably for pasta round two with Mom. "But—"

"Leave it, bro," Devin says. "Don't make her try the fucking potions. She already thinks I should have Amelia popping babies out like they're bursts of air on bubble wrap."

"Speak for yourself," I grumble. "She's been calling me all week for a date with 'some-a nice-a Italian guy from-a Houston for-a date-a.'"

"What did you tell her?" Brody glances at me.

"To kiss-a my-a ass-a." I grin. "Then I hung up. She either forgot, or she's still too mad at my sass to mention it."

Devin shakes his head. "You're as bad as she is. Just find a nice guy and settle down, Noelle."

"Like you are with Amelia, your girlfriend of five years, you mean?"

He doesn't reply after that.

You're never too old for word-spars with your brothers.

And I totally won that one.

chapter **TWO**

I GRAB the chocolate chip cookie dough cupcake with the mini cookie sticking out from the top of the frosting before I've even sat down. Today was obviously Bekah's turn to make the run into Austin to go to Gigi's, because this cupcake is our favorite and, whenever the guys go, there's never two in the box like there is right now.

And I didn't have a receipt for gas money taped to my door.

Sometimes, I think the guys forget I'm their boss. One day, I'll pay them a monthly wage of ten dollars for shits and giggles.

I open my giant planner and scribble as I lick frosting from the cupcake, listening to everyone telling me their current cases for the week. I say current because these things can snap open and shut quicker than a damn oyster having its pearl stolen. Tomorrow, it could be a whole different bunch of cases.

That's also the most exciting thing about this job. It can change in an instant, without you even realizing.

I nod and everyone except Bekah leaves to get on with their work for the day. PI's don't get Saturdays off. Kinda sucks sometimes, the seven-days-a-week thing, but at least I can turn my phone off when I want everyone to piss off. Couldn't do that as a cop.

I grab the lone lemon cupcake from the box and set it in my drawer for later, reasoning that I have thirty minutes of treadmill time penciled in for this afternoon so I can totally fudge the extra cupcake.

Plus, it's Gigi's cupcakes. I think it's actually borderline illegal to justify sneaking a leftover cupcake into your desk drawer for later.

If I didn't do it, Dean would be back in here the second my back was turned to take it. Pain in the ass.

"How did it go with Mrs. Luiz last night?"

Dropping into my comfy leather seat, I sigh. "About as well as if you tried to run my Nonna over with a monster truck."

Bekah winces. "Ouch."

"Yeah. I almost called my brothers to escort her out of the building." I shake my head.

"Where were Dean and Mike?"

"Mike was out working a case, and I think Dean went for coffee. Or he was just hiding from her crazypants. I can't say I blame him." My cell chooses this moment to shrill from my purse. I dig it out from inside one of my Chucks and answer. "Whatever it was, I didn't do it."

My oldest brother sighs. "Really, Noelle? You can't answer the phone like a normal person?"

"Never. What's up?"

"I have one of your clients here," Trent says wearily. "Picked him up because his wife was scared someone was following her."

"This is a new one. Who is it?"

"Samuel Beauford."

"Samuel Beauford…" I mutter, looking at Bekah.

She frowns.

"Oh! His wife is pregnant," I say, snapping my fingers. "But according to fertility tests, he's almost firing blanks, so he's certain she's cheating on him."

"Maybe there was a strong swimmer," Trent replies. "Like The Rock of sperm or something."

"That's what I'm trying to prove. She does nothing but visit Target in Austin, the post office, and browse baby things."

"Great. Well, he wants to talk to you."

"I'm not a freakin' lawyer," I mutter.

"I know. But I can't keep him in for anything because it's the first call. All I can do is give him a tellin' off."

I love it when he talks down to me. "Yeah, I remember. I was a cop once, ya know."

"Seems so long ago," he teases. "Here you go, Mr. Beauford."

Mr. Beauford immediately talks into my ear, his words coming at a mile a minute. I can barely understand a damn thing he's saying, and I have to hold the phone back from my ear a little because, good grief, the man talks ridiculously loudly. Bekah grins from her perch on the tub chairs I have for clients.

"Mr. Beauford," I say as soon as he takes a breath. "We've been following your wife for two weeks now and there's no evidence of her stepping out on you. Please, sir, leave the investigating to the professionals or you're likely to find yourself in jail for a short time."

He agrees and tells me that he'll call in a week for an update. Then I mercifully hang up.

"Some people are certifiably weird," Bekah says, breaking through the silence.

I glance up, rubbing my temples. "Ya think?"

"Damn suspicious, too. And people wonder why we aren't married. No one in this town seems to be able to keep it in their pants."

"Do me a favor and come to family dinner next week and explain that to my nonna." Damn woman won't stop trying to marry me off, lest I become a *zitella*. I swear she thinks that, if I'm not married by my thirtieth birthday—in twenty months—no man will ever want me.

She already thinks the reason I'm single is because I carry a gun and, apparently, men prefer the quiet type.

I'm not sure what men she knows, because my mother isn't the quiet type, and neither is Nonna, and they've both married.

Bekah wrinkles her face. "More dates?"

"Every week. One day, I'm going to find myself a date for family dinner and give the *vecchia* a heart attack."

"Nah. She'd skip the heart attack and go straight into planning your wedding."

I shudder at the thought. "Don't you have work to do instead of scaring the shit out of me?"

She snorts. "All right. I get the message." She stands and tugs her jeans up. "Stop for lunch at twelve?"

"It's a date."

After lunch, I collect my messages from Grecia and return all necessary calls. This means I set up two appointments, give a case update to the wife of a subject, and arrange to have my hair done.

Hey, no judging. PI's need nice hair, too.

"Miss Noelle?"

"Come in." I look toward my door, where Dean's head is poking around it.

I spent the first month of his employment telling him to drop the "Miss" in front of my name, but twelve months later, he still insists on calling me it. It's kind of sweet, really. He's also really big and kind of scary since he's ex-military, and I don't want to piss him off, so I gave up arguing.

"What's up?" I ask as he sits down.

"We have a problem," he replies, his voice wavering.

I slowly close my laptop, eyeing him. There's sweat beading on his upper lip, and his face is pretty pale. Add in the tremble of his hands and I'm worried. Nothing shakes Dean—except possibly spiders, but I'm still confirming that.

"Talk to me, Dean."

"There's a body in the Dumpster in the parking lot."

I blink harshly several times. Did he just say a body? In the Dumpster? In the parking lot? "I'm sorry. What?"

"There's a *dead* body in the Dumpster in the parking lot."

"Like a bird or a deer or something?"

"No, miss. A human body."

Well, snap.

"Okay," I say slowly. "There wasn't one there when I went for lunch."

"Well, Miss Noelle, there is now."

"Let's go take a look." Thankfully, I wore a loose blouse for work today, so I slip my Tiffany-blue Glock 26 into the waistband of my jeans. It's a bit of a squeeze since they're skinny jeans and not made for guns, but it slides in in a hurry.

Dean leads me down to the door to the parking lot. "It ain't pretty."

"Dead people usually aren't, in my experience." Unfortunately, I have plenty.

I see it as soon as I step out the door. The Dumpster is in the far corner of the parking lot to keep any smells away from the building, and a pale, white foot is peeking over the top. A shiver runs through me as I scan the immediate area for anyone, but there's nothing other than the usual driving of cars and people strolling along the sidewalks.

"Miss Noelle—" Dean says softly as I approach the Dumpster.

"Oh, shit," I whisper.

The rancid smell of burning flesh fills the air, and I pinch my nose so I'm not tempted to breathe through it and smell it any more than I have to. The naked body clearly belongs to a woman, but her face is mutilated. Long, gaping cuts crisscross their way across her shoulders and chests down to her breasts. And her breasts... I swallow back the bile crawling its way up my throat.

Her breasts have all but been cut off, and the only things I can see connecting them to her body are ragged bits of bodily tissue. Dark-red, dried blood flakes off her skin in broken patches, and black burn marks char her otherwise perfect, white skin.

Refusing to look any further, I step back and grab my phone. I dial the number for dispatch, and before Mariana can say a word, I ramble, "Mariana, it's Noelle. I've got a ten thirty-three at the agency."

"What it is, honey?"

"A dead body."

"They're on their way."

I hang up and turn to Dean, my hand running through my long hair. "Make sure no one comes in or out of the agency. Tell Grecia to set up the answering machine. The police are going to need to talk to all of us, and this place is now a damn crime scene."

"Got it." He turns on his heel and stalks into the building.

A little more bile rises in my throat, so I step away from the Dumpster. I can feel my lunch swirling in my stomach, and it takes everything I have not to let it make a swift reappearance as I lean against a tree trunk.

It's not the dead body thing. I saw plenty in Dallas. Hundreds, probably. Death doesn't scare me or even faze me. It's *how* she died—it was obviously brutal and slow. Not a way anyone, save the kind of person who did this horrible act, should die. I can't begin to imagine what this poor woman went through.

Sirens blare through my thoughts, and I look up in time to see Brody and Trent making a beeline for me.

Trent's hands curl around my shoulders. "You okay?"

I nod at my eldest brother. "Dean found her. I'm warnin' you—it ain't nice."

He squeezes gently and releases me. Brody steps forward, and they both look into the Dumpster.

"Shit," Brody mutters.

"Yep," I say to myself. "Shit indeed."

Cops swarm the parking lot, and a hint of yellow tells me that they've blocked off my office. Great. Looks like I'm working out of my living room and Skyping my employees for the next couple of days.

Having my workplace as a murder investigation: the last thing I need.

I stand back and watch as the cops do their thing. Glancing at the office, I can see everyone looking out the window of the kitchen to see what's going on. They'll all know by now, but they're also all smart enough to follow Dean's orders and let me deal with this.

"Ms. Bond," drawls a familiar voice.

An unwelcome, familiar voice.

"Detective Nash." I grit my teeth and turn around. "How are you?" I ask politely, my eyes rising to meet the imposing cop's.

"Worse for this," he responds, motioning to the Dumpster. "Do you have anywhere we can talk?"

"In my office." I lead him inside the building, stopping at the kitchen.

Bekah opens her mouth, but I cut her off by raising my hand.

"Can all of you go to your offices? Someone will be in to talk to all of you soon."

A chorus of yeses rings out, and I offer them a tentative smile before leading Detective Drake Nash into my office.

Man, I seriously dislike this guy. Mostly because he's so damn attractive. It's one of those things you can't help but notice. He's the guy who gets everyone's attention when he walks through a grocery store.

It could be the tan skin or the ragged, dark hair that always seems to be shiny. Then again, it could also the glacier-blue eyes that seem to see right through you, or it could be that chiseled jaw. That said, I'm betting it's the biceps.

His being a plain-clothes detective has its perks for the female population of Holly Woods. His shirts are always impeccably fitted, and you couldn't miss the bulging muscles in his upper arms if you were blind.

It's just a shame he's an arrogant asshole. If it weren't for that, we'd get along impeccably. And I don't just mean at work.

"Take a seat." I sit in my big, comfy chair and remove my gun from my waistband.

Drake cocks an eyebrow. Slowly, he lowers himself into one of the tub chairs. "You found the body?"

"No. Dean found it and came to tell me."

"Why would he tell you before callin' the police?"

Now I raise an eyebrow. "Because it's on my property, perhaps?"

"You always keep a gun in your pants?" He nods toward my pretty on the desk.

"Only when I have conclusion-jumping detectives in my office and a dead body in my Dumpster." I smile sweetly, totally hating that he caught me in a stupid moment. Damn it, I know better than shoving a gun in my pants. But, hey—dead body in the Dumpster. Desperate times and all that jazz. "Can you get to the point of this conversation, please?"

Drake focuses his steely gaze on me. "Tim thinks the body was placed there recently."

"It was," I say, confirming the coroner's suspicions. "I threw some trash in it before I went for lunch with Bekah, and she definitely wasn't there then."

"When did you go for lunch?"

"Midday."

Drake glances at his watch. "So she's been there for an hour at most. Did you see her when you came back in?"

"I generally don't gaze at Dumpsters unless I'm using one."

"Your sass is doin' nothing but pissin' me off, Noelle."

I stare at him flatly. "I just saw a mutilated dead body, Detective.

Excuse me if I happen to have a mechanism that helps me cope with such incidents. If it bothers you, spit out whatever it is you have to say and bug my employees so we can get back to work."

"You'll have to close the office for at least twenty-four hours," he says, his voice sharp. "We'll need to search the building."

"How did I know you'd say that?"

"I can get a warrant if I need one."

"Believe me, if my desire to piss you off was stronger than the one to keep my business going, I'd refuse you entry until you had a warrant and gave a flamingo a striptease," I bite out. "As it is, I have a job to do." I pull my spare set of keys from the drawer and throw it at him. "They're all labeled. I'll be outside at four p.m. tomorrow to collect them, and that goddamned yellow tape better be nowhere except for the parking lot."

Drake's lips curve. "You know you can't take anything home with you."

I lean forward. "Do cops have a thing about patronizing ex-cops or is it just the detectives at HWPD? I've already had it from my brother this morning. I'm more than aware that I can't take anything out of the office that's currently in it. Which is why I'll be printing copies of all my current cases to take home so that I can still work."

"It's much easier to do this job when you're not working against an ex-cop."

"If you think this is me working against you, Detective, you don't know me very well." I get up and walk to the door. "Are we done here? Because it looks like I have a busy afternoon, and as pretty as you are to look at, you're not the greatest company."

His smirk comes back as he stands, my keys in his hand, and walks toward me. I pull the door open and glare at him when he stops in front of me. Looking up at him, I'm aware of how much bigger than I am he is, both height-wise and muscle-wise. He has a good three inches on my height and I'm wearing freakin' high heels.

"Keep it that way, Noelle," he says in a husky, dominant tone. "I'd advise you not to work against me. I'd have no problem putting you in cuffs."

"And I'd have no problem spending the night in the lockup for impaling your penis with my stiletto."

He holds my gaze for a long moment. "I want all of your staff out within ten minutes after they've been interviewed. You'll get your keys tomorrow as promised, providing we don't find anything in here."

My body tenses at his insinuation. "My staff aren't murderers, Drake."

"That's Detective Nash."

"Then it's Ms. Bond."

"One day," Trent says, appearing to the side of me, "you two will give up the sick foreplay and just fuck."

"I'd rather shoot myself in the foot," I snap, smirking at the burly man in front of me.

Drake takes a deep breath. "You should. That way, you may think twice before doing it to other people."

"Perhaps. But you still haven't learned not to piss me off when I have a gun in my hand."

"You don't have a gun in your hand, *Ms. Bond.*"

Two seconds later, I have my brother's 9mm dangling from my finger and directed at Drake Nash's chest. Both men tense, and my smirk becomes a grin as I turn to Trent.

"You should really secure that better. I didn't even have to try." I pass it to him and look back at Drake. "Well, Detective? Are you going to stop harassing me and move on to my staff now? I'd like to print my reports."

"Your brother will wait with you to make sure you don't remove anything from your office." Drake's eyes flit across the room then settle on me. "Try not to piss any of my men off, Noelle."

"Ms. Bond," I correct him. "Try not to drink all of my coffee in the kitchen."

"All right," Trent interjects. "Noelle. Inside. You're not doin' yourself any favors."

"Neither is the dead body outside," I mutter, turning away from that bastard Drake Nash and walking back into my office.

chapter THREE

NEWS travels fast in Holly Woods. Especially when there's a murder. Something that happens not regularly, but enough that it's never quiet. I've just never been in the middle of a Holly Woods murder before, much less the investigation.

And definitely not a suspect.

Which is technically what I am, along with all of my staff. And that sucks. I don't have time to be a suspect, and I have even less time to have Detective Drake Nash sniffing around my business. His obnoxious self is a giant pain in the ass.

If he weren't a cop, I'd shoot him in the foot again. I'd enjoy it as well.

Jesus. I really need to stop thinking about shooting the man. It simply isn't going to do me any good, because I might have a bit of a twitchy trigger finger. Which is how he ended up getting shot by me in the first place.

So, yes. No more pointing guns at Detective Drake Nash.

I grab a cupcake from the box and slink down in my seat. Restaurant stakeouts on Saturday nights are the worst damn thing in the world. There are only two or three small-to-medium-sized restaurants in Holly Woods, so they're almost always full on a weekend.

This makes my job very hard when someone I've been hired to

follow goes to dinner with someone other than their spouse. Sadly, nine times out of ten, my clients' hunches are right, and despite the businesslike tone of the dinner meeting I'm observing, there are slight hand brushes and moves like wiping food from the other person's mouth that give it away.

Unfortunately for me, that isn't enough to convince my client that her husband is a love rat. I need a kiss or, at the very least, a blatant tit grab.

Why can't these scumbags make my life easier and just have at each other in an alleyway?

I sigh and grab my can of Diet Pepsi. Stakeouts are the worst part of this job. One day, I'll simply install my own cameras in every public establishment in town and collect the tapes every morning. Then I could technically do stakeouts in my pajamas at home.

Ahh, pajamas.

I glance at the clock. It's almost ten p.m. Yes. I should be in my pajamas, especially after the hellish day I've had. I'm pretty sure all a girl should do after finding a dead body is hide beneath her covers with Jack Daniel's and cake. And then never, ever, ever come out again.

I answer my phone as soon as the screen lights up. "Noelle Bond."

"Why are you sitting outside Red?" *Drake.*

"I'm working. Why do you want to know? Wait. How do you know where I am?"

"Who are you tailin'?"

A face appears at my window, and I drop my phone. I press the button to roll the barricade down.

"That's confidential. What are you doing here?"

Drake leans his forearm across the bottom of the window so I can't roll it back up. "I stopped by your place to give you your keys. We went through your building earlier and it's clear there's nothin' there and that Jane Doe was planted in the Dumpster."

I take the keys he hands me, my eyes narrowed. "Why would she be planted there? In broad daylight, too. It makes no sense."

"That's what we're trying to figure out. Along with her identity. Tim is waiting for dental records before he identifies her."

"Do you know the cause of death yet?"

"Confidential," Drake replies, straightening. "I couldn't tell you even if I liked you a tiny bit."

I smile tightly. "Well, thanks for my keys. I have to get back to work now."

He looks between me and the restaurant. Then his eyes fall on the cupcakes. "Oh yeah. You're workin' real hard over here, Noelle."

Staring at him, unimpressed, I press the window button. He moves his arm as soon as the glass rises, but he curls his fingers over the top.

"Oh, and don't leave town. Your building was clear, but you and your staff aren't."

"I have an alibi, and so does Bekah," I remind him. "We were together."

"Convenient," he drawls.

"I'm not sure I like what you're insinuating." I jab my finger on the window button and it jerks up another centimeter.

"I'm not insinuating anything, Ms. Bond. Merely stating the obvious."

"Merely pissing me off, more like," I say under my breath.

"I heard that," Drake mutters. Straightening, he asks, "What about the others?"

I hover my finger over the window button again. "Maybe you should do your job properly and ask them, *Detective*."

I rub my temples, leaning forward on my desk. The cops didn't do much in the way of tidying after they'd finished ransacking everyone's offices, and Detective Drake Nash took my fucking coffee. The man gets a strange kind of pleasure out of messing with me, I swear.

Because of the lack of fucks given by HWPD's homicide rookies who searched my workplace, we've all spent the whole morning cleaning up and reorganizing all of our files. Neither of which is one of my favorite things, especially since one of my files is missing.

I never throw my files out. Most of them are kept on a flash drive, but I like to print the basic information. It's easier than transferring the documents between my laptop, phone, and tablet, depending on what I'm using. And, uh, what happens to have battery. Call me old school, but it's how I *know* that one of them is gone.

I dial Trent's number.

"Detective Bond."

"It's me," I say. "I have a question."

"Shoot. I'm busy."

"Did y'all take anything from here yesterday?"

"No," he says instantly. "You know I'd have told you if we needed to take something."

"Shit." I bite the inside of my cheek. "Okay. Thanks."

"Whoa, Noelle. Wait. What's up?"

"I'm just a file missing is all. I guess it got lost when y'all tore this place apart. Probably ended up in the trash or something."

"Sorry," Trent says. "Damn rookies don't know how to clean up after themselves."

"And Drake Nash didn't give a shit," I finish for him. "Never mind. I'll keep looking. Thanks." I drop the phone back onto the hook and sit back. Before I have time to think over my newest predicament, though, there are three knocks at my door. "Come in."

"Noelle? Are you busy?" Bekah pokes her head through.

"No, no. What's up?"

"Ryan Perkins is here to see you." She pulls a face. "Grecia called me since your line was busy."

"I was talking to Trent. Why is Ryan Perkins here?"

Six months ago, I busted Ryan Perkins for cheating on his fiancée. Needless to say, my excitement for this meeting is at level zero right now.

"He didn't say. Just that it's real important." She shrugs. "I suggested to Grecia we call the guy who deals with strays, but she told me to stop being a bitch."

I cough to hide my laugh. "Okay. Tell her to send him up. It's not like I have anything else to do." Except look for my missing file. Although I have to admit that my interest is piqued. What could he possibly want me for?

Bekah leaves, and seconds later, there's another knock at the door. "Mr. Perkins," I say, opening it. "Please come in."

"Thank you, Ms. Bond. And please, call me Ryan." He shakes my hand.

"Then call me Noelle." I smile politely and walk around my desk.

"Take a seat. What can I do for you?"

He swallows heavily, and his eyes dampen. "Lena's dead," he whispers.

A chill cascades down my spine.

"Detective Nash came to see me this morning. She's the body your guy found."

Oh. Shit.

"Ryan, I'm so sorry. She was a good friend of mine."

Her boutique stocks the best clothes, and she was always impeccably dressed. She was also one of the sweetest people I've ever met. This isn't fair.

"I can't believe she's gone. My beautiful Lena." He covers his mouth with his hand and looks away.

I wait patiently for him to gather himself again, and when he does, the sadness in his eyes is highlighted by a steely determination that makes his jaw set hard.

"I want to hire you. You have to find who did this to her."

I blink quickly as his words hit me. "I'm not sure I can, Ryan. I'm close to this case, not to mention a suspect in the eyes of HWPD."

"Which is why you have to do it." He leans forward and grabs my hand, his eyes bloodshot and desperate. "Please, Noelle. Please. I'll pay you anything."

I want to say no. I thought I'd left chasing murderers behind when I left Dallas. That was the plan, anyway. I was going to come back to Holly Woods and following cheating spouses and all other kinds of menial little jobs. I was never supposed to do this again—big jobs where it's too easy to screw it all up.

But as I look into the eyes of a man who's just had his heart ripped out brutally, doubt creeps in. One case won't kill me, if you'll pardon the pun. All I have to do is discover the identity of the killer then hand my brother all the information I've gathered.

Shit though. I don't want to be running around after crazy shits again. If I wanted to do that, I'd have stayed in Dallas or trained to be a pre-K teacher.

Ryan Perkins looks at me with tears shining in his eyes, and despite my reservations, I know there's no way I can turn this down.

"All right. I'll do it. You have to understand that I may not solve it and the police are in a much better position than I am to find who killed her," I explain softly. "They have access to forensics and reports I can only get by breaking and entering, and I'm no good to you at all if I'm in jail."

Ryan nods slowly. "I understand. How much is your retainer?"

I tell him a figure two-thirds of my normal price.

"That's not what Julie paid you." He looks at me contemplatively, referring to his ex-fiancée.

"I have a personal interest in this case," is my reply. I want to find Lena's killer almost as much as I want Detective Nash's nose out of my backside.

"Thank you," Ryan says, ripping a check out of his book.

I take the slip of paper and nod. "Thank you." After tucking it into a drawer, I pull a notepad and pen out and pass them to him. "I'm going to need to know everything she's done over the last few days. Who she's been in contact with, if you've seemed suspicious about anything, her schedule—that type of thing. Can I get you a coffee?"

"That would be great," he says weakly, staring at the pad. "I'll write down everything I know."

I pick up the phone and dial Grecia, hoping she already went out to get coffee. "Perfect."

chapter FOUR

M Y teeth nibble at my thumbnail. Dammit. My gut is screaming at me that it isn't a coincidence that I have a missing file, and my gut is rarely wrong. It's why I'm damn good at my job. I swear my gut knows things before they happen.

Shame it couldn't predict a murder, but there we go. I'm not freakin' Superwoman.

Time to figure out exactly which file is missing—and I have a hunch I know which one it is.

I grab my cell phone and lock my office door behind me. Stopping down the hall, I poke my head through the open door. "Hey, Marsh?"

"Yep?" Marshall looks up from his laptop. Actually, laptops. He's surrounded by three of them and somehow using them all at the same time.

"You busy?"

"Not for you, boss."

I smile at my twenty-two-year-old resident geek. "I need you to go through every file on record and see if any are missing. I know it's a big job, but—"

"One is," he says, his eyes on the middle laptop. "There's one less file in the total documents."

Shit. "Can you find which one? I have a paper file missing from my office, and I'm heading down to the basement now to check there."

"Sure. I'll come find you when I have."

"Awesome. Thanks, doll."

I leave him to do his freaky computer thing he does. I don't know if I could run this business without Marsh, and I certainly couldn't figure this out without him. I hired him a year ago for part-time work while he finished his degree in Austin, but instead of staying in the city or going back home to Houston, he came back to Holly Woods and now works for me full time. I'm not exactly sure everything he does to get me the information I ask for is legal, but if I don't ask, I won't feel any guilt.

So I just don't ask.

I unlock the door to the basement I use as a records room. Every case Bond P.I. has ever taken is documented down here, and this room is part of the reason why I use paper copies for my own cases. It means I don't have a whole bunch of printing to do at the end of a case, and if anything ever happened to the electronic things I fight against every single day, I know I have this room.

I skim through the files one by one. An agonizingly long amount of time seems to pass as I go through every single file from the last six months. My organizational skills leave plenty to be desired, so it's not until I get to the last drawer that I know whose file is missing.

My phone rings in my pocket, buzzing against my thigh. "What?" I pull it out and balance it between my ear and shoulder.

"We have a name for our victim," Drake says. "Thought you should hear before the gossip mill churns it out."

"Lena Perkins," I whisper.

"How do you know?"

"Well, for one, Ryan Perkins just came in to hire me."

"What?" Drake explodes.

"Secondly, Julia Owens had me check out Ryan before they got married," I explain, ignoring the random burst of anger. "He was sleeping with Lena. They're married now. Or they were. And that's the missing file I just told Trent about."

"That's no coincidence, Noelle."

"Funnier things have happened," I laugh dryly.

"Hold on."

I go upstairs to Marsh's office and swing my head inside the door, the phone line still quiet. "Did you find it?"

Marshall nods, his shaggy, brown hair flopping into his eyes. He pushes it to the side. "The Perkins file. I'm trying to recover it as we speak."

"If you do, print it and drop it on my desk. I'm going to check the flash drive."

"Huh?" Drake says.

"I was taking to Marshall. He's trying to recover the digital file. It might be on my flash drive but I'm not holding out much hope."

"Noelle, I need that file. Yesterday."

I sigh. "I was afraid you'd say that."

"Nonna, I'm kind of busy right now."

"I have-a you a date!"

I muffle my groan by biting my hand. "I don't have time to go on a date. I just took on a huge case."

"That-a murder one?"

"Yes," I answer hesitantly.

A long stream of angry Italian escapes her. "This is-a why you need a man-a! So you don't have to work-a silly jobs!"

Oh, here we go. "Nonna, my job isn't silly."

"You carry a gun!"

"I'm trained to use it. I could fire a real gun before you tried switching it out for a Nerf gun and a water pistol!" I clap my hand over my eyes. "Anyway. I'm sorry, but cancel the date. My caseload is too heavy to spend evenings frolicking with your Italian blind dates."

Another stream of Italian. With some curse words for added effect. Lovely. "Noella!"

"No, Nonna. I'm putting my foot down." I stomp it for good measure. "No more dates. I don't care if I'm a *zitella.*"

She humphs. "I invite-a him for family dinner instead-a."

"Wait, no!" I shout, but she's already hung up. Interfering old bat!

I groan and bury my face in my arms on my desk. Great. I have three cheating husbands to stalk—I mean, observe—a murder case to solve, my innocence to prove, and, now, Friday night dinner dates.

Just fucking shoot me.

It'd be nicer.

"Busy!" Grecia shrieks outside my door. "She is busy!"

Oh my crap. What now?

"With all due respect, ma'am, I don't care." Detective Drake Nash's voice is strong and firm. "She has something I need."

I groan again. Isn't Sunday supposed to be a day of rest?

I knew I should have gone to church this morning. God is so punishing me right now.

"Quick," I hiss as there's a knock at my door. "Find me a rogue love rat to chase before my pain in the ass comes in."

Bekah laughs down the phone. "Yours are all at home with their families and accounted for."

"Fuck it."

"Noelle?" Drake knocks again. "I know you're in there."

"Gotta go," I grumble, hanging up on Bekah. "Come in."

"This man! He has no manners!" Grecia fumes.

I look at her sympathetically. "Honey, I know. Why don't you take your break now?"

"I will!" She shoots the imposing detective an angry look before sweeping out of the room and slamming my door so loudly that it rattles on its hinges.

I wince as it bounces open an inch before clicking back shut again. For a five-foot-nothin' chick, she's damn strong.

"Thanks for pissing off my assistant. Angry Grecia is so fun to deal with." I roll my eyes and stand up. "You may as well turn around and leave, Detective. I don't have the file yet. It's been wiped from everything, including the flash drive it should have been on. I'll call you if and when Marsh has it."

Drake pins me with his gaze. "It isn't a coincidence that your file on a murdered woman has disappeared entirely from your systems. For all I know, there's something important in there that could crack this case open, so unless you can recite it word for word for me right the fuck now, I'm going to talk to Marshall and hurry his ass up."

My jaw drops. Drake merely stares at me as I gape back at him.

"No?" he asks, his eyebrows raised. "That's what I thought."

With that, he adjusts his gun at his hip and yanks my door open. I stand frozen for a second before I storm after him.

"Detective Nash!" I yell at his back, making Mike look up from his desk on the other side of the hall. "You cannot come in here and harass my staff as they work!"

"Actually, sweetheart, I can. The badge says so. Mr. Wright!" He bangs on Marshall's door.

"No, you can't—especially when they're working for somethin' you want!"

Drake cuts his cold eyes to me and knocks again. "Mr. Wright!"

"Detective Nash." Marshall opens the door. "I'm afraid I don't have what you need, sir, and even if I did, I couldn't give it until Noelle has checked it to make sure it's complete."

I shoot Drake a triumphant yet angry smirk.

"Are you threatening to withhold information from me, Mr. Wright? You do realize I could arrest you for that."

"Seriously?" I exclaim.

"Of course not, sir," Marshall says, ignoring me. "I'm simply saying that I don't have the information you need right now, and I'd hate to give you an incorrect or incomplete file, which would surely impede your investigation." He brushes his hair from his face.

Bekah walks out of her office, her mouth forming an "o" when she sees Drake standing in front of Marshall.

"Detective Nash!" I snap. "Please leave my employees to do their jobs! Marshall," I add, looking at him. "Carry on with what you're doing. Detective Nash knows as well as I do that I can hold that file until the time Judge Barnes signs a warrant and said warrant is on my desk. Everyone else, back to work." I stare at everyone one by one until they're all back inside their offices. Then I take a step closer to Drake. "Again, you cannot come in here and harass my staff. I understand that you want that file, but so do I, Drake, and all that currently exists of it is an empty space where it should be."

"I warned you yesterday not to get in the way of my investigation, but five minutes after being hired by Ryan Perkins, you're already standing in my way," Drake says in a low voice. "Do I need to get that warrant you just mentioned to enter your premises and take what I need when I need it?"

The inflection in his tone makes me fight against a shiver.

"Get it. You can't take what I don't have." I lift my chin so I'm looking at him squarely. "It's just that simple."

A moment passes before he steps forward, so close that my

breasts almost brush his chest. I clench my jaw and ignore the sizzle of attraction that's trailing through my body.

"Stay away from this investigation, Noelle," he warns. "Fucking far away. I don't want to see you near my suspects, the station, anywhere. You understand that?"

"I have a job to do. I'm doing it."

"Then call Ryan Perkins and tell him you've changed my mind."

"You might be the only one with a badge here, *Detective,* but you're not the only one who knows how to investigate a homicide. Apparently, I have more manners and finesse than you possess, and I'm a hell of a lot nicer to people, but I'm not a pushover. I'm sure as shit not gonna have you come into *my* damned building and tell me what cases I can and can't work."

His eyes narrow into angry slits.

"You don't have to like it, but you can deal with it. I will question my own suspects, and if they're the same as yours, then tough shit, big guy. When I have the Perkins file and I've checked it, you'll have it. Same with any information that could drastically change the course of this investigation. As much as I hate it, I'm not the one with handcuffs." My eyes drop to the cuffs on his belt.

"You're a pain in my fuckin' ass, Bond."

"Feeling's mutual, Nash. Now, get out."

"Boss," Marsh pokes his head out. "Got it."

I snap my head around to him. "I might kiss you."

His cheeks pink. "That would be highly unprofessional."

Still, I grab his face and plant a kiss on his cheek. And leave behind a little lipstick. Oops. "You have a…" I point to my cheek and take the file from him.

"The Perkins file?" Drake says, his eyes on the folder.

"No, it's my freakin' dinner reservation," I snap, moving past him.

His arm reaches out, and he curls his hands around my upper arm.

"What are you doing?" I glare at his hand then him.

"You're bringing it to the station."

"I don't even know if it's all there."

"You're bringing it to the station," he repeats lower, stronger. An order, not a request.

Something a little hard to disobey when my skin is buzzing

beneath his grip.

"Can I get my purse before you manhandle me across town?"

His lips thin, but he releases me so I can grab it. No sooner have I locked my office door than he has my arm in his viselike grip again and is dragging me down the stairs.

"Gee, thanks for the gesture, but I can escort myself out."

"I have no problems coming up with an imaginary charge and arresting you for it."

"Do you realize you've mentioned arresting me twice in as many days? Are you fantasizing about me in handcuffs, Detective? Because I'm all for a little kink, but those things hurt like a bitch."

Drake swings me around and my butt bumps into his cruiser. "Yeah? And you'd know, wouldn't you?"

"Actually, I would." I smirk. "If you're a cop dating a cop, it's a given."

Drake's eyes change from angry to smoldering before I've finished my sentence, and he leans in. "Noelle, if the handcuffs hurt, then he didn't fuck you properly."

"Sounds like someone uses his cuffs off duty."

He grabs the door handle, his fingers brushing the side of my ass, and I ignore the sharp breath my lungs are begging me for. "Get in the car, Bond."

"And here I was thinking you were about to promise to show me how to use handcuffs properly in bed."

He tugs on the door so I all but fall against him. I'm only steadied by the grip he still has on my arm, although it's softened a little now.

"If I ever get desperate, I have your number."

He's lucky he moves away, because I'm two seconds from jabbing my heel into his foot and giving him another scar to go with the bullet one I gave him twelve years ago.

"Good to know I need to change my number," I mutter, settling into the car. At least he opened the front passenger's door and not the back.

Sitting in the back would make everyone we pass assume I'm being arrested for murdering Lena, and if that happened, my dad would cause a riot at the station, my mom would cry, and Nonna would scream in expletive-laden Italian that she was right about her little *zitella* having a dangerous job and my gun permit has lead me astray.

And nobody, and I mean nobody, needs that in their life.

Nobody else, that is.

I don't need to hear their complaints about it. I have enough of my own to go around. Maybe I should raffle them off.

"Earth to Noelle." Drake snaps his fingers an inch away from my nose.

I blink sharply and turn to him. "What?"

"I hope your excuse for ignoring me for the last five minutes is because you're thinking about the case."

"Uh…I'm spacey, okay? Don't judge. Some of my best moments are when I'm thinking about cupcakes."

Drake mutters something under his breath and gets out of the car. At least I'm still holding the Perkins file. To be honest, I was so wrapped up in imagining Nonna tearing the police department into lasagna noodles that he could have taken it and I wouldn't have noticed.

I really have to work on my skills of observation and focus.

"Hi, Noelle." Charlotte, the station receptionist smiles at me.

"Hi!" I throw a wave over my shoulder as Drake drags me through his station.

"We're here to work," he mutters.

"And? I don't work with you. I'm on my own time, and you're not paying me for this."

"Think of it as pro bono for the NWPD."

"Ha!" I snatch my arm from his grip as we approach his office. "Working pro bono for *you*? I'm getting a whole list of things under the title 'Prefer To Shoot Myself In The Foot Than Do.'"

"Yeah? Getting long, is it?"

"Every single one of them involves you, so you could say so."

"Sit down, Bond."

Sigh. I was supposed to be the Bond *girl*. Not just Bond.

Still, I sit down in one of the chairs opposite Drake's desk. He unclips his belt and lays it on the desk. Then he parks his butt in his chair and looks at me expectantly. I set the file on the wooden surface before me and pull my purse onto my lap. His eyes get icier and more intense as I pull out my clear lip gloss, coat my lips, then drop it back into the depths of my purse.

Shit. I think it went inside my sneaker.

"Testing my fuckin' patience, Noelle."

"Ms. Bond, Bond, Noelle… One day, you'll decide what to call me," I sigh, setting my bright-blue accessory by my feet on the floor. "Your language is awful, by the way. Are you supposed to swear on duty?"

His response is in the hardening of his eyes.

"Jesus. You need a cupcake. Or sex," I finish under my breath. Then I flip the file open and let my eyes fall to the words on the page.

As I read through it, I remember everything about the case. Julia, my client, had found some expensive underwear in a bag and expected Ryan to give her it for their anniversary. When he didn't and her birthday had passed too, she checked, but they were gone. He also worked late three times a week, and with their wedding only three months away, she'd gotten suspicious and hired me.

Obviously, I proved her suspicions. Easily and quickly, too.

"Is it all there?" Drake asks, his eyes still burning into me.

"I think so," I say hesitantly. "Let me finish."

The problem with being an ex-cop is that I know the law inside out. I can't see right now how this file will help solve Lena's murder. All it's going to do is add Julia to their suspect list—if she isn't already there. I mean, this *is* a great motive to murder Lena. Especially since Ryan used the wedding he'd planned with Julia to marry Lena.

But I also know that I can't not hand this over to HWPD. Drake is already eying his handcuffs, and despite my jokes, I know he won't hesitate to use them and make some menial bullshit charge stick to get me out of his way until he's solved the case.

Still though… "Is Trent in his office?"

"Have you finished?"

"Yes. He helped me out a little on this and I need to speak to him about something."

Drake's eyes narrow. "He should be there."

Bingo.

HWPD can have my file—because I want something, too.

I run down the hall to Trent's office. Well, I teeter, because no one can run in heels.

"What the hell are you doin'?" Drake thunders after me.

Trent opens his door and groans. "What are you doing here?"

"I have evidence." I slip past him and flatten myself against the wall. "Could give you a suspect."

"Hand me the fucking file, Noelle Bond," Drake growls.

In my most immature move for a while, I shove the file up the front of my shirt and look at my brother. "You want the file?"

"Noelle, don't fuck around," Trent warns.

"You can have it. But I want the autopsy report."

"You know I can't—"

"And I'll babysit. On a weekend. Twice." Jesus, this is an expensive autopsy report.

"Or we could get a warrant." Drake's anger is vibrating through the room.

"You could," I reason, "but everyone knows Judge Barnes plays golf on a Sunday and doesn't have his phone anywhere on his person. So you couldn't get one until tomorrow afternoon at the earliest, because tomorrow morning, he's in court with the guy I busted for dealing drugs last month."

That was a fun case. My client had thought her boyfriend was cheating, but he was running a drug-dealing business. Apparently, HWPD hadn't been able to solve it and I stumbled on it by accident.

"The same guy *your* colleagues couldn't identify," I remind them smugly. "So you can wait twenty-four hours and miss a lead, or you could just hand me that report and have it right now."

If Drake's eyes could kill, I'd be ashes on the carpet right about now.

"Fine," Trent sighs. "Fine. You can have the report."

"Great. You get it while I copy this."

"Copy it? Trent, do you have any idea what you're doing?" Drake looks between us. "You can't seriously be giving her the report."

"My clients' files are confidential. Did I forget to mention you need more than a simple warrant to get them?" I smirk over my shoulder.

"Noelle, I'm going to seriously arrest you one day."

"Again with the cuffs." I walk across Trent's office and start up the copier. One by one, I photocopy every page of the report and compile them in order.

"Here," Trent says, handing me several sheets of paper attached together by a clip. "Complete autopsy report."

"Complete report on the infidelity case." We switch at the same time, and I scan the cause of death. "She was poisoned?"

"It was likely what weakened her for the killer to torture her," Drake says softly, but there's still a sharp edge to his voice.

Hemlock poison.

"And she wasn't raped?" I look up from the paper.

He shakes his head. "No sign of sexual activity at all."

"So, why the mutilation of her breasts? And her…lady parts."

"That's what we're trying to figure out."

I swallow. Jesus—I didn't even deal with murders like this in Dallas when I was a rookie officer in homicide. I quit before I made it to detective.

The irony that I'm now technically one doesn't escape me.

"Okay. I'm going to take this back to the office. Thanks." I tuck the autopsy report into the Perkins file and hug them to my chest.

At least, I'm taking them back to the office after I've spoken to Julia.

chapter FIVE

"NOTHING! She has an alibi. She was working, and she showed me a picture of the roster to prove it. Whoever killed Lena, it wasn't Julia in a fit of jealous rage."

Bekah licks frosting from the side of her hand. "Do you think Drake will be pissed that you gave him a dead-end suspect and got a crap ton of info out of them?"

I shrug a shoulder. "Probably. He's always pissed at me, so I don't see how it makes a difference. I'm just going to have to get my information through Brody now. Maybe Devin, but that'll be tough because he's not working the case."

"Kinda sucks that Julia has an alibi."

"You wanted her to be the killer?"

"Well, no. I like her. It would just be easier, right?" Bek drums her fingers against the desk.

"Yeah. She was the perfect suspect. She has the best and only motive I know of right now, but also an ironclad alibi. I asked her boss after she'd left and she didn't leave during her shift."

"Not even for a minute?"

"Nope. So I can cross her off my board." I reach behind me and put a big, red cross through Julia's name. "Which leaves Dean, Mike, and Marshall. Oh, and Grecia."

"Are you kidding? Grecia has only just mastered lifting the kettle.

She's not strong enough to kill someone. She's, like, five foot one and ninety pounds of taco and quesadilla."

"She can slam a door like nobody's business though." I sigh and conference-call everyone.

A chorus of hellos rings out.

"Can y'all come into my office now?"

A second chorus, this time of yeses, and I hang up.

"What are you doing?"

"Getting everyone's alibis. The good Detective Nash and my brother didn't share *those*. Come in!" I call to them at the knock on my door. When everyone's inside, I take a deep breath. "I need y'all to tell me where you were at the time of Lena's death and the time she was deposited in the Dumpster. Dean?"

"I was at home with Emily when she died, and I found her when I came back from the store," he answers.

"And your wife can verify it? So can the store?"

"Well, sure, Miss Noelle. I saw your brother's wife at the store with their youngest."

Okay. He's good. Alison will confirm that with a quick text message.

"Thanks. Mike?"

"I was at home when she was killed and out working a case when she was left here," he replies, his eye twitching.

"Alone? Both times?"

"Yes, ma'am."

"Okay. Grecia?"

She sniffs. "I was here. Eating lunch in my office and watching a sitcom."

"Did you buy lunch out someplace?" I glance at Bekah, who's writing everything down.

"Chuy's. And the manager was in there, so he can confirm I was there."

"And the night before? When she was killed?"

"Getting my beauty sleep." She sniffs again.

"Okay. Marshall?"

"I was at home with my mom on Friday night and here working on something for Bekah on Saturday when y'all were at lunch."

"Ooookay." I breathe out slowly and nod. "Thanks. Y'all can get back to work now." Then I wait until the door has been shut for several moments and there's no noise outside before meeting Bekah's eyes.

"Uh oh," she whispers.

"Mike is lying. So is Grecia. I'll call Danielle and Alison tonight to confirm Dean's alibi, but we can rule him out, I think. Same with Marshall, but you call his mom. Her number is on file."

"You really think Mike and Grecia are lyin'?"

I nod sadly, a heavy feeling in my stomach. "Whether it's to do with Lena or not, I don't know. But they definitely weren't where they said they were."

"Grecia said she was at Chuy's. You want me to confirm that?"

"Already done," Drake Nash drawls from the doorway.

"Were you a boomerang in a previous life?" My eyes find his. "You just keep comin' back here, huh?"

"Can't stay away," he says, sarcasm heavy in his tone. "Grecia was at Chuy's when she said. I already called the manager."

"Told you," Bekah muses. "Ninety pounds of taco and quesadilla."

"Probably Corona, too," I reason.

"Whereas we're a hundred and forty pounds of cupcake and margarita," she sighs.

"Probably forty-five at this point if we're honest with ourselves, and that's pushing it."

"I've never known anyone to go off on a tangent as much as you two. You especially," Drake snaps, looking at me. "You're investigating a murder."

"No shit. You fancy yourself as the next Sherlock? 'Cause Cumberbatch is way prettier to look at," I lie, my hackles rising.

Truth is, not many people have anything on Drake Nash in the looks department. Especially not when he's rocking a five-o'clock shadow the way he is right now.

Shit me. If I didn't think I'd be tempted to uppercut him, I'd probably run my fingers across that stubbly jaw and purr.

"You're kind of cute when you get defensive," he replies with a smirk. "Do you realize your 'potential' suspect was a total dead end?"

"After I talked to her, I did."

"I knew you didn't come straight back here." His eyes glint with annoyance and amusement. "Since you know how she died anyway, and I'm assuming Rebekah does, too"—he cuts his gaze to her for a brief second before it finds its way back to me—"Tim is putting hemlock poison, ingested, as her cause of death on the death certificate. Toxicology reports found it in her stomach. All the torture was inflicted on her as the poison killed her."

I shudder. The first thing I did when I got home yesterday was research hemlock poisoning, and I needed a good measure of Jack Daniel's once I'd finished to wipe the memory of Lena's body and her suffering from my mind.

Every part of the hemlock plant is poisonous. It can take as little as fifteen minutes for symptoms to set in, but when they do, they're horrific. The muscles weaken at a fairly rapid speed, causing extreme pain and paralysis. Sight can be lost as the muscles deteriorate and die, but the mind stays fully awake until the moment of death.

Basically, Lena Perkins was fully aware of every ounce of torture her killer was inflicting on her. She felt the poison threading through her veins and leaking out into the rest of her body, freezing her inch by inch until everything but her mind was rendered useless.

She absolutely knew she was dying.

I wouldn't wish that death upon my worst enemy.

"Poor Lena," I whisper, breaking eye contact for a moment. "So, what are you doing here?"

"To tell you that I meant what I said. Stay away from my investigation, Ms. Bond."

"Detective Nash, please be assured that I have no desire to be a part of it. I have everythin' I need from the HWPD." I pat the autopsy report with a small smile. "Now, be a doll and keep out of *my* investigation."

Slowly, Drake backs toward the door. He pauses and points at me, his biceps flexing. "Remember—you get anythin' at all that could tell us who the killer is, you call me."

I stand sharply and flatten my hands on my desk. I focus on him with angry eyes. "I'm a private investigator, but I'm not stupid. I'm not tryin' to step on your toes. I'm tryin' to do the job I've been trained to do. So, if you don't mind, I'd appreciate if you'd go and do yours and refrain from insulting me every time our paths cross, or I'll report you for police harassment."

"Are you threatening me, Noelle?"

"You bet your fine ass I am, Drake. Now, get out of my building before I have my two-hundred-and-eighty-pound ex-marine help you remember where the door is."

I stare him down for exactly fifteen seconds before he turns and leaves.

"Sometimes," Bekah says, "you're real damn lucky your family is on the police force."

Tell me about it.

I've decided that I've had just about enough of Drake Nash thinking he can control every inch of my investigation by sticking his nose into it. He—and, by default, the HWPD—are so far up my freakin' backside that I'm starting to get piles from trying to get rid of them.

And, really, it's not my fault that my file has given them nothing to work from. I could have warned him, but eh. He's such a righteous bastard that it was much more amusing seeing him figure it out himself. Even if he is determined to get me off this investigation.

I'm trying to figure out what kind of women Drake works with, because if they roll over backwards for him, I'm on the fence as to whether or not they're cop material. There's doing as you're told and then being bullied into doing something.

Drake is undoubtedly attempting to bully me into stopping. Unfortunately for him, I'm not afraid of him or of his scare tactics. They're pathetic, and he's beginning to look a lot like a petulant child.

Maybe he just doesn't like the competition. Maybe he hates the fact that someone in Holly Woods doesn't trust the police force to find the murderer, but they trust a poor, little woman to do it.

News flash: I'm not a poor, little woman. I'm a twenty-eight-year-old badass who has more guns than probably should be allowed on one permit. I'm not planning on bringing that up with the Government any time soon, but by badass, I mean I have three guns within grabbing distance at all times.

I don't believe in overkill.

After Drake left, it became clearer than ever that what the big bad detective is scared of is being made to look a fool by the little private eye. If I solve this case before him, then he's going to look like the world's largest idiot in front of his bosses.

I'm not interested in feeding his ego. I'm interested in finding the asshole who killed my friend.

"Lena's store goes to you now, correct?"

Ryan nods. "I don't know what to do with it. She ran it by herself…but I can't stand to sell it."

"That's okay," I soothe him. "You have plenty of time to figure it out. Now, I hate to ask you this, but did Lena have any enemies? Business deals gone wrong? Maybe some dissatisfied customers?"

"Not that I know of. She'd been trading with the same two suppliers since she opened the store three years ago, and she was the sweetest woman I've ever known." His voice cracks. "Even if something was wrong, she always made sure her customers were happy before they left the store."

That I know to be true. Once, I bought a pair of shoes from her and the heel snapped off the first time I wore them. I let her know next time I saw her, and she all but dragged me into the store to replace them. Then she bought me a coffee to apologize, because that's just the kind of person Lena was.

I know, I know. It makes no sense that she was Ryan's mistress for a while, but that was…well, apparently a very serious burst of desire and emotion. I'm not here to judge, after all.

I thank Ryan, and he leaves. After calling both Lena's parents and sister and getting no answer, I leave messages asking for them to call me at their earliest convenience on either my office line or my cell and give the numbers.

Even the sweetest people have enemies.

Somewhere, Lena must have had one, too. If she hadn't, she'd be alive.

My office phone rings. "Noelle Bond."

"Noelle!" my father shouts down the phone. "Did you threaten Detective Nash?"

Fucking snitch. "Only because he won't leave me alone."

"He's a police officer, honey. He's supposed to bug you when a dead body turns up in your parking lot!"

I narrow my eyes at the door. "There's bugging me and then there's bugging me, Dad, and he's *bugging* my kidneys right out of my body. We've agreed to stay away from each other's investigations now, so it doesn't matter."

"You can't just stay away from his investigation! You're supposed to help him!"

"Noelle? Are you in there?" Devin opens the door. "Dad's just been to the—"

"Is that Dev?" Dad asks as I frantically wave my hand at my brother. "Let me talk to him."

"Can't, Dad. Sorry. He promised to take me to Lena's store so I can talk to her staff."

"I did?" Devin asks.

I stare at him, wide-eyed and tight-lipped.

"Devin? But I thought you just said—"

"Not Dev's investigation. Gotta go okay bye see ya." I hang up and drop the phone into my purse. "Will you take me to Lena's store?"

"Fine. But you have to tell me why Drake just came storming into the station, cursing about 'fucking Noelle' and 'fucking harassment my ass' and 'fucking private investigator.'"

"I might have pissed him off."

"Oh, goodie. You should know that he's currently trying to nail your ass for something so he can throw you in jail for the night, so you've starred there."

"Fuck," I mutter, walking to Grecia's door. "I'm going to be out for a while. If Lena's parents or sister call, tell them to get me on my cell."

"Yes," she replies. "We're out of coffee."

"Mike's gotta lay off it," I growl to myself, walking out to my brother's cruiser. I climb in the front and buckle up.

"All right. If you're making me go in that fancy-ass store, start talkin' about Drake." Devin starts the engine and turns onto the main road.

I summarize Drake's attempts at convincing me to lay off the case, and my brother responds with a giant laugh.

"Jesus. Did no one tell him about your famous temper?"

"I don't have a temper!" I snap. And pause. "I'm simply passionate."

"Passionate. Right. And how do you explain your attitude?"

"Attitude is male-speak for a woman being right all the time."

"Spoken like Nonna's granddaughter," he mutters.

"Heard that."

"You were supposed to."

"Are you engaged yet?"

"Are you dating yet?"

Thankfully, at that moment, we pull up outside Lena's boutique. Sadness pangs my gut as I walk toward the store. It's something about knowing that I'll never be greeted by her smiling face again or I'll never hear her laugh as we discuss Nonna's attempts to marry me off.

Inside, it feels empty without her. The warmth she brought to the air is over, and all her assistant manager, Penny, can give me is a wan smile.

"Hi, Noelle. Officer Bond," she says with a glance to my brother.

"Hey, Penny. How are you?"

She shrugs and pushes some hair from behind her ear, a hand resting on her round stomach. "I'm…lost."

I squeeze the hand she's resting on the counter. "I understand. I need to ask you some questions, if you don't mind. I know it'll be hard, but I want to find this monster."

"Ryan said he'd hired you." She looks down. "If anyone can solve it, it's you."

Wow. No pressure, then.

Drake's voice travels from the back room, and I narrow my eyes as he enters the store next to a sales assistant named Mallory.

His eyes harden when he sees me. "What are you doing here, Ms. Bond?"

"I'm shopping for a new dress," I reply. "My nonna kindly has me a date set up for the weekend."

"That right?" He looks at Devin. "Officer Bond."

"Detective." Devin nods to him.

"Why are you here in a police car, then?"

"Dev often comes shopping with me. You know, to give his opinion on what a good little Italian boy would like." I grin and pinch my brother's cheek. *He's so going to kill me for that.*

"I come under duress and promises of no cop favors," he grinds out, batting my hand away.

I fight my laugh and turn to Drake. "Working?"

"Am I wearing a gun?"

"Three." My eyes flick to his arms.

He stares at me, confused, and I really have to fight my laugh at the look on his face.

"What's the matter, Detective? Can't take a compliment?" I wink.

"Good Lord," Devin mutters.

Penny giggles, and Mallory looks like she wants to shoot me.

Drake's eyes spark, and I know he's finally understood. "If you're trying to distract me, it's not working."

"Not distract you. Throw you off? Maybe."

"You're here to work, aren't you, Ms. Bond?"

"Perhaps I am, Detective Nash, but a girl can talk and shop simultaneously. Killing two birds with one stone is my favorite thing to do." I smile sweetly. "But I wouldn't want to get in the way of your questioning. Please continue."

"Shut up," Devin mutters. "Your niceness is suspicious."

"I'm done here," Drake says, his eyes hot on mine. "Ms. Chandler, Ms. Prescott, if y'all hear anything or think of anythin' that might help me, please give me a call." He slides a card onto the desk and gives a courteous nod before walking past me.

Mallory pouts when he glances at me before leaving the door to shut behind him.

"Jesus, it's hard to be nice to that guy," I breathe. "Okay, ladies. Where were you the night Lena was killed?"

"Are you accusing us of killing her?" Mallory squeaks.

"No," I say quickly. "I'm merely trying to get a picture of her routine. Ryan told me she was here unpacking inventory then went to get some food on her way home, except she never got home. She called him and told him there was a problem here."

"I was here," Penny offers. "One of us always helps her unpack inventory, and it was my shift this time."

"We were both here," Mallory adds. "I needed to change some shifts next week, but she wouldn't let me since she was supposed to take a few days off. She couldn't cover me because her and Ryan's vacation had been booked for weeks." She sighs.

"Did you have a fight?"

"We argued, sure. She's been working less and going away more since she got married. I get it, right? But it ain't fair on us. We've been picking up the workload."

Motive? Maybe.

"When did Lena leave the store?" I ask, sucking my bottom lip into my mouth.

"Around eight?" Penny frowns. "She came back because we'd been sent the wrong amount of the tartan dresses over there in the corner."

I look over. *Oh, they're cute.*

She continues. "She also had a fight with Ryan about the vacation."

Interesting.

I keep my face blank, turning back to her. "When did y'all leave? Where'd you go?"

"Maybe nine thirty? We parted in the parking lot and both of us went home. Lena said she was going to order takeout and sleep on the couch in the staff room," Mallory replies. "She hated going home when they argued."

"Really?"

"Yeah. She was super paranoid that Ryan was cheating on her like he did Julia."

"Mal!" Penny hisses.

"Something to tell me?" I stare at Penny.

"He was," she whispers. "We slept together. Once. Before they got married," she adds hurriedly.

Another motive?

"Just once?" I clarify.

"Yeah. It was a drunken mistake."

"Aren't they always?" Devin mutters.

I flick my fingers against his hand to shut him up. "When did it happen?"

"Maybe a couple weeks before they got married. I can't remember exactly."

"Mhmm." I glance down at her burgeoning stomach. "And that would be…"

Her silence tells me everything I need to know.

"Thanks, girls. I can see you're upset, so I'll leave you to it. But like with Detective Nash, y'all think of anythin', you call me." I hand them two cards from the holder in my purse and grab Devin's arm.

We leave the store to two hushed goodbyes, and I open the cruiser door.

"Did you know that?" I ask my brother.

"Not a clue. And I don't think Drake does, either."

"Hm."

"What are you thinking?"

"I'm thinking they both have motives. And that I need a cupcake to process this."

Three cupcakes and a measure of Jack Daniel's later and all I've done is make more suspects for myself. Which is a good thing—kind of. Dean and Marshall have been wiped off the board, but Mike and Grecia are still very much up there, now accompanied with Penny, Ryan, and Mallory.

If Ryan knew that Penny was pregnant with his baby, he may have wanted Lena out of the way, and the same for Penny. She may not have wanted Lena around in case she found out, because I'm assuming she hadn't. Both of them have strong motives and weak alibis. They were both alone at the time of the murder—unless they were together, which could be a possibility. Penny said that they'd only been together once, but then again, she'd slept with her best friend's husband, so she's not exactly a reliable source.

I rub my temples. A continuing relationship would be the strongest reason for a motive. Both of them could have wanted her out of the way.

Mallory has a motive, too, though. Albeit a weak one. Maybe she got mad and came back after she left. But she's tiny. How would she get Lena to take the poison? The autopsy said that it had been in her dinner, so maybe she snuck in, laced her takeout with hemlock leaves, and hid again.

Or maybe Penny did that and Ryan did all the leg work.

After all, the husband is always the most suspicious, and I certainly have reason to be suspicious of him.

Baking a bun in another woman's oven is a big-ass secret to keep from a woman you're paying several thousand dollars.

Of course, that raises another question.

Why would he pay me if he were the killer?

chapter SIX

"**B**RODY. My favorite brother." I lean against the frame of his front door. My smile is so sweet that I'm in danger of rotting my teeth.

"What do you want?"

"I have two questions." I hold my fingers up.

"No. I can't answer them."

"Oh, come on. They're yes-or-no questions. I'll swap you."

He narrows his eyes. "Trent and Drake already fell for that."

"Fine. I'll go first, and if you already know it, I'll go."

He sighs. "Shut the door and spit it out."

I hurriedly close the door and skip into the front room. "Penny Prescott is pregnant."

"Oh, really? The rapidly inflatin' beach ball on her front didn't clue me into that," he says dryly.

"With Ryan Perkins's baby."

"Fuck off." Brody turns lightning quick, dropping all traces of sarcasm from his tone. "Where'd you find that out?"

Aha! "From her, yesterday. When I went to Lena's store. *And* neither of them has an alibi for the time she was killed. They were alone, supposedly."

"You're not saying it to fuck with Drake?"

"No. If I were, I wouldn't have told you, would I? I get how much this could change the investigation, so I'm being the bigger person."

"Because you want information."

"Yes." I grin.

"Spit it out," he sighs.

"Do you know where Lena was killed?"

"No, but a salad inside a kebab containing Lena's DNA and suspected traces of hemlock leaves were retrieved from the store. We're currently assuming that she was taken to an unknown location, tortured, then kept there until she could be transferred to your Dumpster."

"Great. So it was one hundred percent premeditated."

"That's the theory, sis. Yeah."

I sigh. "Great. Random killing?"

"Can't say. It originally appeared that way, but like you say, Ryan and Penny have one hell of a fuckin' motive to get rid of Lena." He pulls his phone out. "Detective Nash? Yeah, this is Detective Brody Bond... I'm bringing Noelle in to talk to you. She found out some very interesting information while talking to Penny and Mallory yesterday... No, trust me, they didn't tell you this... All right." He pockets it. "He said if your ass isn't in his office in five minutes, then he's definitely arresting you."

It just doesn't sound as sexy when the message comes from my baby brother.

"You're kidding me," I hiss, grabbing Brody. "Hide me and get me out of there!"

"You have-a Italian cops?"

"Brody," I hiss again, hitting him. "You cannot let me go in there!"

"Why-a not?" Nonna yells.

"Nonna?" Trent's voice breaks through Nonna's go-to Italian obscenities. "What are you doin' here?"

"Trying to get-a Noella a husband!"

"Kill me," I groan. "Just do it. Right here." I point to my forehead. "You have your gun. Please."

Brody laughs hard and opens the door to the station.

"Noella!" Nonna exclaims. "They have-a no Italian cop-a!"

"Nonna." I fake a bright smile. "What a surprise. What are you doin' here?"

"I try to get-a you a husband!"

"No. I don't believe you," I reply flatly, sarcasm hitting my words hard. I meet Trent's eyes. "Please take her home, Trent. No one needs to be subjected to her husband-finding efforts."

"My granddaughter will be-a no *zitella!*"

"She's not thirty yet, Nonna. Come back to this next year when the matter is slightly more pressin'," Trent intervenes, wrapping his arm around her shoulder. "Let's go get you one of those pies you like from the bakery and take you home."

"No husbands here!" she mutters, trotting past. "I want-a the paper! Lonely hearts section-a!"

"Sure, Nonna. Whatever," Trent responds to her.

"You just lost all babysitting privileges!" I yell after him.

No, no, no. I cannot believe she did this. Dammit, I have, like, eight years before my ovaries send my eggs to the grave, maybe even ten years. This is not a pressing manner. I could even freeze them, right? That's a thing now? This is not serious.

She is not serious, coming into the local PD and searching for a husband for me.

God, she is. She damn well is.

I want a new grandmother.

I turn around and bury my head in my arms on the reception. Charlotte pats my shoulder with a, "There, there, hon," and I take deep breaths. Honestly, the woman knows no bounds. Devin is older than I am and she's not pressing him to marry Amelia. No, she's happy he's found a good Catholic girl. Hell, Brody is single and she's not getting on his back, and he's only a year younger than I am.

But God forbid I should be twenty-eight and not married. God forbid I should be twenty-eight without even the prospect of a husband.

"In my office, Bond." Drake's voice booms through the ground floor of the station.

I flip the bird over my shoulder. Sometimes, a girl needs a moment. Especially when she has to be in an enclosed room with a sinfully handsome detective right after her nonna demanded everyone in the building show her an Italian police officer.

Hands grab my waist and pull me up. Before I can protest, I'm spun around and propelled into Drake's office. He lets me go when I'm in the middle of the room. Then he turns to lock the door.

"I'm pretty sure that was police brutality."

"Noelle, police brutality would be me flipping me over my knee and slapping your ass for keeping important information from me for almost twenty-four hours," he says firmly, his eyes flaring with heat. "Now, talk."

Sensing I'm going to get no sympathy for my predicament with my matchmaking grandmother, I sigh and tell him everything Mallory and Penny told me yesterday. His face gets angrier with seemingly every word I say, but for once, I sense that it isn't anger at me. It's anger at them for having withheld vital information.

Judging by Mallory's face, I'd guess she was too busy trying to convince Drake to get *her* pregnant instead of telling him about Penny.

"How'd you get that out of them?"

"I'm a woman." I perch on the edge of his desk and cross my arms over my chest.

"I noticed." He drops his eyes to my chest, and I let my arms fall back down so my boobs aren't quite so...boobish. With the excessive cleavage gone, Drake meets my gaze again. "Explain."

"It's easier to talk to other women about that stuff." I shrug. "I'm also a pretty good interrogator, which is why I started my business instead of flipping burgers or something."

Drake raises his eyebrows. "So, what else did they tell you?"

"Exactly what they told you, I guess. Your mistake was that you didn't interview them together. They gave each other away."

"Really?"

"Yeah. Women share everything down to their bra sizes with their best friends, and get them together and we can't keep shit to ourselves. Do you know nothing?"

"Evidently so."

"Sit down, Nash," I sigh, swinging my legs from the chair and throwing my butt into it instead. I cross my legs and wait for him to sit next to me.

"You should be aware, Ms. Bond, that swinging your legs so

vigorously while wearing a dress may allow others to see your other items of clothing."

"That was a very formal way of informing me you just saw my panties."

"I try to be polite."

"No, you don't. You purposely go out of your way to be an asshole."

"Only with you." He winks, smirking. "Now, explain to me about woman friendships."

Words you'll never hear another man say. Ever.

"Actually, I have to get back to my office." I stand. Because, hell yeah, I'm kind of totally fucking embarrassed right now. My panties vary from touching-the-belly-button to what's-the-point-in-those? and I so cannot remember what I slipped on this morning.

Basically, the good detective either saw my Nonna-style panties or got himself a good glimpse of my vagina. Neither of which is appealing.

"Noelle," Drake growls.

I roll my eyes and twist the key Drake left in the door. He comes up behind me and closes his hand over mine on the handle. His chest is solid against my back, and I swallow as the close proximity of our bodies causes my heart to skip a beat or two then speed up so my blood thunders through my body.

"If you know something I should know, I advise you to spit it out," he rasps quietly, his breath cascading across my neck.

"I've told you everything I know," I reply quietly, turning my face back toward him slightly.

"You've realized somethin', though, and you're hiding that."

"Women tell each other everything, except for what they don't want someone to know. Mallory knew things about Penny that Lena clearly didn't. That's what I just realized."

"Are you saying…"

"I'm not saying anything. Now, kindly unhand me. I need a cupcake."

He steps back slowly before coming close to me again. This time, though, we're face-to-face and his icy-blue eyes are boring into mine. If I thought my blood was rushing through my body a moment ago, I was sorely mistaken. I can feel it all over, a sweet heat that has every hair on my body standing on end.

Drake drops his eyes to my mouth for a split second. "Nice panties," he whispers huskily.

I snatch my hand from his and step back, disguising my sharp, lusty breath as indignation. "If I wouldn't be arrested, I'd punch you."

His laugh follows me down the hall, getting louder when I snap at Brody to move his butt.

If Mallory knows things about Penny that Lena didn't, then it stands to reason that Lena may have known things about Mallory.

"Marsh!"

"Boss." He pokes his head out of his door.

"Do we know if Lena Perkins had a life insurance policy?"

"We could in a few minutes."

"That's my boy." I walk out of my office and into his.

Marshall's office is very much like him—small and plain. The only thing in here other than work stuff is a potted plant Bekah insisted he use to brighten it up. Grecia tried talking him into having a sombrero on the wall, but he paled so quickly that we thought he was dying on us. Since then, we've given up on the decorating thing.

"One life insurance policy for Mrs. Lena Perkins, taken out four months ago, covers every circumstance of death," Marshall reads.

"How much?"

"Almost a million dollars."

I whistle low. "Lotta money for a girl who runs a clothes shop."

"Wanna know the best part?" He looks up, a slight smirk tugging at the side of his mouth.

"I have a feeling you're about to mess with me, Marshall."

"The person down to collect the money isn't her husband."

"What?" I shriek, walking around his desk and putting a hand on the back of his chair as I read. "Hmm. Print this."

Seconds later, I have the policy in my hands and I'm knocking on Bekah's door.

"Come in," she calls.

"Read this." I put it in front of her.

Her gaze flicks side to side as she does. "That's a big policy for a chick who owns a clothing store."

"That's what I said. Now, keep reading. To here." I tap my nail against the line.

"Huh."

"Why would Mallory Chandler be down as the recipient of eight hundred and twenty-five thousand dollars in the event of Lena's death?"

"I'm thinking what you're thinking."

"I think we need to talk to Mallory." I grab the policy. "Let's go."

After giving Grecia the usual spiel about messages and requesting that she try to contact Lena's family again, I lead Bekah to her car.

"Where's your crock of shit?"

"On my drive. And I'm still too lazy to go to Austin." I shrug and start the car. "Let's go by the store first. You run in and, if it's Penny working, pretend that Lena ordered something for you before she died but she didn't say when it'd be in. Obviously, it won't be there, so walk out. I'll wait in the car, and if Mallory is working, scratch the top of your head and I'll come in. Okay?"

"Got it."

Luckily, the store is only a couple of blocks away from my office, and we've barely concocted our plan by the time I pull up outside. I pull my phone out and pretend to call someone, watching discreetly for Bekah's signal. It doesn't come.

She walks out and gets in the car. "She's not here."

"Let's try her house." I put my phone in my lap and pull out onto the main road.

Mallory Chandler lives in one of the newer parts of town. Her apartment block is barely a year old, and if I weren't so fond of my little house in the original part of Holly Woods, I'd be jealous. Or I would be if I weren't aware of how much it costs to rent one of these apartments.

I park in the lot, and the shiny, new vehicles hit home how old my crock of shit is. The more places I drive, in my car or Bekah's much newer one, the more I realize I need to go to the dealership.

Maybe I'll get a nice Audi. I already own my house, so maybe I should spend my savings on a car.

"Okay." Bekah scans the list of tenants. "She lives in apartment

8B." She presses the button.

"Hello?" Mallory says through the intercom.

"Hi, Mallory. This is Noelle and Rebekah from Bond P.I. We have a couple more questions for you about Lena."

"Uh, sure. Come on up."

The door buzzes open and we dart through. While taking the elevator up to her apartment, I wonder how Mallory can pay for this. Surely its way out of her budget as a retail sales assistant.

If not, I'm in the wrong damn profession.

She has the door open when we step out of the elevator. "Come in," she says wearily.

"Are you okay?" I ask quietly.

"Just long hours now that Lena's gone. I think it's really starting to hit me, you know? Plus, Ryan came in yesterday and said he's considering selling the store, and Penny's giving me a hard time over telling you about her sleeping with him, and..." She stops and swallows back a sob. "I'm sorry. It's just real now."

"Of course. I'm sorry to bother you again, but I just found something out and I'd like to talk to you without Penny around."

"Sure. Sure." Mallory sits down. "What can I help you with?"

I pull the insurance policy from my purse and set it down in front of Mallory. "What can you tell me about this?"

Mallory draws in a sharp breath. "I forgot all about this," she whispers.

"You knew?" Bekah asks.

"I had to sign it, too," she says softly.

"Mallory, why is it in your name?"

"She seriously suspected that Ryan was cheating on her—or that he would at some point. Her family has a strong history of cervical cancer, and she was afraid that, if she developed it like her sister and aunt did, Ryan would get all the money, but she wanted to have one. She told me that I was supposed to buy the store with the money." She stares at the paper. "Ryan didn't know. About the policy."

How about that?

"Did she think Ryan was sleeping with Penny?" Bekah asks.

"Honestly, I don't know. I think she regretted marrying him as soon as she'd signed the marriage certificate. After all, Ryan and Julia had been together for years before he cheated on her with Lena.

Then they got married so quickly. I think she was preparing for every eventuality. The shop was her baby."

"It sure was," Bekah agrees.

"Will they pay it now that she's been murdered? I-I want to buy the store. I don't want Ryan to sell it to someone else."

"I haven't read the terms, but at a guess, they'll at least need police proof that she was murdered. You'd have to call them." I pause. "Mallory… You knew about Penny and Ryan. Is there anything Lena may have known about you that could have led to her being killed?"

Mallory shakes her head, her sad eyes on mine. "No. Nothin'. I don't talk more than menial gossip. I'm taking my secrets to the grave."

"Wise girl," Bekah notes. "You think she's still a suspect?"

"She doesn't have a solid alibi, so she is. But no, I don't think she did it. I didn't notice a tell when I showed her the policy. If she really hadn't forgotten, I would have known," I muse. Body language has always been my strong point and why, as a cop, I was always taken in on interviews and interrogations. "Same with buying the store. She really does want to buy it."

"Any chance she killed her to get the store?" Mike asks, looking around the room at everyone.

I shake my head and grab a chocolate cupcake. "She genuinely forgot about the policy, and I can't imagine where else she would have gotten the money to do such a thing."

"But her apartment is crazy expensive," Bekah argues.

"Her parents are rich," Grecia inputs. "Her father owns a big construction company in Houston. She moved here to get away from everything. He owns the building she lives in."

"They why would she need the policy money to buy the store?"

"Because other than that, she's independent," Grecia explains.

"Okay. That makes sense now." I frown at the wall.

"How'd you know that?" Dean asks.

"I also enjoy shopping in Lena's boutique." Grecia smiles. "I see Mallory a lot. She's a nice girl."

Huh. Surprises everywhere these days.

"Okay, y'all. If you're okay with your plans for today, I'm going to head home and try to make sense of some of this."

"Sure thing, boss," Marsh says.

The others all express their agreement, so I stand.

"Bekah? Can you give me a ride home? I walked to Brody's this morning."

"Sure."

I grab my things and follow her out to her car. I don't say a word as she pulls away. Instead, I nibble steadily at the skin by my thumbnail and stare blankly out the window.

Something isn't adding up in this case.

I have two prime suspects: the husband and the mistress. They both have the motive and the means to kill her. I mean, I don't understand killing someone to be with another person when divorce is so easy, but hey. Some people are crazy, and hemlock has been implanted in North America for years now. You can drive down a country road and pick it, for the love of God.

But… It doesn't seem like it's enough.

It seems too simple.

"What's your gut telling you?" Bekah asks, parking at the end of my driveway.

She knows me so well.

"That I'm barking up the wrong tree."

"Then we'll look at another angle."

I nod and pat her hand on the gear stick before getting out. She drives away as I fumble in my purse for my keys. Unsurprisingly, I find them in the toes of my Chucks. Along with my phone, a stick of gum, and my favorite red lipstick.

I'm just pulling the keys out when something inside my car catches my eye. Slowly, I move toward the little red vehicle, my eyebrows dipping into a frown.

And I freeze.

My heart thunders in my chest, and I almost drop my keys as I dig my phone out.

"Detective Nash."

"I have a problem," I say shakily.

"Stuck already, Bond?"

"No. There's a dead body on the back seat of my car."

chapter SEVEN

"I HOPE this isn't gonna be a habit."

I look up from my front step at Drake. "You and me both."

"You okay?"

"Honestly? Not really. Another dead body being found on property I own isn't exactly the greatest thing I've ever had happen to me."

"Stupid question," he mutters, sitting next to me. "It's only midafternoon. Your brother has asked that your house be searched with the car so you can at least sleep here tonight."

I lick my lips. "My house doesn't feel that safe right now."

"You got a place to stay?"

"I'll call Bekah. Then someone to install an alarm in this place." I stare at the cherry blossom tree just coming into bloom across the street.

"Good thinkin'. You know it'll be a while before you get your car back, right?" He touches a hand to my lower back. "We can arrange for a rental for you, given the nature of this."

"Fuck that." I snap my head around and look at him. "You can send it to the scrapyard. You ain't getting me back in that damned thing even if you handed me a million dollars!"

"I'm gonna need that in writing."

"Of course you are."

"You know I have to question you, right? Things look suspicious for anyone looking on the outside in."

I lean against the wall and run my fingers through my dark hair. "I worked late last night, and I can get you the tapes from my building to prove it. I left around eleven, came home, downed a shot of JD, and collapsed on my sofa. This morning, I woke with a stiff neck, went to see my brother, then you, then headed back to the office. After that, I visited Mallory Chandler with Bekah, went back to the office, then Bekah dropped me off around two minutes before I called you."

"Airtight alibi," Drake notes, his hand still on me. "Sounds like you've done this before."

I glance at him and open my mouth to snap, but I realize he's teasing me. I sigh. "If you go to the office, Marshall will get you the tapes from last night and a list of everyone's phone numbers to check alibis."

"If only you were this cooperative in the investigation, I might have you in my bed already."

"Seriously? I just found a dead man in my car and you're hitting on me?"

Drake's eyes blaze, his fingers tightening at the hem of my shirt and causing the tips of them to brush my back. "I saw your panties only a few hours ago. I don't care how much you piss me off. You wear panties that nice and I'm going to be preoccupied."

His words jolt through me in a mix of lust and annoyance that counteracts the fear lingering in my stomach. "You're an asshole," I mutter, getting up. "Trent, can I go in and get some things? Please?"

My brother looks toward Drake, and my heart sinks. That's a no, then.

Drake surprises me by cocking his thumb toward the door. "Get in and out before anyone notices," he warns Trent then looks at me. "You take nothing but essentials from drawers. You understand?"

"Understood." I hold on to Trent's arm as he takes me inside my house and upstairs to my room. I shove a change of clothing into my purse and grab my cowboy boots, knowing I have a spare phone charger at the office and I can buy a new toothbrush. I grab my makeup bag as an afterthought from the dresser.

The whole time, Trent's eyes are scanning the house, looking for signs someone's been in here, too.

The thought sends a chill down my spine. This is my fucking space, dammit. No one violates my house unless they eventually want a bullet through whatever limb I aim at when I find them.

"You think they've been in?"

He shakes his head slowly. "No signs of it. In your car, your window was smashed in. That's good for us. We're going to bring some extra officers in to talk to your neighbors and see if anyone saw or heard anything. Someone has to have heard the smash, and if they did, it'll let us know when the body was placed in your car."

I nod, biting my tongue so I don't say what I'm thinking out loud.

It's not a coincidence that both bodies have been placed on my properties once dead.

"I guess there's no chance of bribing this autopsy report out of you," I mutter.

Trent laughs quietly. "You'll have to charm Detective Nash. I'm second-in-command here, Noelle."

"I was afraid you'd say that. Can't you maybe hook him up with the flu or something until the case is solved?"

Trent looks at me like I'm mad.

"Or not," I mutter. "Maybe I should read up on charming people. I'm not that great at it."

"If you're thinking about charming me for the autopsy report, it won't work," Drake says as we rejoin him on the porch. His hands are in his pockets as forensics remove the body and examine my car with a thousand fine-tooth combs.

"Dammit. Don't I have a right to know how he died? I mean, my car and all that."

"Nice try, Bond." He rests his hand on my shoulder. "Do yourself a favor, Noelle. Go chill out and try to relax."

I look at my car and snort. "Yeah. I'll just do that and pretend this never happened."

It definitely isn't a coincidence.

That much has become painfully and somewhat scarily clear since I locked myself in a hotel room with a box of cupcakes and a bottle of JD. So it's not Gigi's, but cupcakes are cupcakes, and since I have no car to get to Austin, I have to deal with it.

I'd only just gotten the images of Lena in the Dumpster out of my mind, too. If that isn't a bitch, I don't what is. Thankfully, I clearly learned my lesson, because this time, all I saw before I called Drake was that the man was clearly dead and covered in blood.

At least he matched the paintwork.

I tip the glass full of Jack Daniel's to my lips and stare blankly at the television. I have all the case files for Lena's murder spread in front of me, but they're all a mess of words and lines. All I can think of is that there were two dead bodies in the space of a week and both of them were planted on or around property I own.

Unless this body comes back as belonging to Ryan Perkins and the murderer is Penny Prescott, the only connecting factor in these cases is...me.

And I'm enough of a nuisance that it wouldn't even be surprising.

I don't think anyone hates me that much though, and they're way too early for my birthday.

Not that dead bodies are great birthday presents. I'd rather receive shoes or something.

I roll the glass across my lips from side to side and put my ringing phone on speaker.

"Oh, my baby!" Mom cries.

"I told-a you! No job-a for a woman!" Nonna shouts.

"Honey? Are you okay?" Dad asks, much calmer.

"I'm fine," I reply.

"You had a dead body in your car! How are you fine?" Mom.

A string of Italian. Nonna.

I swear the woman will never speak English where she can use Italian.

"Dad? Can you get away from the crazies?"

There's some shuffling and then I hear hushed words as my father hopefully escapes from them.

"Okay, Noelle. I've locked them in the house and I'm in the car. Talk to me."

"I don't know what to tell you, Daddy. Another dead body has shown up on my property in, like...four days. Or something. It might be five. Six, even. They're all blurring together." I swallow. "Drake took my alibi at the house earlier, let Trent go in with me so I could get some stuff, and I have to head down to the station tomorrow at some point so he can talk to me properly."

He blows out a long breath that crackles down the line. "You wanna come stay at home for a few days?"

"No offense, Dad, but I'd rather ram a stiletto through my baby toe."

"Can I join you, then? Ever since Trent called earlier, your mother has been going crazy. It's a miracle she went five hours before dialing your number herself."

I laugh, but it's hollow. "I'm good. I'm at the Oleander downtown. I have my gun on the nightstand. Don't worry."

"Okay, love. If you want me to come to the station with you tomorrow, I will."

"It's okay, Dad. I just want to go in, do what I need to, and find out if they think the new murder is connected to my case right now."

"Do you think it is?"

I don't say anything. If I say it out loud, then that kind of solidifies that it is.

"Possibly. Or I've just really pissed off someone in town and they want to frame me."

"Not at all reassuring, darlin.'"

I smile at the phone. "I'm gonna try sleep some now, Dad. I'll call you tomorrow, okay? I promise. And try to get Nonna to cancel the whole date at Friday night dinner. I definitely don't have time for it now."

"I'll do my best. 'Night, Noelle."

"'Night, Daddy."

I hang up and gather my papers. I stuff them haphazardly into the folder, something I know I'll regret tomorrow. But right now, I don't care. With the folder on the floor by the side of the bed, I finish the last of my JD, drop the glass on the nightstand next to my gun—double the weapon—and bury myself beneath the covers with the television still on.

I attach my gun to my ankle holster and admire my cowboy boot in the mirror. It hides the weapon perfectly, and I breathe out a sigh of relief.

After I came to the conclusion that there's a high chance I'm more deeply involved in these murders than I'd imagined I was, I spent the whole night tossing and turning. I eventually slept with my gun on the other pillow, my fingers brushing the handle. I got around two hours of sleep before I woke up, my mind buzzing with theories that are mostly total nonsense.

I'm freaked out. I am. I've done this kind of thing before, but never has it felt so personal.

Even if I'm not embroiled in it, the killer is dumping the bodies in my fucking space.

Asshole.

I pack my things back into my purse, relieved when my heels fit in there, too, and go downstairs to hand in my room key. I leave it on the reception desk with a note of my room number just so no one will talk to me. Then I all but run out of the hotel.

The spring sun is warm on my face as I step onto the sidewalk, and I pause to savor it for a moment. The sun really does make a difference to your mood, because there's a tiny lift in my spirits.

My office is only a block away, and I walk down the street until I reach the turn that'll lead me there. Everyone's cars are in the parking lot, including a police cruiser. I groan, recognizing it as Drake's, and push the door open.

Grecia looks up. "Oh! Noelle!" She stands and hugs me tight. "You're okay?"

"I'm fine," I reassure her, smiling. "Can you get everyone to meet me in the conference room across the hall?"

"Of course. Detective Nash is in your office. Bekah let him in," she adds.

"Thank you." I take a deep breath and take the stairs to my office. I dart into the room before anyone notices me and shut the door.

"Noelle."

I turn to see Drake standing. "You're here early."

"I'm useless at the station until we get results back, so I thought I'd see how you're doin' this mornin'."

"In other words, you've come to question me," I say wearily, putting my purse down on the desk.

"That, too. Sheriff wants to know what your connection to the murders is."

"Well, next time you see him, tell him that, as soon as I know, I'll give him a call. Failin' that, send him around with cupcakes and I'll save you the trouble." My phone rings. "Noelle Bond."

"Everyone is downstairs," Grecia says.

"Thank you." I hang up and look at Drake. "Since you're here, I guess you may as well sit in on our meeting."

"I'm honored," he drawls.

"Don't be. Someone's gonna pay if there isn't a big-ass box of cupcakes today."

When he doesn't reply or move, I stop.

"What?"

He frowns at my feet. "You're wearing boots."

My eyebrows shoot up. "You want a gold star for that observation, Sherlock? Your powers of deduction truly amaze me. I finally understand why you're off beat and the top detective in homicide."

Drake smirks, his eyes showing the laughter he's struggling to contain. "You're always in heels."

"I wear Chucks when I have to observe clients," I correct him.

Sighing, though, I reach down and pull my gun from the boot. His eyebrows go up, his smirk growing, and I put it back.

"But neither Chucks nor heels hide a gun, and I have no issues shooting my way out of this situation."

"I don't doubt it," he murmurs, following me downstairs.

I've barely stepped foot in the conference room when Bekah is running at me. She wraps her arms around me, and the force of her attack pushes me back into Drake. He steadies us both by grasping my waist and holding me there.

Bekah talks a mile a minute, ending with a shout of, "Why the fuck didn't you call me, you dumb bitch?"

I laugh and extract myself from her arms and, more regrettably, from Drake's warm, large hands at my waist. My arms for once empty of files, I sink into the seat at the head of the table. Drake hovers behind me like a security guard, and it's kind of annoying. Mostly because I'm pretty sure he can see down my tank top, and I accidentally packed my date-only push-up bra in my hurry yesterday, so I have a badass cleavage right now.

Everyone asks me questions at the same time, the noise cutting through my thoughts, and I whistle sharply to cut through the noise. It works, because everyone falls silent pretty swiftly.

"What y'all are askin', I can't answer. I don't have the details, and it ain't gonna do you any good starin' at Detective Pain-In-The-Ass behind me. He doesn't know either, and he's already told me he ain't gonna tell me." I get a prod between my shoulder blades for that.

"When I know the identity of the victim, I'll run it by Noelle and see if there's a connection with Lena Perkins. We'll take any necessary steps from there, but what she shares with y'all will be on a strictly need-to-know basis, so don't expect the information you have for Lena. If there's a connection, Judge Barnes is ready to sign an order to ban any member of the public from hiring you to work the case."

"Excuse me?" I stand so quickly that my chair falls over. Annoyance threads through my body as I stare Drake down. "Who the hell do you think you are?"

"The detective in charge of both cases," Drake responds, his voice even but his gaze hard. "That's part of the reason I'm here."

"Well, break it to me gently, Detective." I turn around and look at my team, my hands hitting the table hard. "Hit me with what you're working on today."

Mike starts. "Two infidelity cases. Surveillance and report writing. Should have one wrapped up tomorrow, and I have a meeting scheduled for three p.m. with another prospective client."

"Good. Dean?"

"Much of the same, except my case is up in Austin. I'll be there all day, tracking some businessman. His wife thinks he's hiring hookers."

"Any evidence yet?"

"Nope. The strip clubs are some of the better surveillance I've carried out though." He grins.

I shake my head, smiling, and turn to Bekah. "Bekah?"

"Kickin' your sorry ass and finding out more about both Mallory and Penny."

"Can't wait. Sounds good. Marsh?"

"Doin' whatever everyone else tells me to. Other than that, World of Warcraft."

"And to think that's what I pay you for." I roll my eyes as everyone laughs. "Grecia, did you get Lena's family yet?"

"No. I did find their last known addresses though. They're in Austin."

"Perfect. Dean, could you swing by and see if they're in? If not, post my card through the letterbox with a note. This is bugging me."

He nods to agree.

I run my fingers through my hair. "I'm going to spend my morning with my best friend here behind me then get a cab up to Austin to buy myself a shiny, new car. I'm not into having a coffin for a vehicle."

Dean and Mike snort, and Drake coughs behind me. Marshall and Bekah look at me oddly.

Cop humor.

Need it to stay sane sometimes. Now is one of those damn times.

"And for the love of God, if anyone sees my nonna shouting about Italian men, no matter where you are, please promise her that I'm going to confession tomorrow and I'll apologize to God for having a dangerous job that will mean I'm a *zitella* for the rest of my life."

Bekah giggles in the corner. "No one in their right mind is stupid enough to do *that*."

I pause in the doorway then incline my head in agreement. "Get to work, y'all, or I'm cutting your wages."

"Ruthless," Drake laughs from behind me.

"Dog-eat-dog world," I mutter. "Lemme grab my purse."

I dart up the stairs and grab my purse from the desk. Then I lock the door behind me. Pausing when I notice some scratches by the lock, I frown, but I shake it off pretty quickly. It's more common for me to hit the handle with the key than it is the lock the first time, especially after a sugar high.

Speaking of a sugar high…

"Y'all owe me cupcakes!" I shout, leaving the building. I stop and shove the door open again. "Without charging for gas money, you goddamned cheapskates!"

Laughter follows me down the path to Drake's cruiser. Assholes.

They should know better.

Good news is I'll be in Austin later, which means I can buy Gigi's. And so is Dean. Which means he can buy Gigi's, too.

I really need to get ahold of someone there and get them to open a small store in Holly Woods simply for my convenience. I'd probably keep them in business single-handedly.

Lies. I'd probably quit and work there instead.

Mmm.

"You're drooling."

I snap back to reality and wipe at my mouth. No drool there. "Ass—this isn't the turn for the station."

"Someone's observant this morning."

"Why are you taking me on the road to Austin?"

"Because all three of your brothers spent thirty minutes this morning arguing over who was going to take you to Austin to buy a new car. Since I have to question you anyway, I thought I'd save everyone the headache and do it myself."

"Aw, are you being nice to me, Drake?" I grin, shifting in the seat slightly.

His eyes quickly cut to mine. "You had a rough night. Just doin' my job."

"In that case, I wanna stop by Gigi's because—"

"They forgot your cupcakes. Yeah, Noelle, I heard. The whole fuckin' block heard you."

"I could fire them for that," I say seriously.

"Is it in their contracts?"

I pause. "I need to update their contracts."

Drake shakes his head, but his lips twitch. He has a really bad poker face. But his biceps make up for it.

Sweet hell, what is my obsession with this man's biceps?

The curving bulge… The vein that trails along the inside of his arms…

Jesus. I'm making out with his biceps in my mind.

What is wrong with me? People are dying and I'm thinking about licking his arm.

I snap my eyes away from his very delicious-looking arms, mentally slap myself around a little, and wriggle my foot in my boot. The gun gets a little uncomfortable after a while, and it's kind of a

65

tight squeeze.

"You can take the gun out, you know. I have two on my belt."

Involuntarily, my eyes flick to his pants. His belt. Shit, no, that's his crotch.

Why can't belts be around necks?

Why the fuck am I even thinking about this?

Self-preservation, you wonderful thing, you. Not.

I pull the gun out of my boot, but I leave it on the floor by my feet. Call me paranoid, but it's the floor or down my bra. Gotta be able to grab it in a pinch, after all.

Drake glances at me but doesn't say anything. Maybe he gets it—I don't know. It's cop instinct to have a gun nearby. At least, for me, third-generation cop, it is. My granddaddy never went anywhere without his, Dad still doesn't, and all three of my brothers have them permanently attached to their sides. It's practically in my DNA.

"Get on with it, then," I demand. If I'm going to be stuck in a car with Drake Nash for forty-five minutes, we better actually talk. I don't want to spend more time with him than I absolutely have to.

"Your alibi has been confirmed." Drake scratches at his temple and rests his hand on the gear stick. "Honestly, there isn't much I can ask you until we get the results back from Tim and toxicology."

"And even then, all I can know is the name of the victim." I look away. "Great."

"I can't give you the autopsy report when we have it," he says slowly and quietly. "But I can tell you that preliminary findings show that we're looking at the same killer for both Lena and our John Doe. Their bodies were mutilated in…*similar*…ways."

My hand covers my mouth. I don't have to be Albert Einstein to figure out that what Drake means is that the victim's genitalia has been ripped to shreds. In this case, his penis.

Jesus, I feel sick.

Tension threads through the silence, tightening the atmosphere in the car. It wraps its way around my body, squeezing my neck until I can't breathe. Every word Drake says confirms my suspicions that I have something to do with this.

"So, he was poisoned, too?"

"We're assumin' so, yeah."

I lick my lips again. My chest is so damn tight that it's burning, and there's a big-ass lump in my throat that won't seem to go down. Or, indeed, come up. I'd take vomiting right now over this horribly sickened feeling. I honestly feel like I'm about to vomit anyway. My stomach is churning ferociously, and I shift in my seat.

My foot moves closer to my gun. Again, I know he notices, but in typical Drake fashion, he says nothing. Just quirks his eyebrow.

We're thinking the same thing. I know we are. There's a reason there's an elephant on the back seat. It may as well be bright pink with green and yellow polka dots, singing the national anthem for how obvious it is.

Drake clears his throat. "You got any enemies, Noelle?"

"I piss people off a lot, but they ask for it." Ain't that the truth. If you hire me to find out if your spouse is cheating on you, don't be mad at me when I give you an answer you don't like.

"Anyone hate you enough that they'd want to try to frame you in this? Involve you at the very least?"

"Apart from you?" My tone is dry. "Not that I can think of."

"Not that you can think of?"

"Ask Grecia. She fields all the pissed-off calls because there's a slim chance I have a bit of a temper."

Drake coughs to cover a laugh. "A slim chance, huh? Can't imagine why you're not allowed to talk to angry clients."

"Oh, I can deal with clients. It's their spouses that piss me off. If you don't do the dirty, I can't catch you. It's their own damn fault."

"Can't argue with that kind of logic, I guess." This time, he lets his laugh go.

I don't think I've heard him laugh properly before. It's low and rich, the deep sound rumbling through the air between us until all the hairs on my arms are standing on end.

"What?" I half smile, glancing at him through a curtain of hair. I push it from my face and sweep it around my neck. "It's true. If you don't cheat, you won't get caught. The problem with the guys I bust is that they're not sorry they did it—they're sorry they got caught."

"Have you ever been caught tailin' someone?"

"Once. I got my heel stuck in a drain and she came out of the restaurant. That was awkward." I screw up my face. "I should probably wear my boots more."

"Is that why you carry a pair of Converse in your purse?"

"You know about my Converse?"

"It's a running joke with your brothers."

Bastards. "They're just jealous because they never learned to walk in Mom's heels. Or got the ass to."

Drake's laugh rumbles again. "They wore her heels?"

"We played princesses and knights, but we were all princesses." I sigh. "They're good brothers. Sometimes."

"They look out for you." He prods my thigh just as his phone rings. "If I didn't respect Trent so much, we'd have given each other a few black eyes by now. Can you get the Bluetooth device from the glove box?"

I shoot him a confused look. What did he mean about Trent?

"Bluetooth piece, Noelle!" Drake snaps.

"Shit." I pull it out and hand it to him.

He fits it to his ear and taps the green accept circle on his phone. "Detective Nash… You have? … Do you know? … Fuck… Okay, thanks… Yeah, it helps. I need to read it though. Can you get it e-mailed to me? … Thanks, Trent… No, not yet. Later… All right. Thanks." Drake hangs up and removes the earpiece.

I stare at him as he drops it into my hand. He doesn't say anything, but his eyes have hardened, and his normally curved, pale-pink lips are in a thin, straight line.

"Put it back." His words are sharp, and his jaw snaps shut as soon as he's said the last word.

Doing as I was told, I gently place the small device back into the box. The tension is back, this time stronger and tighter. Pure frustration is radiating from the tautness of Drake's body, and when I focus my gaze on him, I see a vein bulging in the side of his neck.

He flexes his wrists on the steering wheel. "Stop lookin' at me like that, Noelle."

"I'm not stupid. I know why you didn't let me listen."

"It's confidential. You know that."

"Bullshit!" I bang my hand against the dashboard and twist. "You got the autopsy report. You know who the victim is."

He nods—barely.

"You're not going to tell me, are you?"

"It's not a conversation we can have in public. We'll talk when you have a car and are back at your office."

I'm the connecting factor. I know it.

"Fuck the car! Turn off now and turn the fuck around!"

He swerves onto the shoulder and jams on the breaks. The seat belt stops me moving forward, but the shock comes from when Drake turns around. He clasps my jaw in his hand and forces me to look at into his eyes. They're full of anger, and they're glaring at me with the force of that.

"Noelle, for once in your fuckin' life, listen to me. You can't do your job without a car. So you're gonna get a car. Then we're gonna go to your office, and we're gonna talk. Do you get that, cupcake?"

I curl my fingers around his wrist as my own anger flares to life inside me. "The term of endearment does nothing to soften your big dominating act," I bite out, tugging his hand from my face. "But you're right. I can't do my job without a car. So we'll get the car and go back. But we get cupcakes, too."

Drake's nostrils flare, and he pulls back onto the road. "Fine."

"From Gigi's."

"Fine."

"And you're buyin' 'em."

His jaw twitches. "*Fine.*"

I get out of his cruiser in the parking lot, the proud owner of a brand-new, silver Audi TT to be delivered tomorrow morning and the even prouder owner of a half-empty box of Gigi's.

I slam the door shut, holding my cupcake box tight, and storm to the building. The whole way back from Austin, I tried to convince Drake to tell me, at the very least, who the victim is, but he refused. He said that, if the guy is connected to me, he couldn't deal with a freak-out in the middle of a road while he was driving.

Naturally, I completely disputed that I would have freaked out. I might have let out a long stream of curse words, possibly some in Italian, but I wouldn't have freaked out.

He maintained that he didn't want to scare me.

I argued that two dead bodies on my properties in a week is enough to freak out a fucking abominable snowman in a blizzard.

"Noelle," Drake calls after me, narrowly avoiding the main door slamming in his face.

"Hold them," I order when Grecia holds my messages out.

She freezes as I storm past her and up the stairs.

"Noelle—"

"Later!" I yell at Mike, jamming my key into the hole and turning it violently.

"Noelle!" Drake finally growls.

I shove the door open so harshly that it slams into the wall behind it and then fix him with my gaze. "In there. *Now*."

His chest heaves, and a long moment passes between us as he stares at me, both Mike and Bekah staring at us from their office doors.

"Did I not make that clear, Detective?" I tilt my head to the side. "Now means now, not in five fucking minutes."

Drake's in front of me in two long strides. "Watch your damn attitude, Noelle," he warns me quietly, his breath skating across my cheek. "You might get away with sassin' your family, but you won't with me."

"When you're on my property, I'll do whatever the hell I want." I lower my voice. "And you might not realize it, but I've been shitting myself ever since I saw that body yesterday, so unless you want me to rip out a pair of stilettos and tear you a new asshole until you're forced to tell me what I need to know, you'll drag your ass into my office."

"Another threat." He whips his handcuffs out and dangles them in my face. "Want me to use 'em, *ma'am*?"

I step closer to him, moving the cupcake box out of the way of our bodies, and fix him with a stare that I know is as potent as his. "I *dare* you to try, *sir*."

We stand off against each other, barely a few inches separating our bodies. My heart is thumping in my chest, and hell, I'm turned on. My lower stomach is burning, and the heat is seeping between my legs because all I can think about is Detective Drake Nash putting me in handcuffs.

He lowers the restraints and attaches them to his belt again. Then he nudges me away from the door and slams it shut with his foot. I open my mouth to speak, but he grabs my arm and spins me against the solid wood surface. I gasp and drop the cupcake box as my back collides with the door and his chest presses against mine.

"Don't ever dare me, Noelle," he whispers, his tone thick with a seduction that crawls over my skin and joins the heat between my legs. "Because if I get you in cuffs, there'll be no trying about it. You'll be beggin' for it, babe. Keep getting up close and personal and that'll be sooner rather than later."

"You wish," I breathe. *Yes. I do. I damn well do.*

He dips his head so his mouth is hovering above mine, and every breath coats my lips. "I couldn't give a fuck if we're smack-damn in the middle of a murder investigation. You keep pushin' me the way you are and I *will* take you. I'm not afraid to give you a real reason to shout my name."

"You give me a hundred reasons every day."

"'Bout time I gave you a good one, don't you think?"

Good logic. Bad execution. "No. I don't. I think you should tell me what I need to know."

"I just did," he murmurs.

"Drake!" I shove at his chest and slide out from between him and the door. My heart is going freakin' crazy, and I can't hear a damn thing except for the thundering of my pulse in my ears. Turned on is not what I need to be right now.

I run my fingers through my hair and pick my cupcake box up off the floor. The frosting of the lemon one is smudged on the inside of the lid, and I groan. Dammit. Now I'm mad *and* turned on.

I carefully set the box on my desk and grab the lemon cupcake. It's smudged, so I may as well eat it. "Well. Talk."

Drake puts his hands on hips, and with his legs slightly parted, he looks…powerful. In fact, the simple movement means he's filling the room simply with his presence, and as his mood changes, so does the atmosphere.

His eyes meet mine, and the heat is still there, but it's masked by a seriousness that makes my stomach clench. Not in a good way.

"Noelle… Does the name Daniel Westwood mean anything to you?"

I draw in a sharp breath and drop the cupcake.

Drake steps forward. "Noelle," he says softer.

"Yes," I whisper.

chapter EIGHT

"I NEED to know how," he says slowly, coming toward me.

I close my eyes. "He was under surveillance three months ago. Claire Santiago was cheating on her husband with Daniel."

I hold my hands up as Drake approaches me, holding the pose for a second as I catch my breath and push my hair from my face. My fingers fall through to the ends, and I take a deep breath then turn quickly.

"Marshall!" I push his door open without knocking.

He looks up instantly. "Boss."

"I need the Santiago-Westwood file. If it's gone, recover it. Run background checks on both Lena Perkins and Daniel Westwood. Credit records, school records, driver records, medical and dental records—everything, kid. I want to know when Lena started her period and how many inches Daniel Westwood's cock was when you're done. Got it?"

Marshall's eyes flick to Drake, who's standing behind me.

"Don't," I warn him. "I don't care and I don't want to know. What HWPD doesn't know won't hurt them."

"Pretend I didn't hear that," Drake mutters.

I ignore him. "Just get that information for me. I want their fucking life stories on my desk within the hour."

My tech kid meets my gaze and nods once. "You'll have it."

"I better." After spinning on my heel, I push Mike's door open. "Mike!"

His head snaps up. "Yeah?"

"You worked some of the Santiago-Westwood case with me, correct?"

"Yes, ma'am."

"You got your notes still?"

"They're at home, but I sure do."

"Go. Get them and leave them on my desk," I order, turning before he can reply.

"Need me?" Bekah appears in her door seconds before I'm about to shout her name.

"Bekah." I focus on her. "Find Penny Prescott and Mallory Chandler. I want to know if Lena and Daniel Westwood are connected. I want to know if they so much as pissed in the same goddamned sandbox when they were four years old. Got it?"

"Got it."

"From now on, all other cases are on the back burner until this is solved." I reach behind me and grab Drake's shirt. "You. Come with me."

"Kinky."

"Bite me."

"Still kinky."

Without turning, I snatch his handcuffs and storm toward the basement. Drake simply laughs and turns the light on when we reach the top of the stairs.

I'm glad he can laugh.

I'm still stuck on the fact that I have two dead people who were once under my watch.

Drake takes his handcuffs back before I unlock the drawer the Santiago-Westwood file should be stored in and flick through each brown envelope, my heart stuttering each time I read a name that isn't the one I'm desperate for.

The drawer clangs when I slam it shut. I fall against the filing cabinet, dropping my forehead to it. The metal is cold against my skin, but the feeling doesn't last long as my emotions take over.

I feel exposed. Frustrated. Violated.

And real fucking mad.

I slam my foot into the bottom drawer, denting it, and shove off it. "Fuck! It's gone!"

My fingers sink into my hair, and I tug hard, as if the sting on my scalp can take away the cluster of clashing sensations fighting for dominance in my body. Unbidden tears burn the backs of my eyes.

Drake starts to say my name, but I shake my head and take the basement steps two by two. Thank God for my boots.

"Grecia." I stop in her doorway. "I need you to check the January-to-March flash sticks for the Santiago-Westwood file."

She has the drawer open before I've turned around.

That's why I pay her.

When I get up to my office, there are records for both Lena and Daniel sitting there plus Mike's notes on the case. He covered enough pivotal surveillance ops for me that I know there's good stuff in his notes. Attached to the top of Marshall's findings is a note saying the Santiago-Westwood case is missing from the database, but he's doing his best to recover it.

Right now, I'm not holding out much hope.

"How did Daniel die?" I ask Drake, perched on the edge of my desk.

"Same way as Lena. He ingested hemlock leaves and was tortured as the poison took hold. Again, no idea where the torture took place or where he was kept till he was dumped in your car, but a salad was found at his apartment laced with the leaves." Drake picks up Marsh's findings on Daniel with one eyebrow arched high. "Do I wanna know how he got all this?"

"If you have to ask me that, then the answer is probably no." I skim Mike's notes. Finding nothing, I switch it for Lena's records. "Okay."

I walk to my standing whiteboard. I grab a pen and draw a line down the middle. On one side, I write "LENA" and, the on other, "DANIEL."

"What are you doing?"

"Similarities. I'm a visual person." I glance over my shoulder. "I'm going to read out parts I think are important for Lena and tell me if they match with Daniel. All right?"

"I'll read Daniel and you tell me if they match. My case."

"Fine. Okay. Whatever. Go." I sigh and uncap my pen.

"School. Daniel stayed in town his whole life."

"Elementary, middle, and high?"

"Yep."

"Lena, too." So they grew up together. "College?"

"Austin."

"Lena went to Houston," I muse.

Together, we run through every place they could have coincided until my phone rings.

"Hold on. Noelle Bond," I say, lifting the receiver to my ear.

"Lena's mom is on the other line," Grecia babbles. "No files on the hard drives."

"Shit. Okay. Switch her over." I cover the receiver and relay the information to Drake.

He frowns as Lena's mom comes on the line.

"Ms. Bond?" a hesitant voice says.

"Mrs. Young. I'm so glad you called," I say honestly.

"I'm sorry for the delay. My husband and I went to stay with friends for a couple of days after, you know." Her breath hitches. "How can I help you, my dear?"

"Your daughter's husband came to see me the day after Lena's body was found and hired me to find the person who did this—"

"Ryan! Ha! That no-good asshole. Excuse my language."

My eyes widen at Drake. "Please don't worry, ma'am. I was hoping you could tell me how their relationship was. It's always beneficial to hear an outsider's point of view."

"It was…shaky at best. Lena was worried about how stable their marriage was given how their relationship started."

"Understandable."

"Ryan didn't like how social she was. She dedicated her life to her store, and he hated that she spent a lot of time there. He also accused her of cheating on him more than once, which only added to her suspicions."

"Really? Mr. Perkins unfortunately didn't relay that information to me. Please don't take this the wrong way, ma'am, but was there any truth to the accusations?"

Drake's eyes narrow, and he moves to sit on my desk.

"Ryan's? Of course not!" She gasps. "It was darn ridiculous. Lena and Daniel have been best friends since they were five."

"I'm sorry. Did you just say Daniel?" I scramble for a piece of paper, and Drake leans in. I hit the speaker button.

"I did, dear."

"Daniel who?"

"Westwood. He must be devastated."

I draw in a sharp breath and stare at Drake.

"Ms. Bond, are you there?"

"Yes. Yes, I am. I'm sorry, ma'am. What were you saying?"

"Just that Daniel must be hurting right now. Do you know how I could contact him?"

"Mrs. Young?" Drake takes over as I lean back in my seat and cover my mouth with my hand. "This is Detective Drake Nash. I'm the lead detective on your daughter's case, and I'm working with Ms. Bond on some aspects."

"Oh, Detective. It's nice to finally speak to you."

Apparently, I'm not the only one who hasn't spoken to her family.

"And you, ma'am. I'm afraid I have some news about Daniel."

"Oh no," she whispers through the line.

"I'm afraid Daniel's body was found yesterday, and I have reason to believe that the murders are connected." He pauses as she cries out. "I understand this is a real hard time for you, but it would help me and, indeed, Ms. Bond if you could come into the Holly Woods PD tomorrow morning so we can talk."

"Of…of course," she sobs. "I can be there at ten. Th-thank you for your call, Ms. Bond."

"I'm sorry for your loss, Mrs. Young. Both times," I reply softly as Drake hangs up. "Well, shit."

"Shit indeed." Drake looks out the window at the spring sunshine breaking through the trees then back to me. "I think I need to have a word with Ryan Perkins."

Sometimes, the obvious things are ignored because the finer details get in the way.

Like a much-needed girls' night with my best friend and sister-in-law has been ignored because of the whole "dead body" thing.

Tonight, we're at my place, which means copious amounts of sugar and swooning over Sean Connery in Goldfinger.

Yes, yes, I still pretend I'm Pussy Galore. Don't freakin' judge me. She had great hair.

Alison, my sister-in-law, snaps her fingers in front of my face. "I have enough of this case from my husband. I don't want it from you when I'm shaking up margaritas." She wiggles the cocktail shaker in front of my face to make her point.

I hold my hands up. "All right, all right. I'll try to stop thinking about it. Besides, I have my alarm system now."

Why I didn't have one before, I don't know. Maybe because the most notorious murder in Holly Woods' history was when Bert Stanfield was killed over a barrel of beer and a cow.

Plot twist: he wasn't. He shot himself after mixing up the moonshine bottle and the vodka bottle.

So, yeah. I never felt the need for a full alarm system in my house. There's always been one in the Bond P.I. offices for obvious reasons, but who in their right mind would break into a cop-turned-PI's house?

Precisely.

I wouldn't.

My phone rings, and I groan when I see Nonna's name flash up. The woman is seventy-five. She shouldn't have a damn cell phone.

"You should answer that," Bekah says.

Alison glances at the screen. "God yeah. She knows I'm here tonight. She'll just call me and interrogate me about finding you a husband."

"Freakin' hell," I mutter before answering. "Hi, Nonna."

"Noella! You having fun-a at-a girl's night?"

"Yes…" I answer slowly. And suspiciously.

"*Buono!* I want to tell-a you something."

"Oh no."

"*Sì!* I canceled Friday night-a dinner with-a Christofordo!"

"The date you set me up with?" *What a name, my friends.*

"*Sì!*"

"Well, *grazie,* Nonna. I appreciate it."

"I promise-a him you go out-a with him after you solve-a the murder!" she reels off excitedly. "*Sì?*"

I clench my teeth in a pained expression. "We'll see, okay?"

"*Sì!*" she shrieks. "*Ciao!*"

"Bye," I mutter, all but throwing my phone down the back of my sofa. I summarize the conversation, much to Bekah and Alison's amusement, and hold my cocktail glass out for a refill of margarita.

Girls' night is just about the only time you'll get me drinking something other than Jack Daniel's, and even then, it's because of peer pressure.

And I'm simply too lazy to make margs for one.

"I want to be her," Bekah groans as Sean flips Pussy over his shoulder onto the hay bales.

I sigh. "Me, too. Damn my lack of actin' skills."

"I auditioned for a Bond movie once," Alison says. "Then I got there and realized I was too darn Texas to be a Bond girl."

"So jealous," I mutter. "Really, Daniel Craig doesn't hold a candle to Sean Connery, but I definitely wouldn't mind getting shot by his gun."

We three stare at each other for a second before we collapse into giggles. I spill a little cocktail. I've never pretended to be balanced, especially when giggles ensue.

We laugh and laugh, fueled by the alcohol swirling through our systems. Every time I think we should stop, Bekah makes a shooting motion with her fingers and we laugh all over again.

You know you have the best girlfriends when you're all knocking on thirty's door but feel like you're eighteen when you're together.

Bekah's phone pings on the coffee table, and she leans forward to grab it. Seconds after swiping the screen, she groans. Alison and I share a look.

"Uh…" Alison's eyes flick to her.

Bekah sighs. "I joined Tinder. You know, the dating app?"

I nod. Tinder has popped up more than once in infidelity cases.

"My cousin met this really great guy, so I figured I'd try it out. I have nothing to lose, right?"

"So, what's the problem?" Alison asks.

"The guys are…creeps," she whispers. "They say some real odd stuff. Like, listen to this." She picks her phone back up and reads, "'I've been feeling a little off all day, but you just turned me on.'"

I purse my lips to fight my giggle. "Oh, wow. Romeo, eat your heart out."

"It's not even the worst." Bekah's face wrinkles up. "Listen to this one: 'Your body is sixty-five percent water, and honey, I'm thirsty.'"

"How did you answer *that* one?" I snort.

"I told him he could turn on the tap and get one hundred percent water if he needed a drink that badly."

We all laugh. Then Alison reaches over and taps my arm. "Hey, why don't you join, Noelle? It would keep Nonna off your back."

"Oh! Do it!" Bekah exclaims. "Then you're kind of actively datin' and she can't go on too much."

I raise an eyebrow skeptically. "And I suppose Tinder just happens to be full of men with Italian blood."

"Let's find out!" Alison grabs my phone, and I lean over as she downloads the app.

This is going to end badly. Not least because I don't have the time to date on account of my job, but because I'm happy not dating. I agree to Nonna's dates once, maybe twice, a month to keep her happy, but as soon as I mention what I do, the guy basically jumps out the window.

Apparently, my job is intimidating.

I say that those men are boys playing dress up with Daddy's clothes.

"We need a picture of you. Do you have a good one on your phone?"

"Maybe when you get past some of the images of cheating spouses." I wince when she shoots me a dark look. "Okay, okay. I'll go take one."

"Put lipstick on!" Bekah shouts as I leave the room.

I look to the ceiling as I make my way upstairs to my bathroom. I rifle through my makeup bag and extract my lipstick. My phone buzzes from next to the sink just as I smack my red lips together.

Drake.

"What?"

"That's professional," he replies.

"I'm not working. I'm at girls' night getting manhandled into joining Tinder. What do you want?"

He doesn't say anything for a second. "Tinder? That dating app?"

"It's a long story. I'm supposed to be taking a profile picture right now. According to Alison, a cheating couple using a leather whip won't cut it." Shame.

Another silence. "I'm not sure how to reply to that."

"You could just tell me why you're callin', ya know." *Duh.*

"I spoke to Ryan earlier," Drake finally says. "You should probably have a meeting with your client."

"Or you could save me the awkwardness of seeing his serially cheating butt and just tell me how it went," I say hopefully.

"Confidential. I brought him in for questionin'."

"You did that deliberately, you bastard!"

I can almost hear him grin down the line.

"He's jumped so far up my suspect list that he's the only one on it, Noelle. I wanted that shit recorded."

And I can't get access to those tapes unless the HWPD hires me.

No way. Rules and restrictions like needing warrants to access information will make this way harder.

"That's a shame," I sigh. "I was going to copy all the information on Lena and Daniel for you. You know, the info you'll need to get warrants to access at the station? Oh well. I guess you don't need it on file."

"Noelle—"

"Sorry, Detective. Gotta go." I hang up with a shit-eating grin and snap my profile picture.

There. If I have to do it, at least I'm actually smiling.

chapter NINE

PPARENTLY, Detective Drake Nash doesn't take well to threats.
I mean, I wasn't threatening him. I was promising that he
wouldn't get the information, but whatever. He also mentioned
something about blackmail, but he knows as well as I do that it won't
stick because I didn't *technically* blackmail him.

I did for the autopsy report, but he gave me it, so that's moot.

I erase all the angry messages from both my cell and my office
phones. The machine kept cutting him off, and he got progressively
more irate with each message he had to leave. I'm doing everything I
can not to burst into crazy laughter.

To be fair, I was going to give him the information. He could
have applied for a warrant to get it while he already had a head start.
I want this damn case solved as much as he does, and clearly, the
connection between Lena and Daniel is a pivotal point in the case.

Unfortunately, I just don't think the connection between them is
what it seems to be.

That would be just too simple, and if I learned anything in Dallas,
it's that murder is anything but simple.

Even the most cut-and-dried cases have a string of complications
simmering beneath the surface. There's always a motive beyond
the obvious, something you'll never consider until it's too late.
Sometimes, you don't understand until death is staring *you* in the

face. Sometimes, in that situation, you'll make the wrong call. You'll make a move too early and blow everything.

Sometimes, even moving ten seconds too early can cause an explosion where there was supposed to be a simmer.

That makes cases like this precarious. If we move too early, we could lose the killer. If we go too late, we could have any number of dead bodies on our hands. The second our murderer so much as thinks we're onto him, then it's case over.

If I learned anything else in Dallas, it's that killers can disappear as quickly and quietly as they take a life.

I've put off calling Ryan Perkins for three hours now. His number is scrawled on top of the case file, but I'm too chickenshit to dial it. I don't want to know about his relationship with Penny.

I try not to be judgmental in my job. It's the hardest thing in the world, because sometimes, people need a damn good judging. Ryan Perkins is one of those people. It's one thing to cheat on your fiancée with another woman. Not right, admittedly, but it's one thing to do it. It's another thing entirely to marry your mistress and then knock up her best friend.

I mean, come on, man. If you're gonna cheat, use a goddamn condom at the very least.

It strikes me that Ryan isn't the brightest star in the sky.

The moon seems to be brighter.

I take my scissors and cut across the top of the packaging on the new flash stick. I do this four times and insert every one into my laptop, using every USB port. Of course, the laptop freezes, so I remove the sticks, restart, and insert again one at a time.

Each time I push one in, I copy files over. Three months of each year onto each stick, exactly the way they were before. As the files transfers, I pull my sticky labels out and identify what files are where by writing the first letter of each month in tiny letters on the bright, white surface. As another three months of files transfer onto another stick, I cut the label and press the relevant sticker onto the right flash drive.

A knock sounds at my door. "Boss?"

"Two seconds, Marshall." I pull the device from the USB port once the files finish moving and gather all four drives. Then I drop them into my purse, open my drawer, and shove all the packaging into it.

No one on my team knows about these sticks. No one outside my team does, either. Hell, I even turned the security camera in my office off before I sat down to do this. I'm fed up with my files disappearing when I need them.

"Come in," I call.

Marshall opens the door with a grim expression.

"Don't say it," I order quickly. "If you don't have the file, leave right now."

"It's like it never existed," he says quietly, shutting the door behind him.

I bang my fist against my desk. Shit. All I have are three albeit detailed surveillance ops written up in Mike's almost-undecipherable handwriting. No background, no interviews, no images…

I fold my arms on the desk and bury my face in them. A quiet groan leaves me as I process this information.

Whoever the killer is, they know we recovered the information about Lena Perkins and the police have the file. Whoever they are, they've been inside my building, and they've wiped clear every trace of Claire Santiago and Daniel Westwood's affair.

Good fucking job, asshat.

I'm angry so much lately that I'm beginning to wonder if my body thinks I'm having a perpetual period. The hormones would explain a lot, for sure.

Apparently, assholes have the same effect as a surge in estrogen.

Still, though, it doesn't add up to me. It should. It's simple, right? In theory, Ryan got Penny pregnant, and when he couldn't work out how to break up with Lena, they devised a plan to kill her. Their alibis are each other, and yeah, the hotel confirms their arrival, but it's one hour after the approximated time of death.

Then they—or someone else—dumped her here, on my property, the next day, for whatever reason.

But Daniel… He's a wildcard. Kind of. Maybe Ryan was overcome with grief after having killed Lena, went on a jealous, angry rampage at the man he believed had been sleeping with his wife, and killed him in the manner he had Lena.

Yet…why would he kill him if he wanted to break up with her? Wouldn't infidelity on her part be the easy way out of the marriage?

I tap my pen against my desk.

Sure it would be, but cheaters… It's one rule for them and another for another, right? So, in Ryan's mind, he could grow a mini Perkins in his second mistress's belly, but the second Lena offered her vagina up for occupation, it was out of order.

Again, it's a crime driven by anger.

Maybe Ryan couldn't take that Lena wanted someone more than him.

Maybe Penny hated that Ryan loved Lena more than her and that she'd always be in her way.

Maybe nobody knew what they really wanted.

And maybe, just maybe, I'm totally wrong. After all, I can push it to the side, but I can't ignore the fact that there's no DNA tying either Ryan or Penny to the murders. That I know of, at least.

Maybe there is something. Maybe there's more than meets the eye to this investigation, and Holly Woods Police Department and Detective Drake Nash are keeping it to themselves. It wouldn't surprise me in the slightest.

Drake Nash has a particular set of skills. Actually, he has several.

The man is a fantastic cop. There's no disputing that. He takes no shit and cuts to the chase before his opponent has even thought about running. He's quick-witted and determined.

The man wrote the book on seduction. With his delightfully killer biceps, cocksure smirk, and eyes that are connected to his cock by some magic thread, he could melt a ton of metal to his bidding in seconds.

The man is intelligent. He barely seems to think before he connects people or situations together, but that intelligence makes him arrogant. He always thinks he's one step ahead when, maybe, he's a mile behind. But he doesn't see that.

He doesn't see that, once, I was a fantastic cop. That, now, I'm a fantastic investigator. He doesn't see that, like him, I take no shit and make no time for excuses. My wit almost destroys his on a regular basis, especially when he talks about fucking handcuffs.

He doesn't see that, as a woman, I'm a master of seduction. I know my body. I know my curves and how to exploit them to my advantage. I can flutter my lashes and pout my lips to rival Dior's catwalk models if the situation calls for it.

He doesn't see that my body makes me intelligent. He doesn't see how I use it to my advantage and almost strangle information from my source. Detective Drake Nash has no idea how I can manipulate someone until I've drained every ounce of information from their body.

Detective Drake Nash has no idea who he's up against.

He has no idea of the power of my mind or my body.

At this point in my investigation, with my privacy violated in a brutal way, with my freedom abused and my workplace contaminated, he has no idea what lengths I will go to if it means I can solve this case.

Quite frankly, I don't give a shit if I embarrass his ass in front of the sheriff or at the county fair. I couldn't give a flying hippo if he stares at me when all is said and done and despises every vein that pumps blood through my body.

I don't care if my heart does some bullshit skip-a-beat thing whenever he walks within ten yards of me. I don't care if my skin tingles at the barest touch from his skin against mine. I sure as hell don't care if my pussy goes into overdrive when his body is flush against mine.

If I want that, I'll take my nonna up on her dates.

If I want that, I'll reply to the guy on Tinder who just asked me if I rose from Hell because I'm "looking hella horny" right now.

If I want that, I'll let Drake take me with those darn handcuffs he's so fond of.

But I don't. Not for a second.

I don't do my job to fall in love. I don't do it to be second to a man—or, indeed, first to one. I do my job because there isn't a thing I'd rather do than this.

And if that means stepping on Detective Drake Nash's toes, then so be it.

I grab my phone and dial Ryan Perkins's number. He doesn't pick up, so I dial again. And again. And again. Finally, the answer machine makes way for his voice, and before he can speak, I say, "I think we need to talk."

He's drawn. He looks like a man who's had his heart broken then tugged through the wringer a million times over.

I don't anticipate my estimation to be that far off reality.

"Ryan," I say softly yet firmly. "I need to know everything. You know that. I can't help you unless you help me."

"Four months ago." He looks out the window, the bags beneath his eyes more pronounced than they were when he saw me a week ago. "That was the first time. It was at a party. I don't remember where. Lena was tired and wanted to leave, but she told me I could stay, so I saw her into a cab safely and stayed."

"And?"

"Penny was there. She…tempted me. I gave in. We went to the room I'd booked for me and Lena and spent the night together. I regretted it instantly, Noelle." He meets my eyes. "I fucking loved Lena. I still do. But she got busy with the store, and Penny told me she was pregnant, and I didn't know what to do. So I had two relationships. I told my wife I loved her with the same mouth I kissed her best friend with."

"And?"

"And then I lost the person I love most."

I take a deep, slow breath. My eyes flit over every inch of his face, examining his expression from the downturn of his lips to the creases by his eyes. There's no twitch. He doesn't look away for a second despite my intense scrutiny. His lips don't move even a millimeter.

"Talk to me about Daniel Westwood." I lean back in my seat. "What was Lena's relationship with him?"

Ryan's nostrils flare, but the sadness remains in his eyes. "They grew up together. Separated for college. He came back to town and they reconnected," he explains, a robotic, dull tone to his voice. "They were best friends, but they took it to the extreme. If she had a bad day, she'd call him instead of me. She'd have nights out with him and not me."

"So you found solace in Penny," I summarize. "You assumed your wife was finding comfort elsewhere, so you did."

"No—"

"Yes," I interrupt, leaning forward. "Your mistake, Ryan, was not trusting Lena. It was putting her into the bracket you put yourself. Maybe it was easier to speak to someone other than you. Maybe she didn't want to worry you with her issues. Maybe Lena was so much herself that pushing her burdens onto you was too much for her to bear. Maybe, just maybe, she wanted you to ask her."

"Stop."

"What if Lena needed her best friend? Women don't all have female best friends. Brody is my brother and my best friend. I go to him before Bekah sometimes. What if Lena was too afraid to trust you? What if she feared what you know to be true? What if she was so afraid of you being unfaithful that knowing she had problems with her business tipped her over the edge?" My gaze hits him with the force of a ten-ton truck. "What if, Ryan, her telling you about her being in debt tipped you over the edge and you left her?"

"Never!" He shouts it. No, he roars it, his chair clattering to the floor as he stands. "I'd never fucking leave her."

"But you'd fuck her best friend."

"I loved Lena!"

My door bangs open, and Mike and Dean fill the space where it just was. "Miss Noelle?" Dean asks, his muscles taut.

I hold my hand up. "So, why'd you cheat on her?"

He steps toward me, and in the same moment, Dean and Mike jolt forward and I slam my hands on my desk.

"I have three guns I could grab in a second. You wanna step forward again?"" I lift my brows, and Ryan freezes. "You know you're the prime suspect, don't you?" I continue, my hand on the weapon concealed at my hip. "For both me and the police. You have every motive under the sun, Ryan."

"So arrest me!" he shouts, tears filling his eyes.

"No." I smile sadly. "I don't think you did it. I don't believe you killed her, so I won't tell them to or let them arrest you. You don't look like a murderer to me, doll. You look like a man who fucked up and now has to bury the love of his life."

Everyone in the room freezes. Mike and Dean are still holding fort at the door, their arms tensed and ready for a fight.

"I'm right, aren't I?" I push Ryan. "I can't help you if you don't help me, honey. You want me to find Lena's killer, you'll sit down and tell me everything you hid before."

Ryan looks at my impromptu bodyguards, his own body tight and ready to fight his way out of here.

"Y'all can fight it out, but all it's gonna do is call the cops here and make you look even guiltier." I slowly sit back down, my eyes still connected with Ryan's. "This conversation is on camera. You really wanna help me, help the PD, help Lena…you're gonna talk, Ryan. You're gonna sit your ass down and talk right now or I'm telling my team to get Detective Nash, Detective Bond, and their boys in this office to lock you up. Now, sweetie, what's it gonna be?"

With three pairs of eyes and a camera focused solely on him, Ryan Perkins sets his chair right and sits down.

chapter TEN

"HE threatened you?"

I roll my eyes. "God, Devin, no. He just tried to intimidate me."

"I hear-a you taking the Lord's-a name in-a vain-a!"

"Has no one procured legal tranquilizers yet?" I look at all three of my brothers and Alison. "Why is she still making my life hell? Doesn't she know Brody is single?"

"Ahh, but I'm a year younger than you," he sniggers. "Besides, you're a woman, Noelle. You should be married by now."

"Go on," I threaten. "Keep it up. You know I can shoot better than all y'all put together and I won't hesitate to do it."

"One day, you won't threaten such stupid things."

"*Cazzo no.*" I stare at the large, Drake Nash shaped figure in the doorway. "What are you doin' here?"

"Noella!" Nonna strolls into the front room with pasta sauce at the side of her mouth.

"I cursed in Italian!"

"Noella," she repeats, this time with anger lacing the extra syllable she insists on adding to my name.

I push myself up with a fake cough. "I think I'm sick."

"Sit the *cazzo* down!" Devin and Brody shout synonymously, each one of them snatching an arm and yanking me back onto the sofa.

"Y'all are only speakin' Italian to please the *pazzo vicchia senora!*"

"Your switch from Texan to Italian is somethin'," Drake says, grinning as he takes a seat.

I fix my gaze on him. "*Io castrare te, stronzo,*" I snap, to the amusement of both Nonna and Mom, who steps up behind her.

"Noelle." Mom looks at me with that shut-the-hell-up look only moms can give. You know, the one that makes you wanna hide behind the sofa despite being a grown woman.

I tighten my jaw shut as Drake's grin widens even further. Crap, I'm twenty-eight and being totally embarrassed by my mother. Didn't she lose the right to do that when I turned twenty-one?

"I see-a why you have-a no husband," Nonna pipes up. "You have-a no idea how to speak-a to a man."

"I wouldn't call Drake Nash a man," I grind out.

His grin falls, his eyes chilling until their blueness reaches glacier quality. "Don't you have a cheating spouse to be following?"

"Don't you have a murderer to be finding?"

"Noelle," Dad says firmly. "You can take your hand off your gun, sweetheart. You're a little outnumbered."

Reluctantly, I pull my fingers away from my waistband and tuck them between my thighs. Just in case my finger gets twitchy. "Yet I have a better aim than you all put together," I mutter in frustration.

"Only because Dad took pity on you and thought you needed more target practice than we did," Trent grumbles.

"Aww, poor big bro," I coo, reaching for his cheek.

He knocks my hand away to Alison's giggles.

I continue. "Did nobody teach little baby Trent how to shoot a bull's-eye?"

Devin looks at the two terror children in the corner, his lips forming the widest, cockiest smile I've ever seen. "Someone did."

Trent leans over me to thump him in the arm, but I block his swing.

"Hey, now!" I protest.

"Thought you had a better aim than all of us!" he vents.

I ball my hands into fists and slam them both down onto my brothers' thighs, making both of them cry out in pain.

"*Cagna!*" Trent hisses as I jump up and away from both his and

Brody's attacks. Sure—he refuses to curse in English, but Italian is all good until his kids learn it.

I hold my hands out to the sides and smile sweetly. "And to think—I *meant* to do that. Another two or so inches outward…" I whistle innocently and shrug my shoulders.

"Noella! Trent! Brody! Devin!"

"The hell did I do?" Brody exclaims, looking at Nonna.

She furrows her brow, her dark hair perfectly pulled back from her still-youthful face. "You all are children!"

"I'm thirty-three!" Trent protests.

"You no-a act it!" she retorts, straightening to her full five-foot-two height and slamming her hands onto her hips.

That's it, Nonna. You stare down that six-foot-three police officer grandson of yours.

"And you!" she says, rounding on me.

Oh, shit.

"You-a the worst!" Her finger points at me and she waggles it with far too much enthusiasm, if you ask me. "You wind-a them up! All-a time! No wonder you-a single! No man want-a your attitude!"

I catch Drake's grin from the corner of my eye and shoot him a glare before turning puppy-dog eyes on Nonna. "Aw, Nonna, that's so sweet. Don't you know that the guys all say I get my attitude from you?"

Immediately, she bristles, and all three of my brothers sit bolt upright, as if someone just sent an electrical charge shooting up their spines.

"Aha! You think-a that? She has-a same attitude as-a me?!" Nonna shrieks.

"Mamma, maybe you need to lie down," Dad interjects, stepping in front of her. "Just for a half hour."

Nonna narrows her eyes, but Dad lifts his eyebrows and twists her toward the door before she can argue. After one final angry stream of Italian about how no one in this country or family respects her, Dad all but frog-marches her up the stairs and out of earshot.

"Nonna says bad words," Aria says from the corner, her large, dark eyes the spitting image of Trent's.

Trent winces. "Nonna is bad sometimes," he answers, opening his arms for his daughter to climb onto his lap. "How did you know?"

"Sometimes, you and Mom yell bad words at each other. They might be Italian, but, Dad, I'm not stupid."

I cough to cover my amused snort and look away. That's what you get for trying to pull the wool over a ten-year-old's eyes, Trent Bond.

"Dinner's ready," Mom says, breaking through the awkward moment caused by Aria's announcement.

We all get up and head to the dining room, and despite my best efforts, Mom directs Drake in the empty seat next to me. I stare at her flatly as he tucks his legs beneath the table and deliberately kicks my foot with his.

"The hell are you? Twelve?" I hiss, kicking him back.

"Thirty-one," he replies, his light-blue eyes devoid of their previous chill. Now, they glimmer with laughter. "And yourself? Still on the brink of puberty?"

"Twenty-eight." I grab my wine glass and throw half of it back in one go.

Mom notices, her eyebrows shooting up.

"What?" I ask her.

"Nothing," she replies, her pearly-pink lips curving into a smile.

I drop my eyes to the red smudge on my glass and rub at it with my thumb. Damn that man. What is he even doing at family dinner? I was always under the impression that family dinner is for family, girlfriends, fiancés, and husband/wives.

Oh. Hell no.

The crazy witch upstairs is trying to set me up with Drake Nash.

"Nonna!" I slide my chair back. "I swear to god I'm gonna beat your Italian ass into next week!"

Devin grabs the back of my chair and stops me from running upstairs at her. "Noelle," he says through laughter.

"God will probably thank me for it!"

"She's just being nice."

"Nice? No. Nice is her nose up your business instead of mine. Nice is her nose up Brody's backside inside of being up in mine all the time!" I humph and drop back into my chair.

"Shut up and drink." Brody shoves my glass toward me.

"I love you, Brodes, Dev, but I swear to God that both of you are ten seconds away from my drink in your faces if you keep siding with the crazy old bat."

"You only have one drink," Devin observes.

I grab Drake's full beer bottle. "Yeah?"

"Put the bottle down, Noelle," Drake drawls. "Devin, let her go. We all know she's as dangerous as a snail in a heatwave."

I slowly cut my eyes to him, grabbing my fork and jabbing it into my spaghetti with deliberate force. "Are you sure about that, Detective? Because there are nine people around this table right now and only one of us has given you a bullet in your foot."

Drake smiles slowly, and the curve of his lips and the glint in his eye are so fucking sexy that I want to smear my pasta sauce all over his hot little face. "Yet only four of us have a gun about their person."

Slowly, I lift my wine glass to my lips and sip, despite the fact I only just wiped my lipstick mark away. Dad chuckles from the end of the table, and Devin's cough is enough to make me fight against the smirk that wants to form.

Oh dear.

Drake Nash doesn't know me very well at all.

I glide my foot up his calf, making sure to show him I'm wearing boots. "You sound so sure, Detective."

"You're wearing boots."

"Cleverly observed."

"Aunt Noelle always carries a gun in her boot," Aria states a mere second before sucking up a strand of spaghetti with a giant slurp that sprays marinara sauce at her brother.

"Does she now?" Drake asks, his eyes trained firmly on mine.

"Yep. She says every woman with more sense than all the men in her family put together carries a gun, because a real woman needs to be prepared for everything."

"And?" I prompt her, never breaking Drake's gaze.

"And no matter how dangerous a man is with a gun, he'll always be impulsive, but a woman will always be more calculating and therefore more dangerous than a man can ever dream of being."

"When the hell did you teach her that?" Trent booms.

"Ask your wife." I grin, lifting my wine glass once more.

Oh, shoot me. One woman surrounded by four cops, a florist, and a pensioner who fancies herself a matchmaker? I had to learn somehow, and if that meant playing Poor Little Noelle until I whooped ass at target practice, so be it. And if my sister-in-law is happy for her daughter to learn the way I did, then, well.

She's more a Bond than my brothers are.

"Touché," Drake hums. "One gun or two?"

"Take a ticket and get in line, Drake," I whisper back. "You're not the only man waiting to find out."

"I could demand you tell me."

The threat in his tone makes me laugh. "You could. But you won't."

"You sound real sure there, Noelle."

"Oh, I am. Real sure, that is." I twirl some spaghetti on my fork and seal my lips around the metal prongs, sucking the yummy pasta into my mouth. A string of spaghetti falls loose, and I suck it up with one sharp breath. Then, with his eyes still focused on my lips, I say, "If you were going to demand I tell you, you'd have done it instead of staring at my lips like they were on your dinner plate instead of a Bolognese."

His eyes snap to mine, ice-blue frustration and lust warring with each other. His look is intense, but my tongue darts across my lips anyway. He gazes at me and opens his mouth to say something, but Nonna bursts into the room with yet another stream of angry Italian, complaining that her segregation will make her dinner cold.

Her rant cuts Drake off, and I deliberately turn my body away from his, well, because I'm a fucking child. And the look I just saw in his eyes said he was definitely not about to demand I show him the contents of my boots.

More like he was about to demand I show him the content of my panties.

For real this time.

I finish the rest of my wine and don't argue when Brody fills my glass. For all of his jokes, he's my best friend, and if anyone around this table has to see how much Drake affects me then, well, it may as well be Brody.

I tip the glass to my lips right away, much to my baby brother's amusement. And my elder brothers' disdain, but whatever. They know what to expect after having lived with two Bond women before I was born.

We Bond women breathe cupcakes, wine, and profanity. And marriage. Unless you're me. Then you breathe all but marriage.

I sit in silence as Nonna catches up on everyone's lives, because the kids' school tests have changed since she called two days ago, and like there's been another suspect in the murder everyone except Devin seems to be working on.

"Did you know-a Lena bought all-a her salads from Rosie's Café?"

"What?" Drake and Trent ask simultaneously.

"She and Rosie were-a good friends," Nonna sniffs. "Every day-a she was there!"

I narrow my eyes. "How do you know that?"

"I like-a her coffee."

"Every lunchtime?"

"*Si.*"

I grab my napkin, tap around my mouth to wipe away any stray pasta sauce, and reach for my glass. "Thanks, Nonna." Then I throw the rest of my wine back and push my chair out.

The reaction of my brothers—and the way Drake's face sets into a mask—tells me that they had no idea about Lena's eating habits.

"Did you drive?" Mom asks.

"Nope. Apparently, my brother has been stalking my Friday night habits." I cock my thumb toward Brody, who grins. "Picks me up like a good little Bond boy so there's no drinking and driving."

"I will drive," Silvio, my four-year-old nephew offers, holding his arms out like he's holding a steering wheel.

I look over at my olive-skinned, tiny nephew. "It's okay, cutie. Uncle Brody will take me home."

"I got it," Drake offers, pushing his chair back. "Mrs. Bond, your Bolognese was to die for, but I'm afraid I can't eat another darn thing. So I'll make sure your daughter gets herself home safe."

Mom blushes. *What the hell?* "That's very kind of you, Drake. Thank you."

"Yeah. Kind." I roll my eyes and stand. Focusing on my niece and nephew, I give them my weekly warning about being good, and they agree wholeheartedly. Little shits. Good thing they got my cute.

Nonna eyes me speculatively as I shrug my jacket on, and I stare at her, daring her to say anything. Anything at all. Just even goodbye.

When nothing happens and Drake passes me my purse, I give her one final glance.

"Drake," she calls.

"Yes, ma'am?"

"*Sei italiano?*"

Oh, fuck no. "We're going. *Caio!*" I shove him out of the house and slam the door shut behind us. I've had more than enough abuse from my family tonight. Drake Nash does not need to be subjected to such a horror.

I take a deep breath and climb into his truck, dumping my purse at my feet. I get the feeling that that was a very narrow escape. It's one thing for Nonna to invite him to dinner, but it's another entirely for him to be even one-hundredth Italian.

If the woman sniffs Italian on his breath, she'll hound his ass until, in this case, we either marry or I kill him.

The latter is the more likely option. Let's be honest—we can't be together five minutes without jumping down each other's throats. And sadly, it's not a physical jump.

Sadly? This wine is going to my head.

"Your grandmother is…something," Drake notes, his voice hesitant.

Oh, good. He understood her last question.

"Oh, she's a lot of freakin' somethings. Not many of them good." I push my hair from my face and let out a long sigh. "Did she invite you tonight?"

He nods. "After her performance in the station the other day, it was obvious why she invited me. Trent said I should come just to get her off my back. Yet there she is asking me if I'm Italian."

"Oh, yeah. She's like a bloodhound. As soon as she sniffs potential husbands, she's asking the guys to run background checks and research their family trees." I shake my head. "She's fucking crazy."

Drake's lips curl into a smirk, and he glances at me. "Good thing she hasn't researched my family tree. I wouldn't have made it out alive."

"If you have Italian blood, stop the car. I'll walk home. Screw that."

He laughs, deep and goose bump inducing. I fight my shiver.

"I won't tell you then," he says through his laughter. "And I certainly won't tell your nonna."

I shift in my seat as he pulls onto my street and parks behind my car on my driveway. "Save yourself, Drake. Leave town. I'm already fucked. I won't drag you down with me."

Another laugh. He unclips his seat belt and turns to me. My front porch light is on, and the dim glow casts shadows over his face, making his eyes seem brighter than should be possible. I swallow when he leans forward.

"She's wasting her time," he murmurs, his eyes hot on mine. "I might be a quarter Italian, but you and I would be locked up on attempted murder charges by the end of the first date."

"You clearly have a different idea of wasting time than she does. She and Nonno fought every day. And when I say fought, I mean she threw plates and he screamed that he was divorcing her 'crazy fuckin' ass' because she would give him a heart attack before he was fifty."

"Did he?"

I smile at the thought of my late grandfather. "Never. They hated each other for at least two hours a day, but the way they loved each other for the other twenty-two canceled that out." I shrug. "Even if she did give him that heart attack. Never quite managed to kill him, though."

"Sounds like a pretty fucked-up marriage."

"You're familiar with my family, aren't you?" My lips twitch as I meet his eyes again. "Nonna thinks the best kind of love is the one where you hate each other at least once a day. Something about caring enough to get pissed off."

"Touché." His smirk mirrors mine. "Don't worry, Noelle. I'll keep my heritage under lock and key, just in case."

"That's very thoughtful of you. I'd hate to have to shoot you again."

The glint in his eye… It's almost like he wants me to. Challenging and daring and heated.

"I'd have to arrest you if you did," he says in a low voice that flows over me like ice-cold water on a red-hot summer's day. "Speaking of shooting… How many guns do you have with you right now?"

I reach down and grab my purse, then sit up to unclip my belt and open the door. Swinging my legs out, I glance back at him. "Two. I knew you were coming for dinner." I grin and jump out.

Drake roves his eyes down my body. "Where is it? The one not in your boot."

I run my fingers through my hair, smiling. "Somewhere you'll never find it." Then, with one last look, I tug up my tank top to cover my cleavage and turn toward my house. My hand is diving into my purse to find my keys when Drake calls my name. When I turn, he's leaning out of his window, looking at me seriously. "Yeah?"

"Make sure you set your alarm system tonight," he says, a darkness I don't like in his tone. "And lock every door."

"Should I ask my neighbor if I can borrow his guard dog, too?" I joke.

Drake's answering silence lets me know that he thinks that might not be too much of a bad idea.

I swallow. Hard. He knows something I don't. Something about me.

"Thanks for the ride home."

"You're welcome." He waits until I'm inside before he pulls away.

I set the alarm system and yank the deadbolt on the front door. After checking that my back door is locked, too, I kick my shoes off, remove my gun from the ankle holster, and grab my phone. It's only eight p.m., so I dial Ryan's number as I pull the bottle of wine out of my fridge.

"Noelle? Is everything okay?" he answers.

"Yes. I have a couple of questions. Are you free?"

"Sure."

I balance the phone between my ear and shoulder as I pull a glass down. "Do you know if Lena bought her salad from Rosie's the day she was killed?"

"She did. She called me when she was there. I didn't think that was important."

"Neither did I," I say under my breath. "So, she picked it up, right?"

"She went in to order it and had it delivered since she's just down the street. She did that a lot."

"Why didn't she just call?"

"You already know we'd been fighting all day. She called me to tell me she was staying at the shop because there was stuff to do and didn't want to have the conversation with the girls around."

That makes sense. "Okay. Thanks. This helps fill in some blanks."

"Is everything okay?" he repeats.

"Yes. I'm just trying to get a solid timeline together is all. Sorry to bother you on a Friday night."

"No worries, Noelle. You can call any time."

Nice to have permission for something I already plan to do, I guess. "Thanks, Ryan. Have a good evening." I hang up and carry my wine to my front room. After turning the TV on for background noise, I curl up on the sofa and pull my little Tiffany Glock from my chest. I set it on the side table next to me and sip my wine.

Just before Lena was killed, she'd gone to Rosie's to call Ryan and order dinner. That would have taken ten minutes at most, so when she got back, she told Mallory and Penny to go. Rosie's salads are all fresh, so it would have taken fifteen minutes to prepare, and around three minutes to deliver down 21st to the boutique.

Which means the salad was somehow poisoned during its delivery. And taken from Rosie's salad container and put into another. Otherwise, HWPD would know exactly where Lena ordered her salad.

Why was the container changed? How did the salad *get* tampered with? Who delivered it? Why has no one come forward to say that something happened that night? Who was watching Lena to know that? Was it planned or was it simply an opportunistic moment to kill her?

And how the hell did Daniel Westwood, her best friend and fellow cheatee, get poisoned?

chapter ELEVEN

I SAUNTER into Rosie's Café before the morning rush and set my purse on the counter. Rosie Martinez, plump with slightly greying hair, turns and shoots me a big smile that's reflected in her hazel eyes.

"Well, good morning, Miss Noelle. How are you?"

"I'm very well, thank you, ma'am," I reply, my eyes dropping to the pastries. "How are you?"

"I'm just fine, thank you." She wipes her hands on her apron. "What can I get you?"

"I actually hoped you could answer a couple of questions for me if you have time."

She waves her arms around the café. "No one here but you and me, sugar. What's botherin' you?"

"I found out last night that Lena stopped by and ordered her food the day she died," I say softly, bringing my eyes to Rosie's. "I'm trying to piece together how your salad got the poisoned leaves in. I can't work it out."

Rosie sighs and pushes a few loose strands of hair from her face. "Miss Noelle, I wish I could answer you. Daniel took a few salads out, only he never came back. Never answered his phone or nothin'."

"Daniel?" I frown. "Westwood?"

"Yes. He helped me out here on some evenin's. My back ain't what it used to be," she chuckles. "He was around for deliveries, sortin' that there stockroom out the back, and little bits of handy work. Touchin' up paint spots, puttin' up a picture—you know the type? He was a good boy," she finishes on a soft tone. "Of course, he never answered his phone."

I reach over the counter and gently tap her hand. "He was a darlin', for sure." Except for the part where he fucked another man's wife. "Have you found some extra help again?"

"No, ma'am. I just haven't had the time."

"I know someone who would be willing to help. Marshall isn't the strongest, but he'll do until you can find a replacement. I'll talk to him when I get back to the office."

Her face brightens. "Oh, you're a good girl, Noelle. No wonder your grandmother is fixin' to get you married. You'll be a good wife."

Oh, sweet Jesus.

"I'm waiting until she can find a man who can handle me, ma'am." I grin. "She's not doing too well on that."

The bell over the door rings, and I turn just in time to see Detective Nash and Detective Bond The Eldest walk into the café.

"Why am I not surprised to find you here, Ms. Bond?" Drake drawls, his hands on his hips, his eyes burning into me.

"Because you're following me?" I ask, raising an eyebrow. "How on Earth am I supposed to know that, Detective? I was just about to order coffee for all my staff. They're workin' real hard right now."

"I'm sure you were," he replies, disbelief thick in his tone. "Are you meddling in my investigation?"

"No, but you sure are meddling in my morning coffee consumption." I sniff and turn back to Rosie. Shit. Now I have to pay for six cups of coffee. Sigh.

"I'll be right with you, Detectives," Rosie says, acknowledging them. "What can I get you, Miss Noelle?" She winks.

"A regular latte, a large cappuccino, a double espresso, and three large vanilla lattes, two of them skinny. Please." I tick the orders off in my mind to make sure I have enough coffee for everyone. Yep. Nailed it.

"Of course there's one full-fat vanilla latte," Trent notes.

"Oh, bite me." I roll my eyes and step to the side as Rosie turns to make my order. My eyes flit to the pastry cabinet.

"You'll regret it tomorrow," my brother warns, trying not to laugh.

"Oh, I already regret it," I mutter. I should have known that these buffoons would turn up first thing this morning to talk to Rosie. But I figure I have at least an hour on them to figure out what the hell happened to Daniel Westwood.

God, it would be so much easier with his autopsy report.

"Get much out of Rosie?" Drake asks, his eyes telling me that he's got my number.

"I don't know what you mean, Detective. All I've said is that I'll send Marshall around to help her with her deliveries now that Daniel isn't with us."

Drake's eyes go cold, and I swear he gets an inch taller when he straightens. "Daniel?"

"Do you need a hearing test?"

"Don't fuck with me, Noelle."

"Wouldn't dream of it," I reply, a sassy smile on my face as Rosie puts my coffees in front of me. I grab a large cup holder tray and say to her, "Could I get one of those chocolate croissants, too? And two of the hot bacon-and-cheese braids?"

"Of course." Rosie bags them all up separately and gives me my total.

I hand her my card, fully aware of the two men staring at me—one with a lot more anger than the other. Rosie hands me the receipt, and I scribble my name on the signature line before handing it back to her.

"Thank you, ma'am," I say to Rosie then turn to Drake and Trent. "Have a good day, gentlemen."

Trent simply shakes his head as I pick my pastries and coffees up. Drake, however, pins his eyes on me. His gaze follows me as I walk to the glass doors of the café and lean back against them to open it. I pause just before stepping out to shoot him a wide, I've-got-*your*-number smile with a touch of smugness.

His jaw tightens, and the angry glint in his eye only serves to make me laugh. Hot damn, it is just too easy to wind that man up. And way, way too fun.

I walk down the street and take the turn that'll lead me to my office. My visit to Rosie's, for all the questions it answered about Lena, has done nothing but give me another hundred and one more questions about Daniel. Holly Woods is a small town—surely, if he had been missing for a few days, someone would have known? Then again, his best friend was just killed. It would have been easy to assume he was hiding out as he coped with that.

I just can't help but think that something is missing.

Why them? Why steal my files? If the files hadn't been stolen, with Daniel's still floating around somewhere in the universe, it would be much simpler.

What the hell is my connection to these murders? Aside from the obvious, which is far too obvious to even be a possibility.

I open the door to my building and walk into Grecia's office. It's empty, so I put her croissant and coffee on her desk before heading into Dean's office down the hall. He takes his coffee with a kiss to my cheek and a promise to do the next Gigi's run for free. Bingo.

"Oh, hey," I say to Marsh, walking into his office and handing him his espresso. "Rosie needs a little help a few evenings a week running deliveries and helping her sort stock since Daniel died. I told her you might step in for a couple weeks until she can find someone to replace him."

"Sure," Marsh replies without looking up from his computer. His fingers are flying across the keyboard, his eyes flicking back and forth behind his glasses. "Thanks for the coffee."

"Are you playing World of Warcraft again?"

"No, boss. I think I could be close to recovering the Santiago file."

I blink. "Oh. Well. I'll leave you to it."

"Thanks."

I shoot one last glance at him before pulling his door closed some. The kid is some kind of technological genius, I swear. I can just about work my cell phone—there's no way I can search for files in the netherworld of the Internet.

"Breakfast." I drop Bek's pastry and coffee on her desk in front of her.

She looks up from the file she's reading and wipes fake drool from the corner of her mouth. "You went to Rosie's? You're the best boss ever."

I laugh. "So you say. I was coerced into buying them when my brother and Detective Nash showed up."

She narrows her eyes. "What aren't you telling me?"

"Let me give Mike his coffee." I put my drink and pastry on her desk, too, and back out. Mike's door is partially open, and as I approach, I hear a high-pitched giggle.

"Wouldn't go in there," Marsh warns, glancing up at me through the gap in his door.

"Why?" I turn and frown at him.

"Actually, you probably should. And remind them that I can see it."

Can see what?

I pause for just a second. Then I knock twice on Mike's door before pushing it open.

Holy shit.

My mouth goes dry as I take in the scene before me. Grecia. Sitting on his lap. Kissing. Quite feverishly if her hair is any indication.

She gasps and jumps up, frantically reaching up to smooth her hair out, and Mike stands, straightening out his shirt collar.

"Explain. Now," I demand, staring at them both. "How long has this been going on?"

"A few weeks," Grecia mumbles.

"And you didn't think to tell me?"

"Most workplaces don't allow it," Mike reasons. "We thought you might be…the same."

I put his coffee down and rub my temples. Why did I never make this policy a thing? "Okay. One, if I were like that, you'd both be fired right now. Two, y'all hidin' this shit is not okay, especially not when you're makin' out like a couple of teenagers on my damn time. I pay you to do your jobs, not get each other excited. Not to mention Marshall can see this on the security cameras."

Blood rushes to Grecia's face, and she covers her mouth with her hand. I guess she forgot that little gem.

Something niggles at the back of my mind, and I narrow my eyes. "I knew you were lying about your alibis. You were together the night Lena was killed, weren't you?"

"Yes, ma'am," Mike mutters.

I run my hand through my hair. "Okay. I cannot deal with this right now. Mike, your coffee is there. Grecia." I look at her. "Yours is on your desk with a pastry. I want you in that room for the rest of the day unless it's absolutely necessary to leave. And absolutely no more fucking make-out sessions when you're at work. Y'all do what the hell you want at home, but not here. Keep it separate. And if I ever, ever find out you're breakin' my rule, you're both fired. Got it?"

"Yes, ma'am," Mike repeats.

"Yes, ma'am," Grecia echoes.

I look at Grecia pointedly and point at the door. "Downstairs."

When she's gone, I turn to Mike. To his credit, he looks fully ashamed.

"Noelle—"

"Now, don't be givin' me your excuses, Mike. I ain't interested. What I am interested in is you recreating the last few days of Daniel Westwood's life. Turns out Rosie sent him to deliver Lena's salad the night she died and never saw him again. Find out who the very last person to see him was. Keep your mouth busy talkin' instead of kissin'." I glance at his mouth, which is smeared with a little lipstick. "Just make sure you wash your face before you leave your office. You look like you got in a fight with a makeup counter."

He nods and rubs at his lips. I turn on my heel and stalk toward Bekah's office, stopping at Marshall's and telling him to keep an eye on those two. He agrees with a grunt. At least, I'm assuming he's agreeing.

He better actually be looking for that file and not playing his dumb video game or I will cover his office in pretty potted plants.

"Did you know that Grecia and Mike were bumping uglies?" I ask Bek, closing her door.

"Fuck off!" She claps her hand over her mouth. "I mean. No."

I fight my laughter. "Yeah. I just walked in on them kissing in his office."

"No!"

"Yep."

"What did you do?"

"Tore them new assholes and told them that, if they make out at work again, they're fired." I shrug and sit down. "Marshall is on perve-duty."

Bekah laughs. "Right. Oh, wait! Were you right about them lying about their alibis?"

I grimace and nod. "It's a shame my spidey-senses didn't pick up on their secret relationship. More to the point, how did they keep it secret?"

"Yeah. Everyone knows everything here. It's already halfway around town that Detective Nash had dinner at your parents' last night and drove you home. I dropped by the store before work and was cornered, like, six times and questioned." She rolls her eyes.

"Wait, what?" I frown. Quick enough, realization sinks in. "Oh my God. Does everyone think we're dating?"

"Nonna's going into the station and yelling about Italian cops and his going for dinner look kinda suspect."

"I cannot catch a break, can I?" I sigh heavily and tear off a piece of my pastry. I chew it angrily, thinking about my nonna and her meddling ways.

Great—let's add some romantic rumors into the mess that is my life right now. That's what I need.

"And you know Nonna will hear those rumors and not consider where they started," Bek continues.

"Oh God," I moan, sinking down in my seat. "I'm debating my mental health at the time I decided to come back to this damn town."

She grins. "Look on the bright side. Drake isn't in here, yelling at you for obviously beating him to the punch in the investigation."

"Yet." I point another torn bit of bacon-and-cheese goodness at her. "Let's not jump the gun on that one."

My best friend laughs. "Why were you at Rosie's, by the way?"

Oh, of course. The real point of my being in her office. I tell her everything we learned last night at dinner and what I found out this morning at the café. Obviously, that ends that part of our conversation. Because there pretty much is no more information about anything at all that means we can make sense of what we found out.

"Why didn't we know that Daniel was working for Rosie?" Bek muses, twisting her lips to one side in a thoughtful pout. "Wouldn't it have come up on the background check you had Marsh do?"

"I don't think it was anything official." I get up and walk to her window. Her office looks out over the trees behind the building and onto the park behind it. "I think he just helped her out a few nights a week and she gave him some cash at the end of each evening."

"Isn't he a little old for a job like that?"

"Yeah. But Rosie is close friends with his mom, so maybe he felt obligated to." I shrug. "I don't know, Bek. The only real suspects we have are Penny and Ryan. They are literally the only people I can think of who would have a motive to kill both Lena and Daniel."

Bek chews on her thumbnail. "Did anyone see Daniel after he disappeared on the delivery run?"

"I have Mike looking into that. But if not, this investigation is so full of dead ends it's unreal."

Two quick knocks bang at Bek's door.

"Yeah?" I call, craning my neck around to see who's interrupting me.

Dean steps in. "Miss Noelle. Miss Bekah."

"What's up?" Hopefully not another dead body.

"I've been looking into Lena's life like you asked, to see if she had any enemies." He pauses, and after a moment, I nod for him to continue. The man has the manners of an angel. "It turns out she was married in her senior year of college."

"She was married *in* college?" I frown, turning fully in the seat. "She didn't stay in Houston long after her graduation. They must have been granted a quickie divorce, right?" I glance at Bek, and she shrugs.

"Well…" Dean coughs. "That's the thing, Miss Noelle. She never was divorced."

I put the phone down and sigh. No, the lady at the record office said. Unless I'm a police officer with a warrant, I have to wait for marriage records like everyone else and pay the rush fee that isn't actually a rush fee.

More like a rip-off fee.

The thought makes me groan, and it sinks in that I may have to go to HWPD with this information. Dean only knows because he dug deeper than he normally does, which makes me think the police *don't* know that Lena was married before. Which means I'm potentially in possession of case-altering information.

I drum my fingers against the table and stare at the park beyond my window. It's as busy as you'd expect for midafternoon on a Saturday—dog-walkers, elderly couples, moms and dads with little kids, a few groups of teens.

I lift my phone back up and dial Marshall's code.

"Yo," he answers sharply.

"Can you see if there's any record online of Lena Perkins being married when she was in Houston?"

"You askin' me to hack?"

"No. I'm asking you to see if there's an online record. It's not my business *how* you do that."

"'Kay." He clicks off, and I shake his mood off.

The kid has had a stick up his backside all damn day, but he's working desperately to recover the information we need, so I'm trying not to be mad. But still—he talks to me like trash again and he's gonna know about it.

My phone rings, and instead of picking it up, I hit the speaker button. "Noelle Bond."

Brody's voice fills my office. "Drake is mad at you."

"You say that like I should be surprised." I laugh. "Drake is always mad at me."

"Yeah, well, he found out you weren't at Rosie's for coffee this morning."

"Really? He believed that?"

"No. He's just real pissed you lied to him."

I shrug a shoulder. "And it's taken you…seven hours to call me and tell me he's mad."

"Yeah. I'm only tellin' you because he's on his way to your office."

"What the hell for?"

"Presumably to threaten you yet again about 'meddling' in his investigation."

I roll my eyes. "Noted. Thanks, Brodes. I'm ready for the bear when he shows up."

"And by 'I'm,' you mean you and not your gun, right?"

"Aren't they the same thing?"

"Noelle!"

I grin and hang up before he can give me his inevitable warning. Oh, come on. I wouldn't actually shoot Drake Nash.

Would I?

Well. Maybe.

Depends on the mood he catches me in. Luckily for him, I'm

pretty amused right now.

My phone rings. Yet again.

"Noelle Bond," I sigh.

"Heads-up: Drake's cruiser is outside," Bek says. "And he looks pissed. Hot but pissed."

"Fifty bucks on him threatening to arrest me."

"Fifty bucks on him actually doing it," she retorts. "You're on."

"Have you not heard of appointments?" Grecia yells in the hall, and I put the phone down. "Or manners?"

"Is Ms. Bond here, Ms. Gonzalez? Yes or no."

"Yes! But you must have an appointment to see her!"

My door slams open, my wall only saved from certain destruction by the handle by the angle it opens at. It bounces back immediately, and the only reason Grecia isn't whacked in the face is because she steps back.

I look up straight at the powerhouse that is Detective Drake Nash. His hair is curled and falling across his forehead, and those glacier-blue eyes are so angrily intense that I can physically feel his emotion radiating from his body. The force is so strong that shivers cascade down my spine one after another, a cascade of mixing emotions that make absolutely no sense to me.

"Come on in, Detective Nash, by all means."

chapter
TWELVE

"CAMERA. Off." His words are sharp, nothing short of demands he expects to be obeyed as quick as a snap of a finger. "Now." "Me. Noelle. You. Rude." I sit up straight and meet his eyes with the same steely determination he's staring at me with.

His eyes flare as he storms to the corner of my office where my security camera is hanging. Within seconds, he's reached up, turned it off, then spun it into the wall so there's no way Marsh can see anything if it's switched back on.

"Can I help you with anything, Detective? Possibly a lesson in speaking eloquent English?"

"Do not fuck with me, Noelle." He slams his hands down on my desk and leans over it toward me. "What were you doing in Rosie's this morning?"

"Why do you insult my intelligence by assuming I don't know that you already know the answer, Drake?" I stand too, flattening my hands on the desk to mirror his. I kick my chair out behind me and shake my head to pull hair away from my eyes. "You knew what I was doing the second you walked in. Pulling the dumb card does nothing for you."

"You knew we'd be in to question her. Why did you go?"

"Because I'm being paid a lot of money to find the person who killed Lena Jenkins. We're doing the exact same job, and by the sounds of it, I'm leaps and bounds ahead of you despite the resources you have at your disposal. I am, for the most part, workin' off my intuition. You're apparently hoping for the killer to walk through the doors of Holly Woods Police Department and turn themselves in."

"Do not—"

"Fuck with you? Sass you? Grab you by the balls and twist them?" I hiss, cutting off his low growl. "Too late."

He inhales sharply through his nose, his nostrils flaring with the intensity of his breath. His eyes—Jesus, his eyes. They sear into mine, and the passion and determination glaring from them is almost suffocating. I want to cover his eyes with my hand just so I'm not smothered by the power of his gaze any longer. I want to close my eyes and look away and not be so totally overwhelmed with the sheer emotion he's throwing my way with just a stare.

"Again, Detective," I say slowly and quietly, pushing off the desk and walking around it. "I do not appreciate you bursting into my office and yelling at me like I'm a petulant schoolchild. I have no idea what kinda saps y'all work with at the police department or what kinda women y'all got that roll over like little dachshunds expectin' themselves a belly rub when you call for 'em, but you ain't gonna find one here. I'm conducting my own investigation whether you like it not, and not once have I stepped on your toes. In fact, I've been nothing but fucking cooperative to your rude ass."

"Watch your damn mouth, Noelle Bond," Drake says low, his tone full of threats and barely restrained anger. "My patience where you're concerned is just about at the breakin' point, and when it reaches it, you ain't gonna like me very much."

"So save yourself a job and cuff me. See what the hell happens when you do that."

He stands and turns to me, eclipsing me in height and width. "Are you threatenin' me, ma'am?"

I take another step toward him despite our size differences. "Fuck yeah, I'm threatenin' you, sir. Except my threats are closer to promises, so try it and see how well it ends for you."

The minute distance between our bodies is swallowed by his single step toward me. If I were to reach out just a little, my fingers would brush his inevitably toned stomach.

"You have five seconds to take it back before I make good on my threat, Noelle."

"You have five seconds to get your ass the hell out of my goddamned office before I break your kneecaps."

Within two seconds, Drake Nash's arms are around me and he has both of my wrists secured at the base of my back with one of his hands. The other is pressed between my shoulder blades, an open pair of handcuffs just close enough that I can feel the chill of the metal through the light material of my shirt. He's so close that I can feel every contour of his body pressing against mine, and the heat of his breath flowing across my skin sends my body temperature up several degrees.

"Do not tempt me," he whispers hoarsely in my ear. "Do yourself a favor and refund Ryan Perkins his money. Then get your ass out of this investigation. It's too fucking dangerous for you, Noelle. You have no idea what you're up against."

"Don't ever underestimate me. You may be able to restrain me without trying, but I sure as hell ain't afraid to fight your fine ass and pin you to the ground," I grind out. "I'm not the cops who work under you at the station. They might whimper when you so much as glare at them, but you can have those handcuffs at my back, Detective, and I'm still gonna be ready to twist your balls off and hand them to you."

"Listen to me," he says, his voice still hoarse. "Stay. Away. You're connected to this. I don't know how yet, but you are, and every time you drag *your* fine ass into another branch of this case, you're puttin' yourself in danger."

I swallow and meet his eyes, my heart thundering in my chest. "I always liked to live on the wild side. Ask my family. I'm the kid who ran across the road without looking and ignored the 'do not feed the animals' signs at the zoo. I'm doing my job. Just like you are. Try to remember that I'm trained the same way you are."

"Dammit, Noelle!" Drake snaps, letting me go, his handcuffs clattering to the floor between us as he pushes me backward. "You're askin' to sign your fuckin' death warrant. Do you know that? It doesn't matter if you have a gun on you or have them hidden in your office, car, and at home. This killer isn't playing by the rules. They've ambushed and poisoned without the victim even knowing it. This is a cold, calculated murderer on our hands, and your pretty little blue Glock inside your pants isn't gonna save your ass from a poisoned fuckin' salad!"

His words cut through me with their honesty. Because I know that, really. But the blood that runs through my veins—it's cop blood. It's blood that flows for justice and retribution, and the heart that pumps it around my body beats for righteousness.

"I know that!" I shout, running my fingers through my hair. "But someone I know, my *friend,* was murdered and dumped in my parking lot. Someone I followed, someone I had to chase and spy on. Then her best friend turns up dead. In my car. My fucking car! Someone else I had to follow and dig up dirt on." I take a deep breath. "You don't do this job and not get enemies, Drake. I have a helluva lot of enemies—people who hire me then hate me. You know how you deal with your enemies? You don't run away. You stand ten feet away from them, laugh, and give them a big ol' fuck you. This person who's doing this? They're my goddamned enemy, and I'll be fucked if I'm gonna sit here in my office like a good little girl and let them think they've won, because the only way they'll win this is if I'm the one poisoned, cut up, and laid out to die wherever they dump my body!"

Three steps.

That's all it takes for him to close the distance between us and slam our bodies together.

That's all it takes for my body to be against his, for his arms to be around me, for his hand to be in my hair, for his mouth to be dropping harshly and relentlessly onto mine.

I wind my fingers into his crisp, white shirt and succumb to the kiss he's just planted on me. There's nothing else I can do. His body is strong, and his grip is tight. Leaning against him, pulling him closer, and tasting him as deeply and as ferociously as he is me are the only things I'm physically capable of doing right now.

My blood is humming through my body at a speed I didn't know was possible, and I feel nothing but lust and adrenaline and the sweet sensation of pleasure and relief throbbing its way through me from my head to my toes. The intensity of my feelings surprise me, and when Drake pushes me against my desk and my ass perches on the edge of it, I don't complain.

I curl my hand around the back of his neck.

I fall victim to his almost-deadly assault.

I allow his touch to brand my skin.

I sigh inside with his angry, passionate kiss that burns my lips with each touch.

I surrender—hopelessly, entirely, completely and utterly and devastatingly. To his touch, to his kiss, to his unrelenting power and dominance over my body.

And this is everything I never thought it would be. Everything I never thought *would* be. Drake Nash's kissing me was too much of a thought to comprehend, but now, it's a reality, and oh God, it's better than a dream could ever be.

His lips are soft but harsh, and he tastes like coffee and cupcakes. Triple-chocolate torte cupcakes. Rich and decadent and temptation at its finest.

I breathe him in. Just breathe, continuing to let him kiss me, tease my skin with his fingertips, and ignite a fire so strong in the depths of my belly that I feel it pounding between my legs with every stroke of his tongue against mine.

And I don't want him to stop.

Not ever.

I just want him here, me on my desk, his body between my legs, us separated by layers of clothing, while he kisses me like the thought of me being dead is too much for him to bear.

Not a kiss driven by anger or frustration or the tension that's been close to snapping for days now.

Just because imagining me dead bugs him. As a person. Not as a police officer.

"Boss? Is everythin' okay? Your cameras went off. Then I heard shouting then nothin.'"

I shove Drake away from me at the sound of Marshall's voice and glare at the thankfully still-closed door. "I'm fine," I say a little too breathlessly. "Detective Nash and I just needed to discuss something confidential."

"Right. Well, I tried calling your line."

Oops.

"I've recovered some of the Santiago-Westwood file," he says.

Drake's eyes bore into the side of my head as I jump up and adjust my pants. Running my fingers through my hair, I stroll across the room and open the door a crack. "Thank you." I take the file. "And the other thing?"

"Nothing, boss," he replies, adjusting his glasses. "I don't know where Dean found that, but I can't seem to."

Hmmm. "Okay. Thanks, Marsh."

"You're welcome. Remember to turn that camera back on when you're done. Just in case something else happens and your office is broken into for files."

"Thank you, boss," I tease him with a smile. "I'll turn it back on. No worries."

He nods once, smiles, and disappears back into his office. Slowly, I close my door and lean against it, closing my eyes for just a second to gather myself.

"Santiago-Westwood file?" Drake asks, his voice rough.

"Some of." I open my eyes, my heart beating hard as soon as I meet his gaze. "You're welcome to look it over with me, although I have no idea if any of this will be useful."

He waves his hand toward my desk. "Sure."

I walk around to my side and sit in my chair, laying the file on my desk. Drake rounds the desk, too, and leans over my shoulder to read. I can feel his body, hot and strong over me, but I tamp down the lingering memories from the kiss we just shared and open the folder to the first page.

I skim-read it, knowing that, if there's anything majorly important, it'll jump out at me. Line after line, I read, feeling the memories about the case come sinking back.

That's the thing with this job—the cases might all be the same in technicalities, but the details are all different. For instance: Ryan and Lena almost always went to exclusive hotels in Austin. Daniel and Claire always hit up a town around forty-five minutes from here.

I wonder if Daniel and Lena knew about the others' extracurricular activities. If they were both partial to the other's sordid and immoral activities.

That bugs me. Almost as much as having Drake's bicep touching my shoulder.

I swallow hard and inch away from him. *What the hell was I just thinking, letting him kiss me?* I'm done reading, but he clearly isn't. So I'm stuck. With him behind me. Just staring at me.

Wait. No. What?

"Is there something on my face? Why are you looking at me like that?"

Drake's lips twitch up to one side. "For the last few minutes, you've moved farther and farther away from me."

Clearing my throat, I meet his eyes. "Well. You are a little close."

His smile grows. "Noelle," he murmurs, "not ten minutes ago, you had your legs wrapped around my waist and your tongue in my mouth. Little late to be worryin' about personal space, don't you think, cupcake?"

"Okay! One—stop with the cupcake nickname!" I slam my hands on the desk and get up, moving away from him. Ignoring the speedy pound of my heart, I push my hair from my eyes and point at him. "That…serious lapse in judgment…ain't ever gonna happen again."

"You're right."

"I'm…" I frown. "I am?"

"Sure you are." He takes a few steps toward me, his lips still curved in that annoyingly sexy twist and his eyes dancing with laughter. "Next time, it won't be a lapse in judgment."

I blink harshly and clear my throat again. "Perhaps for you. For me, it will never be anything but." I smile tightly, ignoring the clench of my stomach when he drops his eyes to my mouth, and ask, "So, did you see anything in the file that you think could help?"

Anything to change the topic of conversation. I know for a fact he wouldn't have. The file is full of nothing but Claire Santiago and her various comings and goings. Nothing at all on Daniel.

"No. But I'm gonna need you to copy it anyway, just for the case file."

"Obviously." I take the folder from him and turn to my printer-copier-scanner thing I don't know how to work apart from printing. I stare at the machine for a second and run my tongue across my teeth.

Yeah. About this.

A low whistle leaves my pursed lips as I perch on my desk and reach for my phone.

"You don't know how to work it, do you?"

"I can work the printer," I reply defiantly.

"The printer ain't gonna get me a copy of this, Noelle."

"Sure it is. I just gotta turn my laptop on and print another." I shrug, slipping past him. My butt has barely touched my chair before the file is unceremoniously whipped from my hand and Drake moves across the room to the printer-copier-thingymajig Marshall talked me into buying everyone.

He presses some buttons on the pad that's sticking up, lifts a lid I'm not sure I ever knew existed, and slips the top sheet of the report in facedown. Another button, some clicky noises, and the whir of the printer and the machine spits out a sheet of paper.

"I could print this quicker," I grumble as he replaces the sheet.

"I know. I'm just enjoyin' how real fuckin' awkward you look right now." He shoots a smirk over to me and carries on with what he's doing. "Plus, the fact that you can shoot any gun given to you but can't work a three-in-one printer is pure gold."

I glare at him, putting every ounce of annoyance in my body into my gaze. Something that's real hard when I can still kinda sorta feel him kissing me. And touching me. And this was not on my to-do list, dammit.

"Done." His voice cuts through my musings. "This one is yours."

"Thank you." I take the file and set it on my desk. "If Marsh recovers any more, I'll let you know."

Drake nods once, his eyes firm on mine as he tucks his file under his arm. "And the other thing you asked him about?"

"Huh?"

"When he gave you this"—he taps his fingers on the file—"you asked him about 'the other thing.' He said no and that he didn't know where Dean had found it."

I suck my lower lip into my mouth as I consider what to tell him.

What to tell him.

Oh, sweet Jesus, Noelle.

I know the rules—anything I come across that could impact the official investigation definitely needs to be passed on to the HWPD. As much as I hate it. Mostly because I have a serious competitive side, and dammit, I want to work out who this murderer is.

Not catch them, mind you. That's all down to Drake, my brothers, and their cronies.

"Lena Perkins is married."

Drake laughs. "Yeah. Her husband is your client, remember?"

"Technically, he's not," I reply slowly, thinking over every word. "She apparently got married in her senior year of college. And she never got divorced."

His dark eyebrows pull together, creases lining his forehead. "Are you tellin' me Lena and Ryan ain't married?"

"Dean seems to think so." I stand and move to my window, looking out at the park for what feels like the hundredth time today. "But that's it. Literally. After that…the trail goes cold until she returned to Holly Woods."

"When did she come back?"

"A few months after graduation? I think. I was already in Dallas. She was here when I came home for Thanksgiving, though, so she certainly didn't stay in Houston long." I take a deep breath and turn around.

"Did you call the reference office?"

I roll my eyes and turn to him. "I'm no amateur, Drake. It was the first thing I did. Unfortunately, I'm not a cop, so I can't get a warrant, which means I have to wait in line like everyone else waiting for documents they need."

His eyes flare. "But the certificate is there? They have it?"

"She says there's one on record—maiden name Lena Young."

"Come with me."

The ride to the station is tense and full of silence. Drake grips the steering wheel steadily the whole way back, and I'm guessing that it's tight because his knuckles are white. And his jaw is clenched—devastatingly tight. Like, I'm wondering if he has any teeth left by the time he pulls up in the HWPD parking lot.

Drake gets out of the car and slams the door. The loud noise makes me jump, and I follow him into the building. Every door he comes across, he slams it, and by the time we make it to his office down the hall, I think he's rattled every hinge in his path.

Trent's door opens and my brother pokes his head out. "Don't tell me he finally arrested you," he groans. "I don't have time to bail you out today."

I poke my tongue out. "No. For once, I'm not the reason he's mad."

"You think," Drake snaps. "You should have told me right away!"

My jaw drops. "I would have if you hadn't been yellin' at me!"

"Wait—what's happened?" Trent intercepts us.

"Lena Perkins isn't Lena Perkins," Drake replies, a muscle below his eye twitching. He explains the rest of the story.

"And you didn't say anything right away?" Trent glares at me. "How long did you know?"

"Not long!" I protest. "I was going to call you whether or not I got the document." I shrug. "And I would have told this idiot sooner if he hadn't have strolled into my office like he owns the damn building and started yelling at me." And kissing me.

Yep. We definitely won't mention that little incident to Trent.

"I need a warrant." Drake cuts his eyes to me although he's speaking to Trent. "Get Brody on it and get it signed off before Judge Barnes takes off for his Saturday evening dinner and dance with Mrs. Barnes."

"Got it." Trent disappears back into his office, the door closing behind him.

"There's no point in rushing," I mutter, following Drake into his office. "The offices are all closed tomorrow."

He narrows his eyes. "But it doesn't mean I can't have it on their front desk at eight a.m. on Monday morning."

But I bet I can find out before that.

"Okay." I shrug again. "Why did you need me down here, then?"

He shuts the door and locks it. *Oh, shit.* That never ends well for me. I swallow when he turns and walks past me. Slowly, he removes his guns and sets them on his desk. Then he leans against the edge of it and stares at me. His arms bulge as he crosses them over his chest.

"Like it or not, it's clear we're gonna have to work together on this," he says, each word slow like he's still testing them out in his mind. "Your team—somehow—seems to find things mine can only dream of."

"They don't always do it legally."

"What was it you said before? What the HWPD doesn't know won't hurt them."

I tilt my head to the side and regard the dominating man before me. "Are you tellin' me to break the law, Detective? Because I don't think that's in your job description. Quite the opposite, in fact."

Drake's lips curve upward, and his eyes sparkle with amusement.

"Absolutely not, Ms. Bond. I'm merely stating a fact or two. Clearly nothing I say to you is going to change your mind about continuing with this case…"

His pause makes me smile. "I'm sorry—am I supposed to justify that asinine comment with a response?"

"Touché," he mutters, still smirking. "As I was saying, you're not dropping this case, but it's not safe for you to work it. And I know what you're gonna say"—he holds his hand up to stop me when I open my mouth—"so the only way to keep you safe and let you have your way is by us workin' it together."

"Contrary to your belief, I can actually look after myself."

"I'm not disputing that, Noelle. I'm sayin' to you, sweetheart, that it ain't safe for you to work this case. No matter how good you are with a weapon."

"I don't know that my safety needs to be a concern of yours. I already have three brothers who worry about me. I don't need a fourth overbearing man in my life, thank you."

"And your dad?"

I shrug. "He's a smart man. He worries, but he lets me handle stuff. Then, when I fuck up, he laughs and says, 'I told you so.' It works."

Drake shakes his head and stands, walking over to me. "Fine. Have it your way. You pretend I'm not worrying about your safety and look at it pragmatically." He grabs my shoulders and steers me toward a chair in front of his desk. I drop into the seat, and he perches on the edge of the table again. "Our investigations keep crossing. Your team finds things mine doesn't. Mine…probably doesn't find anything yours can't," he admits with a slight laugh.

I grin. "At least you know I have the best."

He inclines his head in agreement. "I have access to documents and findings you don't. You also have a particular skill set. Something my female officers don't have."

"Which is?"

"You're a total bitch."

"Do you *want* me to break your kneecaps?" I push up out of the chair, but with barely a touch to my shoulder, he pushes me back down.

Okay. Maybe I am a little.

Drake laughs. Bastard. "Not in a bad way. At least, most of the time. For what it's worth, that just then? The bad way."

"Explain what you mean before I make good on that threat, douchewank."

"Douchewank?" He raises an eyebrow, pauses, then shakes his head. Again. He does that a lot around me. "You're a bitch because people look at you and see the sweet Southern girl with good manners and a smile for everyone. They don't look at you and see the calculating, suspicious investigator dissecting their every word or action. They see the Noelle you want them to see—and she isn't the version of you with a gun tucked into her pants."

I get up and look at him, my hands on my hips. "I do what I have to do get my job done."

"People underestimate you, Noelle," Drake says huskily, standing once again. "They don't do that when they look at my team. Even when they're undercover—they know they're cops. Even people who know you don't really know you."

"What can I say? I've got more layers than Hell."

His lips twitch. "The only way we're going to catch our man is by working together. I can't allow you access to my case files, but I can't stop you from reading them on my desk or in my car—"

"Again with the law-breaking suggestions."

"Another," he murmurs with that smile. "I'm not your favorite person, and you're sure as fuck far from mine, and I'm pretty damn sick of you meddling in my investigation, so it's easier to invite you into it and have both of us on the front line of the case."

"You're not my boss," I warn him. "I won't take orders from you."

"There's only one kind of order I could give you and have you obey and it doesn't involve the workplace." His low laugh sends shivers down my spine. "I won't tell you what to do, Noelle. For the most part, our investigations will remain separate, but every evening, we'll convene to share notes, and we'll keep in contact during the day about any new revelations. Does that sound fair?"

"And you won't dispute my staff's maybe not-so-legal methods of getting information?"

"If it blows open this case, then no."

I take a deep breath and meet his eyes. If I ignore the lust and annoyance and determination there—and I am—they're completely honest. And if I have to be honest with myself, I know he's right. We may as well combine our investigations.

"As long as we avoid lapses in judgment," I whisper then clear my throat.

"Absolutely." He smirks again. Seriously, he's a total bastard.

"Fine. We'll work together." Ugh. "I feel a little sick from agreeing to that."

Drake's smirk becomes a mischievous grin. "No sicker than I felt proposin' the idea. I'm gonna get this certificate Monday morning and we'll work on Lena's life in Houston—see if there's a connection to Daniel."

I can't help my smile. I can't. I slowly walk backward, bringing my thumb to my mouth. "I'm going to Houston tomorrow. You can wait until Monday morning or you can come with me."

His smile drops. "I'm comin'. You can't go alone."

I roll my eyes.

"Trust me, Noelle. When I say it ain't safe, it ain't safe. You're embedded so deeply in this investigation that your connection is deeper than just coincidental discovery places and being hired by the victim's husband."

His words send a chill through me—one that crawls and twists its way across my skin until I'm all but shivering. "You think I'm in that much danger?" I ask softly.

His lips' thinning is his answer.

"Then I guess you better come with me. Meet me at my house at six a.m. Look like…well, not like a cop." I shrug and turn to the door.

"What exactly are you hopin' to find in Houston?"

"The truth," I say, opening the door and meeting his eyes. "You say everyone who looks at me underestimates me. Tell me, Detective. Do you?"

He looks at me stonily, the twitch of his lips to the side his only movement. "You surprise me on a regular basis, Ms. Bond, so yes. I probably do underestimate you."

"You're smarter than you look."

"I think that was a compliment."

"Oh, it was." I match the curve of his lips with my own. "My nonna is a pain in my ass, but she taught me several things. My favorite? A smart man, a good man, will always underestimate a woman. Not because he thinks she's worthless or beneath him, but because he knows she's on a pedestal towering above him. Remember that."

chapter THIRTEEN

SIP my coffee and flick through the papers one more time. It's an act solely designed to pass the time until the very late Drake Nash actually shows up. Apparently, the good detective isn't too fond of six a.m. and also does not answer his phone before six thirty in the morning if the caller is Noelle Bond.

That said, he assured me at six forty-five that he would be at my house by seven thirty. It's now seven twenty-five and I'm reading the notes Dean managed to dig up on Lena's relationships in college. Except the husband. Because, you know.

In the age where the social media websites are everyone's personal dictionaries, such a huge life thing doesn't seem to be documented.

Which tells me that Lena had something to hide.

My phone rings from its hands-free perch on the dashboard. I frown, expecting to see Drake's name come up, but the number is unfamiliar.

"Noelle Bond," I answer, staring at the screen.

"Ms. Bond? This is Mrs. Young… Lena's mother. I'm sorry to call so early."

I sit up straight. "No problem, ma'am. Is there somethin' wrong?"

"Oh, no, no. I just wanted to let you know that the police are releasing"—her voice falters—"Lena this morning. Finally. We're having a funeral—in two days. At the old chapel just off Oak Avenue.

I know you were friends…"

Wow. HWPD kept her for a while. I wondered why I'd heard nothing of a funeral.

"Of course, Mrs. Young. I'll check my schedule and rearrange a few things if necessary so I can be there."

She sniffs. "Thank you, dear. If you don't mind me asking, how is your…search…going?"

"Not at all. Unfortunately, right now, I seem to be asking ten questions for every one I answer, but that's just how these things go." I open my mouth to offer an apology for that, but it occurs to me that, as her mother… "Ma'am, could I ask you a question?"

"Of course."

"I'm headed over to Houston today to talk to some school friends of Lena's. There's only one I haven't been able to find because I can't seem to find any information on him."

"I don't know much about her college years. She was very determined to be independent, as young people are these days."

"You wouldn't have any information on her husband, would you?"

"Ryan? Whyever would you need to go to Houston to talk to him?"

"No, ma'am. Lena was married in college. There doesn't seem to be any record of divorce. She never legally married Ryan."

Silence.

After a moment, I say, "Ma'am?"

"I-I'm sorry, Noelle. I-I didn't know. Oh my." Her voice crack is thick and genuine. "Ryan isn't her husband?"

"It appears that way, yes."

"The s-store?"

"Goes to the man I can't seem to find, I assume. If they never divorced, he's her next of kin."

"Are you searchin' for him today?"

"Yes. I'm gonna do everythin' I can to find him," I promise her, glancing up when Drake opens the car door. I glare as he slides in almost sheepishly.

"If you find him, could you pass on my details? I'd like to meet him."

"Of course. I'll call you soon." I hang up and look at the detective hiding behind dark aviator sunglasses, his tan body hugged by a bright-orange polo shirt and dark, tight Levi's. "Well, good mornin', Detective," I drawl. "So kind of you to accompany me today."

"Late night," he grunts. "Tried trackin' down the husband."

"Any luck?"

"None." He sighs and takes the coffee cup I hand him. Mercifully, it's still hot. "It almost feels like the information has been hidden deliberately, ya know?"

"But by who, and why?"

"If I knew, I'd know the husband's name." Sarcasm drips from his words. "Thanks for the coffee."

"You're welcome. Now, cheer up. I'm not spending two and a half hours in a car with a teenage girl on her period."

Drake shifts uncomfortably. "Your car is real small, you know that?"

I pause, my hand on the keys in the ignition. I look at him, just able to see his eyes cutting to me through his glasses. Sigh. "Do *you* want to drive your truck instead?"

"I would prefer to."

"Fuck me," I mutter, grabbing my purse from by his feet and shoving all of my things except my coffee and my keys into it. "Well?"

"Well, what? Fuck you? Or driving my truck?" He looks at me over the top of his sunglasses, his eyebrows raised.

"Driving your truck," I manage through a clamped jaw. "Ya know, this is gonna be real hard if you keep pissin' me off all day."

He smirks, unlocking his truck. "I'm countin' on it."

It's way too early for sexual innuendos. Not early in the day, because who doesn't like morning sex? Just early in the day with Drake Nash. The man from whom judgment lapses are banned.

I set my purse down by my feet and put my sunglasses on. With one hand clasping my coffee cup like the golden life force it is early on a Sunday morning, I belt up and then grab my cell phone, immediately scrolling through my contacts.

"Boyfriend?"

"Nonna wishes," I snap. "No. I arranged some meetings with old friends of Lena's last night, but since someone decided to sleep in and be ninety minutes late, I have one to reschedule."

Drake chuckles as I dial Regina's number. It goes to voicemail, and I leave a message, asking if she can meet me an hour later still at the cupcake place on Travis Street. When I hang up, I catch Drake's eyes flitting toward me behind his glasses.

"What?"

"What's in the folder?"

I sip my coffee. "The bra sizes and ages of virginity losses of all of Lena's college friends."

"Marshall?"

I shake my head. "Dean. Marsh is still working on collecting files. And probably playing World of Warcraft." I shrug. "I've lightened the caseload until this is over, and Dean has more than a few computer skills of his own. It wasn't too hard for him to find out who her classmates were and track her closest ones down."

"How did he find out who her closest friends are?"

"Do you do any detecting in your job or do you just tell everyone what to do?" I raise an eyebrow. "Social media. It's basically a public diary for everyone who has time to waste."

"I take it you don't use it much," he assumes, ignoring my jab.

"You'd be correct," I answer. "Except Tinder. And I'm still debating the effectiveness of that."

His lips curve up, but he says nothing more. Although I haven't been particularly active on the so-called dating app, I've still seen the messages I've been sent by my so-called matches.

And let me tell you, from some of these matches I've been sent, I can only deduce that Tinder is either permanently drunk, high, or both.

I run through the schedule I plotted out in my mind. First up if she catches my message: Regina, Lena's closest friend and roommate of three years. I figured that, if anyone knows anything about the husband— or even anyone who will—she's my girl.

And given she's my only schedule because there's an ex-boyfriend who expressed the same shock as Mrs. Young at Lena's having gotten married her senior year, I'm really hoping she knows something.

"Cupcakes? Really, Noelle?"

"Look, if I have to suffer for two and a half hours in a car with you before I've even started investigating, I'm gonna need me a sugar fix." I shrug. "Otherwise, I'm just gonna be a total bitch to people who can help move this case forward."

He slides his sunglasses through his unruly hair so they balance on top of his head and shoots me a disdainful look. "Noelle…"

"What?"

"You're lyin'."

"Not about the sugar fix." I sniff and turn away.

Busted. Totally. Typical.

"Why're we interviewin' her at a cupcake café?"

"Because Gigi's is closed today?" I sigh, staring out the window at downtown Houston as we turn off onto one of the ring roads. "I just have a bad feeling about this whole case. I just know that, one way or another, the husband is connected."

"You think he killed them?"

Them. I hate that. "I don't know. It's just a hunch."

"I can't arrest people on hunches."

"I know that. But that doesn't mean I can't bug some people on my hunch."

"Bugging people gets you into trouble in murder investigations, Noelle, and I already told you it ain't safe for you."

I roll my eyes. "Yeah, well, I'm not exactly unarmed."

"Didn't I text you and tell you to leave the gun at home?"

"Oh, that text was you?" I gasp as we pull into the parking lot outside the mercifully quiet café. "I accidentally deleted that before I could read it. Whoopsie." I send him a sweet smile as I hop out of the truck.

I decided to forgo the heels today for cowboy boots. So there's a two-inch heel, but that hardly counts. I can also run in them… And you never know.

Drake mumbles something under his breath and opens the door to the café. A lone woman with long, blonde hair tied in a ponytail at the top of her head is sitting in the corner, and I recognize her instantly as Regina.

"Regina?"

She looks up with violet eyes. "Noelle Bond?"

"That's me." I smile and offer her my hand.

We shake, and Drake steps forward.

"Detective Drake Nash," he says.

"Are you with Houston PD?"

"No, ma'am. Holly Woods, the town Lena lived. I'm off duty."

"Some people think I have a knack for getting into trouble and need supervision," I say. Kinda. I do occasionally. "My brothers are also cops at home and no one could get away, so I'm stuck with Detective Nash for my chaperone."

"It could be worse." Regina smiles, giving him a once-over.

If I cared, that would bug me.

"Okay, Mr. Off-Duty." I turn to Drake. "I need a low-fat vanilla latte and a chocolate torte cupcake. Please."

"Anything else, diva?"

I purse my lips. "Regina? Can we get you a coffee?"

"A cappuccino would be great. Thank you." She shoots a flirtatious smile toward Drake.

I stop my eye-roll. Just.

"I was real shocked to hear about Lena," she says softly when Drake goes to the counter. We both sit. "And you don't know who did it?"

"No. Her childhood best friend was also killed and found not long after she was."

Regina's hand goes to her mouth. "Oh no. Are they related?"

"We think so." My lips flatten into a grim line. "Regina, I need to ask you something. Did you know that Lena was married in her senior year?"

The paling of her face tells me she does.

I raise my eyebrows.

"Yes," she says softly. "I don't know anyone who didn't know."

"Didn't know what?" Drake asks, rejoining us. He sets three coffees on the table and passes me my cupcake.

I thank him with a smile.

"That Lena was married," Regina answers, her eyes moving to

him. "Literally everyone in our class knew. She barely made it through the rest of the year to graduation."

"Why? She was old enough to get married." When Regina doesn't acknowledge me, I cough. Not discreetly.

Her lips twist to the side in something that resembles a disgusted kind of smile. "Yes, but she married her professor."

"Well," Drake says after she's gone. "That was unexpected."

"The twists always are," I murmur, absently licking some frosting off my plastic fork.

"Her professor." He shakes his head. "Who'da thought?"

"Not me." I put some more cake in my mouth and lick the fork again.

"Can you stop licking that fork?"

"No. I eat when I'm stressed."

"You're makin' me fuckin' stressed, Noelle."

I meet his eyes. They're blazing with heat, focused on my mouth intently. And, I, er, stop licking the fork.

"Can you concentrate?" I ask. "This is a huge piece of the puzzle that is Lena's and Daniel's deaths."

"Then stop lickin' the fork."

I slam the fork down and bite into the cupcake and the huge pile of frosting on its top. "Better?" I demand, my mouth full.

Drake's lips twitch. "As long as you don't lick your lips now."

"This is highly inappropriate, considerin' we're colleagues now."

"I'm off duty."

"I am *not*." I pin him with my gaze and slowly, deliberately, lick my lips.

His gaze follows the path of my tongue as it moves sleekly and swiftly across my mouth, and it takes every inch of my willpower not to laugh at him.

"We should talk to the husband," he growls, slowly dragging his eyes from my mouth up to meet my own darker eyes. "Now."

"Do you know where he lives?"

"Can you find out?"

"Yes."

He says nothing for a moment. Then, "Will you find out?"

"I didn't hear a please."

"You fuckin' with me, Noelle?"

"You should know by now that I'm always fuckin' with you, Drake." I grin like the Cheshire cat and whip my cell phone out, dialing Bekah's number. Honestly, with the way this case is going, the only person I trust is my best friend.

"Yo, ho," she answers. "Whaddyah want?"

"An address." I rattle off the findings of our meeting and wait as she looks up the directory online.

"One Professor Warren Gentry, thirty-four sixty Piping Rock Lane, Houston, seven-seven-zero-two-three," she answers. "You headed there now?"

"Yep," I reply. "It's Sunday. We should catch him."

"Okay. Be safe."

"Always am."

Drake snorts as I hang up, because as he's said a million times, I'm not safe. Apparently. Apart from two dead bodies having been dumped on my property, I see no evidence to support his claim. Which makes me think he still knows something I don't.

We drive until we reach the River Oaks area. My eyes widen as we drive through the residential streets. The houses here are fucking huge. Like, mini mansions. They must be worth anything from one to two million bucks.

How the hell does a college professor in art make this much money?

"How the fuck does a college professor make this much money?" Drake asks, verbalizing my thoughts.

"If I knew, I'd be switching professions like three years ago," I hum, staring at the beautiful houses.

They vary from two to three stories, but almost all are several windows wide with winding driveways, each varying in length. Their front yards are immaculate and well-tended without as much as a grass blade out of place. Lord forbid a bird poop over their yards—they'd probably pull out platinum-plated rifles and shoot the poor little shit.

Why didn't I pack those fucking heels?

Surrounded by houses and people who obviously drip diamonds and wealth, I feel like a hillbilly in my goddamned cowboy boots. So what if my jeans fit perfectly and my white, three-quarter-length shirt hugs my boobs?

I realize now I dressed for information and not sophistication.

Let's hope Professor Gentry is somewhat of a darn letch, or we're screwed.

Drake slows as we approach the house. The large, red-brick façade is preceded by its long, double driveway that ends at a double garage. He looks at me as if to ask whether or not he should pull up on the driveway occupying only one car, and I shrug my shoulders. How the hell do I know proper procedure?

I'm generally climbing the trees of houses like this—and before I started doing that, I was in a marked cop car and could park wherever the fuck I wanted.

Shrugging once, the detective eases into the driveway and pulls up behind a deep-blue Chevrolet truck. After a glance at me, Drake jumps out of the car and comes around, opening my door.

"Remember, I'm off duty. I can't ask him a thing or Houston PD will be onto my ass."

"I know jurisdiction," I hiss through a clamped jaw. Why can no one in my life remember that I was a cop only two years ago?

"Just reminding you," he says in a low voice, stepping back and allowing me to exit the truck.

He follows me to the front door. It looks heavy, and the paned glass windows inset into the wood mean we can't look through without any distortion. Clever yet classy. I like it.

Drake reaches around me and pushes the doorbell. The classic "ding dong" rings out through the house, and a few moments later, a man appearing to be in his early forties opens the door.

"Can I help you?"

"Mr. Gentry?" I inquire.

"And you are?"

"Noelle Bond," I reply, pulling my private investigator ID out. "Ex–Dallas PD and private investigator at Bond P.I. in Holly Woods. Can I come in for a chat?"

"And the gentleman accompanying you?"

I just know that, if I were to turn, Drake's lips would be curving.

"Detective Drake Nash. Homicide, Holly Woods PD. Off duty, of course."

I bet he even pops his collar.

"And the matter is concerning…" Professor Gentry trails off.

"Lena Gentry," I reply, keeping my eyes firm on his.

Never look away from a man asking questions—especially if you know he has answers to *yours.*

The man before me visibly balks at the sound of her name. His eyes flit between us, terror rampant in them. Slowly, he brings his fingers to this throat, and stammers, "It's…it's been a long time, Ms. Bond. Forgive my rudeness."

"Not at all, Mr. Gentry."

"Doctor," he corrects me, the word almost a whisper. "I received my PhD not long after she left me."

"I'm sorry. Dr. Gentry. We really do have some questions for you."

"Of course. Come in." He steps to the side and sweeps his arm in a welcoming motion, but I notice the rigid way he holds himself. Like he's not really comfortable at all. "Is she in some kind of trouble?"

I look at Drake as I realize that this man has no idea his wife is dead.

"We should take a seat," Drake suggests in an odd, bossy way.

Dr. Gentry nods and leads us to a bright room filled with plants and two wicker sofas with cushions tied on. He takes one, leaving me and Drake to fill the other.

"Dr. Gentry, I'm afraid your wife was found murdered approximately twelve days ago."

I freeze as the words wash over the man opposite me. First, his eyes widen. Then his mouth drops. His hands go to his throat as if he can barely breathe through the news before they drop to his lap as the hopelessness of this situation falls over him. Tears fill his soft, hazel eyes, although I suspect they are more regretful than sad.

Eventually, Dr. Gentry sits forward, his hands trembling as he clasps them. "How?"

Drake gives him a basic rundown of the case, omitting all information about Daniel, I notice. I try not to give him a suspicious glance because Dr. Gentry strikes me as the kind of person who would notice that right away.

He asks all the right questions, and Drake answers them all while

I quietly look around. There are pictures of a little girl, from birth to around age six. My eyes linger on one specific frame—the little girl, the double of Lena, sitting on her lap. A heavy weight sits in my lower stomach as the pieces fall together in my mind.

No.

"When was the last time you saw Lena?" I draw my attention to the somewhat distraught man in front of me.

"Just before she died," he replies quietly, his eyes falling to the very same photo I was just looking at. "She was here for Melly's birthday."

"Who's Melly?" Drake asks.

"Their daughter," I answer, focused on Dr. Gentry.

He confirms it with a single slight nod.

"You have custody?"

"Full," he replies. "Lena suffered severe postpartum depression. In and out of hospital. She couldn't trust herself around Melly, so she agreed to let me raise her and have visitation rights. She came every week, like clockwork."

"That must have been hard for you."

"Yes, it was. It is. But I coped because I knew Lena couldn't look after her. My parents have been big helps. She's there right now."

I nod slowly. "My sister-in-law suffered after her first. It was tough, but she manages it now."

"Lena couldn't. No matter what she tried, she was physically incapable of coping. She moved out not long after our agreement and went home."

"Did your relationship break down?"

"Of course." He holds his hands out. "How could we have a relationship if we only saw each other three hours a week?"

"Why didn't you divorce?"

"I-I wanted to." He sighs heavily. "But I just…couldn't. I loved her. I always hoped she'd be able to beat the illness and come home to us. It's all I wanted." Again, his eyes drift to the photo.

"The last times you saw her," Drake inputs, "did she seem different? Agitated? Scared of anyone?"

"No, sir." Dr. Gentry shakes his head. "She was just…Lena." Tears fill his eyes.

I nudge Drake's arm. "Thank you for speakin' with us, Dr. Gentry. I'm sorry we had to meet under such bad circumstances."

Lena's mom's words come back to me. "Here." I delve into my purse and scribble her details on the back of a receipt that was languishing somewhere beneath a half-drunk water bottle, Chucks, and a candy bar wrapper. "This is Lena's mom's phone number. She wanted me to pass it on to you."

"She told me her parents had died," he whispers, taking the sheet.

"Well, I assure you, sir, they're very much alive." Drake shakes his hand. "I'm told her funeral is tomorrow morning. I'm sure Mrs. Young can give you more information."

"Thank you. For stoppin' by. I'll... Please keep me involved in this investigation."

"Of course." We exchange cards, and I tuck his into my purse. Out in the truck after saying goodbye to him, I look at Drake. "He's involved in this. Not directly. But he's...somewhere."

He looks at me funny as he pulls back. "That makes no sense, Noelle."

"I know. But my gut... I don't know. Ignore me. I need to think about what I do next."

"Which is?"

I chew on my thumbnail and grimace. "Tell my client that the woman whose death he has me investigating isn't really his wife."

chapter
FOURTEEN

My conversation with Ryan went about as well as the winter Olympics in Australia. It occurred to me on the way back from Houston that I needed a copy of Lena and Dr. Gentry's marriage certificate as proof for when I told Ryan. Dr. Gentry willingly scanned it and e-mailed it to me without asking why I needed it, and the printout I gave Ryan lasted all of ten minutes before he angrily tore it up.

Long story short, he had a police escort out of my office, and I'm now fired.

Which was happening anyway. Let's be honest. The woman lied to him. To all of us—but to him the worst.

Briefly, I wonder if Julia will ever forgive him.

Probably not when it gets out that Penny's baby is Ryan's and his penis is a rogue animal incapable of staying inside its cage.

I sigh and stop into Rosie's Café on my way home. Right now, I need a big ol' vanilla latte and perhaps a slice of pie…or ten. That's equivalent to one Gigi's cupcake, right? To me, it is.

"Goodness, Noelle! Did you hear?" Rosie gasps as soon as the door shuts behind me.

"Hear what?"

"Lena! Married. With a baby!" She shakes her head and pushes some stray hair from her face. "Why, I can't believe it. How did she keep that secret?"

"I don't quite know," I say quietly. "Can I get a low-fat vanilla frap and two slices of your cherry pie?"

"Sure thing, sugar." She busies herself with my order. "I'm so darn confused. And Ryan—that poor boy! How'd he cope with the news?"

"Not well," I admit. Although "not well" is somewhat of an understatement.

"And the case? He hired you?"

"Hired me, fired me." I shrug and hand her a twenty.

She clutches a hand to her chest and leans forward. "But you are still investigating?"

I take the box containing my pie and bring my coffee to my mouth, my lips slowly curving at the sides. "Now, Rosie," I say, heading for the door. "I never outstep my bounds. I'm surely sittin' by and lettin' the police finish out the investigation."

Rosie shakes her head, grinning. "Surely, Noelle. I believe you, sugar."

With a wink, I push my way outside, the bell over the door tinkling. Back at my car, I nestle my pie box onto the passenger's seat and deposit my coffee cup in the cup holder in the center console. As I drive home, my mind wanders.

How *did* Lena keep her other life a secret?

And how does Daniel fit into all of these things?

It crosses my mind that I haven't spoken to Claire Santiago, the woman whose toyboy he was. Of course, I know that their relationship disintegrated when I informed her husband. She groveled—a.k.a. gave him a ton of blow jobs and participated in his dream of a threesome with a woman from out of town—and their marriage is back on track.

There are some damn weirdos in this town, I tell you.

But, still, if Claire and Daniel had any semblance of a relationship left…

I pull up in my driveway and text Bekah before I get out of the car, telling her to call Claire and see if she saw Daniel before he died. That done, I tuck my phone between my boobs, balance my coffee on top of my pie box, and walk to my house.

I've barely opened the door when I get the sense that something is wrong.

I carefully set the box and coffee down on the hall table, looking through the house. "Hello? Is anyone here?"

Silence answers me.

Clearly, I'm working too much right now. I need a day off. If only the murderer could come clean.

Shaking my head, I grab my treat and coffee and take them into my front room. I pull my boots off and remove my gun from its holder around my ankle, setting the bright-pink weapon down on my coffee table.

And I wonder why people underestimate me.

A pink 9mm tucked into six-hundred-dollar cowboy boots.

I have to be the girliest badass in Texas.

The thought brings a smile to my face as I head into my kitchen and grab a fork from the drawer to eat my pie. I'll also be the biggest girliest badass in Texas if I keep up this cake addiction I have going on, especially if my caseload means I can't get my ass to the gym.

Mind you, this case has me running around so much that it doesn't matter.

Ah—the *old* case. Lena's murder is no longer my case. Officially. I'm in way too deep to get out. Although using my common sense and stepping away from this investigation like everyone is telling me to will mean I don't have to see Detective Dreamy.

Detective Dreamy?

Holy shit. I glare at the pie.

"How much damn sugar is Rosie putting in you? I'm freakin' hallucinating now."

Or not.

Drake is kinda dreamy. And then, of course, he opens his mouth and ruins the whole thing.

I sigh, digging my fork into the sticky cherry goodness. Typical of most males, though. They're real pretty till they talk to you.

After one slice of pie, I'm definitely full. I close the box and set the fork down, grabbing the notebook I always keep in the drawer of my coffee table. I unclick my pen, and leaning back on the sofa, I call forward every fact I know about this case.

Two people I know have been murdered, possibly connected via me, possibly not. Both in the same brutal way, both deliberately positioned on property I own. Both once busted for being bits on the side.

One by one, I write down every last piece of information until I have nothing more than what I started with twenty minutes ago.

"Ugh!" I throw the notepad and pen to the floor and drop my head back. I rest my arm over my eyes and take a deep breath.

This is entirely useless. There are so many questions I have yet to answer. Did Lena and Daniel have a relationship past friendship? Did he see more than he should have that night he died—more than just being the guy her dinner was taken from? What's the real connection between them? Why did Lena lead a second life in Houston? Why didn't Daniel turn up until a few days after Lena if he was killed the same night? Where were they killed? Why were they killed? What's the motive for it? Was it truly Ryan Perkins feeling unhappy about their relationship? Was it Penny, wanting to have a life with Ryan but couldn't see one unless Lena was dead? Was it Lena's husband, Dr. Gentry, sick of her screwing around with him? Was it one of Lena's debtors?

But poison… That's a woman's weapon. Simple yet deadly and incredibly easy to administer. You can kill someone over weeks or months, even years, or you can have them dead in seconds. You can kill slowly or quickly, painfully or painlessly.

Which pins the head on Penny again.

As her assistant manager, she would have had more than enough chances to kill Lena. But if that were true, why not kill her over time? Get her coffee and poison it? It would be easy to lace a coffee jar with poison and only use that for one person by means of hiding it between cups.

Then there's Mallory—she's inheriting the life insurance policy. The substantial one, too. That's a great motive. A lot of money. Enough for her to step out from beneath her father's shadow. But again—why a quick-acting poison and not a long one?

Or maybe there's someone in Dr. Gentry's life. Someone who's mad that Lena won't divorce him and let him be happy despite his protestations that he always hoped she'd go back to him and Melly.

These thoughts whirl aimlessly around my head, one after another, colliding but never separating. They're almost suffocating in their intensity, their confusing and nonsensical jigsaw-shaped pieces never quite fitting together.

Whatever it is, something in this case just isn't adding up. Everyone has motive and means—until you bring in Daniel.

Why kill him, too?

Why not let him live?

I ponder these last two questions for an endless amount of time before, finally, I grab my gun, check that my alarm is set, and go to bed.

In my dream, I've solved a murder, eaten Gigi's, and had another serious lapse of judgment with Drake Nash. Several lapses, actually. And one was very, very fucking serious. Sweat and hair-pulling and naked-body-and-orgasm kind of serious.

In reality, there's a bang from inside my house, and I jolt awake. The hairs on my arms stand on end, shivers cascading across my skin with lightning speed. I grab my gun from the nightstand and hold it in front of me, ready to shoot any fucker who gets in my way.

My heart pounds ferociously as I quietly step off the final stair and look around. The house is deathly silent as I move into the living room. I turn the light on. Empty—if you ignore the mess. DVDs removed from their cases, paper strewn everywhere, and when I move into my office, it's much the same. The contents of my desk are covering the chair and the floor. Some of the sheets are crumpled, others simply thrown carelessly, and there are files and folders brightly decorating the sea of white.

"Motherfucker!" I whisper, clenching my jaw and walking out of the room.

In the kitchen, moonlight illuminates the scene through the large window over the sink. A chair has been knocked over—that was the bang I heard. Several kitchen drawers are also opened, their contents spilled onto the countertop. Moving into the utility, I see what I was looking for.

The door leading into my yard is slightly ajar, and instinct tells me to check the lock. There are scratches on the plating around the keyhole, just like there are on my office door handle.

Anger filters through me like nothing I've ever felt. This shit is fucking personal now. When I find who did this, I'm going to put a bullet through their head so they can't damn well do it again.

My house. My space. My sanctuary.

Completely violated.

I take a deep breath to rein my emotions in and look at the clock on the kitchen wall. Three thirty in the morning. Keeping my gun close to me, I turn on the yard light and make sure I really am alone before I head upstairs for my phone. The deck is clear, and so is the grassy area just beyond it. The shed though…

Barefoot, I slide through the gap between the door and the frame and pad across my yard. The shed is completely untouched from what I can see.

Happy there's no one here—sad there's no one for me to shoot at—I run back into the house and up the stairs. I grab my phone from under my pillow and dial Trent's number, slowly moving through upstairs, which is, thankfully, untouched.

"Noelle?" he answers groggily. "What—what time is it?"

"Th-three-something," I answer, my jaw chattering. The adrenaline is rushing out of my body at a speed faster than I can deal with, and the reality of what's happened sinks in.

Someone broke into my house.

Oh God.

"What's wrong?" His voice is clearer, stronger, more demanding. His cop-mode.

"Someone just broke in," I whisper, feeling my throat clog. "To my house."

"Grab your gun. We'll be there in five minutes."

"Noelle!" Dad yells, my front door slamming open.

"I'm here," I reply.

He takes one look at me sitting on the stairs, my knees to my chest with my arms wrapped around me, and sits next to me, his arms wrapping around me. "*Bella ragazzo*," he murmurs, pulling me into his chest. "You're okay? You're not hurt?"

I nod. "They knocked over one of the chairs in the kitchen. They must have panicked and ran. They didn't come upstairs."

"Noelle!" Trent's voice thunders through my hallway.

"Jesus, I'm right here," I say, standing up and going right down. "And yellin' at me ain't gonna make me appear any faster if I weren't."

My big brother looks at me. Then, in one swift movement, he pulls me into him. He squeezes me tight, and we repeat the conversation I just had with Dad.

Seconds later, Brody and Devin appear and I have the conversation again, and then my house is swarmed by cops. They ask questions and take photos and explore my house. I stand quietly near my family, still wearing my Snoopy shortie pajamas. At least I kept my bra on last night.

Sometimes, you just have to think of things other than the tragedy unfolding before your eyes.

Round and round the HWPD go. More questions, more photos, and fingerprint sweeping until there's layers of fine, black dust across my house.

"Y'all are gettin' that cleaned, right?" I give the lead guy, Detective Rory Spencer, a hard look.

"Yes, ma'am." His lips twitch up. "Someone will be by this mornin' to see to it."

"Good."

Dad laughs and rubs my back. "Why didn't your alarm go off?"

Holy crap. My alarm!

I rush over to the main box by the front door. It's completely disabled.

"Noelle!" Devin snaps. "Did you forget to set it?"

"No!" I turn to look at him. "I set it every night. And I know I definitely did last night."

"Maybe there was a delay—the guy got there before it went off," Brody suggests.

"What kind of alarm has a delay?" Dad asks, coming to look at me.

"Not mine," I murmur, wrapping my arms around my waist. "But it was definitely set. I'm more likely to forget to turn it off, not turn it on."

A shadow falls over me from the doorway. "Just can't help gettin' into trouble, can you?"

"*Vaffanculo*," I snap, turning to Drake.

His hair is messed right up, and the jeans he's wearing have a tear in the thigh, his T-shirt crinkled and his underwear band just showing above the waistband of those torn jeans, which are oddly sexy. Memories of my dream flood back, and I fight the blush wanting to color my cheeks bright pink.

"What are you doin' here?"

He nods toward Trent. "He called me. Told me you were in trouble. Again."

"If you're gonna start givin' me shit, *Detective,* take a fuckin' number because someone already beat you to it. I can only take so much crap, and my quota for today is already overflowing."

"Then I'll make sure I hold in my crap until tomorrow morning."

"Please do." I turn away from him as Detective Spencer comes back and tells me that they're done and someone will be over to clean my house up of the awful powder by lunchtime. I hand him a spare key from the kitchen drawer and watch as everyone trails out.

My father and brothers all check another ten times that I'm okay, that my guns are loaded, and that I'm not going to have a serious mental breakdown if they leave.

"You're stayin' at home tonight," Dad orders, standing in the doorway. "Home, home."

My worst nightmare, but it's useless to fight him on this. "Okay, Daddy."

He steps forward to kiss my forehead, shakes Drake's hand, and then leaves, closing the door behind him. I take a deep breath and look around the mess that is my house. I don't even need to ask who did this. It was the murderer—or whoever's been cleaning my files out.

And I know exactly what they were looking for.

"You all right?"

I shake my head. No. No, I'm not fucking all right. I'm as far from all right as I can possibly be right now.

"They take anything?"

I shake my head again. I'm not sure I can speak right now. The tightness of my throat combined with the rolling of my stomach has me desperate for oxygen. I take another deep breath in, but it's not enough, and it leaves me too quickly, and I need more—more air, more air, more air.

The room. It's spinning. My lungs burn. My mouth is dry. My eyes are wet. My cheeks are hot.

I can't—

"Noelle." Two large, rough hands frame my face for a second. "Breathe."

I fall against Drake's chest, hot tears spilling from my eyes and rolling down my cheeks. My breaths are giant, harsh gulps that have me trembling against the warmth of his body.

He gently wraps his arms around me, but his hold is anything but. It's tight, and the safety that quickly engulfs me slows my breathing just a little. It's like everything else but his embrace blurs slightly, and the feeling of being entirely cocooned by his anchoring hold is overwhelming in the best kind of way.

"Hey," he says once my breathing has returned to normal and my crying has slowed. "Better?"

Oh, good grief. I just sobbed all over Drake Nash.

"Yes. Thank you." I straighten and step back.

He loosens his arms around me but doesn't let go. "Are you sure?" His eyes search my face, glowing with concern.

"Yeah. I just…" I sigh heavily and wipe at my cheeks.

"Your badass gene calmed down."

I glare at him—or try to. His fingers twitch at my sides just before he drops his arms, and the way his lips pull up makes me smile a little, too.

"I think most people refer to it as adrenaline," I comment.

"But not many single women check out their own house during a burglary when there's a chance the suspect is still there."

"I had my gun." I chew the inside of my cheek and look away.

"Precisely. Your adrenaline is a badass gene that flares the fuck up every now and then."

Moving toward the desk and gathering some papers up, I smile a little again. "I'm surprised you're not yellin' at me for not calling someone right away."

"Noelle, sweetheart, if I thought tearin' you a new one would make the slightest bit of damn difference, I would. I didn't come over when Trent called because I was angry. I came 'cause I was worried about you."

"Right."

An awkward silence hangs between us for a long moment before Drake comes up beside me with a stack of papers. "Anything missing?"

I shake my head. "Not that I know of."

"Do you know what they could have been looking for?"

"I have a damn good idea."

When I don't speak for a moment, he asks, "And that is?"

"Wait here." I close one of the drawers. Fisting the bottom of my pajama top, I turn and walk out of the room. I'm totally aware of the fact that his eyes are firmly on me as I walk away from him—just like I am about the fact that my butt cheeks are possibly creeping out from beneath the bottom hem of my shorts.

But hey. I wasn't exactly expecting company in the middle of the night.

In my room, I crawl up onto my bed and bend over, grabbing the pillow from the side I don't sleep on. Then, without a care, I shove my hand inside it and pull out the flash drives I've had hidden there ever since I bought them.

The sound of a throat clearing behind me has me jerking to the side and sitting up straight.

"What are those?" Drake asks, pretending to look at my hand. Instead, his eyes are focused on my chest.

"Flash sticks," I answer, centering myself and standing up in front of him. "Here." I put the drives in his hand with enough force that his eyes quickly pull themselves upward to meet mine.

"And why would they be looking for these?"

"Because," I say, walking back downstairs. "Those drives have every Bond P.I. case on them."

"And by every, you mean…"

"I mean I turned off my surveillance camera in my office, copied everything over in private, then brought them home with me," I tell him as we enter the kitchen. "If another murder happens, I don't want to be running around like a headless warthog on steroids looking for a goddamned file. I want to know I can pull it and all its details in seconds."

"I'm impressed."

"I don't doubt it," I reply dryly, shoving cutlery back into its drawer so there's enough space for me to clean out the coffee machine and make two cups. "Take them. Keep them at the station."

"Are you admitting that I'm right?"

"That I'm not safe?" I pause in my cleaning of the machine and glance at the glacier-eyed detective with a stance so powerful that he fills the room with just his charisma. "Absolutely. You are right. I'm not safe—but I never claimed I was. I claimed I was strong enough to protect myself. And I would have if the assdouche had hung around for long enough."

He laughs, sitting at the table in the center of the room. "Not doubtin' that for a second. Your badass gene sure knows when to come to life."

"Badass gene or not, I'm an Italian-Texan woman in a family full of cops. I'm passionate and shoot before I think. You only fuck with me if you're stupid."

"Some would call that 'passion' anger or attitude."

"No, I don't get angry, or mad, or pissed. I get passionate." I glare at him and put a mug of coffee in front of him. "*Capisce?*"

"*Capisce,*" Drake replies with a grin. He tucks the flash drives into the pocket of his jeans and picks his cup up. "You realize it's five thirty?"

"Really?" A glance at the clock confirms the time. "Crap. The cops were here for ages."

He nods solemnly and drinks slowly. Tension settles between us, lingering in the air, its threads pulled so tight that just one breath a little too harsh would break it. My eyes flick around the room as I will myself to look anywhere other than at him. The wall, the trash can, yesterday's water glass next to the sink, the crack on the cabinet door I really need to replace.

Avoidance. Like the tension will dissipate of its own accord if we simply ignore the fact that it's there.

Drake's fingers slowly wrap around the mug, each long, roughened digit easily curving without so much as a twitch about the heat.

I blink harshly and look away from his hands. Jesus.

"I assume you're still refusing to step away from this case."

I inhale slowly through my nose. "The fact that you question that shows how badly you underestimate me."

"Fuckin' hell, Noelle! You were crying in my damn arms not

thirty minutes ago!"

"And?" I glare at him. "We're closer than ever to finding this killer."

"How the hell have you worked that out?"

"Because every time someone has been killed, my files have gone missing!" I yell. I rub my hand down my face and take a deep breath. "And now, someone has just broken into my house to steal copies of my files. Files no one knew about. Which means I'm being watched."

"And they're going to kill again."

I lift my mug to my mouth. "Bingo."

chapter
FIFTEEN

STARE numbly as Lena's casket is lowered into the ground. Bekah's hand is warm in mine, and she lends me her strength with a gentle squeeze of my fingers.

I never knew how hard it would be to watch a friend die. Not to say I've never known anyone who's died. Hasn't everyone by the time they're in their late twenties? Hell, I lost more than one or two colleagues when I was in Dallas. I am the reason one of them died. One bad call on my part destroyed their life and changed the course of mine. One bad call I tend not to think about or dwell on.

But to see someone you grew up with, someone you counted amongst your closest friends... For them to die... It's heart wrenching.

It doesn't matter that the Lena I thought I knew was a different woman. Maybe her heart lay in Holly Woods while her legacy lived in Houston through her daughter. Who am I to know which one of her was real? Who am I to judge the decisions she made without full disclosure of her reasons?

Just because her life was a lie doesn't mean the relationships she forged were.

Dr. Gentry and Melly are standing by the priest conducting the ceremony, dressed head to toe in black just like the rest of us are. Melly stares somberly at the casket, silent tears running down her cheeks, and my heart clenches at her bravery.

The poor girl never deserved this. Melly *or* her mom.

I take a deep breath as the first dirt is scattered across the top of the casket and the little girl leans over to throw a white lily on it. Smoothly, Dr. Gentry draws his daughter into his arms and holds her tight.

"Poor thing," Bekah whispers, echoing my thoughts as she rests her head on my shoulder.

I nod in response. My throat is too tight to speak, the sadness of the day and lingering fears of last night feeling all too heavy inside me. Add to the fact that, because of last night, I haven't slept since I was rudely awoken by my intruder at three thirty and I'm goddamn exhausted.

People slowly disperse from around the graveside, including Dr. Gentry and Melly. One figure remains though. I nudge Bekah and she lifts her head, looking in the same direction.

"Ryan came?"

"Apparently," I mutter, releasing her hand.

His harsh look at the coffin doesn't go unnoticed by me, and neither does the tense way he holds himself. Shoulders back, fists clenched, jaw tight—all of these things are contradictory to the tears in his eyes. I take a few slow steps toward him, and like he can feel my eyes on him, he glances my way.

"Ms. Bond?" A tall, thin woman blocks my way, her deep Southern twang familiar to my ears. One look at her confirms my suspicions.

"Mrs. Young," I reply, offering a sincere yet sad smile. "I'm so sorry for your loss."

She takes a deep breath and dabs beneath her eyes as a man several inches taller than she is but much more rotund wraps his arm around her shoulders. Mr. Young, I presume.

"Thank you, darlin'," Mrs. Young whispers hoarsely. "Sure is hard, sayin' goodbye to my baby."

"I can't begin to imagine."

"Geoffrey Young," the man says, sticking his hand out. His eyes are the same startling color as Lena's were. "Lena's father."

"Noelle Bond." I shake his hand. "Private investigator, unofficially finding the schmuck who did this."

His lips twitch. Just barely. "Well, Ms. Bond, thank you for your efforts. I assume, given the latest news, that Ryan fired you?"

"Of course. But my daddy didn't raise me to be a quitter, sir."

"Then come along to the wake. It's just a couple of blocks down, at the Dorchester, in the bar. Miss Marcie put on a real nice spread, and we're payin' the first round as a thank-you for seein' our baby on her way to Heaven. I can't have you workin' without payment."

"Oh, please, sir—that isn't necessary."

"I insist. Come on down." He softly pats my arm and squeezes his wife, looking at her lovingly. "We wouldn't dream of lettin' you do this for free."

Mrs. Young nods, her eyes rimmed in red, a handkerchief to her nose.

Aw, damn.

I leave the Dorchester with a check in my purse for half the cost of my usual services. Actually, less than half of it. And that was after they pushed me up from my initial offer of zero dollars.

Turns out Mr. and Mrs. Young have a butt-load of money, and they aren't afraid to throw that at someone who could find the person who killed their daughter.

I admire their resolve. I do. I just detest the fact that the check was literally tucked into my purse before Mr. Young zipped it up and disappeared into the throng of people with his wife. And believe me, I looked for them. For an hour. While I happily sipped on my free wine and then proceeded to drink two glasses of not-so-free wine.

Some private detective I am. Can't even find my dang clients in a crowd.

In all honestly, if I hadn't had a call from Grecia saying that the office had been broken into some time this morning, I would have stayed for a fourth glass.

A glass I could use given the fact that it's the fucking afternoon and they just notified me.

"You," I say, pointing at my little Mexican. "Coffee. My hand. Now." I make a grabby motion at her.

"Two cups," Bekah mutters, and I wonder if maybe she had a

little too much wine to have technically driven across town. She's a cheap date.

"Two cups!" I yell after Grecia. "Marshall!"

"Boss." He appears out of nowhere, a head above me, skinny yet muscular. He adjusts his glasses. "Three files are missing. Totally wiped from the server. And the flash drives Grecia keeps are gone."

"And why the fuck did no one call me before now?"

"You were at the funeral—"

"Which ended two damn hours ago!" I shake my arm, dislodging Bekah's grip on me. Mike and Dean come into my peripheral, and I glare at them. "Please tell me y'all called the cops."

Silence rings out.

I take a deep breath and pull my cell out. "I need you."

"Now there are some words I wasn't expectin' you to say," Drake laughs, his tone husky.

"Cut it, Romeo," I snap. "My office was broken into."

"On my way."

I throw my phone back into my purse and focus on Marshall. "Files?"

"Melissa Hooper, Killan Jefferies, and Rita Owens," he responds, ticking each one off on his fingers.

"I want financials, medical records, education—the full fucking shebang, Marshall. Now."

"Yes, boss."

"Meanwhile," I say slowly but angrily, staring at each of my employees, taking my coffee from Grecia, "Y'all better come up with a damn good excuse for Detective Nash as to why you didn't call him." I turn to Bek. "Deal with him when he gets here. I ain't in the mood for his shit."

"And when he starts demanding files?"

"He won't," I reply confidently, knowing he already has them on the flash sticks I gave him this morning. "Now, I'm gonna go drink this and take a nap on my chaise."

I stomp up the stairs and unlock my door with a little too much enthusiasm. I close it with just as much. Too much. Way, way too much, if you consider that the bang from the slam ricochets throughout the building and makes my door jump back open.

One final shove from my heel closes it. I throw my purse on top of my desk and gently set the mug down. Then I flatten my hands on the smooth wooden surface. Taking a deep breath as I lean over, I close my eyes and try to calm the buzz of anger threading through me right now.

My office and my house broken into on the same day, within hours of each other.

And no one fucking told me about the former.

I sigh and beat down the sugar craving taking the place of my anger. Damn, I could use a cupcake or two right about now. Even some candy. Like some Twizzlers or something. Ooh, no—those peanut butter egg things Reese's do.

Thank God it's Easter next weekend and they're still selling them.

I pull my heels off and haphazardly leave them lying next to each other on the floor. Then I clear the papers from my chaise and fluff up the throw pillow before lying down and closing my eyes.

Sleep doesn't come to me.

My mind works overtime, spinning back and forth and whirring until my thoughts are nothing but white noise ricocheting off each new thought that dares to enter the whirlwind. Nothing makes sense. A murder in a small town where everyone knows everyone else's business—it should be simple.

Someone has to have seen something. Someone has to have some kind of idea about what happened the night Lena died and Daniel went missing. And that's what's truly bugging me—if Daniel had been attacked before he went missing, then surely someone saw something. Sure, at the time he would have been delivering Lena's salad, it would have been dark, but hell, our shops stay open late. Especially in the summer and during vacations.

Like Spring Break, which is in full swing.

Clearly, thinking myself into insanity isn't solving this case. But neither is anything else. And now, I have three missing files, and any of them could be the next victim.

In theory, at least. My gut isn't agreeing. I can't help but think…

"Knock, knock."

I open my eyes and turn my head toward the door. It's wide open, and Drake is filling the empty space. *Should have locked that.*

"What?"

"Sleepin' on the job?"

"Supposed to be," I mutter grumpily, swinging my legs around and sitting up. "Did you make my staff squirm?"

"The correct answer is, I believe, no." He smiles.

"Not in this case. I'm pissed with them for not calling me or you." I stand up. "Did you get the security tapes?"

"Disabled," he replies, sitting down on one of my tub chairs and putting a small box on the desk.

My eyes focus on the white bow on top. "Is that—"

"A cupcake? Yes. Brody stopped by and got it on his way over here."

"God love him." I snatch up the box and open it, perching on the edge of my desk. I rest my bare feet on the empty chair and pull the cupcake out. The bright-pink frosting teases me from its home on top of the soft, cakey goodness, and I swipe my finger through the frosting and insert it into my mouth. I sigh happily as I lick it off my finger and repeat.

Sugar.

It feels good. Tastes, I mean. And feels. Oh, hell, who am I kidding? Cupcakes are like sex for stress. Just a lot cleaner and slightly less pleasurable.

Drake clears his throat, and with my finger still in my mouth, I cut my eyes to him. "Can you stop doing that?"

"Doing what?" I say around my finger.

"That," he replies, his voice much deeper than it was a second ago.

The lusty look in his eyes sends a bolt of heat through me. "Oh," I squeak, dropping my hand. "Sorry. You're right. I shouldn't be eating while we talk. That was rude of me."

He runs his tongue across his top lip, staring at me intently. "It's not the damn eating that's bothering me."

"No?" I scoop some more frosting up on my finger, widening my eyes innocently. "Then what is?"

He stands just as I lick my finger clean. "You enjoy fucking with me, Noelle?"

"It's quite fun." I shrug a shoulder, my eyes staying on his despite the fact that he's towering over me now.

"Fun?" He knocks my feet from the chair, the sharpness in his word making me freeze. My stomach clenches as he flattens his hands either side of my butt on the desk. "You think drivin' me damn insane is fun?"

My lips tug up. "Are you telling me it ain't?"

He holds my gaze for a long moment. A long, tension-filled, goose-bump-inducing, blood-thrumming moment. "You know somethin'? I don't like you very much." He leans in the barest amount. "In fact, more often than not, I can't fuckin' stand bein' around you. But there happens to be a part of me that likes you a whole fuckin' lot. And that part of me is real convincing. "

My legs ache with the desire to open, wrap around his waist, and pull him against me.

Sweet Jesus, I want to know just how much that part likes me.

"Why, Detective, you sure know how to flatter a woman," I reply, my voice thick but steady. "I don't much like you either, so I'd prefer you to have a little *guy-time* with that *part of you* that likes me and kindly talk some sense into it before I have to disappoint it."

Drake trails his fingers up my arm, his touch featherlight but strong enough that it sends a shiver down my spine. I fail to mask it, and he smirks. His hand slides over my shoulder and cups the back of my neck just before his fingers knot themselves in the hair at the top of my neck. My heart pounds, and it takes every bit of strength I have not to let my breath out in a quick exhale.

"Trust me when I say I don't need any *guy-time* with my cock. It has more than enough girl-time."

"Then get it some girl-time and have some sensed fucked into it."

"I hardly have time," he murmurs into my ear, "when I'm trying to find a murderer."

"Looks like you're tryin' real hard right now." My words are said through clenched teeth in a bid to calm my erratic breathing. "In fact, you try real hard whenever I'm around, I've noticed."

His thumb brushes my hip. "What can I say? I'm a sucker for the forbidden."

"Proven by the fact that you're this close to me."

"You're not exactly pushin' me away, are you?"

I shiver again at his lips touching my ear. "You're far stronger than I am. There's no way I'd be able to push you away."

Drake shifts slightly, and *ohsweethell*. His erection brushes my thigh. No, that's no damn brush. That's a freaking bruising prod.

I clench my fists because just how big is that?

I haven't been laid in a while. Don't judge me.

"You should go," I breathe, not moving.

"I should."

"So do it."

"I can't."

And just like that, his lips move across my jaw and cover mine. I can't even squeak a protest. His mouth is hot and demanding, every sweep of his lips something between a promise and a beg. It's the kind of kiss that gives and takes at the same time, the kind that makes me whimper when a low, growly sound vibrates from his tongue to mine.

I'm alive everywhere as I grab his collar and push myself against him. My skin is on fire with the mixed feelings of anger and helplessness and powerlessness combining with the lusty desire bordering on desperation.

And sweet Jesus, this man can kiss like nobody's business.

I could drown right here in his kiss and never feel the desire to come up for air again.

"You're okay?" he asks in a rough voice, one much quieter than I've ever heard him use with me.

"Caught off guard," I mutter.

"No. After this morning. And everything."

"Are you worried about me?"

"I just told you I don't like you very much."

"That doesn't mean you can't be worried. I don't like you, but if you got your head slammed by a rock, I'd be marginally worried about your well-being."

"I'll make sure to call you should that ever happen."

"Awesome. But yes. To answer your question. I'm fine."

"You have your gun on you, don't you?"

"Possibly two," I admit with a smile.

He finally lets go of my hair, only to touch my sides by my breasts. I draw in a breath, and his lips curl as he slides his hands down my body to where my guns are hiding at my hips.

"Dress hid them well."

"I dress for practicality."

He steps back, bends, and picks up my heels. "Yes. Practicality."

I snatch them from him, my lips still tingling. "Mostly practicality."

I clear my throat. "Why did you come in here again?"

"To ask you to come to the station and catch us up on what you can remember about the cases where the files have gone missing."

"Right now?"

"That's the idea."

I sigh and slip my shoes back on before grabbing my purse. "Fine. Let's go." I reach to the side and grab the cupcake box on a whim.

Drake holds my office door open. "You should probably wipe that lipstick smudge before you go down."

I look into his smug eyes and dip my finger into the cupcake frosting again. "And you should try not to lie to me when you buy me cupcakes."

"Touché, Ms. Bond."

"Always is, Detective."

I dump my overnight bag on my childhood bed in my parents' house. I'm trying to be good and understand my father's need to have me at his side tonight, but after so many years of being independent, it's hard.

Plus: Nonna.

She needs only her name as an explanation for my incredible lack of desire to be here. In fact, I'm amazed she hasn't taken the liberty of inviting her own guest for dinner. And by guest, I mean date for her poor *zitella* granddaughter.

If I don't have wrinkles, I don't need to be married. Even if I do, I don't need to be married. I have three brothers to call when something breaks—if I haven't already fixed it myself—and a vibrator for orgasms. I don't understand why I need someone under my feet twenty-four-seven. The likelihood of her finding someone who accepts me, guns and all, is incredibly low anyway.

Her heart is in the right place. Her heart is also in the wrong place. *Bless* her heart.

I sigh and sit on the corner of my bed. It's almost exactly the same as it was when I left for college. My brief summer back at home before I joined the police academy in Dallas barely warranted unpacking, let alone a redecorating party. No matter how much my family convinced me to stay.

The far wall is still covered in New Kid on The Block and Backstreet Boys posters, faded with crinkled edges from how many times they were tacked on after they fell down. My dresser top is littered with bangles overflowing from the bracelet arm, and more than one necklace is tangled amongst the photo frames.

I get up and walk to it before picking up a knotted tie of necklaces. The cheap finishes stand out, as do the ones on the bracelets. Now, either I'm a jewelry snob or my teenage self needed to get her ass to a Kendra Scott or Alex and Ani store freaking *stat*.

"Noella!"

Oh, here we go.

"Nonna?" I poke my head out of my room.

"You help-a me cook!"

"Do I have to?"

"*Si!*"

"Freakin' hell," I sigh, closing the door behind me.

As I make my way downstairs, I hear my mom and the crazy old lady going at each other. It makes me want to run like hell and hide in the attic with the old boxes of Italian photographs Nonna refuses to get rid of.

"Liliana!" Mom yells, running her fingers through her hair the way I do when I'm stressed. "I said I was cooking tonight!"

"No!" Nonna shouts, rolling out some dough. "I cook!"

"I said I would!"

The faint scent of garlic assaults my senses. "Wait. Nonna, are you makin' garlic bread?"

"I wanted to buy it," Mom sighs.

"Buy it!" Nonna scoffs, smacking her fist onto the thick pile of dough on the counter. "You no-a buy garlic bread! You bake-a it!"

"So, you're baking garlic bread?" I ask again.

"It's time consuming!" Mom slams the fridge shut and pours a glass of wine, splashing some on the counter as she does. "Buy it! I'll concede to the lasagna, Liliana, but the garlic bread is ridiculous."

"No! Buying it is-a *ridicolo!*"

"Hey!" I yell over them both, slamming my hand on the kitchen table.

They both stop and look at me.

"Nonna, are you making garlic bread?"

She blinks heavily mascaraed lashes. "*Si,* Noella."

"Mom, let her make the bread. I love that stuff."

Nonna smiles smugly, cutting the dough and rolling it into baguettes. Mom frowns at me as I pour myself a glass of her wine.

"Noelle, you've never complained about store-bought stuff."

Nonna opens her mouth to, presumably, tear me a new one, but I hold up my hand.

"Mom, don't drag me into this. After twenty-eight years, I've accepted that y'all ain't ever gonna get along, but don't use me to point score. I love you the same."

"Twenty-eight!" Nonna tuts as if I just reminded her how old I am. "*Hai un appuntamento con un bel ragazzo cattolico italiano ancora?*"

"No, Nonna. I do not have a date with a nice Catholic Italian boy yet. I'm pretty busy finding a murderer, or did you forget that?"

"*A marone!*" she exclaims, shaking her head. "No wonder you have-a no date!"

"I have no date because there is no one I want to date." Not least the man who manhandled me on my desk earlier today. Whose kiss I might be replaying a few times in my head.

"You need-a man!" she continues, ignoring my protest. "None of this-a silly gun business! No-a killers! No-a cheaters!" She turns, waving her basting brush at me. "God-a judges you!"

Oh, Nonna. If only you knew.

"Not as much as he judges you for enforcing your will onto me."

She gasps, clasping her hand to her throat and clawing at her pearls. "*Noella! Si prende quella schiena!*"

"I ain't takin' that back!" My twang kind of stands out when I'm angry. "God is happy for me to shoot Lucifer's minions. He told me over wine and cupcakes."

"Noelle," Mom warns, but I hear the laughter in her voice.

Nonna gasps again and repeats her previous statement.

"Are you gonna stop tryna set me up with your boy toys?" I ask, leaning against the counter and sipping my wine.

"I take-a you to confession on Sunday!" she threatens, slamming the over door with gusto. "You can tell-a Father Luiz about your-a sins!"

"Oh, goodie. You should warn him it'll need to be a private session."

Her eyes bug. "You have-a sex outside marriage! I knew-a it!"

I roll my eyes. "Okay, Nonna, seriously. To do that, I'm gonna need a boyfriend. I don't have one of those. You should talk to Devin about sex before marriage. Not your angelic, single granddaughter."

She grips her pearls again. "Devin! He have-a sex?"

"He's been with Amelia for five years. Of course he's havin' freakin' sex!"

Mom puts her fingers in her ears. "La, la, la, la."

"You should-a be more like-a Trent!" Nonna comes toward me. Brandishing that fucking basting brush. "Married, babies! Settled! No guns!"

"Trent has a gun!" I protest.

"He-a cop!"

"I'm a private investigator. I need a gun."

"And it got-a your house-a broken into!"

Well, she does kind of a have a point there.

I look at Mom. "Where's Dad? I can't take this anymore."

She smirks. "In his workshop. Cleanin' his guns."

"Thanks." I grab my wine glass and make for the back door.

"I bet you wish you'd sided with me on the garlic bread now, huh?"

"Shut up."

chapter SIXTEEN

ORBIDDEN. What did Drake mean when he said that he was a sucker for the forbidden?

Did he mean me? Because I'm pretty sure I don't have a barbed-wire fence surrounding me. I mean, sure, he's a close friend of all my brothers—probably Trent's closest friend—but that isn't a reason to be forbidden. We're not freakin' teenagers.

I can make out with whoever I want.

Not that I actually want to make out with Drake. I mean, he renders me almost catatonic before he makes his move, so I don't actually have a choice about it. I just have to go with the flow. Like Jell-O.

Jesus. Now I'm putting sugar and Drake in the same thought train. I need to solve this murder, and soon if I want to retain any sanity. I'd really like to go back to unequivocally hating the man. It made my life much easier than what it is right now.

Because as nice as the random kissing thing is, he's still an asshole.

An asshole who brings me cupcakes, granted, but so are my brothers.

"Brody just called," Dad says as soon as I walk into the kitchen. "Daniel's funeral is tomorrow."

"Oh, it's a happy week in Holly Woods," I mumble, grabbing a mug down from the cupboard and putting it in the coffee machine.

"Same place as Lena's?"

"Yes. And he said to call him when you wake up."

"Got it." I set my phone on the counter, dial his number, and put it on speaker.

"Hello?"

"How's my favorite brother?"

"How's my least favorite sister?" he retorts.

"I'm your only sister, *idiota*."

"Unfortunately," he drawls, the sound of a car door closing echoing down the line. "You called just at the right time. I just got to the station."

"Why did I need to call?"

"Dad told you about the funeral?"

"Yes. What's up?"

"We think Lena might have been divorced from Dr. Gentry after all."

I meet Dad's eyes across the room, and he raises his eyebrow. "Don't go anywhere. I'm coming down." I hang up and slide my full coffee cup to Dad along with a travel mug and a sweet smile.

He shakes his head but uncaps the travel mug anyway, and I kiss his cheek as I run out of the kitchen and to the stairs.

I take them two at a time, the sound of my bare feet slapping against the bare wood sharp. Nonna opens her bedroom door just as I close mine, and I breathe a sigh of relief. No one approaches her before she's had her coffee on a morning. It's akin to approaching a hungry lioness and twerking.

How could Lena have been divorced?

I quickly shake the question out of my mind, lest I end up standing in the middle of the room and mulling over possible ideas instead of getting dressed and going to find out the real explanation. I dress as fast as I just ran up the stairs and apply the bare minimum of makeup. Reasoning that I'm going to the police station and don't need my gun attached to me, I slip it into my purse and pull out my lace-up, military-style, heeled boots and tuck the bottoms of my jeans in.

Satisfied that I look halfway human, I brush my hair on the way out of the door.

"You can go home tonight! Your mom told me about Nonna's

grillin.'"

"Thanks, Dad." I kiss his cheek and grab the travel cup full of my coffee. "I'll get my things later."

"I'll be here," he replies, waving as I close the door behind me.

I slide into my new car and set my purse on the passenger's side, putting the travel cup in the center console in the cup holder. After a sip though. I need at least a tiny bit of caffeine running through my veins before I can be trusted with something as powerful as a damn car.

Unfortunately, in the car, my brain whirrs back to the fact that Lena could have been divorced. This case just keeps getting more and more fucked up. I could understand it in a city, maybe, where everyone is anonymous. You can hide anything in cities as long as you leave it there.

I know. I have plenty of secrets left in a big city.

But in small towns?

The shit you bring to a place like Holly Woods stays in Holly Woods. Small towns are a dangerous place to have secrets, mostly because the concept doesn't exist. You can't have secrets in a place where everyone knows everyone and everything about everyone is known. By everyone.

So how in the hell did she keep this secret?

I pull into the parking lot of the HWPD building and push the door open. Charlotte smiles at me as soon as I walk in, and I lean against the reception counter.

"Can you tell Brody I'm here?"

"Sure thing." She picks her phone up and presses two numbers. "Detective Bond? Noelle's here." She looks at me and puts it back down. "He'll be out in a few seconds."

"Thank you. Has Nonna been in here causing more problems?"

Charlotte's dark eyes glitter. "Not since Trent pulled her out of here."

"Great. Can you ban her from the building, or…?"

She giggles. "I don't have that power. I just answer the phones."

"And tell us all what to do," Brody offers, opening the door and stepping into the reception. He smiles at Charlotte.

She returns it, pink coloring her cheeks, and I fight the urge to raise my eyebrows in interest.

My brother looks at me and says, "Well?"

"Coming, coming. See you later, Charlotte." I skip through the door, Brody sweeping past me as soon as he's closed the door.

I've never much thought about my baby brother as a man, but seeing him now, confident and strong and leading me through the police station, I see he is. He's not the shy, gangly teen I remember. He's a muscular, self-assured gentleman. Which means I can tease the hell out of him.

"Well now, Detective Bond, I do say that Miss Charlotte is rather sweet on you."

Brody looks at me flatly as he closes his office door. "Sure she is. That's why she can't say a word to me."

I grin and sit down. "Brother dearest, that's exactly why she can't say a word to you."

"We're not here to discuss my private life." He coughs and sits down. "You're here to find out about Lena."

"I am. But a little sibling teasing never went amiss."

"You're testin' my patience real good, Noelle."

"Aw, Brodes. C'mon. You know I'm your fave."

"Lena got divorced," he says, his eyes, which are the exact shade of mine, hitting me hard. "We have the documents."

I stare at him flatly. Documents? How? There shouldn't *be* documents. There was never a divorce.

"There was," Brody argues. "You said your thoughts out loud."

"Oh." I should get a handle on that. I'll be in trouble a whole lot if that keeps happening. "Well? Tell me about these documents."

"We spoke to Dr. Gentry this morning. He's as shocked as we are."

"Wait—you're saying the man didn't know he was divorced?" But I know that. He was sure they were together. In fact, he was entirely adamant he didn't want to divorce her.

"Either that or he's a real good liar." Brody sighs and sits back. "He admitted that divorce was something they'd both considered. They went to lawyers, split their assets fifty-fifty for a clean and easy split, and the papers were sent to Dr. Gentry. He signed them, but he never gave them to Lena."

Why would you go through all of that to just not hand your wife the papers? All of that time and money?

"He still hoped she'd come back," I say softly. "He never wanted to say goodbye to their marriage. So, how did she get the papers?"

"She found them and stole them. The dates on record are not long after the original file. It really was an easy one."

"How did he not know?"

"She intercepted all the mail. It was summer vacation and Lena stayed with them for a few weeks to be there for their daughter."

I look out the window. The police station is on the opposite side of the park to my office, but the view is much the same as mine. The play area, the dog walkers, the trees, the flowers, the water fountain in the center of it all. The familiar sight brings comfort to me.

Swallowing, I look at my baby brother. "Who was she, Brodes?" It comes out a whisper.

He pats the hand I have on his desk and looks at me with sympathy in his eyes. "That's what we're trying to figure out."

I'd give just about anything right now to clear out my savings account, fly off to some Caribbean island, and hire a cabana boy to fan me and bring me fruity cocktails.

The twists and turns in this case are getting to be too much—and so are the emotions. Telling Ryan Perkins that his wife was actually his wife wasn't the easiest conversation I've ever had. In fact, it was downright fucking hell. Pulling out the divorce papers not even a week after I'd shown him the marriage certificate shocked him. It's a wonder the man isn't entirely screwed in the head after all of this.

It makes me wonder who else knew about all of this. The secret marriage, the secret divorce, the marriage to Ryan.

It really sucks when the person who'd know it all is dead.

Daniel is my obvious choice. There has to be some kind of record about this somewhere.

I lean back in my seat and tap my pen against my lips. I've written everything down for what seems like the fiftieth time, but I'm not getting anywhere. Despite Drake's assurance that my working with the HWPD would give me access to some files, he hasn't shown me a thing, and I barely trust him enough to give me the information I need. I wouldn't put it past him to omit any information he didn't deem necessary for me to know.

Like if anything turned up in Lena's or Daniel's apartments.

I dismiss the thought as quickly as it popped up. No, that's silly. I can't break into their apartments. Just because I'm no longer required to uphold the law doesn't mean I want to break it.

Do I?

"Agh!" I flop forward and drop my forehead to my desk. Maybe I have to break the law to uphold it.

It can work that way, right?

It's not like I'd be taking anything. I'd just sneak in, have a little snoop, and slip back out. Easy peasy. I'd barely be five minutes.

But Lena shared her apartment with Ryan. Which would mean I'd have to get there when he wouldn't be there.

Dammit.

Wait.

He just told me that he's spending the night in Austin for business. I'm sure his business is inside Penny's vagina, but whatever works for him right now works for me.

I pick my phone up. "Dean, I need a favor."

"What is it, Miss Noelle?"

"I need you to tail Ryan Perkins."

"What for?"

"Doesn't matter. He's going to Austin. You're still working that infidelity case right?"

"Yes," he replies slowly. "And that's all I'm working."

"I'll pay you overtime. And won't bug you for cupcakes for a week."

A moment of silence. Then, "You got it. What am I tailing him for?"

"Just watch him. Call me as soon as he looks like he's coming back to Holly Woods, okay?"

"Okay... Miss Noelle, what are you up to?"

"My job." I hang up and dial Bekah's extension.

"What's up, buttercup?" she answers cheerily.

"What are you doing right now?"

"I should be working, but I'm eating Twizzlers."

I roll my eyes. Of course she is. "Wanna go do some investigating in places we probably shouldn't?"

"So, breaking and entering."

"You said that, not me."

"Whatever. Where are we *investigating*?"

"Lena's and Daniel's apartments."

There's a scuffle and a bang. "Let's go!"

"This is insane," Bekah whispers in the elevator. "If we caught, we're screwed."

"Nah. I'll get us out of it."

"Having three family members in the police force does not give you a free pass to break the law," she mutters grumpily.

"Then go back to the office and I'll do this myself," I hiss.

"Are you kiddin'? Someone has to have your back, and as your best friend, this asinine task falls to me." She sighs and pushes her bangs from her eyes. "Let's go snoop. Investigate," she says quickly when I glare at her. "Investigate."

The doors open, and I shake my head, walking out into the hallway. Lena and Ryan's apartment is 3B, so I straighten and walk toward the door like I'm supposed to be here. Then I pause.

I didn't actually consider how we get in.

Bek stops at my side and whistles low. "How do we get in?"

"Shut up."

"It might be unlocked," she says. "After all, this is Holly Woods. Who locks their doors?"

"Me."

"But you're like a dead body magnet and your house has been broken into. I'd whoop your ass if you didn't. Lena and Ryan, however..." She leans forward and pushes the handle down.

Sure as hell, the door opens.

"Oh, yes!" I whisper, excitedly grabbing her arm. "We're not breaking in!"

"We're not supposed to be here," she reminds me as we walk in. "You of all people should know it's still breaking and entering."

"But the door was open. I'll argue technicalities." I sniff and tuck some hair behind my ear.

Looking around the apartment, I take a deep breath. It's cozy. That's about all I have to say. There's nothing really stand-out about it. It just looks like…an apartment. There's a decent-sized TV, a games console and games. There's a bright afghan slung over one cream armchair, and pictures of Ryan and Lena adorn the walls and counters and windowsills.

If I didn't know she was a compulsive liar, I'd say these two really loved each other.

"What are we looking for?" Bek asks, closing the door behind us.

"Good question," I mumble. "Uh, anything that looks like it could solve this case."

"Nothing too out-there, then."

Damn her sarcasm. "Just keep an eye on the door. I'll look."

I walk into the kitchen and open the drawers, hoping to find some documents or something. Doesn't everyone have a kitchen drawer jammed with bills and bank statements and invoices? I thought that was, like, a thing.

Not the Perkinses, anyway. Either they're real organized or I'm super lazy.

The kitchen turns nothing up except for a fridge covered in pictures attached by various magnets. I pause and look through them. Lena and Ryan, Lena and her family, Lena and Penny and Mallory. Lena at the front of her store on the day it opened. I tilt my head to the side and focus on the calendar on the wall next to the fridge. Every Saturday is crossed out on Lena's column. The day she was never in the store.

That's when she went to Houston to see Melly.

What did she tell everyone when she went?

"Hey, Bek?"

"Yeah?"

"Can you call Mallory Chandler? I want to know what she knows."

"You want me to tell her to come see you at the office?"

"Yes. Please." I proceed to the bedroom. This is more than a little awkward, and I make sure to keep my attention away from the bed.

Because. Ew.

I slowly open the drawers on the nightstands. There's nothing except the usual suspects. Chap Stick, condoms, pills. Nothing in the drawer on the other side, either. The bathroom also comes up empty, so the office opposite the bedroom is my last hope for something.

"Someone's here!" Bek hisses, grabbing me from behind.

I clamp my hand over my mouth and look around. "Closet!" I whisper, opening the door.

We both step in and, after I close the door, crouch down. A high heel pokes me in the ass and a dress almost smothers me, but I manage to pull my phone out of my pants pocket and look at it. No missed calls from Dean.

That means it isn't Ryan. So who's here?

Drawers open and close somewhere in the apartment, and Bek shuffles closer when it becomes evident that whoever's here is looking for something just like we were. Which means there's something here to find.

If only, like this person, I knew what it was.

"Fuck it!" *Penny.*

Bek grips me tight and opens her mouth. I shake my head, clinging tight to the closet door handle. God bless walk-ins.

"Where is it?!" Penny exclaims, more drawers opening and closing. There's silence for a second, then more drawers open in the bedroom. Right in front of us.

I shake my head again at Bek. Her hands are trembling, but I squeeze one tight and she holds her breath. Dammit—what was I thinking bringing her with me?

That's right. I wasn't.

A phone rings, and Penny answers with, "I can't find it!"

Bek and I share a look.

"No, Ry! I've looked everywhere, just like you said you did. The policy isn't here... I've already checked the store. You know that... No, Mallory said she didn't know anything about it... Okay... Sure. I'll drive in now... See you soon."

The policy.

The sound of footsteps echoes through the apartment, followed by the sound of the door opening and closing. We wait for an excruciatingly long minute before we get out of the closet and straighten up.

"The policy?" Bek asks, frowning.

"The life insurance policy," I reply, putting my hands on my hips and looking around.

"Why would they want that? They being Ryan, too."

"Let's go," I say, not wanting to be here any longer. God knows who else could be after that. When we're in the elevator, I look at my best friend. "Life insurance policies are generally made out to your spouse. Right?"

"Right."

"Ryan obviously knows that Lena was in contact with an insurance company about it. It made sense because of the debt she was in with her store—maybe she was paranoid about someone killing her."

"They did."

"Well, yeah. But that wasn't connected. Anyway…" We get into her car. "What if Ryan knew about the policy but didn't know anything about it? Now that she's dead, he's thinking he has the store, all her assets—which don't seem to be many—and her insurance payout."

"Except there's no policy."

"Except there is. It just doesn't have his name on it." I shift in my seat. "When did you say Mallory was coming in to see me?"

"I didn't. But she should be there already."

"Then put your foot down, Bek!"

She does. We make it across town, breaking several speeding limits in the process, and when I walk into my building, Mallory is sitting in the lobby with Grecia, talking about the newest stock inventory and the cutest little black lace dress Grecia would love.

"Mallory?" I interrupt their conversation. "Do you want a coffee or anything?"

"I'm fine," she says hesitantly, swallowing. "What's up?"

"Let's go to my office." I lead her upstairs and shut the door behind us. "Take a seat." I nod toward my tub chairs.

Mallory sweeps her hair over one shoulder, her eyes warily focused on me. "What's wrong?"

"Why didn't you tell me about Lena's past?"

chapter
SEVENTEEN

CAN'T help but think we could be much closer to solving this case if Mallory had just told me everything in the first place—or even told the police. It's not like she hid a tiny bit of information, either. She hid something huge. Massive and explosive kind of huge.

Change-the-course-of-this-investigation kind of huge.

I look at my feet, which are propped up on my coffee table, and wiggle my painted toes. Well, I say painted. They're closer to chipped than painted. Which reminds me that I have to reschedule my hair appointment for next week since I forgot about it today.

People getting killed is starting to really piss me off.

At least I managed to get my things from my parents' house earlier relatively unscathed. And by relatively unscathed, I mean I only heard my mom and my nonna yell three times and Nonna promised me she has me a date to take me to church on Sunday.

If there's anything worse than her dinner dates, it's her church dates. As long as he doesn't suggest a quickie in the back room like the last one did, I might leave with some semblance of sanity. It's still a long shot, but I'll take it.

Alison slumps onto the sofa next to me and hands me a cocktail glass. I pat her leg, thankful my brother picked someone awesome to marry. And by awesome, I mean someone who will make me margaritas and watch trashy TV with me just because it gets her away from her hellions. Hellions that include my brother.

I'm not even paying attention to the show. I'm just staring blankly at the television as I try, still unsuccessfully, to make sense of this case.

"You need a break," Alison announces.

"Yep. But it's out of the question until this is done. You know that."

"I know. We're still going for a girls' weekend when it's done."

A whole weekend away from Holly Woods and Drake Nash? Sign me up. "I'm in."

"Of course you're in. It's nonnegotiable. I'd take you even if you fought." She grins.

Her smile is infectious, and I find my own lips curving up. "If you could outfight me, you would, at least. But props for your enthusiasm."

"I'd give it a damn good try," she muses, sipping on her cocktail. "Or I'd just get Trent to do it."

"Nah. He's too afraid to fight me ever since I was sixteen and almost broke his arm." I giggle when she widens her eyes at me. "Of course he didn't tell you."

"What—how?"

"He was annoyin' me. Something about me dating, I think. Anyway, I snapped and put him in an arm lock until he squealed. It was fun. He'd just graduated from the police academy, top of his class, and his little sister had just bested him." Another giggle escapes, and I sip my drink.

"No wonder he never told me!" Alison breaks into laughter. "Oh my. He's not gonna live that one down."

I grin and get up as there's a knock at my door. "Please don't. He threatens to revoke my gun permits if I bring any of that up." I open the door.

"Any of what?" Drake's voice cuts through my amusement.

I turn, swallowing. "What are you doin' here?"

"Hello to you, too. Can I come in?"

"Do you have to?"

"Not really. We can have this conversation standing here, but unless you want the whole block to know what I'm about to tell you…"

"Is it work stuff?"

His eyes darken with heat. "I'm not here for a booty call."

Alison coughs from the front room and stands up. "I should probably be getting back now. And not telling my husband that I'm leaving his sister alone with the guy he answers to every day," she adds on a mumble, making me narrow my eyes at her. She kisses my cheek. "There's still half a pitcher in the kitchen. Maybe put it in the fridge for tomorrow. Bye, Drake."

"Bye, Alison," he says, a confused look on his face as she gets into her car. When my sister-in-law has pulled away from my house and disappeared around the corner, Drake turns back to me. "Well? Am I allowed in?"

"Are you sure you're not here for a booty call?"

"Noelle."

I sigh and open the door fully. "Come on, then."

He stalks past me and into the front room, where he proceeds to sit down on the sofa. In my space. Where I was just sitting. I take a deep breath and close the door. Then I grab my half-full glass from the coffee table. I drink it in one go, ignoring Drake's chuckle as I storm past and refill it in the kitchen.

"That much of a bad day, huh?" he asks, his eyes on my glass.

"And it *just* got better!" I inject every ounce of sarcasm my body is capable of into those five words.

"It's always thrillin' to know I brighten your day, cupcake."

"Oh, you do. You're like my own personal solar eclipse."

His lips pull up into a smirk, his eyes dancing with laughter. "You wound me."

"My gun is next to me," I warn him. "Don't make me give in to temptation."

He laughs, his head going back onto the cushions of the sofa. I try to ignore the flutters in my stomach at the sound and curl up on the corner of the couch. I bring my glass to my lips and sip demurely, wanting to chug the whole thing down instead.

"Keeping Up With the Kardashians, huh?"

I look from the TV to Drake and back to the TV again. "Blame Alison. I only watch E! for Total Divas."

"Total Divas? That's that WWE thing, right?"

"The reality show? Yeah."

Drake nods. "Nikki has a real nice ass."

"Really? You're here to discuss the anatomy of divas, huh?" I raise my eyebrows.

Another laugh. Note to self: Margaritas and Drake's laughter do not go well together. Or they go very well. It depends how you like your butterflies in your tummy. I happen to not like them. At all. In the slightest. Especially if they involve him.

"No, not at all." He smiles and shifts so he's facing me. "We found out something real interestin' today."

I look at him expectantly, and when he doesn't reply, I say, "What was it?"

"Wondered how long you'd wait," he teases. "We finally got a look at Lena's will. Ryan may have been her husband, but he isn't the owner of the store."

What? "Who is?"

"Who *was* is what you should be asking."

"Daniel?" I gasp, leaning forward and almost spilling my drink. I switch hands and lick the liquid off the back of my hand as Drake continues.

"Got it in one. Now, we're trying to figure out the legalities. Her will states that, in the event of Daniel's death, the store goes to her parents. It should be simple, but Daniel's will states that everything he owns at the time of death goes to *his* parents, with the exception of his motorcycle, which belongs to Lena."

"So…Lena's parents could have his bike, and his parents could have her store?" When Drake nods, I wrinkle my nose. "What sense does that make?"

"It doesn't. Perhaps that was the point. Maybe their final wishes were supposed to make as much sense as their deaths."

"They couldn't have planned these," I point out, setting my almost-empty glass down. "How could they have thought for a second they'd be brutally murdered? And by the same person? It's illogical, Drake. There has to be something bigger at play here than just two best friends screwing around. You don't fuck around with your will."

"I know that. You know that. But these wills are three years old. The only thing that makes sense is that Lena stipulates that her daughter owns twenty-five percent of the store, with Dr. Gentry handling it on her behalf until she turns twenty-one and can either sell or step into the business herself."

Another nail in the screwed-up coffin that is Lena Perkins's legacy.

"When were both wills written?"

"Three years ago, like I said."

"What date?" I run my thumb across my bottom lip, ignoring the way Drake's eyes flick there. "Was it the same date?"

"Let me find out." He pulls his phone out. With his eyes still on my mouth, he dials a number and then holds the device to his ear. "Charlotte. Yeah… Check the dates on Lena and Daniel's wills… Uh huh… Interesting. Thank you." He puts the phone on the table and looks at me. "May twenty-seventh. The same day. Signed by the same lawyer."

"They wrote them together." My gaze drifts away and falls on the credits of the Kardashians. "Holy shit. Drake," I grab his arm. "Is there a history of mental illness with Daniel? Do you know?"

"No idea. Why?"

"I didn't see anything in the files Marsh gave me, but what if the wills were the result of a suicide pact?"

He opens his mouth to argue, but I clamp my hand over his mouth to stop him.

"It's not unrealistic. They've been together their whole lives. We already know Lena suffered postpartum depression. It's not outside the realm of possibility that Daniel suffered depression too and they decided this!"

Drake narrows his eyes. "You sound way too excited about this possibility."

"Cop problems," I mutter. Or in this case, ex-cop problems. Running my top teeth over my bottom lip, I suck the soft, tender flesh into my mouth and then release it slowly. The idea holds merit. It's entirely realistic. "I need to go to the office, check on Daniel's medical records."

I move to get up, but Drake grabs my arm and tugs me back down. I squeak when my butt hits the sofa. He doesn't release my arm when I give it a good shake, and I narrow my eyes.

"You've been drinking. You ain't goin' anywhere until you've slept it off."

"I'm fine. I've only had three glasses."

"Three glasses too many to be driving."

"What would you rather I do? Sit here like a damn lemon while the answer to one of our questions is sitting in my freakin' office?" I sigh when he finally releases my arm and run my fingers through my hair. "It's only a few blocks. You could even drive me."

"Noelle."

"It's not that far."

"Noelle."

I graze my teeth over my lower lip again. "Come on, Drake. Don't you want to know?"

"Noelle!"

"What?" I finally focus on him and his blazingly hot gaze.

"For the love of God, shut the fuck up."

I open my mouth to argue, but he silences me with a kiss. Instead of speaking, I gasp, the ferociousness of his kiss reawakening the butterflies in my stomach and sending a thousand different types of shivers cascading through my body.

Drake's fingers curl around the back of my neck, and mine curl around his, because goddammit all, I need something to hold on to if he's gonna unleash his magic mouth on me right now. There's no way, not even sitting down, that I can cope with the wonders of this man's kissing ability without holding on to him like he's my anchor to the here and now.

And that's what he is. When he kisses me this way, deeply and deliciously and fervently, desperately and wonderfully and harshly, the touch of his fingers is the anchor I need to stop myself from flying away with the ecstasy of his mouth on mine.

His teeth graze my lower lip as he lightly tugs on it, and I gasp again, the opening of my mouth providing him with exactly what he needs. His tongue collides with mine and our kiss deepens and he pushes me back and I feel him everywhere.

Like a freezing winter breeze, Drake Nash swirls around me, the very touch of him crawling across my skin so closely and chillingly that it elicits goose bumps on every bare inch of me. And every inch that's covered, too.

His mouth—it's sweet and forceful. I'm entirely helpless to the assault of his kiss. And even if I could fight this, I don't think I would. His fingers are twining in my hair, and mine are in his, and his strong, powerful body covering mine has my heart beating triple time and my legs twitching with the desire to wrap themselves around his waist.

God. I want this man close to me. Over my clothes. Under my clothes. Everywhere. Just everywhere.

I want Drake Nash everywhere on me.

He stops, his mouth hovering above mine, his breath mingling with mine in the barely there gap between our lips.

"You stopped," I breathe, feeling more out of control than I have in a long time. "Why did you stop?"

"I really fucking hate you," he rasps.

"I really fucking hate you," I reply, not brave enough to open my eyes and look into his.

"Good. Then that makes this a whole lot damn easier." He wraps an arm around my back and tugs me down flat on the sofa, moving with me and touching his mouth to mine once more.

Now, his touch is hotter. His fingers move across my back, sliding under my shirt. My skin sears at the touch of his fingertips against me, and I arch my back, pushing my body against his, begging for him to stop yet pleading for more as he steals my breath with every relentless kiss.

I tug at the collar of his shirt, because hell, if he's touching me that way, I wanna touch him like that, too. The material scrunches beneath my fingers, and when it's up around his chest, I trail my hand down his front. It dips with every bump of muscle on his lightly sculpted body, and my whole body tingles. My pussy throbs with the potential of what could be lower—beneath those pants—and I slide my hand around his back as he inches his hand up mine and toward the strap of my bra.

His fingers wrap around it, and I hold my breath, waiting for him to click it open. Just waiting.

But that's interrupted by a buzzing between our thighs.

He growls when he sits up and pulls his phone from his pocket. "What?" he snaps into it.

I cover my eyes with my hands, because did I just almost make it to second base with him? And would I have let him hit a home run?

Fuck yeah, I would have.

That man's mouth is like… Fuck.

"On my way." He shoves his phone into his pocket and looks at me, remnants of my pink lipstick on his stubble and his eyes as dark as ice blue can be. "You need to come with me."

"Whatever it was, I didn't do it," I automatically say, scooting back and sitting up.

"Noelle, trust me, babe, you did fuckin' do it. But that ain't what that call was about."

Don't look down, Noelle. Whatever you do, don't look down at his pants.

I look down. Holy shit. I really did do it. And now, I do really want to do it.

That is one majestic, hard cock. And it's still inside his pants.

"Not helping," he growls, which snaps my eyes back up to his.

I swallow.

"My cop instincts are fightin' real hard with my male instincts right now."

"Male instincts?" I ask, looking back down at his erection. *Sweet baby fucking Jesus.* "What are they?"

"They're the ones tellin' me to rip off your clothing, bend you over your coffee table, and fuck you until you can't breathe."

I inhale sharply. "Thought you hated me."

He grabs my chin and pulls my face to him. "Trust me. I can make a fuck punishment as well as pleasurable."

"Punish me and see where that gets you," I whisper, meeting his eyes.

"Every time you speak, you just tempt me into pulling out a pair of handcuffs. You know that?"

"Don't you have cop instinct to work on? I'm sure your urge to cuff me will still be there tomorrow morning."

"You're right. I do. And you're still comin' with me."

"I told you," I say as he stands and I sit up fully. "I didn't do it."

"No, but our murderer tried to. We've got a woman in the emergency room with hemlock poisoning."

chapter EIGHTEEN

I FOLLOW Drake into the emergency room after a quick stop off at his house so he could grab his holster, "work" gun, and badge. Apparently, he hadn't foreseen a poisoning when he'd come to my place earlier.

When he's found out where we're going from the receptionist, he drags me toward the private room where Trent and three other officers are. Trent raises his eyebrow at me, but I simply glare at him.

"She supposed to be here?" one of the other officers asks. I've never seen him before, and judging by his baby face, he's a rookie. "Sheriff didn't say nothin' 'bout a woman meetin' us here."

"Hey!" I snap. "*She* could have her gun from her boot and a bullet between your eyes before you could reach for your own. She'd also hate to have to prove you right, so how about some respect?"

Drake's lips twitch.

"She is my sister," Trent says, addressing the young officer. "And she happens to be an ex-cop and the finest private investigator for a hundred miles. Show her some respect or you'll be back on the beat rounds before you can apologize."

"Sorry, ma'am," the rookie says immediately.

"Damn right you are," I mutter, folding my arms.

"Try not to kill my staff, Ms. Bond," Drake says.

Sure. I'm Ms. Bond *now*. "Noted, *Detective*."

Trent coughs and draws me away from our staring match. "Drake. We have a Ms. Portia Robinson being admitted for hemlock poisoning. She only ingested a small amount of the poison and was able to call nine-one-one before it took full effect. She's being treated right now and is expected to make a full recovery. We can go and see her soon."

Drake looks at me. "You wanna question her?"

"Sure. Why not? I'm not a cop and supposed to be finishing my margarita at home, but hey!"

"Don't sass me, Noelle," he says. "I'll have you arrested for impeding my investigation."

"It's hardly impeding your investigation when you won't question her yourself," I sigh. "But yes. I will talk to Portia. I happen to know her very well."

"Hey," he says to the other officers. "Go get a coffee or something from the cafeteria. We'll let you know if we need you."

They file out of the room.

As soon as the door shuts, Drake's eyes focus on me. "You 'know her very well'?"

I swallow and perch on the edge of the bed, fully aware of his and Trent's eyes on me. "Yes."

"Fuckin' hell, Noelle. Don't tell me she's a case," Trent says.

"She was a mistress," I reply, looking out the small window that faces the parking lot. An ambulance comes speeding past it and out onto the main road. "Recent case. Maybe a month old. Kieron Vaquez wanted to know if his wife, Diana, was cheating on him with her boss. The irony is that Diana had hired us, too, and Kieron was the real cheater."

"With Portia."

"Yes. It was a cut-and-dried case."

"Do they have anything to do with Lena or Daniel?" Drake asks.

Slowly, I bring my gaze from the window onto him. "That's the funny thing, isn't it? I don't even think Portia knew either of them."

Concern darkens my brother's eyes, and Drake's jaw tightens.

"Go and talk to her," Drake orders. "Now."

I hover outside Portia's room. After speaking to several nurses and either pretending to be family or having Trent back me up as part of the HWPD, I finally got the correct directions to her room. And here I am.

Putting off going in to speak with her because I'm more than a little afraid of what I'm going to find when I walk into that room. Will she be in pain? Will she be partially paralyzed? Will she be sick for the rest of her life? Will she even want to talk about it?

Unfortunately, I'm not gonna find anything out by standing here like a goddamned lemon waiting to be made into lemonade. I'm only going to get the answers I need by walking through the door and asking the questions.

I take a deep breath and knock lightly on the door before pushing it open slightly. Peeking through the door, I see Portia lying on the bed, pale and tired but awake.

She turns her head and faces me. "Noelle," she says quietly. "Come in."

"How are you feelin'?" I ask stupidly, closing the door behind me.

"Like someone just tried to poison me." She cracks the barest of smiles. "Say, could you ask the police if your hunk of a brother, Brody, could come question me? My day could use some brightening."

I smile. "I would, except they've sent me in to ask you some. If you feel up to it right now, that is."

"Sure. Don't have anything else to do."

"Great." I sit in the chair next to her bed. "Talk me through your evening—from when you got home."

"I got in from work, called my mom, then went into the kitchen. Paws—that's my cat—had taken it upon himself to eat the salmon I'd set out to defrost for my dinner, so I decided to call for takeout." She takes a moment, and I hold my breath. "I called up that new pizza place on the corner of Eleventh. You know... Fernando's or something?"

"Sure, I know it."

Nonna was complaining just last week that they couldn't claim to be an Italian restaurant when the owners didn't have a drop of Italian blood between them. That, and she was most aggrieved that a second, unneeded Italian restaurant had opened in town. She might be planning to run them out of town when she isn't setting me up on dates.

"Well, I called, ordered, then poured a glass of wine and got changed." Portia takes another moment to breathe, this time reaching for the small cup of water on the table.

I pass it to her and she smiles gratefully.

"What did you order? Just a pizza? Or maybe a salad?"

"Oh, just the pizza. I raid Mom's veggie garden every week to get my salad items."

My stomach twists. "So, you made your own salad?"

"Keep a small bowl in the fridge, always."

"What did you eat first? The salad or the pizza?"

Portia closes her eyes. "I opened the pizza to let it cool for a moment. The crust is stupid hot on the fingers, you know? So I grabbed some salad and had a few bites."

I swallow. "How'd you know somethin' was wrong?"

"I started feeling like I couldn't breathe, and my toes started to tingle. I'd only had a couple bites, so I called nine-one-one and, well, here I am. Just escaped a poisoning."

And torture by means of genital mutilation to the death.

"Thanks, Portia. I'll let Detective Nash and my brothers know everything you just told me." I pat her hand. "Is there anyone you want me to call?"

"Your brother." Her lips quirk despite her eyes still being shut.

"I'll see what I can do." In my next life. "Thanks for speaking with me. I'll leave you to rest."

"Thanks, Noelle. And do me a favor?"

"Which is?" I ask, my fingers on the door handle.

"Find the motherfucker who tried to kill me."

"That's the plan." I walk through the door and close it behind me, leaning back on it and shutting my eyes.

Victim number three: someone I once tailed as she screwed one of the mayor's right-hand men behind his wife's back. Someone who is connected to me because they were a mistress. Someone not connected to Lena and Daniel in the slightest.

Which means I, and I alone, am the single connecting factor for these murders.

Sure, I suspected it. Maybe I even knew it in my gut. From the very beginning, I was connected to this case deeper than just investigating. But now, to know one hundred percent that I'm in the middle… It's terrifying.

I'm more than a little scared. I'm terrified to be alone and terrified to be with anyone in case anyone else gets hurt.

What if the next victim isn't someone I once watched? What if the next victim is one of my friends? My family? *Me?*

A shudder racks my body. It feels as though a thousand ants are crawling across my skin as the thought that I could be next washes over me. That maybe I was always the target. I inhale desperately through my nose as my lungs constrict and my throat feels dangerously tight.

No.

I won't succumb to this fear. I won't let this panic take over, because I am a strong woman, dammit. I won't let this fear overrule my determination to find the person behind all of this, even if that means I'm walking into a potentially dangerous situation. It happens all the time in movies and everything is okay.

Yeah, yeah. My life isn't a movie, but it's a comforting-ass thought right now, so I'm going with it.

I'll be like Scarlett Johansson in Avengers. Tied to a chair and about to be knocked off—then I'll come whoop some ass like the badass I supposedly am.

Except I'll probably shoot someone instead of whooping ass. Because, you know. I'm Southern. That's what I do.

"Noelle?" Drake's voice cuts through my comfortingly random musings, bringing me out of my head and back into the here and now.

I push off the wall and meet his eyes. They're soft and concerned, yet they're edged with pure, hard determination, and the contrasting combination seems to make his irises glow in a bright burst of color in the otherwise bland hospital hallway. The power of his gaze is entrancing, and my cheeks are burning beneath his concerned scrutiny, but I can't look away.

"Noelle?" he prompts, stepping closer to me.

I run my fingers through my hair and repeat everything Portia just told me, including the difference in the way she was almost killed.

"Okay. I'll have someone go over to her place and dust it for fingerprints."

"'Kay. I'm going home to bed." I walk past him, wrapping my arms around myself.

"Hey," he calls when I'm by the door. "What did you say her connection to the other victims is?"

I pause, glancing at him over my shoulder. "I didn't."

"What is it?" His eyes narrow into suspicious slits, and his usually plump lips thin.

After swallowing hard, I reply simply, "Me."

chapter
NINETEEN

"**Y**OU have got to be freakin' kiddin' me."

Bek winces. "No."

I press the heels of my palms into my eyes and take a deep breath. "A lost cat? Who they're not even sure belongs to them?"

She shrugs and puts the file down. "They said the cat has been coming around for six months. Their daughter started feeding it, so it kept coming back. Even named it Tabby."

"Original," I mutter, opening the file and flicking through it.

"They haven't seen it for a little over a week and she's worried."

I run my eyes down the first page. "They seriously hired us to find a cat based on a seven-year-old's worries? Why can't they just buy her a goddamned kitten? Or get one from the rescue center in Austin?"

Bek shrugs. "Apparently, the mom hates cats."

"Yet here I am, holding a check signed by her, to find a fucking cat."

"Yes, ma'am."

"Ma'am me again and I'll break your nose," I say automatically, slipping the check into the file and holding it out. "No. This is utterly ridiculous. I did not start this agency to find a cat that doesn't even belong to the owners."

"You didn't start it to find a murderer, either."

"And your point is?" Very good—that's what.

"You're currently looking for a murderer."

I stare at her flatly and wave the folder. "My answer is still no."

She takes it and holds it to her chest. "So, you're going to crush a poor little girl's heart because this wasn't the investigation included in 'Bond. P.I.'? What if the cat was homeless and they became his new family? What if he's stuck somewhere, injured? Or run over?"

"Or back with his real owner," I add drily.

"She still deserves to know." She sniffs, turning away. "Remember when Coffee ran away? Your cocker spaniel? You enlisted everyone in town to find the dog that had crept beneath your mom's new deck."

She moves toward the door. One step, two, three...

"Aw, screw you, you ho." I sigh. "Fine. Take the damn case. Look for the damn cat. On the side. Do you understand? A missing cat is not our flippin' priority!"

Bek turns, grins, and flounces over to deposit the check on my desk. I snatch it up the second it hits the wood and stuff it in my drawer with the two checks Mike brought to me this morning. My best friend opens my office door and shoots me the kind of smile that reeks with smugness over her successful manipulation of my emotions.

Bitch.

"You're the best boss ever."

"Yeah, whatever. Get out." I wave my hand at her, but I'm grinning.

She responds by blowing me a kiss, and I just about manage to hold my laughter in until she's shut my door. Damn her. I can't seem to say no to her.

Besides, she's right. I tantrummed the mother of all tantrums when Coffee went missing and enlisted the help of everyone from Rosie at the café to the mayor. Luckily, I was a pretty cute kid, so no one was mad when we found her beneath the deck.

That and everyone's scared as heck of Nonna.

Wise people.

I get up and grab the sheets for my new file from the printer. When Mike brought me a new infidelity case this morning with the offer to handle it, I all but snatched it out of his hand and set Marsh to finding me all the information I need.

It's dangerous. I know. I shouldn't be taking any cases right now, but once Dean reminded me that he was the lead guy on Portia's case, my brain justified it as okay. Justified it as I'm not fully connected to her case and her attempted murder in a bullshit form of denial. I'm going with it though. Because, if I don't, I might crawl under my covers and never come out again.

So here I am, slipping my new Louboutins on—it was a freak yet calming purchase at full price. Don't judge me—ready to go find me a cheating bastard husband.

Sounds like a damn good day to me.

Ignore that the Louboutin website is still an open tab on my phone browser. And so is Neimans. And possibly Victoria's Secret.

Evidently, I shop when I'm stressed.

With my mind on that cute, lacy, pink underwear set I saw on the VS homepage this morning before I left my house, I grab my keys, purse, and phone and make my way out to the parking lot.

"Shall I hold your messages?" Grecia asks, glancing up from her romance novel.

Do my staff members actually work around here? "Please. And if you have nothing to do, the basement could use some organizing." I smile sweetly.

She closes her phone. "Okay, but you bring back cupcakes."

"Like that was ever in question," I reply, walking out the door and wistfully wondering whether or not this case will take me into Austin so I have a legit excuse to drive to Gigi's. Although, given the fact that I had to suck it in to button my favorite light-blue jeans this morning, I should probably use that as the reason not to.

I sigh and get in my car, double-checking that my little, blue gun is tucked into its hiding place in my purse. A feeling of safety washes over me when I see the Tiffany-blue handle peeking out at me.

The fact that I could kill someone in a second is oddly comforting. And slightly disturbing. Both that I could kill someone and find it comforting.

Perhaps I should close down the VS tab and open up a Google search for "psychologists in Holly Woods." You know, after I've purchased the cute underwear.

My priorities are pretty fucked.

I can't help but think that my priorities fit in real well with the rest of my life right about now.

"Hello," I say, catching my phone on the first ring.

"Noella!" Nonna's voice booms around my tiny TT, and I wince. "I have-a you a date!"

Despite my best efforts, I can't hide my groans.

"No! Listen, *bella*," she implores. "He is-a cop in Austin! He no-a scared of your gun!"

"Hmm," I reply. "You realize it's not my gun he should be scared of, but me?"

She laughs. "You no-a scary! His name is-a Giorgio. He take-a you for dinner tonight!"

"Wait, what?" I break a little too hard at the intersection. "Are you being serious?"

"*Si!* He take-a you to Giovanni's! The real-a *Italiano* restaurant!"

"Nonna, what if I had plans for tonight? You know I'm busy with work right now." I pull away and take a right. "I don't have time for your crazy dates."

"He is-a very nice! Respectable. You will go!"

I clench my jaw. "Fine. Fine, I'll go. I'm not promising that I'll be nice!"

She mumbles something in Italian before sighing dramatically. "Is-a best I get," she finishes. "Seven! You be there!" Then she hangs up on me.

"*Cazzo*," I mutter, pulling up across the street from my guy's office building. Which just so happens to be next to Melanie Lyons's little bookstore and coffee shop. Damn, she makes the best carrot cake in town. And sitting here in my car would be suspicious, right?

Oy vey. Looks like I'm going to have go in. What a darn shame.

"Noelle!" Behind the counter, Melanie looks up from her book and shoots me a dazzling smile. God only knows how she's never married. With her long, Barbie-blond hair and the closest-proportioned body you'll get to the doll, she's more worthy of a Hollywood movie than a Holly Woods coffee and bookshop. "How are you, honey?"

Did I mention she's also illegally sweet? Yeah.

"I'm good. How are you?" I smile. "Ohh." I pause, sniffing. "Is that—?"

"Mom just made a fresh carrot cake," she confirms, a knowing twinkle in her eye. "I'm guessin' you're here to work."

"I am." I perch on one of the stools she keeps to the side of the counter. "Can I have a vanilla latte and carrot cake?"

"Regular?"

"Uh…I should probably go for no-fat with the cake." I grin.

She smiles knowingly. "Brody was in here yesterday and almost bought you carrot cake. Just before he went to the hospital." She froths the milk and raises her voice. "Poor Portia! Do y'all know who did it?"

I rest my chin in my hand and shake my head, my eyes on the building on the other side of the street "No. I have next to no leads, and if the cops have any, they ain't sharin' 'em."

"Bummer." She sighs. Melanie Lyons is also known as the Holly Woods Gossip Queen, and her store the Gossip HQ. "Hey, did you speak to her secret boyfriend yet?"

I drag my eyes from the realtor building and toward Melanie. "Her whatty-what, now?"

She giggles. "Secret boyfriend. She comes in here every day on the way down to that fancy-ass boutique of hers—ain't nobody got time for that designer business in this town, I tell you—and she's been real happy lately." She leans forward just as I tuck my designer shoes beneath my stool. "So the other day, I ask her why she's all happy, and she tells me she's got herself a boy toy. Or, to be exact, a toy boy. But she wouldn't tell me who. Like I can't keep a secret or something.'" Her eyes glitter with her own laughter.

I smirk. "I wonder why," I say, taking my coffee. "How long has she been seeing him?"

"Who knows, honey? Could be a week, could be a month. How she kept that secret is beyond me. I got eyes all over this town keepin' tabs on them there relationships."

"Hmm. Hold that thought." I pull my phone from my purse and bring my call log up. My finger hovers over Drake's name for a second before I scroll to Brody, then Trent, then ultimately end up tapping Drake's name. Dammit.

"Detective Nash," he answers curtly.

"Ms. Bond," I say sickeningly sweetly. "I have some information for you."

"It better be good," he replies more softly this time.

"Portia has a secret boyfriend."

"Come again?"

"Portia has a secret boyfriend."

"Didn't see anythin' in her house."

"Hence the secret part of my sentence." I roll my eyes. "Y'all checked her phone records yet?"

"Are you questionin' my competency, Ms. Bond?"

"Not at all, Detective. Have you?"

His breathing is all I hear for a few seconds before he says, "No. I'll get Brody on it."

"You do that." A grin spreads across my face.

"Is that everything?"

"Yes, sir."

"Great. And aren't you supposed to be working instead of sitting in a bookstore?"

"I am working," I argue, looking out the door and catching the end flash of a cop car. "Aren't you supposed to be working and not stalking me?"

"I am workin'. And my stalkin' you keeps getting interrupted, remember?"

I shudder at the memory of his mouth on mine and his body over mine and his hands splaying across my skin and... "Goodbye, Detective." I hang up, unwilling to go down that street.

If I hafta go on Nonna's dumbass date tonight, I do not want to think about getting naked and doing the horizontal tango with one Detective Drake Nash.

"Mel?" I ask, turning my attention to her. "What do you know about Barry Quentin?"

"The realtor across the street?" She leans in, grinning widely. "I know he's a cheating son of a motherfucker. Seen him leaving the office with some black-haired woman for the last couple weeks."

I open my file. "How many times?"

"Twice a week, maybe? Always at the end of the day. I'd bet she's his assistant."

Ugh. That old gem. Can't cheaters be original these days? Come on, man. Screw the cleaner or something. Who wouldn't want to get hot and heavy in the company bathroom? Secretaries are so overrated. I always feel like a total fraud when I have to tell someone their other half is doing their bitch.

Sigh.

"Any idea who she is?"

"It'll cost you a date with Brody for me to find out."

"I could look online, you know."

"I know. But I'll also find out who Portia's secret boyfriend is…" she trails off, leaning forward and smiling sweetly.

I shake my head, but I'm smiling, too. "Now, Mel, put those weapons away. You know I don't swing that way," I tease, and she sighs dramatically and tugs up her shirt. "I'll do it, but I need the names before I set you up, okay?"

Her smile brightens. "Okay!"

Good thing I know that Brody has had a crush on Mel since he was fourteen.

"You call me when you know anything," I tell her. "And what time do they leave?"

"Six thirty, give or take a few minutes," she answers.

Shoot. My date is at seven. But if I get dressed before I leave and go to the restaurant straight from here… "Thanks, Mel."

"I'll call you!"

I know she will.

This is ridiculous.

"I'm not going," I say to my mirror.

"You are!" Bek's voice crackles through the speakerphone. "Come on, Noelle. You haven't been on a date in months."

"There's a reason for that."

"Using your gun as a reason for not dating is unacceptable."

"No, it's a real thing," I argue, pulling yet another dress over my head and throwing it on my bed. "Because it's better than the whole 'I have nothing to wear' excuse that all the women in the world use."

"How can you have nothing to wear? Your closet is bigger than my living room."

"Shut up," I mutter, grabbing the phone and walking into my closet. "If I wear red, I'll have to wear my new Louboutins, and that'll make me look like I like expensive things. But if I wear that blue dress with the cut-out panel on the back with those cute nude heels I got from Macy's last summer, maybe I'll look cheap. But then again, if I wear that black off-the-shoulder dress you made me buy two years ago that I haven't worn yet, I can wear any shoes with it. But there's also that pale-pink one with the pleated skirt that makes my complexion look good, and those Prada heels I bought just after Christmas will go so well with those."

"Noelle, hon, never go on a date again."

I groan and lean against the doorframe. "See? This is why I don't date. Why I can't date. There's no such thing as too many shoes or clothes until you have to impress a man."

My best friend laughs. And laughs. And laughs. "Since when did you care about impressing a man?"

I purse my lips, staring at the pretty, red bodycon dress that's been sitting in my closet for six months, unworn. She's right—when did I? I dress for me. I buy pretty things because I like pretty things. They make me feel good. Expensive shoes make me feel sexy. Nice dresses make me feel feminine.

I guess that's the thing about being a confident, independent woman. Everything you do is for you.

I like being me.

"Okay. I'm going to wear the red dress with my new Louboutins, and if he thinks I look expensive, then he probably can't afford me, right?"

"There's my best friend. She got buried beneath some Mean Girl shit right there."

I laugh, pulling the dress from the hanger and tossing it over my shoulder. "Okay, Rebekah, I'm going on this godforsaken date. If you don't hear from me tomorrow—"

"You're shacked up with a hot Italian-Texan cop and I should let you sleep in. Got it."

"I don't sexytime on the first date!"

"What about that guy you slept with just after you came home?"

"You mean when you dragged me to Vegas? Oh, Bek, what happens in Vegas stays there. In the Holly Woods dimension, I didn't sleep with the red-hot dancer from the bar, okay?"

"Sure. If that's what you wanna believe, girl. I'll go with it." She laughs, and I do, too. "I'm going. Be good. Get pics of the cheating husband. Stay out of hot cop's pants."

"Yes, boss," I say sarcastically.

We say goodbye, and I throw my phone onto my bed. I give my closet one last glance before grabbing my sparkly, black clutch from the shelf and slamming the door to the damn thing.

A man must have created walk-in closets. No one else would employ that level of torture on a woman once she's filled it.

With my hair still wet and knotted on top of my head, I glance at the clock and note that I have all of forty-five minutes to get ready before I have to go spy on Mr. Quentin and his Black-Haired Bimbo. *Cazzo.* I tug the dress over my head, covering my sexy, black lingerie, and smooth it down my thighs.

I twirl in front of the mirror. Damn. My butt looks kinda good in this baby.

I should wear it more often. Although I'm not sure the knee-length, tight fabric would be conductive to climbing trees to spy on sex trysts.

I blow-dry my hair with one hand and apply my foundation with the other. Overall, it's kind of awkward, so I drop the blow-dryer before I apply my mascara. I'm blessed with thick, dark lashes that are naturally curly, but hey.

Mascara is a girl's best friend.

After wine and cupcakes.

And shoes.

Speaking of shoes… I put my Louboutins on and stare at myself in the mirror. I was right. This looks too expensive. Like I'm trying. Which I am, but I'm not.

Jesus.

I sit on the edge of my bed and push my hair from my face, looking at myself in the mirror. What's my real issue with this date? Because Nonna did it? Because it's one of her harebrained schemes to have me married by the age of thirty? Because I don't have time for it because of work? I have paychecks to sign and files to look through and cases to approve and a murderer to find.

Or is it because the person I'm going on a date with isn't the person I want it to be?

I resist the urge to slap my cheek to knock some sense into me. The person I want it to be? Is that supposed to be Drake? Sure thing— the man makes my body come alive like a fucking box of fireworks in the middle of a bonfire, but I can't stand him. I want to wring his neck with my heels and shoot my cute little Glock into his foot in a repeat of my sixteen-year-old self.

So why the hell am I not comfortable with this date?

If this were multiple choice, I'd tick off all of the above. And scribble out the last before filling it in and scribbling it out and filling it and scribbling it out…

I stand, grab my favorite red lipstick—recently recovered from one of my Chucks—and apply it smoothly. Any more thinking and I'm going to be canceling with a phantom stomach bug or something. Which, come to think of it, doesn't sound like a bad idea. Although, if I just suffer through this one date, Nonna will get off my back for at least two weeks.

And, oh God, those two weeks would be worth it…

I snatch my keys from the counter, shove my wallet into my clutch with my phone, and make my way out to my car before I change my mind.

I can't shake the terrible feeling I have about this date, but that probably comes from Nonna's track record. She, unfortunately, believes that any man who is Italian will be a good enough husband. Now I know my generation is a touch shallower than hers, but come on. I want to be attracted to and turned on by a man.

Anyone who brings me cupcakes is a bonus.

Why does my mind keep going back to Drake?

Fuck you, brain. Fuck you ten bazillion times.

I spend the next few minutes repeating that mantra in my head as I drive back toward Melanie's place. The realtor opposite is still bathed in light, and I park outside the coffee and bookstore while I wait for whoever is in the building to vacate.

Three raps on my window precede the door opening and my blond friend sliding in. "Suzie Carter. Single mom, twenty-six, moved to Holly Woods six months ago when her baby daddy got locked up for arson. Got a job working for Quentin and Jones almost immediately and has been seeing Barry Quentin ever since."

"You star." I scribble that down on my pocket-sized notepad. "How does no one who she is?"

"She's pretty quiet. Keeps herself to herself. Apparently, she doesn't want to bring any bad juju to the town her daughter is in love with."

"Makes sense." I snap my notebook shut and pull my phone out.

Mel moves to open the door and get out, but I grab her arm when the door to the realtor opens.

"Sit," I hiss, tapping the camera con on my phone screen. I position myself in such a way that I could be texting or something.

"Smart," Mel hums approvingly as I snap a photo of Barry with his arm tight around his assistant.

"Shh." I angle the phone slightly to get a better lighting. Early April is the awkward time of year where it's not quite dark and not quite light at this time. Thankfully, it's almost always the lighter side.

Which is exactly how I get the shot of Barry Quentin planting a smacker onto Suzie Carter.

"Holy shit," Mel breathes.

"Welcome to my world." It's all I need to say as I tuck my phone into my purse again, watching as Barry and Suzie get into his car for what is presumably a "late night at the office."

Again with the originality. You'd think there'd be some better excuses than that by now.

"Thanks, Mel," I say, smiling at her. "Any idea who Portia's secret boyfriend is?"

"No. But one of my girlfriends goes to pottery glass with her down at Marcie's place, and their class is tonight, so she's gonna ask some questions since Portia won't be there."

"Okay. I have to go deal with Nonna's latest date."

"Thought you looked hot." Mel winks teasingly, then she gets out of my car and shuts the door.

I roll my eyes as I head down the street to the restaurant. Giovanni's is the quintessential Italian restaurant, from the one hundred percent Italian family that runs it to the Italian-style décor and totally Italian menu. It's my favorite place to have a date, and I think Nonna books it for that reason.

"Ahhh, *Signorina* Bond," my favorite server, Alonso, greets me. "You are here for Nonna, *si*?"

"*Si*," I sigh. "Your lack of surprise astounds me, Alonso."

He grins, switching to his native Texan accent. My twenty-five-year-old friend totally puts on the accent for the benefit of the customers, but he's as country as they come. "I'm still askin' for that date, Noelle. She's a tough customer!"

I laugh. "She sure is. Maybe when you start datin' women, she'll let you take her precious grandbaby on a date. Until then, she's offerin' you Brody!"

Alonso laughs. "I assume you're with the handsome gentleman, Giorgio."

"So she tells me."

"May I say you look stunning tonight?"

"You may. But I'm still not settin' you up with Brody," I tease him, knocking him with my elbow.

"Damn," he shakes his head. "What I'd do to make that man gay."

I cover my mouth with my hand to hide a very unladylike snort. "Will you show me to my table? It's one of Nonna's famous *appuntamenti al bio.*"

"Ahh. Her blind dates. She did good with this one, my friend. Very good. He is over here." He takes my elbow and guides me to the back of the restaurant.

And, uh, yeah. Nonna did good. She clearly took my moaning seriously, because this man is hot. Like, Italian-Texan hot. "Hello I have the genes and complexion of an Italian man mixed with the hardworking sexiness of a Texan" hot. Dark hair, dark eyes, light-olive skin, plump lips…

"*Signor,* this is Noelle, your date for this evening," Alonso says with a little flair, encouraging Giorgio to stand and kiss my hand.

I smile. "Giorgio, it's lovely to meet you."

"And you, Noelle. Your grandmother did not say you are so beautiful." He smiles widely, sitting opposite me.

My cheeks flush slightly. "Nonna didn't tell you a lot, I'm sure," I reply. "But thank you."

"Can I get you some wine?" Alonso asks, looking between us.

"House white, if that's okay with the lady," Giorgio says, looking to me.

"Fine." I smile at him and Alonso. "Thank you."

He disappears in seconds, leaving us alone.

"So," Giorgio says to fill the awkward silence, "what do you do?"

So much for his being comfortable with my carrying a gun. Like I am right now.

"I'm a private investigator," I respond, smiling, wishing I had a wine glass to hide behind when his eyes widen. Alonso? Hello? Now would be great. "Nonna tells me you're a police officer."

Giorgio recovers. "In Austin. Private investigator. That's interesting. How did you come about that?"

"I was a police officer myself, in Dallas. Let's just say that a case I was working went very wrong and I felt some responsibility and came home." I look away but pull myself back. "I don't talk about it much. I loved my job as far as finding whodunit went, so private investigating is the perfect job for me."

He smiles, and it's kind of dazzling. "Interesting. What do you mostly work on?"

"Infidelity." I fight my smirk when he blinks hard. "Although we were hired to locate a missing cat earlier today, so we take on a little of everything."

"Riveting." His dark eyes glitter across the table.

Alonso pours us two glasses of wine, leaving the bottle in an ice bucket. When he's gone, I sip my wine slowly and meet Giorgio's eyes. "What do you do?"

"I work homicide," he says slowly. "We actually received word about the poisoning case you have here."

Indignation filters through me. If the Austin PD has been notified, it means the mayor doesn't think the HWPD can handle it. This has only happened twice in my lifetime—and the second time, my grandfather shot the previous mayor's front window in and the statement was retracted.

He argued it was the window or Nonna.

I'm not one to get easily riled—I'm also a chronic liar—but when someone says my brothers can't do their jobs, I get very pissed very easily. And this, the mayor calling Austin PD to be on guard in case they're needed less than a mile outside their jurisdiction, makes me very damn angry.

"You look angered by that," Giorgio notes.

Observant, this one.

"I'm actually working that case." I smile, although it's tight. "The husband of the first victim hired me. Then his parents after him."

"He fired you?"

"Can I take your order?" Alonso slips in, his smooth yet fake accent cutting through the tension.

I avoid the appetizer but order my main course—the same seafood pasta I always do—and hand him my menu. Once Giorgio has ordered and handed Alonso his menu, I push my hair from my face.

"Have you seen the case particulars?" I ask, noting the tic in his jaw.

"No."

"Then I can't discuss it, really. But, yes, for reasons given in the case files."

"Noelle," he says, leaning forward, his voice softening. "You seem real perturbed about me knowing about this."

I take a deep breath and realize I'm taking my frustration over the mayor's actions out on my date. Awkward. "I'm sorry. My brothers are on the police force here. For y'all to know about this up in Austin… It rubs me the wrong way."

"Oh. We aren't called in to investigate. Just to monitor the situation in case the murders leave the HWPD's jurisdiction. Also to keep our eyes open."

"That's better news." I smile more softly. "Sorry if I snapped."

"It's okay." He returns the smile, this time softly touching my hand. "You're beautiful enough to get away with it."

I blush and turn away. So I can shoot someone but not take a compliment. It's a serious issue in my mind. Plus—a compliment from a hot guy Nonna approves of? Blush-worthy, I tell you.

Leaving behind talk of work, we discuss our hobbies and all of that other awkward shit people do on the first date. Which is, incidentally, one reason why I hate dating. With a passion.

I discover that Gio, as he insists I call him, loves tennis. And I, well… I can hold a racket and at least attempt to serve, so I guess we kind of have that in common. He loves animals—all of them—and I can just about stand Bekah's eight-year-old mopey-ass cat.

Alonso brings our dinner, and we continue our discovery mission. Because isn't that what first dates are? Discovery missions? It's where you get out all the happy, sparkly bits about yourself and leave the blackened bullshit to be discovered when the honeymoon period of the relationship is all said and done.

Gio likes cars. I like shoes. Gio likes traveling and big cities and expensive wine. I like expensive wine, but I'm done after a flight to

Vegas and can only take big cities in moderation. He likes movies over books, and despite my affinity for the Bond franchise, I'm picking a paperback over a DVD case every time. Or a Kindle over a Blu-Ray.

He detests social media aside from Facebook, and my phone buzzes with a Tinder notification.

Really, we don't have much in common. But I like him. And if the smile on his face is anything to go by, he likes me. And who needs things in common, right?

I mean, we both like guns. And each other, apparently. That'll do.

I'm just finishing up my dinner when my phone buzzes in my purse. I ignore it only for it to ring a second time. I smile apologetically at Gio and steal a glimpse at the screen. Drake's name flashes up, and I tuck the Samsung back in. But it buzzes for a third time.

"Shouldn't you get that?"

I look up at Gio. "I'm sorry. I feel so rude, but I think it could be work related. Do you mind?"

"Not at all." He gestures to my purse. "Take all the time you need."

I grasp my purse, tugging my phone out with another apologetic smile to him. This time, it's the HWPD number calling me, and I answer as I open the restaurant door.

"Noelle Bond."

"Why the fuck are you ignorin' my calls?"

Oh. Someone is on his man-monthly.

"Actually," I say to Drake, "I'm busy."

"Too busy to know I have a member of your staff brought in for questioning?"

Bolts of annoyance as fierce as lightning spear through my body. "Excuse me?"

"Marshall. He's been seeing Portia Robinson for several weeks."

"You have got to be kidding me."

"Do I sound like it?"

"I'm coming down. Don't you dare question him until I'm there." I hang up just as he protests, but I don't care.

Marshall is her secret boyfriend?

I run back through the restaurant toward my table and stop in front of Gio. "I'm so sorry," I breathe, "but I have to run to the station. The detective in charge has taken one of my staff members in for questioning and I'm about to wring his ass out."

"Detective Nash?" Gio asks, standing. "Let me take you." He motions for the check.

"It's okay, really. I have my car in the lot. I'm just sorry I have to run out on you like this."

"Don't be silly. Let me take you down. Wait, please," he tells Alonso. He opens the book and tucks in his card. "Return immediately, please."

"Of course," Alonso replies, dipping his head slightly.

I watch as he runs away with the bill then look at Gio. "Honestly. It's okay. How much do I owe you for dinner? I can write you a check, or..."

"Noelle," he says quietly, touching my upper arm. "Nothing. It is my treat and an honor to take you for dinner. Now, please allow me to escort you to the station where your staff member is."

Clearly, he's not going to take no for an answer. "Okay."

Gio takes his card from Alonso, and with his hand on the small of my back, he guides me out of the restaurant into the balmy evening. He leads me toward a parked, navy-blue Chevvy truck in the corner and opens the door for me. He even gives me a hand getting in.

I don't need it, but it's kind of nice to see that gentlemen still exist. Even if this is Texas and gentlemen are supposedly the norm.

"You look like you're ready to kick some ass," Gio notes, climbing into the driver's side. I guess, in retrospect, his one glass of wine to my two makes him safer to drive than me.

"Oh, I am." My lips thin as I say it. "And Detective Nash knows it."

chapter TWENTY

"**W**HERE is he?" I demand of Charlotte, slamming my hands on her counter.

"Down the hall, to the right—interview room three."

"He's started?"

"He's crazy, but he isn't stupid, Noelle," she says, her lips twitching. "Detective Nash knows that everything you have to say to him can't be said over the phone."

"He's learning, then," I snap, pushing off the counter.

Gio follows me down the hall, and I ignore the interested look from the receptionist as he does so. He touches his hand to my back just as we turn the corner toward the interview rooms, and it feels as though his fingertips burn through the material of my dress.

Well, burn is relative. They're warm. Obvious. That's it.

There's no damning skin tingle. But there's enough. I'll take enough.

The first person I see as I approach the interview area is Trent. He stares at me for a long moment before his eyes flick knowingly to Gio.

"Detective Messina. What a surprise," Trent drawls, his eyes falling back onto me.

I lift my eyebrows and shoot him a shut-the-fuck-up look.

"Detective Bond. Of course. I should have made the connection." Gio's fingers tighten on my back.

I wonder if my brother knows more about the man our grandmother decided to set me up with than she does.

"It's a common surname," Trent replies. His smile is tight, and it's an obvious attempt at keeping his jaw slack. Unfortunately for him, my brother has never been very good at hiding his emotions. "You're forgiven for your oversight."

Tension rockets between them as Gio's tense smile matches Trent's.

I brush my hair away from my eyes. "Hello? Can someone please explain to me what the hell is going on here and why the ever-lovin' fuck y'all called my tech whiz in for your dumbass questionin'?"

Gio snorts behind me, a sound cut short by my brother's harsh look.

Huh. Something tells me that they know each other.

"Hey!" I snap, clapping my hands "Y'all are trippin' if you think I'm standin' here in these fuckin' shoes for shits and giggles!"

"I should have known it would be you makin' a scene here." Drake's voice drawls as he shuts a door and appears in the hallway. Tight, white shirt. Perfectly pressed, black dress pants. Shiny, black shoes. Badge attached to the pocket of his shirt.

"Well, I warned you about harrassin' my staff on my premises—"

"And I'm not—"

"So a smart cop such as yourself should have anticipated me being a drama queen down here when you pull my guy in," I finish, glaring at him. "I want an explanation. Now."

"I don't have to give you shit, Noelle, and you know it." His glacier eyes narrow.

I step toward him, my finger pointing at his chest. "No, you don't, but I expect a goddamned reason why he won't be at work tomorrow morning like he should be."

"That's his job," Drake hisses.

"But I'm talkin' to you, and I'm tellin' you to answer my damn questions before I demand to sit in there in lieu of his lawyer and advise him to tell you to shove your questions where the sun doesn't fucking shine until his lawyer does get here," I hiss back.

My heels make me almost as tall as he is, and we're so close that, with each angry breath Drake takes, his chest is close to brushing mine. Close enough that I can feel the vibrations of his movements through the tense air between us. Close enough that, if I breathe in at the same time he does, my breasts brush his chest.

Our gazes battle it out for the longest, most breathtaking moment. Until his eyes skirt over my shoulder to Gio standing behind me.

"Who the hell is that?"

"My date," I reply tightly, "which you so kindly interrupted."

"Your date," Drake repeats. His voice is flat, monotone, but his eyes betray the flare of anger that makes his jaw twitch.

"Yes, sir. Is that a problem? Because I can ask him to leave while we continue this conversation."

"Please do."

I roll my eyes and turn away, my heels clicking against the laminated flooring as I gently take Gio's arm and pull him to the end of the hallway. "I'm so sorry. Detective Nash and I don't particularly see eye to eye on many things. He's also an arrogant bastard, so I could be a while, and it isn't fair to expect you to wait for me to be done."

"It's okay." Gio brushes some hair from my face. "Your brother will take you home?"

I nod. "Thank you for a lovely evening. And if we do this again, I'm paying."

His face breaks out into that dazzling smile again. "When we do this again, I'll hear of no such thing." He leans forward and kisses my cheek, his lips lingering warmly against my skin for a moment. "Goodnight, Noelle."

I smile. "Goodnight, Gio."

He walks around the blind corner, glancing back at me before he's entirely out of view.

The sound of fake vomiting has me turning around.

"I think I'm gonna be sick," Trent says.

"Hey, Dad of Two, remember that next time you join forces with Nonna to get me married!" I walk back to him and smack his arm. "This was her idea, her date."

"Looks like you really hated it."

"I'll have you know, he was the perfect gentleman."

Trent snorts, but Drake interrupts.

"Noelle." He says my name in a short, curt tone that makes me feel like I should have picked up the dirty glass on my coffee table before I left my house a couple of hours ago. "Are you sittin' in on this or not?"

"You mean you're allowing me?" I ask, slowly looking at him.

His eyes don't soften—neither does the tight pull of his lips or his jaw. "You think I'm stupid enough to allow a non-cop to sit in on my interview with someone just because she's his fuckin' boss and let some big-city stiff know about it?"

"No. So, why are you?"

"He doesn't know," he corrects me. "And because I like my balls where they are, so get your ass in that interview room in two seconds or go home."

I stare at him for one whole second before I do exactly as he said and tug the door open to join Marshall in the interview room.

My whiz kid is sitting at the table, wearing a faded Green Lantern tee that's definitely seen much better days. In fact, it's probably seen better years. His hair is wet and tangled, and his glasses slip down his nose. He looks up as I step inside, Drake hot on my heels.

"Boss."

"Hey, kid," I say quietly, hovering in the doorway. "How you doin'?"

"I have no idea what happened, I swear!" He digs his teeth into his bottom lip, and his hands are shaking where they're clasped on the table.

"Hey, Marsh. No one thinks you did." I move to the table and sit when Drake pulls out the chair next to his. Great. Interviewer side. "But you gotta understand that your relationship with Portia means Detective Nash has gotta talk to you."

"I know. Can she stay?" he asks Drake.

"Yes. She'll just demand the transcript of the interview after anyway, so I'm saving the whole department a week's worth of headaches." He ignores the look I shoot at him. "She knows the rules."

Stay quiet. Don't ask questions. Don't interrupt. Don't influence either Drake or Marshall.

Drake clicks the button on the recorder and shuffles the papers on the table. "Can you state your full name?"

"Marshall Leonard Wright."

"Address?"

"Fifty-four Shrewsbury Avenue, Holly Woods, Texas."

"Date of birth?"

"January seventh, nineteen ninety-three."

"And can you confirm for the record that you're not exercising your right to have a lawyer present?"

"That's correct."

I frown but quickly look down so he doesn't see it. He must be truly certain of the answers to his questions, but I know how cops can wrap people up in knots. Marshall is the smartest guy I know—academically and technologically—but he won't stand a chance if Drake pulls out the big guns and decides to question him until they're both shitting armadillos.

Drake kicks me under the table, and the frown drops from my face as I look up. Whoops. Already fucked up.

"Mr. Wright, you're here because it's recently come to our attention that you were in a secret relationship with Ms. Portia Robinson. Ms. Robinson is currently in the hospital, recovering from hemlock poisoning she suffered approximately twenty-four hours ago. We've also been told that you were the last person to see her before she was poisoned."

I bite my tongue. I want to call him out on the technicality that Marsh was the last person to see her before she ate the poisoned salad. She could have been poisoned at any time. But hey...

"I guess so," Marshall replies quietly, looking Drake dead in the eye. "I left her house around four p.m. I was only there briefly."

So Portia lied to me.

"What was the purpose of your visit?" Drake asks.

"To tell her I wanted to end our relationship. I-I met someone online. In Austin."

Interesting.

"Ms. Robinson is twelve years your senior, is she not?"

"Yes, sir."

"Why the attraction to an older woman?"

Marshall shrugs.

"I need you to reply so the machine can hear you, Mr. Wright."

"Sorry." Marsh clears his throat. "I'm not sure. It started as a one-night thing and remained strictly casual. I'm not the only person she was seeing."

"And that didn't bother you at all?" Drake quirks his eyebrow.

"No. Like I said, it was a casual relationship. Neither of us expected anything out of it except something physical. At least, I didn't."

Imagining the gangly, World of Warcraft–obsessed techie in a physical situation has me beating down giggles before they erupt and Drake throws me out.

Drake nods slowly. "Understandable. How long had you been seeing each other?"

"A few weeks."

"How did she take your news?" Drake leans back and crosses his arms. *Hello, distraction.* "Was she upset? Put out? Angry? Distressed?"

"Quite the opposite, I'm afraid, Detective. She was very happy that I'd found someone who made me happy. We parted as friends, on good terms." Marsh pushes his glasses up his nose.

"Sounds like a dream," Drake replies, amusement riddling his tone. Silence reigns as he studies Marshall. His gaze is so powerful that I can feel it, too, and dammit, now I want to look at him.

The air is becoming more and more suffocating as they stare each other off, only blinking occasionally. It's literally like man and house, tornado and wooden shack, bulldozer and brick wall. Drake is, naturally, far more imposing and terrifying than I suspect Marshall will ever be, but he's holding his own despite it all.

Sure, there's a nervous tic just below his eye, and anyone untrained wouldn't notice the bead of sweat on his brow or the way his right hand is twitching with the urge to wipe it away. They wouldn't know the tremble of his lower lip as he fights the urge to say something or the miniscule shift in his shoulders as he desperately wars within himself not to break the eye contact he's so meticulously maintaining.

Son of a bitch!

Drake didn't get me in here to support Marshall. If he had, I would have been on his side of the table. No. The bastard got me in here to read his body language.

And I know exactly what his question will be next.

"Any reason you'd want Ms. Robinson dead, Mr. Wright?"

Fucking son of a bitch.

Except, now, I'm tuned in. My eyes are so focused on Marshall that I couldn't rip them away if I tried, and his every movement, I see it. There isn't a tic or twitch or throb of a vein I don't miss as his eyes widen at Drake's question.

"Absolutely none, Detective."

Drake pauses for a moment then turns to me. "I think we're done here." His gaze drifts to Marshall. "Thank you, Mr. Wright. Someone will be in shortly to discuss with you anything you may know about Ms. Robinson that may help us in our investigation."

Marshall visibly relaxes, and that bead of sweat that was hovering just above his brow slides down the side of his face and disappears into his sideburn. "Of course. I'll be happy to help."

Drake clicks the recorder off and pushes his chair back. He pulls my chair back with a tiny jerk, making me squeak in surprise. I get up with a harsh glare to him then look at Marshall, softening my gaze.

"You good?" I ask him.

"I'm good, boss," he replies, pushing his glasses up his nose again. He really needs to get those fixed.

"Ms. Bond," Drake says sharply, stalking toward the door and yanking it open.

Oh. It's like that, is it? Ms. Bond my left ass cheek.

Drake walks through the door before I've even gotten there, and I have to grab it to stop it from slamming on me. Holy shit, someone has a cactus up his ass tonight.

"What the hell is wrong with you?" I call, anger tensing my muscles.

"I have no idea what you mean," he replies equally as angrily, now drawing the attention of the other staff still working.

"You know exactly what I mean!" My heels loudly tap against the floor as I chase after him. "Pulling me in there just because you didn't want me to bug you for the interview! That's the biggest load of bullshit I've ever heard in my life!"

"Didn't realize you were a walkin' lie detector, Noelle."

"Oh, now I'm Noelle? You need to make your damn mind up about what you're callin' me, Detective."

"Noted."

"Dammit, Drake, I'm talkin' to you!" I grab his arm and yank him so he faces me. "And you're gonna damn well listen to me!"

His eyes narrow into slits, his anger burning through that tiny glimpse, and his eyes are hard, cold, unfeeling. If I gave a shit, I'd be scared of him right now.

"Noelle," Brody says. "Take it to his office."

"I am not your personal fuckin' body language expert!" I jab my finger into Drake's chest, ignoring my brother. "You cannot drag me into your damned interviews just because this two-bit police station can't train someone! You do not have the right to abuse the fuck out of me and my abilities as it pleases you. Do you get that? You want my help, you ask for it. You don't fuckin' manipulate me just because you think you can."

"Oh, I can manipulate you, sweetheart, because I just did." He steps closer, his voice low, and the warning in his tone, the spine-tingling threat, does nothing but anger me. "And you'll watch your language when you speak to me. In your building, you do what you want. In mine, you do what I say, when I say. Got that?"

"Like you do what I say when you're in my office, yeah? I forgot how well you listen to others!" I step back, bringing back the sliver of space between us. "I'm no longer working with you on this case. Bond P.I. will no longer be working with you. You want information, you get your ass a warrant. Until then, you can kiss my sweet ass."

"You sure you wanna play that game?"

"Game? No. I'm not playing. I never have been. So take the game, set, and match, Detective, because I'm out. Lives are at risk, including mine, and I'm not going to waste my time pandering to the most insufferable, arrogant, pigheaded fuckwankingdouchebag I've ever had to—"

He slams his body against mine and fists my hair, his mouth forcing itself onto mine and cutting off my tirade. It's short and harsh and hot, the kiss almost bruising in its intensity, and it's like everything has stopped, the world stilling on its axis. No more ticking clocks, no more wondering about tomorrow or next week or next year. Just now. Here, now. This second. This very moment.

This very touch that is equal parts thrilling and terrifying, because no one should ever be able to make someone feel like there is nothing left in existence but one simple kiss.

Drake releases me as quickly and harshly as he grabbed me. My heart thunders in my chest as he storms down the hallway and makes the turn to his office. The sound of his door slamming ricochets through the silent police station, and it's only now that I realize what he's done.

He just kissed me. In front of everyone. Including at least one of my brothers.

Oh, hell.

I touch my thumb to my mouth and take a deep breath, knowing that one pair of eyes on me is stronger than the others. And the person they belong to is grinning like he just stepped out of Wonderland.

"Well," Brody says through his smile. "About time that happened. Maybe y'all will finally figure your shit out."

"Don't count on it," I murmur, grabbing my clutch from him. "I need a ride home."

"Sure." His grin widens.

"A silent ride home."

"Damn."

chapter
TWENTY-ONE

I F life were simple, I wouldn't have a job.

That's the conclusion I've come to this morning after calling two poor, cheated-on spouses and asking them to come in for their answers. That's also the conclusion I've come to as I've thrown this murder case file in the trash three times and picked it up every time.

If it were simple, I'd know who the killer was. I'd know why these people were killed—and, in Portia's case, almost killed. If it were simple, I'd know the who, what, where, why, and when of every single detail.

If it were simple, I wouldn't see Drake's eyes every time I close mine.

I slap my cheek for what feels like the tenth time in the last hour and attempt to focus on the file in front of me. It's entirely useless though. My mind is filled with the craziness of last night, the revelation about Marshall, and the fact Nonna has called an impromptu family dinner in approximately four hours to discuss my date last night.

My date that ended up with me being kissed by another man.

Yeah. It's no wonder I'm single.

I drop my head to my desk and rest my cheek against the cold surface, facing the park. Sometimes, I miss Dallas. Small-town blood runs through my veins, but I miss the electric life of cities. I miss the anonymity that comes with living in an apartment block bigger than

209

the town center and not knowing every single person you pass on the street.

I miss the huge police force and the fact it was incredibly easy to avoid my ex-boyfriend after we broke up. It was also really easy to avoid him after the time we slept together after we'd broken up. It was even easier to avoid the rookie officer I found him shacking up with after we'd broken up for a second time.

Actually, she is the reason we broke up for the second time.

There, I could go somewhere and be left alone. I could disappear for however long I needed—work hours not included in that—and just breathe and live and fall into silence. I could switch the world off and allow my mind to go over whatever case I was working on. I could sit and just think until I came through with a thought that could change everything.

Here in Holly Woods, it's an impossibility. If my staff doesn't need me, it's the police, and if isn't the police, it's my family. If I turn my phone off, they come to my office or house, and if I try to hide in Austin, they send out a goddamned search party.

Just once, I'd like to be able to disappear and allow the hive that is my mind to breathe.

The case and the deaths and the attempted death and the suspects and the lies and the truths and the unanswered questions—they don't connect in any way. Usually, serial killers, like I can assume this person is, have a strict plan. Their MO doesn't change and they aren't afraid of being caught. They're methodical and almost OCD in their actions. But this guy isn't.

Why did Portia suspect she was being poisoned? Hemlock is a fast-acting poison. She's lucky she caught it before her throat swelled.

Why was Daniel caught in the aftermath of Lena's death? Was it a coincidental act because he saw who the killer was when they intercepted his delivery of her salad?

Why was Lena killed? Did her multiple lives finally catch up with her?

The ridiculous lack of DNA is the biggest hindrance we have. There's nothing to connect anything in any kind of way. Only the manner of death and the placement of their bodies.

If Portia had been killed, where would her body have been placed? In my shed? My house?

And if I'm really right and I'm the one single thread holding all three victims together, then I need to carry my gun with a bullet in the chamber all the time.

"Why," I say as my office door opens after one single knock, "would Portia be targeted? What's her connection to Lena and Daniel?"

"She has a thing for younger men." Devin answers smoothly, closing the door. "She and Daniel had a previous relationship several months ago."

"Huh." I lick my lips, still staring out the window despite the ache in my back. "And Lena and Daniel?"

"You know it."

"So she was married to Ryan but seeing Daniel. Ryan's fears were entirely justified, it seems."

"As the story goes." He hits the cushion before he sits down. "It wasn't a new thing. Lena and Daniel were in a very open, very happy, very private relationship. Had been for a number of years."

Slowly, I move to sit upright, looking at him. "So, what are you sayin'? Are we looking at a lover? Past or current? Someone angry with their relationship?"

"Like Ryan?" He raises his eyebrows. "Yes."

I flip through my call log and hit Ryan's name, tapping the speaker button as the call connects. "Ryan. I need you to answer something for me."

He hesitates, before he says, "What is it?"

"Did you know that Lena and Daniel were in a relationship?" When he doesn't answer, I say, "Ryan?"

"Yes." His voice is thicker than it was a moment ago, and I swallow at the thought that he's crying, because the single word was packed more emotion that I'd thought were possible. "Yeah, I knew. How could I not? They spent so much time together. They were more than friends."

"So, why did you marry her?"

"She said yes. She never backed out. I thought that maybe, if we were married, she would learn to love me more. That I'd be enough for her."

"Oh, Ryan," I say softly. "But you weren't."

"No. I never was. She knew about Penny, you know. She just

didn't know about the baby. I denied that. She didn't care. She was happy with our relationship. She'd go do her thing with Daniel when she was taking inventory and I'd see Penny. Then we'd come home and fuck each other with our anger and sleep it off."

"Thank you. That's all I needed." I hang up and look at my brother. "What kind of relationship is that, Dev?"

"A seriously fucked-up one," he replies, leaning back. "But you'd know about that, wouldn't you?"

My eyebrows shoot up. "Come again?"

"Drake."

"I have no idea what you're talking about."

"Don't shit me, Noelle."

"If I had a relationship that was worthy of conversation with that man, I'd tell you. As it is, I don't, so can we discuss something that's worth my time, please?" I shake the annoyance Drake's name has brought off.

"Jesus, Noelle," he says, leaning forward onto my desk. "You're gonna let him treat you the way he did last night and tell me there's nothing between you?"

Fucking hell, Brody. I'm gonna kill him.

"There isn't," I return, my voice steady and harsh. "I had no desire to participate in his…actions…last night. It wasn't my choice. I didn't want to sit in on that interview, and I sure as hell did not want that pig to kiss me!"

"Yeah," Drake says from the doorway. "You did a real good job of pushin' me away."

"What the hell are you doin' here?" I stand, grabbing my desk as though the wooden piece can anchor me to the ground.

He strides across the room, ignoring my brother, and hands me a small, white envelope. "This is my warrant allowing me to access all the information on the files you gave me before the termination of our agreement. Per your request last night."

I take the envelope from him, swallowing, and force myself to meet his eyes.

Cold. Hard. Unfeeling.

Just like I knew they would be.

"Thank you, Detective. Is that everything?"

"It is. Just remember to call us whenever you find some

information that may pertain to our investigation."

"As I always have."

"Indeed," he says coolly. "You have the direct lines to your brothers. You can call them."

Them. Not *me.*

"I intended on it." I inject a dose of indignation into my voice and straighten. "Kindly call ahead next time you drop into my office. I'm a very busy woman."

"As evidenced by the fact that the very important meeting your receptionist insisted you were in is with your brother."

"Until you know the contents of our discussion, keep your comments to yourself," Devin says, standing next to Drake. They stand almost eye to eye, and the narrowing of Devin's dark gaze matches the angry twitch of his arm.

Drake steps forward. "Remember, Officer Bond, that I'm your superior."

"Remember, Detective Nash," Devin replies, his voice steely, "that you're not *my* superior, and I'm more than certain that mine will accept me defending my sister after the way you treated her last night. So, until you are my superior, step back and stay the hell away from her."

I inhale at the rocketing tension, but my heart misses a beat at his protectiveness. Sure, I can handle Drake and anything he throws at me. But it sure doesn't hurt to have my brother stand in front of him for me and give him a piece of his mind.

"The way I treated her?" Drake questions, his eyebrow quirking. "I was doing my job, Bond, and I was utilizing the resources available to me."

"I didn't realize kissing was in your job description," I murmur, glaring when he looks at me.

"*La famiglia e tutto,*" Devin says, ignoring me entirely. "Family is everything. Do your job, but don't fuck with my sister while you do it. She's the only woman in this town who demands respect, and by fuck, Detective, I'll die makin' sure she gets it from everyone who thinks they're above it."

Drake faces him off for a long time before turning to me and simply saying, "Thank you for your time, Ms. Bond."

I exhale slowly as he walks out of my office and closes the door behind him. The second he leaves, it's as if the room fills with air again, and my lungs burn as I breathe in sharply and cover my face with my hands.

How can one person have such an effect on you? How can they make you feel as though you're going to suffocate just by being in their presence?

And isn't that the thing with Drake? He's either setting me on fire or taking my breath away. Maybe they're synonymous. I don't know anymore.

Maybe they're one and the same where he's concerned.

Maybe he takes my breath away as he sets me on fire. Or maybe he sets me on fire while he takes my breath away.

I just know that he does both, and he does it with alarming ease. Like he breathes it or his heart beats for it. Like he takes every ounce of oxygen from my body and steals it just to give it back and take it away again and again and again.

Like he lives to torture me in the most pleasurably painful way. In a way I didn't know existed.

I didn't know it was possible to want someone and despise them at the very same time.

"Noelle?" Devin says quietly, his rough voice slicing through the silence that descended the second Drake left. "You've been staring at your palms for a few minutes now."

I drop my hands, swiping them at my cheeks, and look at him. I look at Devin's smoothly shaved jaw, his perfectly straight, short hair, and his dark eyes, and a piece of me warms with the comfort and safety that looking at my brother brings me.

"Thank you," I say, my voice breaking halfway through. "For standing up for me then. Even though you could get in trouble."

"Are you kidding? Sheriff Bates is more concerned about the way he treated you in front of half our employees yesterday." Devin grins. "Mrs. Bates also requested the gossip."

I smile, but it's weak. Just like how I feel where Drake is concerned. I'm strong until he touches me. Then I melt into the largest puddle of muddy, clumpy, gloopy glue because he does something to me that infuriates and attracts the hell out of me.

"Well, tell Mrs. Bates I'm sorry, but there is none. And tell Sheriff Bates that big, bad wolf Drake Nash isn't going to scare this little piggy off."

"Then why you cryin'?"

"Hay fever," I lie immediately, angrily swiping at my cheeks.

"Twenty-eight years and she never suffered once. Some jacked-up detective pisses her off and she's a chronic sufferer," he mutters, walking around my desk to me. Then he wraps his arms tight around me.

I return his hold, only lighter, and rest my head on his shoulder. "He's not pissing me off," I sniff.

"She's also a dirty little liar," he laughs, squeezing me. He pulls back, grabbing my arms. "Listen to me, Noellie Bellie."

"You haven't called me that since I was nine," I whisper, smiling.

"Because I save it for the real big guns, yeah?" Dev grins. "Listen to me, Noelle. Don't let him get to you. He's pissed. For some dumbass reason, he's real pissed at you. And men, well... Our asshole gene takes over when we get pissed, 'kay? So just let him be a giant fucktard and keep kicking ass the way you are, and eventually, he'll come around. Eventually, he'll give you the respect you deserve. And if he doesn't, there's a high chance I'll lose my job."

I laugh softly, wiping another tear from my cheek. "I don't know, Dev. What'd I ever do to him, huh?"

"Well, you shot him in the foot for starters."

"Twelve years ago! Damn, y'all just can't get over that, can you?"

"Mostly, we like pissin' him off with it," he replies, his eyes sparkling. "But back to you, yeah? You can do this, sis. You can solve this case, okay? 'Cause it don't matter a damn that you don't carry a badge anymore. You're a cop by blood and that's one thing you got on him. He breathes cop. But you live cop. And living is a hundred times more important than breathing. You can breathe and not live. But you live, so you breathe, and if who could solve this case were a betting pool, my life savings are goin' on you. And those are goin' on a kickass engagement ring for Amelia, so don't fuckin' let me down."

I squeeze him tight, unable to stop the upturn of my lips. Goddamn it, I'm so lucky to have the family I do. I truly am.

"I got it. Now, when are you proposing?"

"I dunno." He releases me and steps back. "Gotta see if I have to bail your ass out of jail first. Not sure I trust you around Drake until he's on his knees and washin' your feet when you solve his case for him." He winks when he gets to the door.

My smile grows. "You're crazy. No bail money, okay? I promise to behave. For now."

"The 'for now' is what worries me." Those are his final words as he scoots through the doorway and closes the door behind him.

Left alone, I lower myself back into my chair. I kick my shoes off and haul my feet onto my desk, pulling my Fucking Brilliant notebook onto my lap. I click my pen and open my notebook to the next blank page, writing the three victims' names and circling them.

Then I open my drawer, pull my neon Sharpies out, and designate each victim a color simply so I can keep track of their relationships.

Daniel and Lena. Daniel and Portia. Portia and...

Lena?

Maybe I should have avoided the second cupcake, I think idly as I throw the wrapper in the trash can and my head lolls back onto my sofa. Especially since I'm still being forced into going to my parents' so Nonna can assault me with her endless questions I could barely give a crap about right now.

I lasted all of ten minutes with my Sharpies and notebook before I packed everything up, said a giant, "Fuck it," and left work early. I figure I have a ton of paperwork-type stuff to do, like payroll and all that crap, so I can be at home, in my sweatpants, and still work.

My intention was honorable, but the reality is that I've done next to nothing. If you don't count e-mailing my accountant and telling him that I'm too swamped to do payroll, so if I pay him extra this month, can he please do it for me?

He, of course, agreed. And I ate a cupcake in celebration of my ability to delegate tasks to others.

I'm sure that's something worthy of celebration. It's kind of like how, next week, I'll delegate the bathroom deep-clean to one of the guys. I conveniently have a nail appointment right before the day I scheduled it.

But that's the fun of being the boss. You can make everyone else do the shitty things you don't want to do.

I wish I could delegate this case though. I wish I could grab one of them and say, "Hey, you're doing this full time and I'm taking your cases." After all, I did allow them to open business back as usual when it became clear we've done nothing but run around in circles since this whole thing started.

No point having four of us on the case when there's barely enough work for one. And it's a good thing, too. Now, without the collaboration with the local police department, I'm back being plunged into the dark.

All I have are the basic facts.

I hope that'll be enough.

I take a deep breath and decide I am most definitely in the middle of a tragedy and desperately need some clarity. Everyone I know is plunged deep into this case. I can't discuss anything with anyone who can bring a completely unbiased opinion to this.

I snatch up my phone and my keys and call my parents' landline, knowing Nonna will answer.

"*Pronto*?" she answers.

"Nonna," I say, pulling away from my house. "I won't be able to make dinner."

"Noella!" she gasps, and I can imagine her clutching her pearls in horror. "Why-a not?"

"I'm going to church."

There's nothing except the sound of her breathing filling my car for a long moment. Then, "*Scusami*?"

I roll my eyes. "I'm going to church, Nonna. I need some peace."

"You want-a me to come?"

"That doesn't exactly fit in with my plan of peace," I respond dryly. "No, thank you. I will be just fine."

"*Si, si.* You find-a clarity on-a your love life, *si*?"

"Yes. That's exactly it. I'm going to have a gossip session with God."

"Ah! He will-a help you! You no like-a Gio?"

"No, Gio was just fine, Nonna. I just want to make sure a second date is the right thing to do right now."

"Ah! I will let-a you go! Go!" She hangs up.

The woman just does not understand sarcasm.

I shake my head and park in the small lot next to the church.

Holly Woods Chapel is just about the prettiest building in town. The classic Gothic style is reminiscent of the time period in which it was built, and careful restoration efforts over the last few decades means that the tall spires, traditional glass windows, and intricate detail on the main body of the church are as beautiful and preserved as they are in the very first pictures of the church.

Leaving my phone locked in the car, I pocket my keys and walk toward the small but imposing building. I've always had a strange relationship with my religion. I'm Catholic by necessity—Nonna would drop dead if we'd been baptized as anything else, and it's the one thing Mom has never fought her on—but I've never truly… grasped it.

Maybe I'm too much of a realistic person. My logical mind and inquisitive nature require steadfast proof, real evidence, and definitive answer. Since religion can't provide any of those, I've always hung in the balance of a believer and a nonbeliever.

I believe in something. I believe that somewhere out there—in the sky, deep in the oceans, in the heart of the forest, buried under the desert—there's something bigger than all of us. I truly believe that, one day, we'll face the consequences of our actions, whether that thing is God, karma, or plain old justice.

Sure. I don't have the proof that there is something there. But I don't have the proof that those things don't exist, either, do I?

I open the heavy wooden door and walk into the church. As I knew it would be midweek, it's empty until Father Luiz holds his midweek session tonight. I like it this way. Silence. Peace.

This is probably the only place I have left to get that.

I walk slowly through the church, my eyes focusing on the large stained-glass window that fills the back wall. The sunlight hits it full on in the late afternoon, and spots of color are dancing around the room, the brightness of the depiction of Mother Mary almost too bright to look at.

It's the only one the church has, but it's the only one it needs.

I take a seat on the third pew from the front and exhale gently. The table set up to the side in Lena and Daniel's memory is reminiscent of a shrine, and I know that Father Luiz will leave it there until their killer is found. He'll believe that, as long as we can see their faces, their spirits will stay with us and justice will be served.

EMMA HART

I hope he's right.

Closing my eyes, I tuck my feet beneath the pew and breathe. The calmness of the building seeps into my skin, and with every exhale, I feel a little of the tension leave my body. If even an ounce of it leaves, then I know I'm much lighter. I wish it would take the confusion and stress and questions with it.

If only I could exhale the questions and inhale the answers.

If only I had the strength to walk away from this investigation.

"Hey, God, Jesus, Karma, whoever you are up there. I know I don't come here as much as I should, but could you help me out a little here? People keep getting poisoned, and it would be really great if you could tell me how to fix this mess, you know? And if you're not gonna do that, could you make my next ten cupcakes calorie-free? It's the least you could do if I have to continue onward in this crazy maze of a case. Also, calorie-free wine and margaritas would be great. I'm just sayin'."

A low chuckle makes me open my eyes, and I see Father Luiz standing at the front of the church. His hands are clasped to his front, and his light-brown eyes are alight with the smile on his tan face.

"Hello, Noelle."

"Father," I say sheepishly. "I didn't realize anyone was here."

"Don't be embarrassed, girl. Your request was very reasonable, and I'm sure you'd get a lot of backing from the other women in town." He winks. "Your grandmother called and said you were coming. I was, naturally, intrigued."

Guilt riddles me. "I don't come as often as she thinks I should, I know."

"Ah, but you come when you need to. And isn't that the beauty of belief? You don't have to be connected all the time to feel the benefits of it. Just because your faith isn't as strong as Liliana's doesn't mean you can't come whenever you must."

"Doesn't it bother you? That people…like me—people who don't feel the same as you do—still find comfort in your church?"

He smiles and takes the seat on the pew next to me. His eyes are fixed on the cross depicting the crucifixion hanging above his pulpit. "Quite the contrary, my dear. I don't judge others for their beliefs— that is not my job. And this church? It is not mine. Rather, I belong to it. It's been standing for years before I was born, and it will stand for

219

many after my death."

"That's a very realistic view."

"Because I am a priest, I cannot be realistic?" His eyebrow quirks despite the fact that he never looks at me.

"Oh, no, of course not."

"Fret not, child. This world… It is a peculiar one, no?" He clasps his hands on his lap. "Belief is relative. Religion is optional. Here is the thing, Noelle—no one can make you believe anything your heart isn't fully into. No one can dictate to you your feelings or dreams. And that means no one can offer you any more or less than your heart declares, as long as your heart is strong."

"What if it isn't though?" I ask, my voice barely a whisper. "What if the person you think you've been is someone other than who you are? What if you don't actually know what your dreams are?"

"Do any of us know it, really?" Father Luiz asks, finally turning to me. "Can any one of us say that, definitively, we know what we want? Or is what we want simply a figment of our imagination, proven or denied at the point where we thought life would serve us our desire?"

Huh. I never thought of that way. I admit that, too.

"My dear, common sense is relative. Religion is relative. Belief is relative. Life is relative. All we can do is wake up each morning, breathe the air we are given, and take hold of life the way it intends us to, whether that be gently or fiercely." He pats my hand. "For me, the Lord dictates my life, but he allows me the freedom to make the choices that ultimately end up at his decisions. If you so believe, you will have the same courtesy. If not, then, well, I believe the good Lord will allow you the same courtesy anyway. Like I, He does not discriminate upon beliefs. He fears nothing, not the least free will. If you have free will, you will always have a semblance of belief in the man I and so many others call Father."

I shift, slightly uncomfortable. I'm not used to such a deep religious conversation. But I can't stop. A part of me wants more.

"What if I have questions without answers though? What do I do then? Do I stand by and wait for innocent people to be hurt, or do I go with my undecipherable gut feeling and risk losing it all, Father?"

His lips curve. "Ah, Noelle, now are you asking me about your job or about your personal life?"

"If I knew, I could answer your question."

"Then it's both." He shifts just a little. "Personally, I go with my gut feeling. I believe in impulses and righteousness. If your gut is telling you something, you follow it. Our instincts are rarely wrong. If they were, we wouldn't have lived so long."

I close my eyes again for the briefest second, allowing his words to wash over me like a cold shower on a red-hot summer day. Everything he said has made perfect sense, and in the strangest way, it has allowed me to organize the chaos of my mind.

"Thank you, Father. I think I know what I need to do now."

chapter
TWENTY-TWO

"Y"OU'RE fucking crazy," Brody declares, slamming his coffee cup down. Dark liquid sloshes out onto the table.

"How am I?" I protest, putting mine down and grabbing a cloth to wipe up his mess. It's a rare moment when all four siblings can get together outside family dinner, and I'm embracing it. "I'm not getting anywhere looking for the killer, so maybe the killer needs to come to me."

"Noelle," Trent says, "do you realize how fuckin' dangerous this is? What if you're in the shower or some shit and you can't protect yourself?"

"I'll carry my gun everywhere."

"Dammit, you're so fuckin' naïve!" Dev slams his chair across the kitchen as he stands. "You think he's gonna bring a bucket and a spade to a gunfight, huh? He doesn't hafta be there to see you die, you fuckin' idiot. He just had to stand at the end of your damned large yard and wait."

"I'm not eating salad," I reply calmly. "So, how can he kill me if his choice is poisoned leaves?"

"And that makes it okay?" Brody explodes. "Jesus, Noelle. Did Drake kiss the ever-lovin' fuckin' sense out of you, huh?"

"Leave him the hell outta this!" I stand, my gun burning into my hip and my muscles tensing. "He's got fuck all to do with this."

"So, where'd my sister go?" Trent thunders, far too loud for nine in the morning. "Where'd my smart, levelheaded, theoretical sister go, Noelle?"

"She grew up!" I yell. "She grew up into an independent person who can handle all the guns y'all got better than you can and you know it. Your baby sister grew up into the kind of woman y'all wish your wives and daughters could be, because she's the woman who takes no shit without givin' it first. And she's the woman who can solve this damn case, if only y'all would trust her with her theory."

"Sis," Brody reasons, "I get it, yeah? The only girl in four kids, the only one to step out of the police force, you have somethin' to prove—"

"My leaving Dallas has nothin' to do with this!" I snap, leaning against my kitchen counter. "That was a whole different situation, and one I don't wanna think about. I don't wanna think about how my two words killed two people and potentially destroyed the lives of hundreds. Y'all get that, huh? Y'all know how I fucked up! Leave it!"

"Noelle," Dev says slowly, coming toward me. "Noellie Bellie, forget it," he whispers, his fingertips brushing my arms.

I'm shaking inconsolably. All I can think of are the lives I lost and the memories I said goodbye to and the families I destroyed.

"Noelle!" he snaps, clasping my face. "You don't get to go back there. We need you, yeah? Fuck Drake. Fuck the sheriff. We need you—the three of us."

"You're the one who's gonna solve this," Brody says softly. "I don't know why or how or when, but you will. You've got somethin' we don't, Noelle. You've got more a desire for the truth than the whole department has. But that doesn't mean you can be stupid about it."

I sniff, hugging myself. "You know that the mayor has contacted the Austin department, right? He's ready to call them in if y'all can't solve this case."

"Which is why we need you!" Trent thunders, his eyes falling on mine. "Dammit, Noelle. We need you safe, not in danger."

"I don't work with the HWPD anymore."

"But you work with me," he argues. "Drake might be my boss, but I'd take my stapler to his fuckin' face as easily as I'd shoot a man who'd point his gun at you. Noelle, it doesn't matter, *bella*. *La famiglia e tutto.* Family is everything. I can get another job. Can't get another sister if this goes wrong."

"You don't even know what my plan is yet."

"Do you have one?"

"Aside from make the killer come to me?" I pause. "That'll be a no. But I figured it was a damn good start, right?"

"Great," Brody mutters. "Not only is her idea dangerous, she has nothing to back it up."

I poke my tongue out at him. "Shut up."

"Well, it's true!"

"Don't start fightin'," Trent groans, rubbing his temple. "Fine, Noelle. For now, we'll go along with your dumb plan. But if you figure out who our killer is before he finds you, you call me. Right away. I'll have some guys step up patrols in the street and around your office building. Write it off as standard protective measures."

"That's hardly going to make a killer—"

"I don't care if it scares them off. I just care that it'll keep you safe for long enough to come up with something to back up your idea."

"And what if it doesn't? What if the killer finds me before I find them?"

The look he gives me is so solemn that a lump forms in my throat. "Then it's your funeral, kid."

Excellent.

I swipe the brush against the wall with a little too much vigor, and paint splashes onto the dust cover beneath my feet. Perhaps painting my office on a spur-of-the-moment decision and moving heavy furniture alone isn't the smartest idea I've had, but I don't seem to getting many of those lately, so I figured why not?

What I did think of is that, if I won't be left alone in peace, I need to keep busy. So busy that anyone who disturbs me will be instantly thrown out.

Which is precisely how I've ended up in an old Backstreet Boys concert tee and tiny, floral shorts, painting my office a delightful shade of duck-egg blue. At eight in the morning, no less.

I dip the brush into the can and hum "Clarity" by Zedd as I

continue my redecoration mission. Who knows? If I still haven't figured this out by the time my office is painted, maybe everyone else's space will get a lick of new color, too.

Lord knows this place needs it. The cream walls were great in theory, at first. But now, they're just damn boring. It's a miracle no one has said, "Hey, Noelle, brighten this place the hell up, will ya?"

Although this building is rather on the large side. Maybe I'll enlist the help of the others, or if I do solve this case, I'll get a decorating company in. I know that Jason Marshall has one.

Maybe I should call him for quotes.

Or maybe I should stop procrastinating and actually think about the case.

It would be a lot easier if I hadn't already thought everything through around ten million times—and that's just from this morning.

That said, I really, really need to come up with a theory of how to bring the killer to me. It's incredibly hard without knowing their motive for having killed twice and attempted a third. I know that the police are following the Ryan-and-Penny trail, but it just doesn't add up for me. The only connection I could find between Lena and Portia is that Portia used to babysit her when she was a teen. Hardly something worthy of killing for.

But according to Brody, Drake is dead set that that's the right angle.

I think Drake is a damned fool. But what I think doesn't matter to that righteous shit.

I huff and dip my brush into the paint again. One passing thought of him and I'm mad. It's like I have a little switch where he's concerned. One side is happy and the other is miserable. The only time it doesn't move is when he's doing something idiotic like kissing me. Then the switch is balanced in the middle.

And this is not solving this case.

"You know, boss, we can hear you singing downstairs. Grecia sent me up to make sure you weren't being murdered." Marshall grins, pushing his glasses up his nose.

"You need to get them fixed," I remind him. "And Grecia should speak for herself. She ain't winnin' American Idol any time soon."

He laughs. "A roller would get that done much quicker."

I look at the brush, look at him, and shrug. "I know. But it's therapeutic this way. A little arm-achy but therapeutic."

"You're not bringing any of that color crap into my office, are you?"

Slyly, I smile. "Oh, yeah. I was gonna call the local kindergarten and invite them in with their crayons."

He widens his eyes, and I'm pretty sure he pales a little.

"Kidding!" I laugh, unable to hold it in any longer. "I'm just kidding. I found a gorgeous scarlet red for you."

"You wouldn't."

"Work with one eye open, kid."

He pauses for a moment then relaxes when he sees that I'm grinning. "I need a new boss."

"Nah. They'd never pay you to play World of Warcraft the way I do."

"Too true."

"Was there somethin' you needed?" I ask when he hovers in the doorway.

"Mallory bought the store."

"Lena's?" I pause, holding my brush away from the wall. A drop of paint falls onto my foot.

"Yes, ma'am. And the first thing she did was fire Penny." He shrugs when I open my mouth. "Store records say that Penny was only ever on a temporary contract despite being the assistant manager. Her employment was able to be terminated at any point. And Mallory did it."

chapter
TWENTY-THREE

WHEN I pull up to my parents' house and see Drake's truck parked at the side of the street, I want to turn around and go home. I wasn't aware he was becoming a permanent staple in family dinner.

It's been two days since our fight at the station, and aside from when he handed me a warrant the morning after, I haven't seen him since. If not for the constant buzzing inside my head, I'd say that the last two days have been rather peaceful.

I wanted to share the information Marshall gave me earlier with my brothers, but I'm sure as hell not saying a thing when he's around. I don't believe that this will impact the investigation anymore; it's more just gossip. Something interesting. Unfortunately, I couldn't get Mallory on the phone this afternoon to verify it, so I'm stuck with the speculation borne from the results of Marshall's spying.

Maybe he plays less video games than I thought.

I wait in my car for a long moment, apprehension coiling in my stomach. Do I really want to go in there? No. Do I have to? Not really. Will Nonna tear out my ovaries and force-feed me them if I don't?

Yes. Just as soon as I've gotten married and given her some more great-grandbabies.

I have a few years of safety, so it might be worth the risk...

After a deep breath, I get out of my car and walk down the path to the house. Mom's flowers are coming out in full force now that it's a lot warmer, and the brightness and inevitable work makes me ever more thankful that I was the kid born with black fingers instead of green ones.

I can't even grow a dandelion in my backyard.

"Her eggs-a getting older!" Nonna exclaims, waving a wooden spoon ferociously in the air. "She needs-a babies!"

"Nope." I turn around and open the front door. Which I just closed a second ago.

"She's talking about Amelia," Drake says, his voice traveling across the living room to my right.

I look at him, wishing my heart wouldn't do that fairytale pitter-patter bullshit. "Well, I can get on board with that."

"She needs-a them soon!" Nonna continues. "You men, you-a okay! You always work. Women? Pah! Tick-a tock-a, Devin!"

I grin, leaning against the fridge. "Ahh. I see you told her you have a ring."

"She keeps insisting I go to her work and propose to her! She's damn crazy!"

"No!" Nonna cries, brandishing her spoon again and sending hot water flinging across the room. "You-a crazy! You need-a babies, too! You need to grow up!"

"You know, Nonna, you're sayin' this to me, but at least I'm planning on marriage." Dev looks at me slyly, taking a few steps away from me. "Noelle is still single!"

"Pah! She-a dating though, *si*?" She looks to me. "Gio is nice, no?" She waggles her eyebrows.

Oh, Jesus. No. "Never, ever wiggle your eyebrows at me like that again," I warn her, shuddering. "And *si*, Nonna. Gio is very nice."

"She's only sayin' that so you'll be happy!" Dev protests.

"Actually, douchebag, we're going on a second date! So ha!"

"*Si, si!*" Nonna claps excitedly. "When? A-where?"

"Uh, next week some time, and I'm not sure. He's going to call me again."

She smiles, her whole face lighting up like I just told her that I'm marrying him and getting pregnant with triplets on my honeymoon. And it isn't a lie. We are having a second date. Email is a wonderful thing.

I nibble on my thumbnail as she turns back to the stove, no longer splashing boiling water or harassing anyone about their relationship status. I feel eyes on me though, and when I glance toward the doorway, I see Drake standing there, his arms folded, his gaze intense beneath the messy hair on his forehead.

I don't know how he pulls off that surfer-esque hairstyle. I just know that he does. It looks good slicked back for work and looks good all scruffy like it is now. Maybe it's his jaw, too. Maybe it works because of how delightfully messy his stubble is.

He really is so much prettier when he doesn't talk.

Mind you, so is Nonna.

"Where's Dad?" I ask Mom at the exact second a shot rings out.

Devin and Drake both stand to full attention, alert, and Drake's hand goes to his hip, where he's no doubt hiding a gun.

Mom smiles and looks at me. "Where do you think?"

"Does he have the targets out?"

She gives me her "of course he has the damn targets out" look.

"He has targets in the yard?" Drake asks, raising his eyebrows.

"Yes," Mom replies nonchalantly. "Good luck trying to take them away. Sheriff Bates is around more often than not. Somethin' about not having the time to go into Austin and those fancy places with all their rules." Her eyes glitter as Drake gets more and more confused.

"I'm goin' out there," I say, grabbing two bottles of water from the fridge.

"Girls don't-a shoot guns for fun!" Nonna shrieks, the spoon coming out again.

"Guess I should get myself a penis, then," I reply, grinning at the look of horror on her face. I close the back door behind me and almost get attacked by one of mom's shrubs. I can't decide whether it's overgrown or just a lethal weapon I'm pretty sure she could be arrested for.

One of the best things about living in a small town is the ability to shoot guns in your backyard. Okay, so I'm not positive it's legal, per se, but like Mom said, the sheriff is a regular staple in our yard, and none of the other cops are gonna say a thing to him. I'm pretty sure most of the force has been here at some point or another.

Gio would have a fit if he knew that this happened.

"Nice shot," I say appreciatively as Dad hits the center of the target.

He looks around, smiling. "Thanks. Joinin' me?"

"Sure." I hand him a bottle of water once he's put his rifle down and he takes a long drink. "You got another target in the shed?"

"Human one. Just for you." He smiles, walking into the brick building that's really an outhouse but claimed by him for all of his things. Except the guns. They stay in the actual house. He sets up the target next to his and walks back. "There you go, Noelle."

"Thanks, Daddy." I bend and pull my gun from my boot. I'm gonna really miss this hiding spot when it gets too hot for my boots.

Dad chuckles and kisses the side of my head, making me smile. "Been a while since we did this," he remarks when I put on my protection, then lock my arms in place, remove the safety, and shoot.

Straight to the head.

He waves to get my attention. "And I'm guessin' you need a chat," he finishes.

I shoot once more, in the shoulder, then again in the thigh before I replace the safety and set my gun on the table next to Dad's. I hang the ear defenders around my neck. He picks his favorite Glock up, and I sigh.

"Can I ask your opinion?"

"Sure."

I explain about Lena's store. "Why would she do that? Take over the store and fire Penny?"

"Was Penny really instrumental to the day-to-day running?"

"I don't know. That's the thing."

"Did Lena know about Ryan and Penny?"

"Yes. Apparently, she was okay with it."

Dad pauses, relaxing without shooting, and sets his gun down in its case. "Maybe it's not a case of Mallory doing it out of spite. Maybe Lena hired Penny and kept her on after the end of her contract as her assistant manager to keep an eye on her. Maybe Lena wasn't as okay as she pretended to be."

"Even though she was sleeping with Daniel?"

"Noelle, I've never met anyone with as many lives as Lena had. So yes. Even though she was sleepin' with Daniel." He rubs his chin. "You know what they say, honey. Keep your friends close..."

"And your enemies closer." I finish the old saying and look out at

230

the target I just shot at. "I guess. That makes total sense. I never really got the picture that they were friends with Penny. Lena and Mallory, that is."

"Then Mallory has no reason to keep her on. Penny obviously isn't a threat to her."

"But she was to Lena?"

"She was sleeping with her husband." He stands and raises his eyebrows. "Of course she was a threat. By all accounts, Daniel's life wasn't very stable. He still lived at home with his mom. He worked odd jobs. Ryan has a steady job, a nice apartment in a good area of town, and enough money for little vacations every couple of months. Which life would you rather live publicly?"

With that last question, he walks back to the house, his words ringing out in the silence.

The answer, of course, is easy.

I'd rather live the life married to Ryan. The stability his lifestyle provided meant Lena didn't need to prop anybody up. They were independent within their relationship—literally. She made enough money to live alone—ignoring her debts—but not if she had Daniel needing her financially. Her marriage to Ryan stopped that avenue from opening up for her.

Smart, really. Deceitful and bullshit, but smart. I'll give her that.

Gotta give her something, after all.

I take a deep breath and push off from the table I'm perching on, replacing my protective equipment I grab my gun once again and reload it, carrying it over to my human target. A few head shots always makes me feel better. I lock my arms and shoot. Shots ring out as I do my best to keep relaxed against the constant recoil of the gun.

When I'm done and I've shot every bullet in my baby into the head of the paper man several feet away, I drop my gun to my side and turn to the table to reload.

"Remind me never to let you stand in front of me with a gun pointed."

I glance up, pushing the magazine back into the gun. "Remind me to put that on my bucket list."

Drake's lips twitch to one side as I reposition in front of the target. "You know, there ain't much headspace left for you to shoot."

"You want it to be your head I'm shooting at?"

"Can't say I do."

"Shut the fuck up, then."

I ignore the buzz of his laughter through the air and aim. And shoot.

This time, when I'm done, there's nearly straight line of bullet holes through my paper man. Including one where his cock should be.

The temptation to laugh is almost too much, especially when I turn and raise my eyebrows at Drake. "Why are you here?"

He pulls his ear defenders down. "Out here?"

"Here." I yank off my ear defenders. "At my parents' for family dinner. Out here, bugging me. Take your pick. I'll take a reason for either."

"Your nonna appears to have taken a real good likin' to me. If I didn't know better, I'd say she's tryna set us up."

"Clearly, she's losin' her mind," I snap, reloading my gun again before tucking it back into my boot. I fold my arms and meet his eyes. "And out here? Why are you here?"

Nothing. Just silence. Just those goddamned beautiful eyes boring into mine.

"No? Okay." I walk past him, pushing hair from my face.

"Don't go out with him again." His arm shoots out to stop me, and his words hit me hard. "Gio."

"Since when has it been any of your business what I do?" I face him, narrowing my eyes as our gazes collide. "Last I checked, I'm a single, grown woman, and if I want to go out with someone, I will."

"He's not the kind of guy you need."

"Neither are you," I reply, running my eyes down his white shirt, which is untucked over his dark-blue jeans. The bottom of his shirt is gaping, allowing me a view of a triangle of tan skin with a smattering of dark hair. I linger there for a moment before pulling my gaze back up. "Yet here we are, having this conversation, you thinkin' you know what's best for me."

"I don't. But I know he ain't it. He won't get you, cupcake."

"Screw your 'cupcake,'" I whisper, my voice harsh. I shove his arm down and away from me, walking past him. "I don't care if he gets me or not. Maybe I'm not supposed to be gotten. I'm not a fucking puzzle waiting to be figured out."

"You say that," he says to my back when I look away, "but you are. You just got a couple pieces missing."

"Then it's a damn good thing you aren't my missing pieces, ain't it?" The words are shot over my shoulder, and I swallow, my stomach twisting as I yank the back door open and every face of my family stares at me. "Sorry, Nonna," I say to her. "But I gotta go."

"Noelle?" Trent reaches for me, but I step out of his reach.

"I cannot be around him," I explain—like that won't bring a whole new barrage of questions. I ignore the worried look from Mom and dart out of the front door before I get commandeered into staying and explaining.

I slam my car door shut and rest my head against the steering wheel. My heart is thumping, and I wish I could say that I don't know why. It's beating scarily fast because I'm mad but thrilled. The feelings mix up into the kind of emotional tornado that rips through your veins without care.

And maybe that's what he is.

Drake Nash is my tornado.

He's roaring through my life, ripping apart my days without care or thought, obliterating any control I think I have and twisting it until I'm so out of control that all I can do is get caught up in his whirlwind.

The fucking bastard.

My passenger's door opens.

"Talk," Alison demands, shutting it after sitting in the seat.

"Drive," I mutter back, jamming my key in the ignition and turning so the little TT starts with a roar.

I pull away from the house and take the turns to my house, not speaking a word to Alison as I drive. She doesn't push me though. She stays quiet as I fume and breathe and sigh and clench my hands around the steering wheel over and over.

I pull into my driveway far too quickly, angrily slamming on the breaks at the last minute. Bekah opens my front door, and it's now that I notice her car parked in front of my house. Shows how observant I am.

"There's cupcakes and wine," Bek offers, opening the door wide.

I storm through, grab a glass of wine, and drink it in a handful of gulps. "Who the fuckin' hell does that total douchecock think he is?"

"Drake," she replies, shrugging.

"What did he do?" Alison asks.

I recap our brief conversation. "Like he thinks he gets to do that! Like he thinks it's fucking okay to tell me what to do when he can't even respect me as a person, let alone a woman with a mind of her own!" My voice cracks halfway through my rant, and I clear my throat.

I am a fucking strong woman, dammit. I won't cry.

"Y'all are so screwed up you don't even know it," Bek says. "You're like gunpowder and a match. You don't even notice it, but it's suffocatin' to be around you both. You just bounce off each other, and when you start fightin', sweet Jesus! It's like there's nothing else other than you two."

"That is not a good thing!" I raise my voice. "I don't even like him, okay? He pisses me off all the time. I wish he would literally disappear from my life and leave me the heck alone."

Alison smiles. "Ah, I remember hating Trent once, too."

"Don't," I warn her, pointing my finger at her face. "I like Gio, okay? He's sweet and thoughtful and easy to talk to."

"You say the same thing about your niece," Alison snorts.

"And Drake is arrogant and pigheaded and stubborn!"

"From the woman who makes backing down and admitting she's wrong a habit." Bek grins. "You don't like him because he challenges you, babe. And that's okay. But for reals, when you two start arguing, I feel like I'm intruding on some freaky foreplay. Then I think I should look away, but it is literal word porn, and hell, if that's voyeurism, I have a new hobby."

Alison bursts into giggles. "It's true. Even you standing there in the kitchen just now... You had that turned-on kind of anger. You know? Where you're so angry you want to shoot them but fuck them at the same time."

"Hey, you should just fuck him," Bek suggests. "You know, angrily. Bed-shakin' kind of angry."

And isn't that the problem? I really, really hate Drake Nash, but I want to jump his bones. In the bed-shakin', headboard-breakin', body-rockin' kinda way.

And that's rather annoying.

"I'm not sleeping with him," I say in a softer tone. "I really do wish he'd leave me alone. He doesn't have a right to tell me who I can and can't see. He doesn't have a right for anything. He's just a guy whose path I happen to cross on a regular basis."

"Yep. And in my next life, I'm a two-headed, three-tailed armadillo," Alison replies.

I inhale deeply through my nose and drop to my sofa.

I am a strong fucking woman. I will not cry.

I *am* a strong fucking woman. I will *not* cry.

I sniff, pressing the heels of my palms into my eyes. "Why do I let him get to me, huh? All the time. He's like a goddamned stink bomb in a basement."

Bek trembles next to me, and I hear a tiny giggle from Alison.

"Stink bomb in a basement," Bek mutters, her voice wobbling with her laughter. "That's it? That's the best you have?"

My lips twitch, but I fight it. "Shut up. I'm in a crisis here."

"Denial isn't a crisis. Comparing a man to a stink bomb in a basement is!" Alison laughs her way through it, and when she sits next to me, I'm sandwiched by my two closest friends, who are laughing like crazy, and it's too infectious.

I wipe the angry, frustrated tears from my eyes and let my own laughter break through. It wins out over my emotions, and I rest my head on Bek's shoulder, letting the amusement run free.

Alison leans forward and pours me another glass of wine. She hands it to me, passes Bek hers, and then grabs her own. "To douchebags."

"Even Trent," Bek adds, lifting her glass.

I want to argue that, but, eh… "To douchebags. They're a great excuse for wine."

Bang. Bang. Bang.

"Go away," I mumble, rolling over and burying my head beneath my quilt.

Bang. Bang. Bang.

Ring. Ring. Ring.

"Screw you!" I yell, shoving my head beneath the pillow.

Ring. Ring. Ring.

"What?" I snap into the phone.

"Noelle?" Trent asks. "Your office was broken into."

chapter
TWENTY-FOUR

IN all seriousness, can people just stop fucking breaking into my buildings?

Is it really that much for a woman to ask? That people just don't infiltrate her privacy? I'm not a fucking Kardashian. I don't want my ass across the Internet. I just want to wake up, eat cupcakes, do my job, and sleep.

That's literally it.

"It's six a.m., and I'm hungover as fuck. This better be a goddamned jewel heist," I tell Grecia when she meets me at the office door.

Yeah, did I mention we cleared out two bottles of wine and a bottle of sangria last night?

Apparently, emotion makes me do dumb shit.

"No jewel heist," Drake says, sitting on Grecia's office chair.

"What in the hell are you doing here?"

"This is relevant to my investigation."

I look at my feet and then pinch the inside of my arm. "Fuck me, I'm not a ghost. Again, what are you doing here?"

"Like I said, this is relevant to my investigation," he repeats, standing up.

"Whatever. Can I get coffee or have your rookie bitches ripped my kitchen apart?"

His lips curve up into a highly dangerously sexy smirk. "You can get your coffee, cupcake."

I'll cupcake his ass pretty soon.

I storm downstairs and into the kitchen, which has clearly been ripped apart. "Y'all gotta teach your bitches how to tidy the hell up!" I shout out the door, slamming it behind me as I turn back into the room.

I put all the plates and bowls back in their places in the cupboard above my head and pull the clean dishes from the rack on the draining board. Mugs, plates, cutlery—they all have their place here. And I put them all back exactly where they belong. Then I pull down the "boss" mug Marshall bought me as a joke for Christmas and turn the coffee machine on.

I rifle through the box of pods and pull a latte one out. It's full of freakin' mochas and cappuccinos and whatever the hell other kinds of coffee you can get. I just drink lattes. Dad calls them a coffee milkshake, but it's coffee. And I can have it strong still. And it's coffee. Who the hell cares what else is in it?

After filling the hot water, I press the on button and lean against the counter as the machine hums to life. The door opens, but I refuse to turn because I know that it's Drake.

The emotion in the room has changed. It's gone from flat with anger to buzzing with tension and conflict and a myriad of feelings I can't decipher while my head is pounding this way.

I'm never drinking sangria again. Or wine. Or alcohol.

I am a dreadful liar.

When the coffee machine stops, I stir in some milk and throw the spoon into the sink behind me. My lips are twitching with the desire to ask what's happened this time. Why I've been hit again. Why people can't just leave me alone.

But I don't. I grasp my mug like it's a lifeline, ignoring the plainclothes detective standing merely feet away from me.

"Your cameras cut out about ten p.m. last night."

"They were hoping I was here," I whisper into my mug.

"Yeah," Drake answers. "Came back on around ten thirty when it was obvious you weren't."

"Any ideas who?"

"From the grainy picture of someone in head-to-toe black? A male. Tall. Lean. Beyond that, no?"

"Sounds like you're coming along fabulously," I reply dryly before sipping on my coffee.

"Trent told me about your idea," he says, stepping closer.

I move away, and he bangs his fist on the counter.

"Dammit, how can you be so fuckin' stupid, huh? Invitin' a killer to come and get you?"

I meet his eyes. "I'm sorry, Detective. I don't answer to you."

"No, but your dead body does."

"Just as well there won't be one, isn't it?" I set the mug down and look at him. "Y'all pullin' some DNA from here or what? Don't tell me there's still nothing after all this time."

"Forensics is on it."

"And if they don't find anything, you should look at replacing your department," I snap, folding my arms. "Are you done here?"

Drake shakes his head. "Noelle, think about what you're doin'. Think about the ramifications of your actions if your plan backfires."

"It won't," I bluff, ignoring the fact that my plan, right now, is actually to wing it. "I'm not like the rookie shits you send into my places to look for shit. I know what I'm doing!"

"Clearly you don't if you think you can trap this killer without a plan!"

"And what does that have to do with you, huh?" I shove his shoulder. "Nothin'. That's what. I'm not a damn kid or a graduate from the police force. I know exactly what I'm doing."

"Then you know how stupid you're being!"

"God, you are infuriating!"

"And so are you!"

"Get out!" I yell, my voice hoarse.

"I'm sorry?" Drake recoils.

"Get out. Of my building," I add, moving toward him as he walks backward. "If you don't have a warrant in your ass pocket, get the fuck out. Now."

He grabs my wrist and pulls me into him. "Listen to me, cupcake. Someone got real lucky last night, and that someone was you. You weren't here when your killer wanted you to be. Yeah, I said yours. They know you're waitin' for 'em. Most nights, you'd be here, right? But last night, because I pissed your ass off, you weren't. Know what that tells me?"

"I'm sure you're gonna tell me," I manage through gritted teeth.

"It tells me this killer is watching you. You ain't safe. They're waiting to strike, and it's gonna be the second you're alone. We're close. I can feel it. You're their target now. And this killer? They want to kill you."

"No shit," I whisper, looking away from him. "I won't back down. I don't care what you say. They can try to kill me. I've dealt with worse."

"Stop being a pain in my ass." He grabs my chin and forces me to look into his eyes and all of their devastatingly icy glory. "Someone. Wants. To. Kill. You."

"I know."

"Yet you don't care."

"I care," I whisper, holding his gaze. "But did you ever think that I'm your best bet at catching this person? If they're watching me, if they want to kill me, they're there. Waitin', like you said. And that means they're gonna come to me. Not you. Not anyone else. Me."

"Yeah, I thought it. But I don't like it."

"Ain't your job to like it, Detective. It's your job to deal with it."

"You're right. It ain't my job to like it, but I ain't exactly dealing with it."

"What the hell does that mean?"

"It means—" He leans in, his touch relaxing just a smidge. "It means that I don't like it. I'm not dealin' with it. And the thought of you bein' in the kinda danger you are scares the ever-lovin' fuckin' shit out of me."

My inhale is sharp and harsh and loud. "I'm no wimp," I reply, trying to ignore the proximity of his lips to mine. "I'm not afraid. They want to come for me? They can. They're gonna get a real surprise when they look down the barrel of my gun instead of into my eyes. Don't be afraid of havin' another dead body on your hands, Detective, 'cause you ain't gonna get one."

"Ain't just any dead body on my hands I'm worried about, cupcake. It's yours."

"Yeah, well, in the highly unlikely situation this moron succeeds, you'll find my body in your hands and my ghost haunting your ass until you join me in Hell," I breathe. "And then I'll never leave you alone, so keep on wishin' for me to stay alive."

"Oh, I am," he replies, his voice soft and gentle and honest. "And when you don't die, we're talkin' about your deluded idea to date Giorgio Messina."

"Deluded?" I move back, making him drop his hand. "We've discussed this. No delusion necessary, thank you."

"We'll see." He releases me entirely, his eyes intense and his presence suffocating and everything about him consuming and disastrously sexy.

I cough, pushing everything away. "You're right. We will."

The office front door busts open and my entire staff comes bursting through it. Bekah looks as rough as I do, her hair mussed, her mascara smudged with purple circles beneath her circles. Dean and Mike look as though someone just threatened their unit or battalion, and Marshall looks somewhat dumbstruck. I'm assuming this staff rally was a last-minute, emergency gathering.

"What the hell happened?" Dean demands, his arms tense, looking like the toned giant he is. "Miss Noelle?"

"Another break-in," I reply with a sigh.

"Was anything taken?" Mike asks.

"Nothing," Trent replies, coming up next to me and touching his hand to my back. He faces me. "It was a straight in-and-out job, sis. I'm sorry. We'll hopefully know more when forensics gets some results back. They pulled some fingerprints from the windowsill."

I sigh, knowing that every member of staff will have prints on that thing. I guess it excludes them though, right?

"Thanks, Trent. Sorry y'all had to come out so early."

"Apologize to Alison," he grins. "She was ready to attack me with the kettle when I left."

"Don't," Bekah groans, sinking into Grecia's now-empty receptionist chair. "Just don't."

Drake's eyebrows go up. "I'm guessin' y'all had some fun last night."

"Well, pretentious detectives bring it out in me." I smile and motion pointedly toward the door. "Aren't you done here now?"

"Here?" he asks. "Yes. With you? No."

I hold his gaze as his words circle me, and once again, I motion toward the door. "Goodbye, Detective. You can see yourself out."

His eyes hold mine for a long moment before he finally, slowly, makes his way to the door. He places his hand on the handle and stops, looking at my staff. "She's not to be alone in this building. Do you understand? A patrol car is outside of her house as of now, and deputies will switch shifts. She'll be escorted between here and there and everywhere else."

"I'm not a child."

"No," he agrees, still not looking at me. "But someone is trying to kill you."

My nostrils flare in anger as he walks through the door, making all of my staff and friends look at me.

"Wanna clue me in?" Trent asks quietly.

"Ask your boss," I grind out, "And get the HWPD the fuck outta my office."

"They're not done—"

"If there were a part of me that gave a single fuck, you could have it. Get. Them. Out. Now."

"Noelle…"

"Warrant," I reply.

"Don't pull that crap with me."

"Then get out." I turn from him to Mike, Dean, Marshall, Bekah, and Grecia. "Y'all get to work. You can leave early tonight."

"Noelle," Trent says.

"No." I look at my eldest brother. "This is my building. Mine. If I want you out, you get out. Got it?"

He takes a deep breath and touches my arm. "I sure hope you know what you're doin.'"

For once, I do.

The board in front of me is covered in Post-it notes. I have a color for Dr. Gentry, one for Ryan, one for Penny, and one for miscellaneous suspects. Simple.

Each one is connected by a relationship timeline, which has been scribbled onto the whiteboard with different-colored dry-erase markers. To anyone else, it looks like a muddle of lines and crisscrosses, but to me, it makes total sense.

On the board next to me, I have a timeline of every victims' last few hours equaled out with the whereabouts of my suspects.

For the first time since this started, I feel like I'm looking at some definitive evidence.

Well, I say evidence.

It's hard to have that when you're basing theories upon Post-its and dry-erase markers.

Still—better than nothing.

I lean back in my chair and tap my foot against the floor. My heels sink into the deep carpet, and I chew the end of my pen. If only figuring this out were as simple as the others.

And why did someone smudge my paint on my wall?

Inconsiderate little rookie-cop assholes.

"Yellow?" Bek pokes her head in my door. "Can you sign off this case? Mrs. Gonzalez wants her daughter-in-law followed. Thinks she's sleeping with her boss."

I wave her in, my eyes on the board still, and grab my pen to sign the bottom of the sheet.

"Thank you." She walks out as quickly as she came in, closing the door behind her.

Relationships are funny things, aren't they? Always twisting and turning... Honest yet so deceitful... Real yet so fake at the same time.

How do you know what's real? How can you separate the illusion from the clear picture? How is it possible to look at someone and know they're being entirely truthful? How can you look at someone and know they are when you're not being truthful?

"Miss Noelle," Dean says, knocking and pushing my door open. "Ms. Oliver wants her boyfriend Lucas investigated."

I wave him toward me the way I just did with Bek and sign the bottom of the sheet.

Today is busy.

I pull the cupcake from my drawer once he shuts the door and dip my finger into the frosting. Mmm, chocolate. With sprinkles. And extra chocolate.

God bless whoever put this one there.

Sneaky people...

I drop it as quickly as I picked it up.

Eating a cupcake I didn't know existed? Am I insane? Paranoid?

Yes. Insane? Yes. Still yes.

Good grief.

Thank God I only swallowed one mouthful of frosting.

I swallow it down with a wash of water from my bottle and revisit my boards. I know I'm missing something, however small it is. However big or small or shiny or dull. There's this tiny little dot in the image that is my investigation that just won't be filled in.

"Yo, boss."

I wave Marshall in, not looking at him. Squares. Bright squares. Relationships. Connected oddly. Yet connected. Somehow. Secondarily. Enough? Maybe.

"Here's the latest on Mallory and the store."

"Thanks." I put my hand on the file when he drops it on the desk and slide it toward me. "You good?"

"Yeah. Are...you? Do you need anything?"

I shake my head. "Not right now."

"Okay."

I breathe in slowly but deeply when he moves away and lean even farther back in my chair. He pauses, something I see in the corner of my eye, but I don't pay attention until he moves again and he opens my office door.

chapter
TWENTY-FIVE

CONFERENCE-CALL everyone. "Y'all can leave now," I say into my speaker. "Thanks for stayin' earlier."

"You sure?" Dean asks. "Detective Nash said—"

"I know what he said. My brother is on speed dial. Don't worry."

"If you're sure, Miss Noelle."

"Positive. I'll call now and they can send someone over if they feel I need it," I lie smoothly. "Y'all take a few hours for yourselves."

"Okay," Bek says slowly. "You sure you're good?"

"Yeah. I'm gonna finish printing out the Delaney and O'Connor cases then head off. I won't be ten minutes after you."

"I'd feel comfortable stayin', ma'am," Dean says.

"And I have my gun. I'm fine. I promise. Detective Nash is a giant worry-worm. Don't y'all worry now."

"You sure?" he asks, his voice more hesitant than Mike's.

"I'm sure as sure can be, doll. You go on." I hang up before they pester me even more. I reach down, hidden by the camera angle, and put my black-and-pink 9mm into the ankle holster I slipped on not long ago. Then I sit back up, brandishing a pen. "Damn things get everywhere," I murmur, putting it into my holder.

Bek opens my door and meets my eyes. Her gaze is screaming worry, and I feel bad for a moment. "You sure you're okay?"

"I'm fine." I smile, holding up my Tiffany-blue Glock. "Just gotta pick it up and I'm shootin' someone. I'm good."

She looks from the gun to me. "Yeah, you're good. Call me later."

I smile and agree. Everyone pokes their heads into my office as they leave, and I tell Dean to leave the office door open just a little. As the last man, he does, and I breathe a sigh of relief as I click my security camera off and dial Drake's number.

My heart is in my throat as I do, but the danger I face right here, right now, is worse than what I could face from him.

"Detective Nash."

"It's Marshall," I whisper.

"Noelle."

"Yes. It's Marshall," I repeat, still whispering. "The killer."

"I'm comin' down."

"No!" I protest, keeping my eye on the security feed on my laptop. "He won't come in."

"You're tellin' me you're bringin' a fuckin' killer into your office, in front of you, and it's okay?"

"No," I reply, still watching. "But I can get your confession. Just trust me, okay? Please. Y'all can hack my security feed. I'll send you the login thingymabobs I've never found. Just…trust me."

"I don't."

"Then learn to."

A door closes somewhere in the building, and I freeze, fear flooding my body.

"He's here," I say basically into the speaker, a tremor running through me.

Jesus, I'm scared.

"Don't hang up!" Drake yells down the line, slamming and banging and yelling happening at his end. "Leave this motherfuckin' line on! You got your gun?"

"Three." Overkill? Eh, maybe.

"Do not hang up," he orders.

"'Kay," I say into the air, setting the phone face down into my open desk drawer.

My door handle squeaks. It's somehow closed since everyone left, but the two-second delay allows me to turn my camera back on, pull my gun from the drawer and stand.

"Put it down, Noelle." Marshall's voice is cold, and his void eyes show nothing of the college graduate I hired a few months ago. They show nothing of the guy I asked to answer a million and one questions and teased about playing video games.

"You don't want to do this, Marsh," I warn softly. I feel sick—my gut feeling just hours ago was right.

His lips curl evilly. He looks different. Cold, calculating. Like a stranger. "I have no choice. By the time your boyfriend gets here, you'll be dead, and he'll wish he fucked you when he was makin' out with you on your desk."

"Well, for one, I severely dislike Detective Nash, so he sure as hell ain't my boyfriend," I respond, "And I won't ask how the hell you know about the desk thing."

"I couldn't let you get too close." He flicks the safety on his gun, the barrel pointed at my face. One shot on target and I'm Sunday lunch for maggots at the Holly Woods Graveyard. "I changed all the records before you asked for them. You're not as smart as you think you are."

"Clever," I soothe him. "And the files that went missing? That was you, too?"

He nods.

"You deleted the files—Lena, Daniel—and then left the false trail. You knew I'd made copies because you reactivated my camera, but you didn't know where I'd hidden them," I guess. "You hacked my alarm system at home, broke in, but I woke up before you found the flash sticks."

Another nod.

"Dr. Gentry. He's your father, isn't he? Your relationship broke down when he met Lena. He married her, this girl only a few years older than you, and you couldn't stand it."

"She ruined my family!" he hisses, his jaw tightening, his fingers clenching around the gun he's holding up. "Put it down!" he shrieks.

I gently place my Glock on the desk.

"Good. Now, stand still. Hands out."

"Doll, don't do this," I whisper.

His hold on the gun wavers, and I take my chance.

"You're scarin' me, Marsh."

"I hate it when you're scared! It makes it hard!"

"Is that why you used hemlock? You didn't have to deal with

them begging. They were paralyzed. They couldn't fight you."

"Yes! Lena was easy. Her stupid split personalities made her easy! She was three people. One with my dad, one with Daniel, one with Ryan." His hands shake.

I drop my eyes to the barrel of his Beretta, which is trembling with his unsteady hold. "And Daniel?"

"He was in the way! He recognized me when I attacked him for her salad. It was unfortunate. But necessary. He was just like her. A life-ruiner."

I can barely breathe, the adrenaline pounding through my body the only thing stopping me from fainting.

"Portia was unfortunate, too. But a cheater. All the same. And you! You let them carry on! Those cases keep your business running. You live off cheaters and liars." Marshall's voice takes on an animalistic tone. "They all died. Except Portia. She realized what was happening before I could burn her like I did Daniel and my dear old stepmother. Dirty whore."

"Marshall, I'm not those people. I do my job, just like you do." I swallow. "Put down the gun."

Where the fuck is Drake?

"No." He tightens his grip on the weapon and moves his finger to the trigger.

Anyone else would miss the tremble on his finger, but I don't.

"If you're gonna shoot me, shoot me," I taunt him. "I won't beg you not to."

His expression morphs, and his finger presses the trigger in what seems like slow motion, the barrel facing right at my chest.

I drop, pull the gun from my ankle, aim, and shoot.

chapter
TWENTY-SIX

M Y door bangs open just as my gun recoils. The bang of the door and the loud boom of my shot ring out through my ears, and I curl into a ball behind my desk. I squeeze my eyes shut as footsteps thunder through my office, deafeningly loud to my ear that's pressed against the floor.

"Noelle!"

"Here," I call back to Drake, sitting up.

There's no pain or aching or stinging, and a quick rubdown of my body with my hands proves that I'm definitely not bleeding.

"Did I hit him?" I ask, using my desk to stand up. I look around, seeing that Marshall is cuffed and has a large, white bandage being held to his shoulder.

Two strong arms wrap around me. My face is buried in a solid, warm chest, one that smells like freshly burned logs and hot apple cider tinted with gunpowder.

"Hey," I say into Drake's chest. "I hit him, right?"

His hold on me relaxes just the tiniest bit. "Yeah, you hit him. In the shoulder."

"Oh. Cool." I want to hug him, but instead, I rest my hands at his trim waist. "Now what?"

"Now, the paramedics come, he gets checked out and arrested," he sighs, letting me go just enough that he can turn and bark orders to someone on the other side of the room. Then, with his hands on my upper arms, he looks at me. "And I need a statement, ma'am."

"Sexy." I roll my eyes. "I have his confession on video, you know. And your unexpected hug."

He pulls me back against him and brushes his lips over mine once.

"And now your unexpected kiss," I mutter. "Thought we were fighting."

"We are. But that doesn't mean I can't be glad you're all right, cupcake." He brushes his thumb down the side of my face. "And swallow my pride 'cause you were right."

"I'm a woman. There was never any doubt about the accuracy of my theory." I sniff in mock affection and look away.

The adrenaline is subsiding from my body now, the recent thundering pound of fear giving way to the dreaded chill of reality. I wrap my arms tight around myself as a shudder rocks me.

"You okay?" Drake asks, his eyes on mine.

I nod. "Just, you know. Coming back down from my heroic high."

"Badass gene strikes again." He lets out a small laugh and shrugs his leather jacket off, swinging it around my shoulders and pushing me down into my chair.

I wobble as I sit down, and my heart sinks. "Aw, man."

"What?"

I lift my foot onto my other knee and stare at the shiny, black shoe, less half a stiletto heel. "My shoe's broken."

"You just shot a man and you're worried about your shoe?" Drake deadpans.

My eyes meet his. "What? He's still alive, and he's arrested, and since I have his confession on camera"—I cock my thumb toward the camera in the corner—"I'm taking five seconds to lament my broken shoe. I'm traumatized. I just shot a man who was my employee. I'm coping with this in my own way."

Drake closes his eyes and takes a deep breath. "Hell if I know why I worried you were dead. The man upstairs would never inflict that kind of pain on himself," he finishes on a mutter, his eyes opening. "Come on, cupcake." He takes my hands and heaves me up. "I'm taking you in so we can close this case."

"Are you going to handcuff me, too?"

"You make me sick," Brody gags as I walk past.

I grin at my little brother then glance back at Drake as I hobble across my hallway and down the stairs. "Well?"

Drake takes another deep breath and all but pushes me outside just after the medics rush in. "I usually like to get past five dates before I handcuff a woman. Unless she's a criminal."

"I did just shoot someone."

"Get in the car, Bond."

"We're *still* fightin'."

"Noelle, we could get married and we'd still fight mid vow."

"You sayin' you wanna marry me, Detective?" I flirtatiously bat my eyelashes.

He scowls. "Move your ass before I spank it."

"Are you allowed to threaten that?"

"Move!"

"Yes, sir."

I hit send on the message to Gio, telling him I won't be able to make our date next week. No excuses—just that I won't be able to.

After Marshall was carted out of my office, I realized that life is short. Cliché as hell, I know. But I didn't. All it would have taken for my life to be over in a blink was for him to gather the courage to pull the trigger all the way.

Luckily for me, he was too chicken for that.

Unluckily for him, I wasn't.

I've seen guns before, sure, but I've never looked at one and thought, *Oh shit. I could die.* That sounds totally dumb, but I've never had one pointed at me as brutally as the way he did, despite his reservations. Despite the fact that I knew, deep down, he wouldn't actually pull the trigger and shoot me.

At least, I'd like to think he wouldn't.

I handed Holly Woods PD my security footage with his confession as soon as I was released from questioning. There was nothing I could tell them that my tape couldn't show them. I told them that—several times—but I'm sure Drake was just being a giant pain in the ass by keeping me there and asking me the same shit over and over.

He's lucky I didn't shoot him. My trigger finger was hella twitchy last night.

Now, it's Sunday, and Nonna has successfully convinced me to come to church with her and thank God for having spared me.

I'm still torn on the whole "big guy in the sky" thing, but I'll go and worship in my own way. I'll thank whoever is out there that saved my ass.

"Gio is-a not for you," Nonna muses, clasping my hand as we get out of my car. "But I like-a the car."

I smile. "I thought you would."

"Is-a sleek. Sexy. Will make-a man fall-a in love!" She twirls, her cane nearly taking somebody's legs out.

"Nonna, control that thing." I grasp the cane and straighten it. "You will behave in here, won't you?"

"I-a always do." She grins at me, which tells me that she's the one who causes any trouble Father Luiz might deal with.

I shake my head and follow her into the church. She sits us in a pew close to the back and closes her eyes. The urge to do the same is tempting, almost overwhelming. Just to breathe in the serenity of this building, one I forgot even existed until just a couple of days ago.

One I want to bathe in, whether or not I believe the stories behind its existence. I don't think you have to believe to respect or appreciate things. I think you just have to accept that there's something other than your own desires out there.

The church fills rapidly, and Nonna pulls me to the side as an imposing figure takes a seat next to me.

I want to groan. I bet this is another one of her matchmaking efforts.

And it is.

So I groan. Because the guy is Drake.

I glare at Nonna. She grins and turns away, making conversation with the woman next to her.

Dammit.

"All right, cupcake?"

"Screw you."

"Can we talk? After?" Drake asks me in a whisper, smiling.

"About?"

"The case."

"Sure." I beat the hint of disappointment down. "Not for long though. I have to take Nonna home."

"Nah, you don't. Trent, Alison, and the kids are on the other side of the church."

"Scheming little…"

"Be nice," Drake teases, knocking my elbow.

I slice my eyes to him, but I have to look away as my lips curve and Father Luiz steps up to start the service.

I'm not sure I listen to a thing he says. Not out of disrespect or disinterest, but because I'm still thinking over the last twenty-four hours and how quickly things escalated. I still don't know all the ins and outs or the connections, but I assume that that's what Drake's going to tell me after this is done. I sure hope it is. I might have come to the conclusion that Marshall was the killer because of the blue paint spot on his back—something that would have had to have happened while my wall was wet, around ten p.m. that night—but I still don't know the details like I want to.

So I sit, praying and singing and listening, until the service is over and people are leaving. I turn to my right to see Nonna, but she's gone, having disappeared into the crowd deliberately, no doubt.

"Come on." Drake takes my hand and pulls me up, leading me into the crowd walking through the door.

We break through the shuffle of people into the bright spring day, the temperature just creeping up high enough that I'd dare to call it summer.

"Slow down," I say, hobbling across the parking lot behind him in my heels. Thankfully, the broken ones weren't my favorite black, Prada, snakeskin ones, so I celebrated this morning by pairing them with my cream dress with the flared skirt.

Drake smirks, glancing at my feet. "No Chucks in your purse?"

I hold the large clutch up. "It's big, but not Chucks kinda big. They're in my car, but they wouldn't match the dress anyway."

His laugh is infectious and tickles across my skin in the best kind of way. One that makes my hairs stand on end with goose bumps and sends tingles down my spine.

"Here. Now, you can sit," he says, opening the door to his truck and holding my elbow as I precariously climb into it.

"Thank you. What did you want to talk about?"

"When we get to your place." He slams the door behind me, and a chill rolls over my skin. He gets in on his side and puts his key in the ignition, bringing the engine to life before he's even closed his door.

One of the perks of Holly Woods being a small town is that it takes barely any time to get from your location to your destination. The church to my house is no different. Unfortunately, you don't have to be crammed in a small space with someone you simultaneously hate and want to sleep with for a long time to get real uncomfortable real quick.

By the time he parks in my driveway, my stomach has twisted with the tension tightening between us and I can barely hear anything aside from my pulse pounding in my ears.

I open the door and swing my legs out, tactfully using the little step at the side to ease myself down onto the driveway. I dig my keys from my purse, ignoring the way his eyes are burning into the back of my head, and insert the right one into the lock. My alarm beeps, so I turn to disable it then walk into the kitchen, dropping my purse on the table.

"Well?" I ask Drake, turning with my hands on my hips.

He loosens the tie around his neck and pops the first button open. "Marshall severely restricted the records you received. He hid the fact that Lena suffered from multiple personality disorder, thus allowing her to compartmentalize the separate parts of her life."

"And by different parts, you mean Dr. Gentry and Melly, Daniel, and Ryan, right?"

"Exactly them. We spoke with her psychiatrist first thing this morning, but she wasn't able to answer whether or not Lena's 'other sides' would know about each other. And as far as we know, it was something she hid from everyone."

"Wow. How old was Marshall when Lena met his dad?"

"Twelve. Just." Drake leans against the counter, crossing his arms. "She was a freshman in college, and that was that. Her doctors found no evidence of any trauma in the past bringing on her disorder, and they studied her extensively for emotional, physical, and sexual abuse. Her disorder was just one of those things, but it was triggered to a serious level after Melly was born."

That makes sense. "So, that's it? The case is closed now, right? You have his admission on tape."

"We do. And it's all thanks to you."

I shrug and look away, grabbing a cloth from the side of the sink and rubbing at an imaginary spot on the countertop. "Would you believe me if I told you it was a coincidence? I just happened to notice the paint on Marshall's shirt as he walked out, connected it with the time of the break-in, and that was it."

"You were right though. The killer would come to you."

"Well. He wanted to kill me." I smile sadly, pausing in my useless cleaning. I glance at him. "Guess it's lucky I'm a damn good shot with a gun and always keep more than one close to me, huh?"

His pink lips curve into a bright smile. "Sure is, cupcake."

"One of these days, Drake Nash, I'm gonna cupcake your ass into next week."

"I know." His smile grows. "Until then, I'm gonna keep calling you it."

"I know." I glare at him. "Was that everything? I have to go and prove to my mom that I wasn't used as target practice for a murdering lunatic."

"In a minute."

"In a minute?" I raise my eyebrows.

"Put the damn cloth down, Noelle. There ain't a mark on your counter."

I open my mouth to argue, but the glint in his eyes makes me shut it. Yeah. Caught. "Fine." I throw it in the sink with way too much vigor just to make my point. "What do you want now?"

He drops his arm and crosses the kitchen, his eyes getting the frustrated glimmer I'm so accustomed to. "I'm real pissed at you."

"When aren't you?"

"Don't ever put yourself in the way of a killer again, you hear me?" He stops in front of me, his eye twitching as he reaches for me. The backs of his fingers brush my cheek, lingering against my jaw. "Two seconds. That's all it would have taken for that to end differently."

"But it didn't," I say softly, wrapping my fingers around his and pushing his hand down. "Y'all gotta stop focusin' on me as some damsel in distress."

"I know you've got your badass gene"—his lips quirk—"but it's my job to protect you."

I swallow. Hard. "Well, the danger has passed, Sir Knight, so it's no longer part of the description."

I turn away from him, but he grabs my arm, spinning me back to him. Our bodies slam together, and I inhale sharply, my skin tingling where his fingers are wrapped around my bicep.

"You think it's just my job? That's the only reason I do it?"

"Yes."

He moves us so my back is against the counter, and he lets me go only to trap me fully against the counter. He leans in, his breath hot on my lips as I fight back the urge to breathe frantically at his closeness.

"Newsflash, *bella*," he rasps, "That time your house was broken into and I came over? It was my day off. Houston? My day off. Every single fucking time you've called me and needed me, I've dropped whatever I was doin'. Know why? 'Cause you bein' safe is more than my goddamn job, Noelle."

There goes control of my breathing. "I didn't call you for the break-in here," I whisper.

"Yet I still came."

"Why? Why would you do that? You don't like me. I don't like you. We're like oil and water."

He moves closer another inch. "I don't like you. You're the most infuriating woman I've ever met. You're almost guaranteed to piss me off every single time you open that sweet little mouth of yours, but for the life of me, I can't fucking resist you."

My eyes flutter shut when the distance between our mouths closes to a single breath. "Luckily, I have plenty of resistance where you're concerned."

He grasps my thighs and lifts, his hold strong and powerful, and I'm catapulted onto the counter. He eases his hands over my legs and pushes them open, stepping between them easily. "Really? Where's that resistance now, huh?"

I say nothing.

"If I pulled this dress off you, tugged your obviously small panties to the side and fucked you right here on the counter, you'd object, wouldn't you? You'd tell me where to go. You'd tell me to stop and leave you alone."

I swallow.

"Come on, Noelle," he breathes, sliding his hands up my legs, his thumbs dangerously close to the triangle of fabric protecting my increasingly throbbing pussy from him. "Where's your fight? Your resistance? Where's the big, fat no you just told me you'd give me?"

And Lord help me, I don't do any of those things.

I grab his face and close that ridiculous distance between us. I press my lips to his and curl my fingers around the back of his neck, the ends of his curly hair tickling my fingers. Drake's fingertips dig into my thighs as he pushes against me, taking control of the kiss and bringing a hand up. He buries it into my hair, his other hand yanking my dress up around my hips.

I let him go and yank at his tie, undoing the knot and whipping it off from around his neck. He smiles against my mouth, but dammit, I don't care.

I hate this man, but right now, I just wish he'd fuck every ounce of that hatred out of my body.

His fingers play with the band of my underwear as mine go to work on the buttons of his shirt. One by one, I undo them as his mouth keeps mine busy with each gentle nip and suck and flick of his tongue.

When the final button is undone, I slide my fingers up his lightly toned body, ghosting them over the hard packs of muscle, and I shove his shirt down over his shoulders. He releases me for a second to throw it to the floor, and the break in the kiss means he's looking at me.

He's looking at me, my heels on, my panties on show, my dress bunched up beneath my breasts.

My cheeks flush beneath his heated look, and he says nothing as he steps forward and curls his hands around the bottom of my dress. He pulls it up, forcing me to raise my arms, and tugs it right over my head, discarding that on the floor, too.

"What are we doing?" I ask quietly, my whole body humming with desire and screaming at me to shut the hell up because it doesn't actually matter what we're doing because it feels fucking wonderful.

"What we should have done years ago." He grabs me and pulls me off the counter, holding me firmly against his body as he spins.

One kick sends a chair clattering to the floor, and my almost-bare ass finds itself planted on the kitchen table. I open my mouth, but he presses a finger to my lips.

"You gonna protest?"

"No."

"Then it can wait. This can't." He kisses me once more, this time deeply. His tongue swipes mine, and I gasp under the force of the kiss, falling back and holding onto him to keep me up.

He leans me back, though, kissing me roughly and quickly in such a way that my toes curl in my shoes. I reach between us and unbuckle his pants, yanking the zipper down so they fall away. Our bodies come together, and I can feel his hard cock against me, pressing against my clit, tempting and sinful at the same time.

I can't breathe—at all. This is wrong. God, this is so wrong. But it feels right. It feels heavenly and thrilling and head-spinningly sexy.

His lips on my neck send shivers cascading across my skin, and the quiver of my muscles as his fingers work their way across my breasts and down my body to my hips is all consuming. His breath is hot and fast and desperate, and I'm sure mine is the same because my lungs are burning, but I don't know if that's fear or pleasure or excitement or all three of those things mixed into one.

I have no idea what I feel. I just feel everything, nothing discernable, everything interchangeable. I feel everything as right mixes with wrong and perspective changes and determination distorts into the strongest kind of blood-pumping desire I've ever felt.

And then he does what he said he would. While I can feel everything without knowing anything, he slides my panties to the side and he pushes his cock into me, and I'm nothing but him filling me until I can't breathe.

I flatten my hand against the table behind me, my other twining in his hair, my legs wrapping around him as he thrusts into me.

I still can't breathe. I can only feel. Be. Gasp. Moan.

This is everything I dreamed it would be but nothing like I thought.

Drake Nash inside me is the cruelest kind of perfection. His kiss is the most delightful kind of pleasure. His skin against mine is the maddest kind of insanity.

He's my nemesis and my ally, my dream and my nightmare, my anger-inducer and my pleasure-bringer.

And right now, he's all of those at once as he moves relentlessly.

His teeth graze my bottom lip and his moan vibrates through my mouth as he pulls me closer to me, pushes himself deeper into me.

My grasp on him tightens until I need both hands. Until I'm pushed so close to the edge that I can't do anything other than hold on to him, my nails digging into his tan skin, my legs squeezing his waist, my pussy clamping down on to him until my head spins and he groans and my body trembles with the edge of my orgasm.

One groan.

That's all it takes.

My whole body tenses as the orgasm hits me like tidal wave, hard and bruising and impossible to fight against. I fall into it, into him, just for this moment, letting it all go as I give myself over to this utter bastard.

My name falls from his lips in a low, desperate rasp that almost sounds like a beg, and he leans me back, holding me tight as my hips tilt up and he rams into me. His harsh movements guide me through my pleasure as he seeks his own, and he buries his face into my neck, groaning once again, but this time, he's coming, letting go the way I just had to.

I drop my head back when the harsh thumping of my heart slows, but we don't move. Drake doesn't move. He stays, leaning over me, holding me tight, his skin searing into mine without a care in the world.

He turns his head so his lips brush me. "Please tell me there isn't a chance of mini yous any time soon."

Oh shit. No condom.

"Don't worry. I'm good," I breathe back, dropping my arm from around his neck and covering my eyes. "I'm a responsible woman."

"Who just had sex on her kitchen table."

"I didn't say I was sensible."

He laughs, the low sound sending goose bumps over me. Damn, I wish he'd stop doing that. I *humph* at his amusement, and he slowly stands, pulling me up with him. He hesitates for a moment then drops his mouth to mine.

I swear I can feel the swollenness of his lips from the harsh way he kissed me. This time, though, the touch is soft but firm.

I bite back a sigh when he pulls out of me and reaches for his boxers. Without pulling his pants up—which are hilariously around his ankles—he bends for my dress and hands it to me. I take it from him and pull it over my head, kicking my shoes off before I slide off the table and ease the fabric of the tight dress over my butt and down my legs.

I step around him, awkwardness descending. The room is rife with it, but I'm almost sure I could step into the yard and still be embraced by the words either of us refuses to say.

"I meant what I said," Drake says when I turn the kettle on. "About Giorgio Messina."

How's that for a post-sex conversation starter? "I'm sure you did."

"Stay away from him," he whispers, coming up behind me. His chest is hot against my back, and he wraps an arm around me, his hand flattening against my stomach. "He's not good for you."

I sigh, pausing with the teabag in my hand. "I canceled our next date. I'm too busy tryin' to stay alive to pander to Nonna's silly little demands."

"What if," Drake murmurs against my ear, "I asked you out? Would you say yes?"

"We'd kill each other in ten minutes."

"But it'd keep your nonna happy. I'm Catholic, and I'm a quarter Italian. She can't complain."

"I repeat: We'd kill each other in ten minutes."

"Isn't that part of the fun?"

"Really? You call that fun?" I raise my eyebrows and turn to look at him, but I can see he's deadly serious. Fighting? For fun? Is he fucking crazy?

But then… Nonna and Nonno—they fought. Every day. Like cats and dogs.

Passionately.

Ridiculously.

Relentlessly.

And they were married for fifty-something years before Nonno gave in to the cancer that ate at his bones.

And like she told me once… It isn't fighting in a relationship you have to worry about. It's when you stop fighting, 'cause that means you've stopped caring. As long as there's something to piss you off that's worthy of complaining about, it means you still care with all of your heart.

I look at Drake, his icy eyes framed with dark-brown lashes, and his sharp cheekbones curving down toward his soft, pink mouth, which is currently turned up in that God-awful, smug smile I can't stand. I look at him, still feeling his naked body against mine, him inside me, his lips burning mine with every begging kiss, and Nonna's words go around and around in my mind.

Hey, he's handsome. Catholic. Italian. It could be worse.

And we're sure as hell gonna fight like cats and dogs anyway. Or, as Bek puts it, like gunpowder and a match.

Maybe that really is us. Maybe, no matter what, Drake and I will always be gunpowder and a match—explosive.

"What'd'you say, Noelle?" he asks, running his fingers through my hair.

"It's real dumb," I reply honestly. "We can't have a single conversation without getting at each other's throats."

Slowly, those damn lips move into a sexy smirk that has my heart hopping. "Who said a thing about a conversation?"

I shake my head with an amused sigh and tap his arm. "I'd tell you to behave if I thought for a single darn second you'd listen to me."

"Never," he confirms.

"Fine," I say before he can carry on. I touch my thumb to his jaw, feeling the roughness of his stubble scratch my jaw. "We'll go on a date. One date. As long as you pay. And there are—"

"Cupcakes at the end of the night. I know."

My smile matches the one slowly stretching across his handsome face. "Okay. But I'm not promisin' I won't kick your ass by the end of the night."

He curls his hand around the back of neck and leans in, his lips barely brushing mine. "I'm countin' on it, cupcake."

To be continued in

coming July 30th.

Sign up for my newsletter to be notified when it's available.

For exclusive peeks at TANGLED BOND, including the first look at the cover and blurb, join my reader group on Facebook

about the
AUTHOR

By day, New York Times and USA Today bestselling New Adult author Emma Hart dons a cape and calls herself Super Mum to two beautiful little monsters. By night, she drops the cape, pours a glass of whatever she fancies - usually wine - and writes books.

Emma is working on Top Secret projects she will share with her readers at every available opportunity. Naturally, all Top Secret projects involve a dashingly hot guy who likes to forget to wear a shirt, a sprinkling (or several) of hold-onto-your-panties hot scenes, and a whole lotta love.

She likes to be busy - unless busy involves doing the dishes, but that seems to be when all the ideas come to life.

Connect with Emma online at:

Website: www.emmahart.org
Facebook: www.facebook.com/EmmaHartBooks
Twitter: www.twitter.com/EmmaHartAuthor / @EmmaHartAuthor
Instagram: www.instagram.com/emmahartauthor / @
emmahartauthor

Made in the USA
Middletown, DE
24 March 2022